Monsoon Memories

Monsoon Memories

RENITA D'SILVA

bookouture

Published by Bookouture

An imprint of StoryFire Ltd.
23 Sussex Road, Ickenham, UB10 8PN
United Kingdom

www.bookouture.com

ISBN: 978-1-909490-05-5

ACKNOWLEDGEMENTS

First and foremost, I would like to thank my publisher, Bookouture, for believing in me enough to agree to publish not only this book but two other books I hadn't even written at the time I signed my contract. Bookouture have been tireless in their efforts to make *Monsoon Memories* the best book it could possibly be.

I am extremely grateful to Oliver Rhodes at Bookouture for his patience and advice, for creating such a fabulous cover, for my brilliant website and for guiding me at every step of the exhilarating journey from manuscript to publication of this book.

I am grateful to Lorella Belli of the Lorella Belli Agency for her guidance and for her efforts in making *Monsoon Memories* reach a wider audience.

A huge thank you to Jenny Hutton, my editor, for all the hard work she put into making every sentence sing at exactly the right note.

I would like to thank Cornerstones for helping me hone the manuscript before I submitted it and Kathy Gale to whom I went for advice after I attended her talk at the Kingston Readers' Festival.

I owe a debt of gratitude to my friend Louise Swain, who asked me to enrol in a writing course, who egged me on and who read my very first draft, which she says she will sell when I am famous.

This book would not have been possible without the support of my family: my mother who believed in me from the time I penned my first poem as a seven year old; my father for filling our house with books even though we could ill afford them; my children who humoured me every time I was faced with rejection: 'When your book is published, we will…' and who proudly told everyone at school that their mother had 'written so many books' when my first short story got published; my husband whose quiet and unstinting support I rely on.

And last but not least, I thank *you* for buying this book and for taking the time to read it.

CHAPTER ONE
Ghosts

OCTOBER

Shirin dreamt of home. Of monsoon showers drumming their rat-a-tat beat on the tiled roof. Of sitting on the veranda sipping hot sweet tea and biting into spicy potato bondas freshly cooked by Madhu. Of Madhu herself, in her pink sari with white flowers, washing clothes beside the well and smiling when she saw Shirin, opening her arms wide and welcoming her in, smelling of washing soap and fried onions and whispering in her ear, 'You came. I knew you would.'

Coconut-tree fronds danced in the wind, displacing drops of rain like the holy water Father Sequeira sprinkled across the pews as he walked down the church aisle on feast days; and the crows that were perched on the branches flew away, black silhouettes against a moody sky.

The tamarind tree in the front courtyard bent like a weary old man from the weight of its ripe knobbly fruit.

Her father, Walter, sat under it on the threadbare rattan stool, absently swatting at mosquitoes as he read his Bible, its pages worn from use; the ever-present bottle of water by his side, within easy reach.

Her sister, Anita, squatted on the veranda, recounting earnestly everything that had happened to her that day and Shirin felt guilty, as she only half listened, nodding at appropriate times, her mind wandering.

Deepak slouched with his gang of friends by the church and eyed all the college girls. He laughed, eyes twinkling— momentarily distracted from his perusal of Anjali, his latest crush, by Shirin's expression when she found the dead lizard he had left as a souvenir in her accountancy textbook.

Her mother, Jacinta, resplendent in her blue-and-gold sari, dressed ready to go to church, entreated, 'I have to attend this parish council meeting, Shirin. Don't you be gone when I come back. Please, Shirin, we have so much to talk about.' Worry lines creased Jacinta's face and Shirin wondered why her reserved, unflappable mother looked so concerned.

Jacinta left, walking down the hill past the mango trees. Shirin saw her making her way between the fields, the green ears of paddy bending gracefully, eavesdropping on whispered conversations. Jacinta looked back at Shirin one last time, a plea in her eyes.

A baby. Red scrunched-up face. Downy golden skin. Mewling minuscule mouth. Toothless red gums. Chubby arms extended upwards, tiny hands bunched into fists. Reaching out.

Shirin woke with a start, hot tears streaming down her cheeks. She reached for Vinod but the empty space beside her told her that he had already left for work. She glanced bleary-eyed at the bedside clock. 8:00 a.m. The phone beckoned. She picked it up, dialled Vinod's number.

'Hello,' he said.

In the background, she could hear chatter and the steady chug-a-chug of the train Vinod took to work—normal, working-day sounds.

'Vinod,' she whispered.

'Yes,' he prompted. He was taciturn, but never impatient.

'Vinod, I want to go home.'

✵ ✵ ✵

The day was populated with ghosts. Ghosts from a past that Shirin had tried desperately to relegate to a corner of her heart. Ghosts that stubbornly refused to stay quiet or hidden and every so often manifested in memories that washed over her and left her dizzy with yearning.

She was waiting, the engine of her old Honda Civic idling, at a pedestrian crossing on the way to work, wishing away the headache that loomed behind her eyelids, when she felt premonition chill her spine. She looked up and her gaze was held by a pair of eyes—cold, empty and yet somehow accusatory—among the press of people crossing the road. She was aware of a rushing in her ears, of her whole body trembling, of her heart screaming against her chest. She wanted to gun the engine and drive away but she was hemmed in by the people ahead and the cars behind. She wanted to get out of the car and run. But what if the Eyes followed?

The last straggling pedestrian crossed and Shirin raced away, breaking the speed limit, constantly checking all mirrors to make sure she wasn't pursued. When the crossing was a safe distance behind, she pulled up at a gas station, taking in the other cars, the people visible through the lit windows of the shop. No empty, threatening eyes. She switched off the engine and locked herself in. Then, with shaky fingers reluctant to do her bidding, she pulled out her phone and dialled Vinod's number for the second time that morning.

'Yes?' His voice was clipped.

'Vinod, I saw...'

'Shonu. I am at a meeting. Can I call you back?'

Why had she called him? She knew how busy he was, how he hated to be disturbed at work. Everything was off-kilter since the dream this morning. And what she had just seen... A hallucination? Something real? Here? Now?

He misinterpreted her silence. 'Shonu, I'm sorry.' She heard voices discussing flowcharts. Male laughter. 'I'll call you later. Bye.' Ringtone loud in her ear. She put the phone back in her bag, unlocked the car and stepped outside on jelly legs. She was a survivor. She wouldn't let what she'd just seen—thought she'd seen?—defeat her. She smoothed her skirt, flicked a sliver of lint off her shirt. A bell tinkled as she pushed open the door of the shop. The Asian man at the till looked up briefly. Drowsy brown eyes glazed with boredom. *Stop this. Stop inspecting the eyes of everyone you see.* She treated herself to coffee and a jam doughnut.

At work she was swamped with concerned queries and advice she didn't want: 'Shirin, you look peaky.' 'What's the matter—you coming down with something?' 'Two ibuprofen and a black coffee, that's what works for me.' And exaggerated winks and nudges with allusions to the night before: 'Enjoyed ourselves a bit too much last night, did we?' 'What was the occasion then?'

She went straight to Kate's office and knocked. 'Have you had breakfast? I got doughnuts.'

'Are you all right, babe? You look like something the cat brought in.'

Kate: witty, straight-talking, Irish; her only friend in the UK. Kate was the one who had interviewed her at CST Solutions, looking for a software programmer to join her team. Immediately after the interview, Kate had held out her hand to Shirin: 'I know I'm breaking all the rules and we're supposed to get back to you after three days, but what the heck—you're on. Welcome to CST Solutions, Shirin. Welcome to my team.' Shirin had stared at Kate's hand, at her beaming face with its faint dusting of freckles.

'The person on the CV, that's not who I am,' she'd said.

'It's not? As long as you do your work well, I don't care who you are,' Kate had replied, a bemused smile on her face. Something in Shirin had shifted then; the chill that had taken root since leaving India had thawed slightly and she'd warmed to this woman with her upturned mouth made for laughter.

Kate was the only person besides Vinod who knew the truth about Shirin's past. She had had to confide in her, when the thing happened with Ian. For Shirin, who had learned the hard way not to trust anyone, trusting Kate with her story was a leap of faith. To her credit, Kate had not been outraged, had not sacked Shirin as she'd half expected her to, had not treated her differently since. And tentatively over the years, Kate had morphed from boss to friend.

Now Shirin asked, 'Do I look that bad?'

Kate nodded, 'Like you're coming down with something. Are you? Do you need the day off?'

'No. I've just had a shock, that's all. A blast from the past.' She tried to be blasé, to put on a smile. It didn't work. Not with Kate.

'What happened?'

The concern in Kate's voice brought it all back. Made her knees buckle. She sat. 'I... I dreamt of home. Woke up aching with longing. I used to have these dreams a lot in the beginning. So vivid. Like I was there. Like that was real and this... this life a dream...'

'But it wasn't only that, was it?'

Perceptive Kate. 'No.' A deep breath. 'On the way here, I was at a pedestrian crossing. I saw...' A pair of eyes. Empty yet menacing. Looking directly at her. 'The Eyes...'

Kate's startled gaze held hers. 'Here? Now?'

'I... I don't know.'

'Was there a face? A person? Anything?'

An intake of breath that came out a sigh. 'Just the Eyes. Like in the nightmares.'

'Yesterday. Did something happen? Something that jogged your memory? Caused the dream and this...'

Shirin met Kate's gaze. 'Her birthday.' A whisper.

Kate's mouth: a perfect maroon-lipsticked O. A couple of years ago, when Kate had had her pregnancy scare with the Boyfriend from Hell, Shirin had told her. The final ugly truth about herself. Her guilty secret. Her biggest regret.

'Does it happen every year?'

'Not like this. The dream perhaps... But not...'

'What you just saw?'

'Must have been my imagination—don't you think, Kate?' It was a plea.

'I'm sure it was.' Kate gave Shirin's arm another squeeze. 'Shirin, it's been ten years...'

'Eleven,' Shirin whispered.

'Eleven then. After all you've been through, what's the worst that can happen?'

Shirin closed her eyes, gripped the arms of her chair. She could think of a few things.

'All right, I'll shut up now. I'm not helping.' And then, very gently, 'Do you want to talk about it?'

Shirin shook her head, no. Kate nodded once, then stood abruptly, clicking her fingers. 'Come on, you need a strong black coffee. And work. Nothing like work to get your mind off all this.'

'Yes,' said Shirin, shaking her head to clear her mind of visions of cold, empty, accusing eyes. 'Nothing quite like work.'

CHAPTER TWO

The Curious Case of the Mysterious Girl from the Photograph

SEPTEMBER

It was when she was visiting her grandmother on a rain-drenched, gloomy afternoon in September and there was nothing better to do than go over old photographs, musty and yellowed with age, that Reena found it. It was tucked away behind one of the other photos in the album. She would never have discovered it if it hadn't been for Chinnu the cat, who squeezed in through the bars of the open window, landed on the album and then proceeded to shake vigorously to rid herself of the raindrops in her coat. Reena squealed. She had been lying on her stomach, legs bent at the knees, feet swinging merrily in the air, on the cool cement floor. Madhu had warned her repeatedly not to do so. 'You're a city girl and not used to these floors. You'll catch a cold. It will seep straight into your chest from the cement. Then how will you travel back home in the overnight bus, tell me?' Madhu had yelled just that morning when she found Reena sprawled on the naked floor.

Reena smiled as she remembered asking her dad once, when she was little: 'Is Madhu your aunt?' Her dad had picked her up and twirled her around, so her dress bloomed in patterned swirls like a Bharatanatyam dancer's, and, laughing, had said, 'No, darling. She's more like a second mum.'

She had scrunched up her nose, puzzled. 'Another mum?' From up in the air, suspended in her dad's strong arms, his face had looked different, wider somehow.

'She came to stay when your Mai was about to give birth to me, to help with the housework. She's never left. She's part of the family now.'

'Why don't I have a second mum?' Reena had asked and her dad had laughed. She had watched, fascinated, as his face became wider as it got closer, until she was so close she could see the tiny hairs curling just inside his nostrils.

'Your mum's a superwoman, that's why. She says she manages quite well on her own.' Reena had wrapped her arms around her dad's neck, had laid her head in that warm safe space just above his left shoulder and breathed in the familiar smell of his sweat.

'Yes,' she had said, voice muffled, 'she does.'

Reena jumped up and pulled the album out from under Chinnu. That was when she saw something peek out from behind the picture she had been looking at.

Wonder what that is, thought Reena excitedly, imagination in overdrive. *Perhaps something of great value that someone wanted to conceal… What better hiding place than an old, woodlice-ridden album of photographs!*

She had just started reading *Nancy Drew* and wanted so much to be a sleuth like her. She knew her mother hoped she would be a doctor, and her father wanted nothing more than for his only daughter to follow in his footsteps and become a computer programmer. But ever since Reena had laid her hands on the first *Famous Five* book at the age of nine, she had wanted to be a detective. Solving mysteries seemed such fun. And there was a dearth of Indian detectives, which was a shame really considering there was so much crime in India, so many unsolved murders.

She had listened enough to her parents' laments after they watched the news or read the paper. Her mother would shake her head sadly and say to Mrs. Gupta next door, 'Did you hear about the poor woman being attacked and left for dead in her flat for hours? Everything taken, even the dog's bowl it seems.'

'Arre Baap re,' Mrs. Gupta would moan, 'I am sure it was the servants. You have to be very careful, Preeti. They are very sly, these lower-class people. Once they know where you keep your keys, God help you…' One of Mrs. Gupta's hands would be clutching her right breast dramatically, checking to see that the keys she kept tucked inside her bra were safe. Reena was sure Mrs. Gupta was aiming for the 'tragic heroine' look, but with her long pointy nose and evil face, she was anything but.

Murli, Mrs. Gupta's cook and Reena's friend, regaled her with horror stories about crimes that went unchecked in his village. In Murli's version, it was the rich people, the employers, who were the villains.

All this only served to make Reena more determined to be a detective. It would have helped if she had a book starring an Indian detective as a guide. The India she knew didn't have moors, gorse, secret islands and open spaces like the England of the *Famous Five* books, except maybe at her grandmother's house. But the open spaces in Taipur were populated with mud, mosquitoes and snakes. She couldn't find a single book, fiction or otherwise, with an Indian girl, boy or adult detective. She had even braved asking the Scrooge of a librarian at her school, who had looked down her nose at Reena with her ogre-like eyes and pinched-together face and asked, 'Who wants to know?' Reena was a tiny bit ashamed of the fact she had fled. But, she reasoned, detectives needed to keep a low profile. They couldn't afford to blow their cover...

In the beginning she had been all for forming a club like in the *Famous Five* or the *Secret Seven* and had spent ages concocting names and passwords. She had given up when she realised that she had names aplenty but a scarcity of friends or siblings who could be coerced to join. Then she started reading *Nancy Drew* and bingo, she realised that she could go it alone. She spent hours practising her signature in her notebook, adding flourishes and titles. She personally liked 'Reena Diaz, Super Sleuth' best. It had a nice ring to it. She decided she would be the first

Indian girl detective. All that remained was to find a mystery. The only problem was that once Reena decided to become a detective, there were no mysteries to be found. No murders or burglaries were reported in the local newspapers or on the TV channels. Even Murli didn't have any more horror stories of unsolved crimes to impart. Her life, Reena was fast coming to the conclusion, was extremely mundane. Nothing thrilling ever happened in it.

And now, thanks to Chinnu, she seemed to have stumbled on something exciting, even if it wasn't the murder she'd been hoping for as her debut case.

Before proceeding any further with the discovery, and wanting to prolong the sense of mystery as much as possible, Reena glanced furtively around her, as she imagined Nancy Drew would. Chinnu was sitting under the wooden bench in the corner cleaning her whiskers busily with her paw.

Her grandmother, Mai, was having her afternoon siesta. She lay on the mat by the front door. Her mouth was open and little snores escaped it from time to time. Her sari was slightly askew, the pink skirt she wore underneath showing. The steady hum of rain relentlessly beating down on the tiles and the steps leading down from the front door served as a familiar lullaby.

Outside, the coconut trees stood out in relief against the blanket of rain which muddied the courtyard that Madhu had diligently swept and tidied just that morning. Dirty little puddles had formed everywhere.

Her parents were out visiting with her father's old school friends. They had tried to get Reena to go but these friends of her dad's did not have any children and nothing could persuade her to venture out into the blinding rain, get wet and muddy only to sit in their house, stare at their walls and listen to her father reminisce about the good old days. Looking at yellowing photographs of people she didn't know to the accompaniment of Mai's snores, while eating hot golibhajis dipped in coconut chutney and sipping cardamom tea was much better.

At least she was dry.

She went to the kitchen, ostensibly to get a tumbler of water, but in reality to check on Madhu. Madhu was sitting beside the hand grinder which she used to pound spices into thick masala for her curries, preferring it to the new electric grinder, which she insisted didn't make a smooth enough paste. Her knees were drawn up, and she was resting her head on them. Strands of grey escaped her bun and obscured her lined face. She was wearing the stained, old apron that she was never without around her sari. She was fast asleep. The kitchen door was wide open and sprawled across the entrance was Gypsy. She was fast asleep as well.

Reena hurried back into the living room. Luck was on her side. Her parents were not due back for a while yet. And it was as if an epidemic of sleep had struck the rest of the household. Even Chinnu was asleep now, lying on her side under the wooden bench, paws stretched out.

Slowly, Reena pulled out whatever it was that was peeking out from beneath the picture she had been looking at—and sighed in disappointment. Just her luck! It wasn't a mystery at all but another black-and-white photograph. It must have slipped behind the other one by mistake. Like the others, this one too was yellowed with age. And, like the others, rot had begun to eat away at it.

She pulled it closer for a better look—and noticed something different. Unlike the other pictures she had spent the afternoon flicking through, this one was creased and worn, as though someone had run their fingers across it many times and then folded it and tucked it away. It was a picture of three children, all of them smiling what were obviously false smiles for the camera. The youngest—the little girl sitting cross-legged on the floor, hair in bunches, flashing dimples—Reena recognised as Aunt Anita, from the countless pictures she had seen of her as a baby and toddler. The boy in the photograph, tummy sticking out, adorable gap-toothed grin, awkward stance, was her father, Deepak, as a child.

It was the other girl in the picture who captured Reena's attention. She was chubby and dark-complexioned. She wore seventies-style churidars and her long thick hair was in pigtails and tied neatly with matching ribbons behind her ears. She had a kind face and an open smile. And she looked very much like Reena herself...

❅ ❅ ❅

Lying on the deliciously cool floor, staring at the photograph, Reena remembered packing her clothes into her case the evening they left Bangalore to come here, desperately hoping for a mystery to sink her teeth into...

Reena's parents had not meant to visit Taipur in September. They had already been in June during the summer holidays. And they did not like visiting during the monsoons anyway.

As her mother, Preeti, had put it to Mrs. Gupta from the flat opposite, the evening they were leaving for Taipur, her nose crinkling disdainfully: 'Stuck in that house all day, nowhere to go, what with the relentless rain. Can't even watch television...'

'Why not?' asked Mrs. Gupta, curiously. 'Doesn't your mother-in-law own one?'

'Oh, no, no...' Preeti hastened to reassure her. She did not want Mrs. Gupta—who always slipped her husband's royal and hallowed ancestry into any conversation—to think that Deepak's family did not measure up. Deepak wouldn't be pleased. 'They have a very big house and are one of the oldest and most respected families in Taipur. And they have one of those big televisions. Deepak's father brought it back from the Gulf. It's huge, really, almost like being in a cinema hall. But you never get to watch. It's the power cuts, you see. Because it is a village, there is no power, either all day long or all night long. And the mosquitoes and all those insects...' Preeti gave a practised little shudder, 'Ohhh... the monsoons attract the *worst* sort of bugs. And the humidity...'

'I don't see why you go at all then, Preeti,' said Mrs. Gupta, delicately taking a sip of her tea, and immediately embarking on a coughing fit.

Reena gulped down a giggle. Mrs. Gupta always did this and any minute now...

'Murli!' Mrs. Gupta called shrilly, summoning her harassed cook, who arrived, head bowed and apologising contritely.

'Is it the tea, ma'am? Too much sugar is it?'

'Too little, Murli. Too little. Pah! The cooks nowadays—you pay them a thousand rupees a month and they don't even know how to make tea! Get me another cup right away. You have made a fool of me in front of my guests. If it happens again, I will sack you. I mean it, Murli.' She waved Murli away and turned to face Reena and Preeti. 'The servants these days...'

'I know,' Preeti murmured sympathetically even though she didn't have a servant, had never needed one.

'Anyway, as I was saying, Preeti, why do you go at all?'

As Murli bent to take Reena's cup, he made a face at Mrs. Gupta behind her back and winked. Reena giggled out loud, unable to hide it this time.

'What's so funny, Reena?' asked Mrs. Gupta, interrupting Preeti who was explaining more to herself than anyone else why they had to go to Taipur during the monsoons.

'Nothing,' mumbled Reena, fiddling with her top, her face lowered so Mrs. Gupta could not see the glee on it.

Her mother continued talking as if she hadn't been interrupted.

'It's the Bandh you see. I can't believe they are having yet another strike! They need an excuse, don't they, to shut down the city. You whisper the word 'Bandh' and the whole of Bangalore shudders to a halt. It's disgraceful, really...'

Mrs. Gupta made sympathetic sounds of agreement.

'So, Reena's off school and Deepak just delivered a release well ahead of time and he's due some time off. You know how he's been working all those long hours and weekends. Some days he's even slept at the office! You are lucky your husband comes home at a decent time, Nupur. You are lucky he runs a business and doesn't work in software, full stop. Anyway, Deepak feels guilty, now that his mother is getting so old and frail, especially after his father died. And of course Anita never visits...'

'You should put your foot down.'

'Well, yes, I suppose I should...'

'And where is Anita nowadays?'

'Oh, you know her. She flits around like a butterfly, never in one place long enough...'

'And what about her husband? Doesn't he get annoyed with her travelling everywhere?'

'They are a modern couple,' Preeti said as if that explained it all.

Reena sighed inwardly. Her mother's comment was like holding a red cloth in front of a raging bull. Now Mrs. Gupta would embark on a monologue on the state of the country and the wantonness of its youth: her second favourite topic after the despicable laziness of servants—and there would be no stopping her.

And sure enough...

'Modern couple...' Mrs. Gupta sniffed loudly, making it clear to all and sundry what she thought of modern couples. 'All those young girls strutting around showing their belly buttons, boys hanging on their arms! No values, nothing. No respect for elders. I saw a couple kissing each other—*on the mouth,* Preeti, in full view of everyone! Chi! I swore loudly and spat on the street right next to them but they didn't even notice. Too busy tasting each other's lunch, they were...' Mrs. Gupta shuddered. She paused to take a breath and her narrowed gaze settled on Reena. 'I hope you don't go about behaving like that, Reena, when you grow up...'

'No, Aunty,' Reena mumbled, eyes down, suitably demure.

'What is this country coming to? Politicians corrupt, young people with loose morals...You know what it is, don't you, Preeti? It's the *influence of the West.* Our impressionable young blindly following what they see on TV, all those half-naked women...'

Reena noticed her mother's eyes start to glaze over. Preeti had come round to Mrs. Gupta's for her daily fix of gossip but none seemed forthcoming. Silently, Reena willed her to interrupt Mrs. Gupta's rant, and for once she did.

'My God, is that the time? Reena, we should be going. We've got the packing to do. Thanks for the tea, Nupur. It was lovely.'

With that they were saying their goodbyes and were out of Mrs. Gupta's flat, across the landing and inside their own.

In the living room, Preeti collapsed onto the sofa and reached for the phone. 'Rinu, go and pack what you want to take with you, sweetie. The bus is at 10 o'clock tonight.

Why they don't have a proper train line connecting Bangalore and Mangalore I don't know. I hate going in that bus; it always gets stuck in the ghats...'

Leaving her mother still grumbling, Reena escaped to her room, lay down on her bed and stared out of the window, not really seeing the blue of the swimming pool which the peon was half-heartedly cleaning, or the landscaped gardens, or the little playground in the centre. 'I liked that plot we saw in Dasarahalli, Deepak,' her mother had said when they came to view this flat. 'We could build a two-storey house and still have some land left over for a garden and it's a quarter of the price of this one.'

'Ah, Preeti,' her dad had beamed, standing in the shade of the palm trees by the swimming pool, and Reena knew then that his mind was made up, 'Ma will be voted president of the parish council when word gets around that we are buying a flat in the same apartment complex as Shivarajkumar. A pat on the back for the Taipur Diazes.' Status meant so much to her dad.

'He's like Mrs. Gupta that way,' her mother had said once, laughing conspiratorially. 'Good job he works the hours he does. If he and Nupur had a family pedigree contest, it would result in a tie...'

Reena had not wanted to move here, despite the fact she was going to have, as her father had said, his eyes sparkling, 'Your own room, Rinu, as big as our entire flat in Hosur Road.'

'But I *like* our flat, Dad,' she had protested. 'My best friend, Divya, lives nearby. Here I will have no friends.'

'You will make some. Who would not like to be friends with you?' her dad had beamed.

Most people, she had wanted to say. *I am not that popular, you know.*

She sighed deeply, worrying the tassels on her pillow cover. She missed Divya sorely, her once best friend who still lived in the old apartment complex. She used to knock on Divya's door and they would walk together to the bus stop. And then Reena had moved to this apartment complex where *film stars* lived, and where her school bus had to make a special detour just to drop her off. There were hardly any other kids living here and the ones who did went to very expensive schools at the other end of the city and would not deign to talk to her. Paradoxically, her classmates, including Divya, assumed that she was too snooty now that she was keeping company with the stars, and would not talk to her either. *What use is status if you have no one to share it with, Dad?*

A lone bird flew past her window—a fan-shaped shadow against the peaceful azure sky, framed by a couple of lazy clouds. Reena wished she could fly too, back to her old flat, to her friend. But then, she mused, she wouldn't have Murli.

She hoped Mrs. Gupta had not meant what she had said about firing Murli. Every time Reena visited Mrs. Gupta with her mother, there was always a little fiasco with her tea. Murli hadn't been sacked yet. Surely that was a good sign.

'Why do you do that? What do you put in her tea?' she'd asked Murli once. She was off school, recovering from the measles, miserable and bored. Murli had come to visit with chicken soup. It was the most heavenly thing she had ever tasted.

'I can't tell you all my secrets, little one,' Murli had chuckled, eyes twinkling. 'Let's just say it's my revenge...'

'But it might get you fired!'

'Oh, she wouldn't dare fire me. No one knows how to make Dal Makhani to her satisfaction quite like me. They are empty threats. She wants to show off in front of her friends. You're sweet to worry about me.'

'I wish she'd treat you better, though. If you left, who'd get non-vegetarian food for me when I am ill?' Reena had said, making Murli laugh. She was on a strict diet on account of the measles. 'How did you manage to smuggle it past my mother, Murli?' she had asked curiously between mouthfuls.

'Oh, I told her it was soup. She assumed it was vegetarian. I didn't lie or anything...' He'd winked at her, his bony face lighting up when he smiled. He was perched on the chair beside her bed, a little slip of a man, wearing a worn white mundu, the bones sticking out of his bare torso, looking at her with such tenderness.

'Aren't you afraid you'll get the measles too?'

'I already had them when I was little. I'm immune to them. You're sweet to care about me. I hope my little girl is growing up with a kind heart just like yours,' Murli had said, a wistful look in his eyes.

Murli's wife and two children lived in a village on the outskirts of Bangalore. Murli saw them once a year, when

Mrs. Gupta grudgingly allowed him a week off work. The first time Murli had met Reena, he'd told her that she reminded him of his little girl, who was her age.

'Don't you miss her, Murli?' Reena had asked.

'Oh, I do, Reena, so much.'

'Then why do you stay so far away?'

'I have to. There is no work in our village. My family lives in a mud hut like the ones you see in the slums in Rajendra Nagar.'

'No…'

'Yes. I save the thousand rupees Mrs. Gupta gives me every month and send it to my wife. This way they can afford to eat and my children can go to school. English Medium, like you. Fees—eight hundred rupees. I want them to get good jobs and live in a big house like you, Reena, when they grow up. If they are educated, not illiterate like me, they can do anything, go anywhere, be anyone…' And Murli's face would glow with his dreams of a better future for his children.

Even though she'd never experienced it, Reena knew all about poverty. She saw it every day, on her way to school, all those slums by the road, the beggars—bedraggled mothers with children on slings around their neck, dirty wisps of hair hiding their sad eyes, knocking on the windows of her chauffeur-driven car as it stopped at a traffic light. If she could, she would have helped them. As it was, she tried to ignore them. She imagined herself to be invisible, or deaf, or in a planet far away, which perhaps in a way she was—cocooned safely in an air-conditioned car, living in a flat in a gated complex with a swimming pool which kept away the riff-raff: the same riff-raff her parents and others in the complex then employed to clean their cars and their houses, to cook their food, wash their clothes and look after their children.

The clock in the dining room chimed the hour, interrupting Reena's thoughts, galvanising her into action. She jumped off the bed, pulled her suitcase out of the wardrobe and started to pack. She overheard her mother in the living room, on the phone to one of her friends.

'The tea was horrible,' Preeti was saying, 'And the way she shouted at Murli! I feel so sorry for him... What? Oh the new decor. I don't think it's any better than the last one. How much did she spend? You're joking! Fifty thousand rupees to redo the living room? But it's just the same as before. Of course I looked. Hardly any difference. Well, personally I liked the old sofas better...'

Packing complete, Reena slumped back into bed and pulled out her notebook—her detective's handbook, as she liked to call it—from underneath her pillow. In four hours, they would be on the bus, on the way to Taipur. She was so looking forward to this unexpected holiday. No homework, no school. A whole week of Madhu's cooking, so much better than her mother's, though Reena wouldn't dream of telling her that. Playing with Chinnu and Gypsy. Going for long rambling walks among the fields, weather permitting. Monsoons or not, Reena liked Taipur, full stop. And, she figured, as she packed the handbook along with the latest *Nancy Drew* in the side pocket of her suitcase, there was more chance of her finding a mystery in Taipur with all those open spaces than here, cooped up in her flat.

And to her great surprise, she did.

SUPER SLEUTH REENA DIAZ AND THE CURIOUS CASE OF THE MYSTERIOUS GIRL FROM THE PHOTOGRAPH, she wrote carefully in her best handwriting in her sleuthing handbook, while squinting at the picture. Yes, the girl definitely looked like her. Hmm... Not bad for a debut case. Not bad at all.

CHAPTER THREE

Sister Maya's Bulbous Nose

Vinod called just as she was starting work on the system test plan for the housing module that was due that afternoon. 'I'm sorry, Shonu,' he said, without preamble. 'I couldn't talk to you just then.'

She could picture him: the stripy shirt he usually wore to the office carefully tucked into his trousers now coming untucked; his grey hair ever so slightly dishevelled from his habit of running his hands through it when he was thinking; his face puckered into a frown as he tried to explain. 'I know.'

'What happened?'

She looked at the test plan in front of her, needing to be reworked. If she started thinking about the morning again, there was no hope in hell of getting it done by lunchtime. But if she didn't tell Vinod, he'd think she was sulking. 'I thought I saw… eyes…' They danced briefly in front of her: menacing, threatening, wanting to unnerve. She kept her mind firmly on the system test plan.

'What? You had the nightmare?' He sounded worried. Guilty.

'Vinod. I'm fine. Truly. I have to go. I'm not cross with you, honest. I'm just busy. I've got to get something done by lunchtime. Speak to you later. Bye.'

She hung up before he could get a word in. Perhaps she was subconsciously annoyed with him. She didn't know and didn't have the time to analyse. Not now, with the team waiting on her to get the plan done so they could begin testing. She switched off all unnecessary thoughts and emotions—she was an expert, after years of practice, at keeping memories at bay—and concentrated on work.

When Shirin got home, she cooked. She made rice with carrots, peppers and cashew nuts. She pounded chillies, cumin and coriander seeds, turmeric powder and vinegar in the pestle and mortar she had bought at Wembley market and marinated the kingfish filets bought from the little Sri Lankan shop across the road in the spicy paste. She made cucumber-and-mint raita to go with the rice. And all the while, Madhu's voice whispered in her ear: 'Too much salt, Shirin. That's quite enough. Add some more chilli powder. A teeny drop of coconut milk for flavour. Yes, that's it.'

When, at the end of their first year in the UK, her fug of depression started to lift, Shirin had tentatively attempted to cook food from home: dishes she remembered eating, that she longed for. They were living in the rented flat in Kenton at the time and the kitchen, populated with strange appliances, seemed alien to her: gleaming white and unsoiled; so different from the cramped kitchen of her childhood, the walls dark with soot from the hearth. Madhu's voice had haunted her then, and if she closed her eyes, she could picture Madhu in her worn apron, wispy hair escaping her bun and getting in her eyes, frying koilolis, stirring pork bafat, grinding spices. All too often, as Shirin had sniffed and swiped at the salty tears running down her cheeks, battling nostalgia, she'd ruined the food she was attempting to cook. So, hard though it was, she learned to ignore Madhu's voice, pushing it away along with errant memories that threatened, and after a while, as the white kitchen became turmeric-tinged and the alien appliances commonplace, as Shirin discovered her own style of cooking, she didn't hear Madhu anymore.

Until now.

Today, it was back: Madhu's sweet, beloved voice, giving her company as she cooked.

'Shonu, I've been thinking,' Vinod said as he came in, and Shirin smiled at his expression as she shoved a plate of piping-hot green plantain podis and a mug of cardamom tea under his appreciative nose.

'Yes?'

'About what happened today,' he said, dipping a podi in coriander chutney and taking a generous bite.

'Uh-huh...'

Vinod chased the last of the chutney with his remaining podi, swallowed, pushed his plate away. 'Her birthday was the trigger?' he asked, his voice gentle.

Reena. Regret. Overwhelming. All-consuming.

'You want to talk about it?' A soft pause. 'About her?'

Kate had asked the same thing. She shook her head, no.

Vinod looked tired all of a sudden. Defeated. Then, 'Shonu, this morning... Was it the nightmare?'

She tried to be matter of fact. 'I thought I saw the Eyes. At a pedestrian crossing on Aldershot road.' She used to see them so often in the beginning. They followed her everywhere and when she attempted sleep, exhausted, they lurked behind her heavy, closed eyelids like a second skin.

'Can't be. Not after all these years.'

'That's what Kate said.'

'You talked to her?' Vinod reached across and gently tipped her face so her gaze met his. She willed herself not to stiffen against his touch. His hand smelt of coconut oil and fried spices—Madhu's smell. She closed her eyes. Something skulked behind closed eyelids, waiting to pounce.

'Good. You need to talk, get it all out,' Vinod's voice. Lips on hers. Pressing down. Eyes. Empty. Mocking. A pungent smell, tamarind-thick, laced with fear—hers. No. Her eyes flew open, met Vinod's gaze. A whiff of musk mixed with sweat. Vinod's scent. She relaxed.

'I... I heard Madhu's voice, after a long time. Years...'

'Heard Madhu's voice?'

'As I cooked. Telling me what to do.'

Vinod nodded thoughtfully. 'Fits in with my theory.'

'What theory?'

'Since your call this morning, I have been thinking,'

'So you said.'

'First you have a vivid dream. Then... the nightmare. And now you're telling me you heard Madhu's voice.' He

ticked them off on his fingers as he spoke. 'All these you
haven't experienced in a while.'

'Yes?'

'Well. They haven't affected you like they used to. Just
think, in the days before... heck, even last year, if this had
all happened in one day, you wouldn't have been so... together, I guess.'

She thought of how, after one of her nightmares,
she couldn't function without a visit to the counsellor;
how, after a dream of Taipur like the one she had had
this morning, depression settled heavy and stifling like
humidity before the monsoons, and she felt parched like
barren fields aching for rain. 'I know.'

'But none of this happened all at once before. You've
had the nightmare, but never on the same day or even the
same week as the dream. And hearing Madhu's voice...'
He nodded, 'A good sign.'

'Your point being?'

The furrows on Vinod's face relaxed into a smile. Tri-
umphant. 'Shonu, it's the healing process, that's what this
is. You are finally ready to revisit your memories; you have
put enough distance between you and your past...'

'You sound exactly like that counsellor I used to see.'

'Well... I am quoting from one of her books...'

And then they were laughing, tension erased, nightmare if not forgotten then pushed aside—for the moment at least.

In bed that night, as Shirin closed her book, pulled
the duvet up to her chin and nagged Vinod to switch off

the light, he said, voice hesitant, 'So, Shonu, did you really mean what you said this morning?' A pause. 'About going home?' He played with her hair, fanned out on the turmeric pillow like shadows dancing in the sun, concentrating on threading strands between his fingers. He did not look at her.

Shirin stalled, focusing on how, even though they had spent the last eleven years in Harrow, North London, they both still referred to India as home.

'I ache to go,' she said finally. 'And I know you do, too.' A whisper. 'I made a deal, Vinod.'

He closed his eyes. 'Yes.'

'I want to break it.' She watched Vinod's eyes fly open, settle on her face. She held his gaze.

He smiled. That beautiful smile. Like the first delicious bite of a perfectly ripe, juicy mango. 'The healing process,' he said.

She smiled.

'When?' he asked.

Her mother's face. The horror, the accusation. 'Soon. Very soon.'

'Invite the memories in, Shonu,' He paused. 'Even the bad ones. Then the past will not have such a hold over you.'

'What I did...' *The baby's cry, a high-pitched wail. And her, running, running barefoot, cars tooting, rickshaw drivers yelling, her hair flying in all directions, nightie soiled. Running.*

'You did what you thought was best.' Vinod said. 'She will understand. One day.'

He knew her so well.

'Part of me was being selfish.'

'Rubbish.' A hint of impatience in her husband's voice. 'Stop beating yourself up. You did what you thought was best, in the circumstances.'

Really?

She looked at Vinod, wishing, as she always did, that she shared his certainty and saw the exhaustion etched in lines around his eyes. Eyes. *Don't think about that.*

'Sleep,' she said.

He reached across to switch off the light.

'Let the memories come. Goodnight. Love you.' He whispered.

A feather-soft kiss on her lips. Darkness. Her husband's gentle snores—phut-a-phut-phut—like the ramshackle Bajaj moped that conveyed Doctor Kumar into Taipur every weekday morning. She fought the weariness weighting down her eyelids, afraid of what might be prowling behind closed lids—another pair of eyes? In the end, weariness won. She dreamt...

Of Sister Maya.

❄ ❄ ❄

Shirin, along with a group of boys from her class, had sneaked out to steal 'bimblis', a sour-sweet fruit, from a tree just outside the school and visible from their classroom. The tree, laden with bimblis, tempted them with its spoils and made their hungry stomachs growl. They had scaled out of the window, jumped over the wall of the school and were enjoying their hard-earned feast when they were apprehended by a tight-lipped Sister Shanthi, their class teacher.

Shirin was marched back to the school, along with the boys (some of them still furtively swallowing the last bits of the fruit), much to their humiliation and the guilty delight of the rest of the class. 'Kneel down facing the statue of Jesus, and recite, "Our Father" and three "Hail Marys" ten times,' snapped Sister Shanthi. And, once they'd done so, brandishing the wooden cane reserved for such occasions, 'Hold out your palms.'

Shirin was at the end of the long line of boys—the lone girl sticking out like a guava in a basket of cashews. Her classmates sitting on the floor in front of them watched wide-eyed—the terror that Shirin felt writ large on their faces. She had never been caned before. She always cried when one of her classmates got caned, and now that she had to face the same thing, she could feel the sobs building in her chest and threatening to overflow. But none of the boys were crying and she didn't want to be labelled a coward and a crybaby.

Anil, the first in line, cried out as the cane came whooshing down on his outstretched palm—not once, as was customary, but twice.

'This will teach you not to run away from school again,' said Sister Shanthi grimly as she started on Steven who was next.

Involuntary tears filled Shirin's eyes. Her palm trembled. Oh, why had she done this? It was sheer agony, awaiting her turn, hearing the yells of her partners in crime, feeling their pain. When Sister Shanthi reached her, she stopped and shook her head in disapproval.

'Shame on you,' she said, 'gallivanting with all those boys. What will your mother say?'

As it was the Catholic 'English Medium' school, the nuns spoke only in English, of course, and the pupils were expected to do so too. And even though Shirin didn't know what 'gallivanting' meant, even though she couldn't fathom why it would warrant such disgust and her mother's displeasure, Sister Shanthi's words hurt more than the caning. Shirin got caned not twice but thrice. As she watched welts rise like Madhu's yeasty dosa mix on her red palm, Shirin thought, *I deserve this, for disappointing my mother.*

But the worst was yet to come. Shirin had just joined the rest of her class when the headmistress of their school, Sister Maya, entered and looked at all of them in turn, until her eyes locked with Shirin's.

'Shirin,' she said, her ugly face looking more ogre-like than ever, 'please come into my office.'

The school building was comprised of two rooms. The larger of these housed the various classrooms, separated by cardboard dividers which could be moved depending on the size of the class. The other room served as the headmistress's office. Scary Sister Maya closed the door to this room while meting out punishments. The rest of the school would hear the wails of the transgressor and imagine the worst. When the child came back out, he or she was so traumatised that they never talked about the incident again. But they were never what the nuns labelled as 'naughty' again either. The nuns were very effective at quashing their charges' spirits.

Shirin could feel scores of terrified eyes on her, as the school collectively followed her progress, pitying her, and at the same time guiltily relieved that it was not one of them. She made her way to Sister Maya's office, her legs trembling, her sore hand held slightly away from her dress so that it wouldn't accidentally brush against it, her eyes fixed on Sister Maya's unyielding back.

Once inside her office, Sister Maya turned to face Shirin, and reached behind her to close the door. As her fleshy hand neared Shirin, she tried hard not to flinch, even as a little stubborn part of her rebelled. *Why only me? Why not the boys as well?* Then the door slammed shut and she and Sister Maya were alone.

Sister Maya stared at Shirin from over the top of the spectacles that were perched precariously at the tip of her bulbous nose. This close up, Shirin could see the tiny black freckles dotting it. It reminded her of pictures of white mushrooms with red dots that she had seen somewhere once. A hysterical laugh threatened to bubble out of her throat—even as her eyes shone bright with tears—but she managed to swallow it down.

'So, miss, who gave you permission to sneak out of the classroom with a bunch of boys and steal bimblis?' Sister Maya asked.

Shirin couldn't reply. Her words stuck in her throat. The acidity of the bimblis, along with the terror she felt, was making her nauseous. She was afraid that if she opened her mouth, she would vomit all over Sister Maya's prized collection of holy statues arranged neatly on her desk.

'I am very disappointed in you. I thought you were a good girl, that you would make your mother proud.' Sister Maya's accusatory gaze bored into Shirin. 'But no, you have to consort with boys and forget all the rules.' She said the word 'boys' with vehemence, like it was a swear word, like Shirin had had a date with the devil.

'Do you know how many sins you committed today? Remember God is watching you, always.' She pointed to the statues on her desk and the huge one of Jesus nailed to the cross that took up most of the wall behind her chair. 'Do you want to burn in hell?'

Shirin could feel God's wrath, His disappointment and the heat of His anger. She could feel the flames of Hell licking her bare feet. She started sobbing and couldn't stop.

Sister Maya snorted in disgust. 'What is the use of crying now, Shirin? You should have thought of the consequences before you ran after a bunch of boys.'

She had to endure many more agonizing minutes of Sister Maya's lecture. When she thought she could stand the guilt no longer and might as well kill herself before the wrath of God did, Sister Maya was finally done. Shirin was asked to kneel down in front of the statue of Jesus on the cross and pray for forgiveness. She was to stay there, on her knees until her mother arrived to take her home in disgrace.

Jacinta found her kneeling on the cement floor in Sister Maya's room of shame, the tears forming two little pools around her knees, her eyes swollen and as red as the welts on her palm. Shirin could not meet her mother's gaze. As Jacinta scooped Shirin up in her arms, something she hadn't done since Shirin learned to walk, she did not say a word.

Her mother carried her through the muddy road behind the school and down the little hill, past the stream and through the thin strip of raised earth just wide enough to accommodate one pair of feet, which separated the verdant fields, just starting to sprout milky paddy.

Shirin held on to her mother, her arms round her neck, sobs coming out in remembered bursts of agony. Jacinta was pregnant with Anita at the time, but she carried Shirin home without a murmur, her breath escaping in short heavy puffs. The ears of paddy, swaying gently in the breeze, mocked Shirin. 'Look at you,' they said, in soft swishes. 'You are a disgrace to your mother. How could you have let her down so? You are soon to be a big sister. What example are you setting?'

Shirin buried her face in Jacinta's warm shoulder, inhaling her mother's familiar smell of Ponds talcum powder mixed with sweat, and refused to look at the fields. She missed the first glimpse of her house, something she always loved, rising up among the banana, mango and guava trees on the next hill, guarded by a soldierly row of coconut trees, and intercepted by mehendi-yellow marigolds and chilli-powder-red hibiscus flowers which her mother and

Madhu had painstakingly planted. Her mother crossed the stream at the base of the hill, walking carefully on the makeshift coconut-tree frond bridge. She carried Shirin past the tamarind tree, nestling halfway up the hill, navigating with an ease bred through years of practice the steep path made from uneven stones and pieces of brick haphazardly put together. As they approached the house, Rex, the stray mongrel Madhu had adopted, who was sprawled on the little veranda outside the bathroom and licking his paws in the sun, came bounding up and started running in circles around Jacinta's legs, tugging at the ends of her sari.

'Shoo, Rex, Shoo,' said Jacinta, the first words she had spoken since she came to pick Shirin up at the school.

Madhu came rushing out of the kitchen, wiping her hands hurriedly on her housecoat, her hair flying in all directions. 'What happened? Oh, Shirin, baby, look at your knees!'

Without a word of explanation, Jacinta carried Shirin in through the open front door and lay her down on the floor of the living room.

Madhu fussed over her. She wiped Shirin's face with a damp cloth and gently cleaned her knees and her sore palm. She applied Boroline—her panacea for all childhood scrapes and hurts—to Shirin's knees and led her into the kitchen. When the peon from school had come to fetch Jacinta, Madhu knew something had happened. She had made Shirin's favourite potato bondas with coriander-and-mint chutney. She sat Shirin down on her lap and fed her. But Shirin, who loved all food, and who had committed this, her first great transgression for love of food, found that she could not eat. But she knew that if she refused to eat, Madhu would worry, so Shirin forced the bondas down through the tears and the fat lump of shame and regret which sat in her throat. Even as an adult, she would never again eat potato bondas without experiencing a slight aftertaste of guilt and shame.

In the days that followed, Shirin worried that her mother was displeased with her and would never love her again.

As always, Madhu sensed her anguish. As she oiled Shirin's long hair with warm coconut oil, Madhu said, 'She looks upset because she is tired, Shirin, not because of you. This baby she is carrying is giving her a lot of trouble. I bet it's another boy.' Shirin could hear the smile in Madhu's voice when she said 'boy', the awe which accompanied the word.

'Madhu,' she whispered, turning round to face Madhu just as she was starting on the second plait, her eyes wide with worry, 'Ma's face, when she carried me, was so... so...'

'Angry?' Madhu prompted, and then, at Shirin's nod, cupped her face in her palm. 'Silly girl, she was angry with Sister Maya.'

'Sister Maya?' Shirin was shocked, sure that for once Madhu had got it wrong. This was her mother they were talking about. Her mother. Who had taught her that nuns and priests were equivalent to God. 'No. I don't believe you.'

'She told me so.' Madhu smiled gently, 'She did not agree with what Sister Maya did but she didn't say anything to her. She couldn't. That's why she was upset.'

Her ma hadn't looked upset. She had looked angry.

'She grew up in a convent, see.' Madhu's voice was soothing.

'Who?'

'Your ma, that's who.'

'Really?' This was news to Shirin. She thought about this for a minute, wrinkling her nose. How horrible, to grow up with nuns! A turquoise butterfly with yellow suns on its wings hovered close. 'Did she not have a ma and da then?'

'She did, but they weren't very nice. So she had to stay with the nuns.'

Shirin was quiet for a minute, pondering. The butterfly landed on the hibiscus plant nearby and Shirin's fingers itched to catch it. 'Will I be sent to live with nuns if I am naughty again?'

Madhu laughed, the sound reassuring Shirin more than the words that followed. 'Of course not, you silly girl! Now turn around. I need to finish plaiting your hair else you will be late for school.'

'I don't want to go to school anyway. Everyone is teasing me, and I have to wear long socks to hide the bruises on my knees, and they *itch*...' All the agony and worry of the past few days burst out in a torrent of tears.

Madhu gathered her in her arms. 'Shh... It's okay, Shirin. Have your bruises not healed yet? Ayyo, poor you! Why didn't you tell me? Let me get the Boroline and some bandages. You sit here... Look; Rex has come to console you. Shoo, Rex don't lick her tears... Does it tickle? Good dog, you've made my Shirin giggle...'

As Madhu tied the strips of cloth she had torn from an old nightie to use as bandages securely around Shirin's knees, she asked, 'So who is teasing you then?'

'The boys tease me to make me talk to them. But I don't want to; I'll only get in trouble.' A hiccup. 'And the girls tease me for gallivanting with the boys...' Shirin interspersed the new English word she had learnt from Sister Shanthi, with her Konkani.

'What's gallivanting?'

'I think it means stealing bimblis. Sister Shanthi used it,' in a whisper.

'Look here, Shirin,' Madhu put her palm under Shirin's chin and tilted her face upwards. 'If your classmates tease you, you ignore them. Why do you go to school? To study, isn't it? You work hard and get good marks. Then won't your ma be so pleased with you? She will be beaming when she sees your report card. And everyone will want to be your friend when you come first in the class!'

Absorbed in Madhu's fantasy, Shirin nodded, sniffing away the last of her tears.

'Now don't let your ma find out, but here is a nevri to eat on the way to school. Isn't that a sunny smile! There's a good girl. Rex will keep you company till Lenny Bai's house.'

❇ ❇ ❇

Shirin sat up in bed and squinted, bleary-eyed, at the clock. 4:00 a.m.

Beside her Vinod stirred, then blinked awake. 'Shonu, is it...'

The spectre of her nightmare slipped under the covers between them like an old intimate.

'No. I'm fine. Just wanted a drink is all. You go back to sleep.' She smiled down at his tousled head.

Reassured, he smiled back, closed his eyes and was snoring in two ticks. She envied the ease with which he could delve in and out of slumber. Sighing, she got out of bed, only to trip over Vinod's book which he always chucked across the room before turning off the light instead of leaving it on the bedside table like any other normal person. 'Oh, for God's sake!' she grumbled.

From the dregs of her dream, Sister Maya materialized. 'Don't take the name of the Lord in vain, child,' she admonished.

CHAPTER FOUR

Super Sleuth Investigates

The first task that Reena Diaz, Super Sleuth, undertook was to make a list of all possible suspects. They were, in no particular order,

1) Deepak
2) Anita
3) Jacinta, Grandmother
4) Madhu
5) Walter, Grandfather—deceased.

She pondered this list for a bit, as she imagined Nancy Drew would. In the end she decided that although it made sense to talk to Deepak and Anita first, as they were the ones actually in the photograph, she wouldn't do so. For one, Anita was not available to talk to at the moment, and Deepak, well, she was worried that he would confiscate the picture and tell her off for poking her nose in matters well left alone. Confiscation of the picture would spell the end of her days as a detective.

Ever since she had found the picture, questions had been buzzing like a convent of nuns chanting the rosary in her head. There would be quite a simple explanation, Reena reasoned. This girl must be some cousin they had all forgotten about. But why would they forget a relative? Or shove her photo behind some other picture, out of sight? Why were there no other pictures of her? (She had sifted meticulously through all the other albums for the rest of the afternoon, in the hope of finding more pictures of this mystery girl.) And why had that particular picture been creased and worn, as if it had once been treasured? And even if they *had* forgotten about this mysterious girl—whom they seemed quite comfortable with in the photo—wouldn't they remember her when Reena grew up to look just like her? Why the conspiracy of silence? Was there a conspiracy, or had they just forgotten to mention her? Had she been so insignificant that she had slipped straight out of their minds?

Reena hoped to get at least some of the answers from Madhu. Madhu was the one her dad and aunt had turned to when they were in trouble. She was the one who had got them out of scrapes without Jacinta—Mai—knowing.

Now all that remained was for Reena to corner Madhu when no one else was around...

Her opportunity came that afternoon. One she couldn't miss. The incessant rain had eased for once, and her mother, bored of sitting at home or visiting her husband's friends, managed to coax Deepak to take her shopping in Dommur.

'Would you like to come, Rinu?' Preeti asked. 'We'll go by rickshaw so you won't get wet or your dress muddied.'

Though the rain had eased, there were dirty red pools of water everywhere. Preeti knew how Reena hated feeling her wet dress lick her bare legs knowing that mud had spattered all over the back, even when she was wearing the ridiculously expensive 'special rain shoes which do not splash' that the salesman had cornered them into buying in that shop in Commercial Street.

'And after we can have masala dosas and gadbad at Aashirwad,' Preeti continued, looking expectantly at Reena.

Aashirwad was the restaurant they always ate at in Dommur. Climbing up the winding walkway, breathing in the vanilla scent of ice cream mixed with the sharp, salty aroma of idlis and sambar, marvelling at the impossibly long paper-thin crispy hot dosas and picking at the black mustard seeds in her green coconut chutney, made Reena feel as if in here, time had progressed in snapshots. She could see herself visiting as a toddler, sitting on her father's knee, fascinated by the shiny stainless-steel tumblers of water and trying to grab at her reflection, even as her father pushed the tumbler aside and her face grew impossibly long and splintered. Then as a little girl in a polka-dot dress and ribbons in her hair, sitting wedged between her mother and father. For some reason, they'd always dressed up to go to Aashirwad. After their meal, her mother bought sambar and rasam powders, malpuris, thila ladus, holiges and raw mango pickle from the shop below to take with them back to Bangalore. Going to Aashirwad was a tradition and she was tempted, but she had more important work to do.

'What do you do here anyway?' her mother asked curiously, but before Reena could concoct an answer, continued, 'God, if your dad launches into yet another lecture on the pedigree of the Diaz family, their distinguished roots in Taipur, I'll kill him... You're sure you don't want to come? You might help prevent a murder...'

'Oh go on, Mum, spend his money. That'll be good revenge.' And then Reena had her brainwave. 'Why don't you ask Mai? It will be good for her. Dad and Mai can reminisce while you shop.'

Mai needed some persuading. She was getting very frail. Madhu helped her into one of her good saris—'The Kanjeevaram silk one I wore for your Roce, Deepak,' Mai said, a far-off light in her eyes as she relived the memory—and off she went, leaning on her son's arm for the walk up the little path to where the auto-rickshaw was waiting.

Once she'd waved them off, Reena, complimenting herself on a job well done and armed with her sleuthing handbook which hid the photograph nicely in-between its pages, went in search of Madhu.

Madhu was washing clothes on the little granite stone by the well, in the shade of the tamarind and banana trees. The heavy thud of clothes hitting stone guided Reena there.

Deepak had tried countless times to get Madhu to use the new washing machine he had had installed in the bathroom. But Madhu was having none of it: 'I wash the clothes, rinse them and then scrub them again. Will that square little box do that? I am not using any fancy machines when my hands will do.' Since then, the washing machine had sat forlorn in the bathroom gathering dust and chicken droppings where the hens perched on it when being chased by Gypsy, the gleaming white exterior fading slowly to dull grey.

Reena sat on the cement rim surround of the well and watched Madhu. Her sari was tied up, the pallu tucked tightly into her waist. Her worn apron was wet and hair escaped the confines of her bun and collected in greying tendrils around her face. Every once in a while she used her arm to push it away, leaving wet soapy smudges on her face. She had finished scrubbing the clothes and was wringing the water out of them by rolling them into a tight cylinder and then bashing them very hard against the stone. The bar of Rin soap that she had used lay on the stone beside her, bleeding dark blue water onto the streaky granite surface. Gypsy, who followed Madhu wherever she went, lay curled beside her feet. She looked lost to the world, except for the deep growl that escaped her every once in a while and the little twitch her nose gave when a fly landed on it. *Do dogs dream?* Reena wondered.

Every so often the spicy, scented breeze stirred the tamarind and banana trees, releasing a little flood of raindrops that had adhered to the leaves. The garden in the front courtyard which Madhu diligently tended was in full bloom, and Reena breathed in the sweet honey aroma of the hibiscus and jasmine flowers mixed in with the earthy smell of rain-washed mud. Bees buzzed, butterflies flitted and a fat frog stirred in the grass next to the well. Reena sighed, for just a moment loath to disrupt the peace and stir up old secrets. The moment didn't last long, however.

'Madhu,' she said, 'I've got something to show you.'

Madhu jumped, startled. Gypsy barked. 'Gypsy, shush. Rinu, you gave me a fright. How long have you been sitting there?'

'Not long. I like sitting here, watching you. It's peaceful.'

'What's that?' Madhu rubbed soapy hands down the sides of her apron and extended wet fingers to receive the photograph Reena was holding out to her. Reena watched as she squinted at the picture, as her smile stilled and her face lost colour.

'Where did you find this?' Madhu asked.

'Oh, you know...' said Reena vaguely, deliberately nonchalant, even though her heart was pounding.

Up until now, though she had wanted to find out more about her lookalike, wanted to get to the bottom of the mystery, a part of her had thought that it was all in her head. The adults would pooh-pooh her wild theories as just that. There would be a perfectly simple and straightforward explanation.

Although she'd hoped to have stumbled on something, now, as she looked at the myriad emotions flitting across Madhu's lined face, as her breath came out in long sighs, as the smile fled her face to be replaced by grief, Reena wished she had never found the photograph. She wished it had remained hidden in that old woodlice-ridden album.

For the first time, she considered the fact that the girl might be dead. But that didn't make much sense either. Why hide her photographs? Why forget her? In Reena's experience, the dead were revered and remembered all the time, even more than the living, she sometimes thought. There was a seven-day mass after the funeral, a thirty-day mass, a yearly mass, framed photographs adorned with garlands taking pride of place next to the altar...

Again she found herself asking the same questions. Why the secrecy, the conspiracy of silence?

Madhu used the pallu of her sari to wipe away the tears streaming down her face.

Reena was horrified. She had never seen Madhu cry. She didn't know what to do. Guilt, sharp and painful bound her to her perch on the rim of the well. Try as she might, she couldn't seem to move to comfort Madhu.

The frog hopped away in wet sticky plonks, drawing arches in the air. Gypsy stirred and ambled up to Madhu, licking away the salty tears which kept on coming.

'Shoo, Gypsy,' Madhu murmured, patting the dog's flank. 'I saved it in a safe place, but couldn't remember where I had put it. I looked everywhere, but in the end had to accept it was lost. And now...'

So the photograph had been Madhu's.

Madhu ran her fingers gently over the girl's face, her hair.

And Reena understood why the picture was worn.

'She had lovely hair, thick and long. I used to plait it for her in two long braids, and tie it up behind her ears.

She always made sure I used matching ribbons.' Madhu smiled. 'She sat so still while I oiled it and combed it, no matter how knotty it was, no matter how much it hurt. And I talked to her the whole time. She was my favourite, you know. It was a secret—hers and mine.' Madhu's voice broke.

Reena waited until Madhu had composed herself somewhat.

She hated herself for doing so but she had to ask. 'Did she die?'

Madhu blanched. Years of living in a Catholic household had rubbed off on her and she made the sign of the cross, her puffy, red-rimmed eyes sprouting fresh tears. She spoke so softly that Reena had to strain to hear. 'No. Thank God, thank Jesus, no.'

CHAPTER FIVE
Blue-Green Soda Bottles

'You're early today, Shirin.' Kate said as she and Shirin took the lift up from the car park together.

'Yes, well, Vinod had a breakfast meeting and I was awake,' Shirin said, yawning.

'Wide awake, I see,' smiled Kate, who always turned up at the office at the crack of dawn—which would have been an extremely annoying trait in any other boss. 'Journey here okay?'

'Yes.' She had sped past that particular pedestrian crossing, ignoring the two people waiting to cross. No haunting eyes.

'It's not the nightmare keeping you up?' Kate's voice was tentative.

Sister Maya's face—thick bushy eyebrows joined together at the top of her frog-like nose; a moustache replete with the beginnings of a beard; moles dotting her face, with curly black hairs growing out of the larger two, located rather symmetrically on either side of her nostrils—flashed before Shirin's eyes. She smiled. 'Not the nightmare, no. An ogre called Sister Maya.'

'Huh?'

'She was my primary school headmistress.'

Kate's eyebrows were two question marks, her lips curved in a bemused smile. A query.

'Memories,' Shirin continued by way of explanation. 'They've been overwhelming me.'

'Since the dream?'

Shirin nodded. 'Vinod thinks it's the healing process. He's read all the books that counsellor gave us. He says I am ready to revisit the past.' Words tripped over themselves in their hurry to get out of Shirin's mouth, a bit like the memories that hovered, ready to spill out at the slightest provocation. 'He thinks it's the only way I can let go. Move on.'

'And what do *you* think?'

Numbers blinked red on the panel by the lift door: 2, 3, 4. 'It doesn't hurt to remember, Kate. Not anymore.'

Kate smiled. 'Good. That's good.'

The lift pinged, the doors opening with a sigh. Shirin looked at the rows of desks, bereft without their occupants. 'Right. Work,' she said.

'If you need to talk about anything, you know where I am.'

'I know. Thank you. For yesterday.'

'Don't be silly. See you around ten-ish for the UAT meeting.'

'Oh, Kate, I almost forgot. That guarantees spec you requested is ready. Shall I email it to you?'

'I think it would be better if we went over it together. Print it off. I'll be at your desk in a tick.'

As she waited for Kate, Shirin clicked on the first message in her inbox, one of those forwarded emails that she usually deleted unread: a photograph of a Stella Artois bottle *sans* label, sitting on a windowsill, a ray of weak winter sun illuminating it, making it glow. To Shirin, it looked just like the blue-green soda bottles of her childhood.

A memory, long forgotten, suddenly vivid: Pelam beach. Sea roaring; sea gulls hovering, scavenging for fish scraps; noisy crows swooping and cackling; men with wicker baskets of churmuri slung loosely round their necks peddling their wares; the overpowering stench of rotting fish masking the salty-sweet tang of sea and the inviting spicy oniony aroma of churmuri; Madhu haggling for fish; Deepak wandering off to the little shop on the far side of the beach, drawn by the soda bottles, meticulously counting out all his pocket money; Shirin and Anita impatiently hopping from one foot to another—they were barefoot and the sand was quite hot, even in the setting sun—urging him to hurry: 'Madhu will be looking for us, Deepak. Quick.' Deepak looking up at the shopkeeper, eyes shiny with hope, 'I have fifty-five paise here. Mummy also said I have five rupees in the bank. Will that be enough to buy the bottle?' The shopkeeper smirking, displaying black, paan-stained teeth,

'Shoo. Go away. The bottles are not for sale.' Deepak's face crumpling. And Shirin, boiling with a rage she hadn't known she possessed, shaking her fist at the leering shopkeeper, using the very bad English word she had overheard once, 'You—you bastard.'

'What are you looking at?' Kate perched on the arm of her chair, looked at her monitor and guffawed, 'A Stella Artois bottle? You in the mood for a pint, girl, at barely nine in the morning?'

'It looks just like the soda bottles of my childhood.' If she closed her eyes, she could see the beguiling crates of blue-green glass bottles outside the thatched entrance to the little shop by the River Varuna, which sold sweet milky coffee, onion bhajis, green plantain crisps and whole clusters of tiny ripe bananas, yellow skin flecked with black, each shaped like the tail of the letter 'y'.

'The bottles were sealed with a marble on top to stop the gas escaping and they used to fascinate us kids. We often tried to prise the marble out, under the watchful gaze of the shopkeeper. We had to pay twenty paise—our sugar-cane juice money—for the privilege.' Sugar-cane juice: thick, frothy, the colour of milk sprouting from between the brown hands of Ananthanna's wife as she squeezed Nandini's udders, sweet as Alphonso mango mixed with honey, served in cloudy glasses that had once upon a time been clear. It was freshly pressed courtesy of the booming enterprise that was Jenna Uncle's sugar-cane machine, headquartered under the shady, all-enveloping branches of the banyan tree beside Muthu, the fisherwoman hawking fresh fish caught that morning arranged in neat piles on a dry banana branch, which slotted onto the two handles of her basket: an impromptu tray.

Kate laid a hand on Shirin's arm and smiled. 'Shirin, your face, it's glowing. From the inside.'

'It's such a relief, Kate, to let the memories come instead of always pushing them away, repressing them.' The Varuna River rippling silvery grey beside the shop with the soda bottles; the coven of crows conversing in their secret language as they perched on coconut trees that bowed down to the river as if drinking from the water; the boatmen humming a catchy, elusive tune as they ferried people across, their dark muscles gleaming, beads of perspiration forming little rivulets down their bare torsos, soaking their colourful lungis. The bus from Dommur, creaking and complaining as it disgorged its straggling passengers, the conductor yelling instructions to the driver to turn the bus around, slapping the back of the bus when it was in danger of going too deep into the river, inadvertently waking the drunk snoring open-mouthed in the back seat; the conductor balancing on one leg on the steps of the bus, his skinny body dangling, yelling, 'Dommur! Dommur!' urging the few people clustered around, dressed in their best clothes for the trip into town, to climb aboard, and, once they'd boarded, blowing his ear-splitting whistle and shouting, 'Right, Poi,' scaring the few crows perched delicately atop the bus into squawking in fright and flying away.

'Earth to Shirin... Shirin, you in there?' Kate gently tapped Shirin's forehead.

'Sorry, Kate.' Shirin shook her head to clear it of the images. 'Was miles away.'

'I could see that,' Kate grinned.

Shirin blinked to rid herself of the sudden urge to run away, to go home. Why did her mind insist on calling Taipur home when it had not been that for years? 'I know—guarantees beckon.'

'Yes, sadly they do. But we are early and you've finished the spec ahead of schedule, so what the heck, you are allowed to daydream for, let's see—' Kate made a show of looking at her watch, '—a minute more.'

'Aw... just one minute?' Shirin feigned a whine and they shared a laugh.

Kate stopped abruptly mid-laugh, clapped her palm on her mouth. 'Shirin, I forgot to tell you before. Jenny's back. She starts tomorrow.'

'Oh.'

'Will you be okay?'

Shirin willed her lips to move, curve upwards in a grin. 'Of course. Shall we begin?' She waved the sheaf of paper she had printed in front of Kate.

Kate looked piercingly at her and nodded, morphing into brisk work mode. 'Let's.'

Shirin let out the breath she was holding, glad of work to take her mind off things. Work was her saviour, and she was grateful to Vinod for persuading her to do the software course during those early dark months in the UK—which had led to this job—when all she'd wanted was to wallow in depression. It had given her a reason to get up each morning, to face the world, to escape her past—however briefly.

She would keep the smile fixed on her face and deal with Jenny tomorrow—but right now, guarantees beckoned.

CHAPTER SIX
Madhu's favourite

'Shirin,' Madhu said. 'Her name is Shirin.'

She was calmer now. They had moved to the kitchen and she was sitting on the cold cement floor, her legs bent and her knees touching her forehead. Her hands circled her knees and she nursed a tumbler of sweet tea in them.

'Who is she?' asked Reena.

Madhu stared at her sharply for a moment and then shook her head, a funny half smile playing on her face. 'Of all the people who could have found it…' she whispered almost to herself.

'I mean she's obviously a relative. Is she my dad's cousin?' Reena didn't want to sound impatient, not with Madhu in this state, but she was a sleuth and sleuths had to follow rules. *Get to the point; don't allow the subject to digress* was one of them.

'She is your dad's younger sister. The one in the middle. First Deepak, then Shirin and then Anita.'

The shock Reena felt must have shown on her face, because Madhu put down her tumbler and gently stroked Reena's cheeks with her callused hands.

'Why doesn't anyone mention her? What has she done?'

Madhu's open, expressive face closed before Reena's eyes. Her lips became a thin straight line. She stood up wearily, went to the sink and deposited her tumbler. Then she turned to face Reena. There was such sorrow in her eyes that it hurt Reena to look.

'It's not my place to say anything, Rinu, to comment on what goes on. I have always felt part of this family, but I did not agree with what was done eleven years ago, with what is still being done.' She sighed. 'I didn't agree then and I don't now,' she repeated.

'But...' Questions scrambled through Reena's head and she couldn't decide which to ask first.

'I could tell you about her if you like...' Madhu said softly.

'Yes, please.'

'Come here then and sit beside me. It's a relief to be able to talk about her at last.'

'Tell me everything: how she looked, how she was...'

Madhu smiled fondly, brushing a wayward strand of hair away from Reena's eyes and tucking it behind her ear. 'Let me get you something to eat first. I could talk about Shirin forever, you know. Stop me when you are bored...'

So, sitting on the kitchen step, eating sannas and dry fish chutney, with Chinnu and Gypsy begging for scraps, Madhu told her about Shirin, Madhu's favourite. The aunt whom Reena hadn't known existed: a dusky, plump, shy girl who felt she wasn't good enough—not nearly as pretty as her sister, and not the coveted male, the son to carry on the family name, like her brother...

'Oh, poor Shirin...' Reena's heart ached for the girl her newly discovered aunt had once been.

'Yes, she was always trying to please.' Madhu's eyes had a faraway expression, as if she was looking not at the fields in front of them, but directly into the past. With an effort, she pulled her gaze away and focused on Reena. 'Right, I have to prepare dinner. Your mum, dad and Mai will be here soon.'

'They will have eaten at Aashirwad.'

'Not your Mai. She likes to have red rice, curds and lime pickle for dinner.'

'Tell me more, Madhu.'

'I thought you would tire of my ramblings and ask me to stop.' Madhu smiled fondly at Reena. 'Thank you for finding that picture. It's been wonderful to talk about my Shirin.'

'What happened, Madhu? What did she do?'

Madhu stood up slowly, joints creaking and stretched. Then she turned to Reena, held her face in her palms and kissed her nose gently. 'I told you; it's not for me to say.'

At least, thought Reena as she came away into the living room and lay down on the mat beside the front door, she had garnered a few facts. She wrote them down in her notebook, below the list of suspects.

Mystery Girl—Name: Shirin

Relationship to other subjects in photograph: Deepak (this detective's dad) and Anita (aunt): sister.

Other: Madhu's favourite.

IMPORTANT: Rift that caused her to be erased from family happened eleven years ago.

'How could they all do this?' she wondered, re-reading what she'd written and correcting the spelling of 'favourite'. How could her dad live his life, visit his old friends and reminisce whilst completely blocking out a major part of his childhood: his sister? How could you forget your sister existed? What had Shirin done to deserve this sort of punishment?

If she, Reena, had had a sibling, she would have stood by them no matter what they did. She longed for a sister or brother. She had hounded her parents for a time, but had given up when the answer was always: 'You are perfect, darling. You are enough for us.'

'Yes,' she had countered. 'But what about what *I* want?'

'When you are older, you can have lots of children,' her mother had said, laughing at Reena's expression of disgust.

Reena pulled out the picture and looked at Shirin again. She looked ordinary and a bit shy. Her eyes were kind. She thought of the story Madhu had told, of a timid girl always trying to please. Had Shirin changed when she grew up? Turned into the monster that sometimes stirred within Reena when she wearied of being the good girl she was expected to be? Sometimes, when her parents told her off without even bothering to *listen* to her, she felt this monster waking, growing, and she lashed out, without thinking, without caring. She had even bitten her mother once. Afterwards, when the monster retreated, she had apologised to Preeti.

Preeti had lifted Reena's chin and softly wiped the tears streaming silently from downcast eyes. 'We all get angry sometimes, Rinu. But it's not okay to hit, bite or lash out physically, however angry you are. No pocket money for two months.' Reena had looked up then, her gaze settling on her mother's face. 'Consequences, Rinu, consequences. Think before you act. Even when you are so angry you want to hurt someone very badly,' her mother had said, gently tapping her nose and pulling her close into a hug. Her mother understood, had known about the monster without Reena ever having to tell her...

She had come to believe that everyone had a monster living inside them. But was it possible for someone to change so drastically, to completely renege on the person they were and become only the monster? Could she, Reena, change too?

And her grandmother, Jacinta: how could she turn her back on her own child, one she had carried for nine months, one she had watched grow from a helpless baby to an independent adult? Weren't mothers supposed to forgive even the worst sins when the perpetrator was their child?

TO DO: Find reason for rift.

Plan A: Madhu. Refuses to tell. Work on her.

Plan B: Mai? Not a good idea. Deepak (this detective's dad)? Even worse. Preeti (Mum)? Does she even know? Aunt Anita? Possible.

Plan C: Find Aunt Anita and ask her about Aunt Shirin.

Reena looked up from the photograph and the past, at the world beyond the front door. While this revelation had turned her whole universe upside down, nothing had changed outside. If anything, the fields looked a more brilliant green than usual, and the flowers in the courtyard shone. It was as if the rain had decided to be extravagant and applied an extra coat of paint on Nature.

Smells and sounds drifted from the kitchen: pots banging, onions sizzling as they hit the pan of hot oil. Reena lay there, with Gypsy, who was sprawled across the steps leading down from the front door, for company and pondered the doings of the adults in her life, people she thought she'd known—until twilight set in, sapping the world of colour; until mosquitoes started feasting on her flesh; until it started raining again, and her parents and grandmother returned from their shopping trip, wet but happy and full of news, bringing noise and busyness into the quiet house.

'You should have come, Rinu. We had such fun. And the rain held off, well until just now.' Preeti flopped onto the mat beside Reena, her face animated. 'I bought a sandalwood jewellery box for Mrs. Gupta. What do you think? Will she like it?'

Reena looked at her mum as if seeing her for the first time. Did she know about Shirin?

Preeti didn't seem to notice that Reena hadn't replied.

'And the food at Aashirwad was great. But there was a fight just outside. When we went in, it was a small spat between two people and we thought nothing of it. But when we finished, we couldn't get out of the restaurant! The entrance was blocked by so many people all arguing and shouting at each other. The little quarrel had ballooned into this huge altercation between the Hindus and the Muslims. We had to leave by the side entrance. As we were leaving, the police drove up... In a way I was glad you didn't come, Rinu. Dommur is changing. Ma said there's been plenty of unrest in the last few months. Isn't that so, Ma?' Preeti turned to include Jacinta who had just hobbled into the room, sighing with exertion, into the conversation.

Jacinta lowered herself gingerly onto the sofa and stretched her legs out in front of her. 'What to do? Things change. It used to be so peaceful around here. Now the Hindus have started complaining about the Muslims' call for prayer. And the Muslims don't want the Hindu crematorium on their land.'

'Their land?' Preeti asked.

'They are claiming Nemar as theirs. They don't want the Aata held there either, which has the Tulu community in uproar.' Jacinta shook her head. 'All these petty disputes! It's shameful. Nobody is tolerant anymore.'

Reena looked at Jacinta's lined, familiar face. *She* had not been tolerant of whatever her daughter had done. What if Reena did something wrong in the future? Would her parents pretend she had never existed and throw her unceremoniously out of their lives like the jar of prawn pickle gone bad that her mother had chucked away before coming here? Sudden tears pricked her eyes at the thought.

'What about you, Rinu? Did you have fun?' her mother asked.

'Yes,' Reena mumbled, hiding her face.

'Anyway, guess what's for dinner? We packed the paper masala dosa from Aashirwad for you. Your favourite,' Preeti announced, expectant joy at her daughter's reaction lighting up her face.

Impulsively, Reena reached up and gave her mother a hug.

Preeti laughed happily. 'If I can guarantee this reaction from you, Rinu, I will get you dosas every time I am out...'

Reena buried her face in her mother's shoulder, drawing comfort from her familiar smell: the faint remnants of sandalwood talcum powder mixed with sweat.

Madhu came in with a tumbler of ginger tea for Mai. 'Madhu,' Jacinta said, 'Bijju Bai's only son, Lucky, has run away with Sumati the fisherwoman's daughter, it seems. Winnie was in Aashirwad. She told me. The shame of it! Bijju will be voted out of the parish council committee of course.'

Deepak walked in, freshly bathed, wearing a lungi and running a towel across his bare torso. 'Who will?'

'Bijju of the big house up the road, who's always bragging about her daughters in America: Shanta this and Jaya that...' She took a sip of ginger tea. 'When is Anita going to have a baby?' she grumbled, irritably, the talk of daughters having reminded her of hers. 'Winnie was asking if there was any good news. "How old is she now? How many years since she married that Hindu?" she asked.'

Uncle Uttam was a Hindu? Why had Reena never thought about this, thought to ask? So had Aunt Anita…?

'It's none of her business,' her father's voice interrupted Reena's musings.

'You know how things are here, Deepu,' Jacinta said wearily. 'I will never live it down. Anita's marriage. Even though Uttam is a Brahmin from a distinguished family. I was only reinstated to the parish council committee when Anita became the face of Ponds.' She sighed loudly at the mention of her errant daughter. 'Will you talk to Anita about starting a family for me?'

So Aunt Anita had *not* had an arranged marriage like Reena's parents. She had gone against her mother's wishes, fallen in love with a Hindu no less. It figured. Her impulsive, daring Aunt Anita would not meekly marry the man her mother chose for her. But *she* was not disowned. So what had Shirin done?

'Yes, Ma,' her dad was saying to Mai.

'Though sometimes I think, was it worth it?' Mai was saying.

'Was what worth it, ma?' Deepak asked.

'All that happened.' Wearily, Mai leaned back in her chair, fingered the rosary beads she was wearing, 'So worried about status. At the cost of… I can't sleep you know, some nights. My back…' She laid a gnarled hand on her hip. 'And then I wonder…'

What did Mai mean? And why was she talking in this strange way, in half-baked sentences?

'Ma, are you applying that balm I bought you? It is very effective you know.' Deepak said.

Jacinta looked at her son fondly. 'You are the only one who has made me proud. Such a good son.'

Deepak preened.

Preeti rolled her eyes at Reena behind Deepak's back. Despite herself, Reena giggled.

Deepak turned to Reena, smiling. 'How is my favourite girl doing?' he asked.

Reena could not bear to look at him. 'Fine. Shall we start the rosary now?'

'My goodness, Preeti! I think Reena should stay here more often. She is actually suggesting saying the rosary instead of pretending to fall asleep while reciting it. What a transformation!' her father joked.

Reena gritted her teeth. Everything about her father irritated her. She had considered him to be a man of principle, a man who didn't lie. And now she had caught him out in a lie of colossal proportions. Something made her ask, 'How many brothers and sisters do you have, dad?'

Deepak stole a glance at his mother, who had gone very still on the sofa. He leaned forward and, with his palm, gently tipped his daughter's face upwards. Reena refused to meet his gaze. He laughed then, a cheery, false laugh. 'You're being silly. You know I have one sister—your Aunt Anita. Okay, let's pray the rosary. In the name of the Father...'

'*Liar*,' Reena thought. '*You liar. How can you lie and pray at the same time? How can you live with yourself?*'

Later, after she had eaten the paper masala dosa her mum had packed for her—somehow it didn't taste as nice as she remembered—she sat on the veranda breathing in the scent of rain-drenched earth mixed with night jasmine, the chattering of crickets and Gypsy's warm weight on her legs for company, and in the light of the flickering bulb crossed out her father's name from Plan B altogether.

Progress so far: Aunt Anita had a love marriage—she married a Hindu (Uncle Uttam) and caused a scandal. *She* wasn't disowned. So what did Shirin do that was so bad that she is as good as dead? Find out.

Reena couldn't sleep that night. She lay on the hard bed, her head spinning with questions, wedged between her mother and Chinnu, who for some reason had decided to come and lie down beside her. As her eyes adjusted to the darkness, she watched lizards expertly bypass the ceiling fan blades as they flitted across the wooden beams in search of food. Outside, rain drummed incessantly on the tiles. Gypsy howled plaintively for a while, echoing the neighbourhood dogs, and then settled down with a few half-hearted whines to sleep. Reena imagined all the nocturnal creatures coming out in the cover of the rain to look for food. She wondered where Shirin was and what she was doing, at that moment. Was she missing her childhood home? Was she even thinking of it? Where was she?

CHAPTER SEVEN
A Cricket Team

'Yes, she's cute, isn't she? Even if I say so myself. It was a real wrench leaving her. But needs must, I suppose. Have to earn enough to pay the childminder at least...' Jenny's tinkly, slightly breathless laughter filled the corridor as Shirin rounded the corner.

She was tempted to turn around, go to the loo or get a cup of coffee perhaps, but she was running late as it was. And she had to get this over with sometime.

Taking a deep breath, she walked up to Jenny's desk, where most of her female colleagues were clustered, oohing and aahing. 'Welcome back, Jenny. You look great.'

'Thank you, Shirin! Managed to shift all those pounds I gained in pregnancy. Just. And you look wonderful, as always.'

'Thanks. And is that...' Shirin was drawn to the photographs of a pink-faced baby covering every inch of Jenny's desk, obscuring her keyboard and phone.

'Yes, this is Mia.'

'She's beautiful.' Shirin couldn't keep the wistful note from creeping into her voice.

'She is, isn't she?' Jenny's voice was dripping with pride. 'It was so hard to leave her this morning. The childminder is lovely, though, and Mia adores her. She went to her without tears. Or a backward glance for that matter...'

'Couldn't say the same about the mother, I bet.'

'No,' laughed Jenny. 'I was a mess when I left her, sniffling in the train all the way here. Wonder what my fellow passengers thought...'

'Oh, don't worry about them,' one of the many colleagues still bunched around Jenny's desk piped up.

When the question came, Shirin was not prepared for it. She had been too distracted by the photographs, unable to stop leafing through them, looking at the chubby white baby with wispy blond hair and imagining instead a tiny brown face mirroring her and Vinod's features.

'So, are you and Vinod planning...?'

She kept the smile fixed on her face. 'We are not quite ready yet.'

'It's never the right time to have a baby, Shirin. You just have to go for it. You know how I kept postponing having Mia. But now she's here, I cannot imagine a world without her.'

She wanted to say, 'You decided to have a baby and—boom!—you were pregnant, just like that. Lucky you.' She said instead, 'This is a lovely one of Mia, on a high-chair, food everywhere. Was she trying to feed herself?'

'Yes, that is a good one. Richard clicked it, I think.' Jenny giggled, diverted.

Shirin heaved an inward sigh of relief. It was over. She was just about to make excuses and head to her desk when Justine, who had been peering at the pictures over her shoulder, asked, 'Don't your relatives nag you to have children?' A pause that lasted a lifetime. 'I have this Indian friend, Priya. Her in-laws started hounding her to have a child barely two months after she got married. It's an Indian woman's duty, Priya said, to produce a son and heir to carry on the family name.'

She willed herself to keep smiling. 'Our relatives let us be.' Eleven years and counting.

'That's good then,' smiled Justine.

'Right. Got to get some work done. Thanks for sharing the photos, Jenny. Mia is gorgeous. Takes after her mum...'

Once safely at her desk, Shirin switched on her computer and got to work, refusing to give in to the pictures crowding her mind: dimpled arms, toothless smiles, grubby faces.

'You saw Jenny?' Kate was at her desk, her voice gentle. Shirin nodded.

'You okay?'

Caramel skin soft as candy floss and smelling of baby: that warm, milky scent; wispy black hair; long-lashed brown eyes; chubby arms extended out to her, mouth open in a pink-gummed, spit-bubble grin. 'I'm fine,' Shirin sniffed.

Kate leaned forward, gave her a hug. 'If you need to talk, you know where I am.'

Lovely Kate. 'I know. Thank you.'

'You've always been there for me, Shirin.' Kate's voice was soft and Shirin knew she was thinking of David. Four years on, and Shirin could see that thoughts of him still hurt. Kate and Dave: college sweethearts, fifteen years together. And then David met Elaine: brunette, bimbo, ten years younger.

'He's a fool, Kate.'

'I know. All men are. Except, perhaps, your Vinod.'

'Oh, he snores.' Shirin wrinkled her nose. 'And will not put his book on the bedside table, throwing it on the floor instead, right where I'll trip on it,' She held up her hand, counting down on her fingers, 'He's always late. He can't cook to save his life. He leaves the toilet seat open. He...'

Kate held her up her hands in surrender. 'Right. I get it. He's not a saint.'

Shirin considered. 'Well...'

'Shirin,' laughed Kate. 'I'll leave you to it.' And, as an afterthought, 'Business spec for Tanner ready by end of day tomorrow?'

'Yes, if not earlier.'

'You're a star,' Kate gave her a thumbs-up sign and was gone.

Shirin went to click on the Tanner document shortcut but some ungovernable impulse took over and she clicked on Internet Explorer and googled 'Deepak Diaz' instead. She scrolled down the list of entries, heart pounding. And there he was: Deepak Diaz, Senior Software Engineer, Hewlett-Packard Global Soft Limited, Electronics City II, Hosur Road, Bangalore. Her brother. So close she felt she could reach out and touch him. His hearty laugh. Those twinkling eyes. That teasing dimple. No picture. No mention of his family. She scrolled down the list, all twelve pages. Nothing more. Which was good. As it should be. And yet...

Why hadn't she done this earlier? What was wrong with her? Why was she doing this at all? A baby: wispy hair, downy skin, huge brown eyes...

And then she was googling 'Anita Diaz', urgently scrolling down the list. Nothing. There were plenty of Anita Diazes but not one of them was her sister. Which was odd. Her Anu: exuberant, outgoing, wanting so much out of life, not settling for anything other than the best. Shirin had expected her Anu to be the first entry on the search-engine list, her name to be everywhere on the Web. Her name. Perhaps she had changed it when she married. Had she married? Uttam? Would she dare, after everything that had happened? Yes she would. What was his surname? She couldn't, for the life of her, remember. But, then again, Anita changing her surname? Giving up her identity? Didn't gel with the Anita she knew. Oh, what did she know really? She had a picture of her sister in her mind that was eleven years out of date...

Waves of regret, homesickness. The dull, familiar ache of loss like a phantom limb making itself felt. This was why she had not done this before, given in to impulse.

But, like pulling a scab off a healing wound, she scrolled back to Deepak's name, the three succinct lines describing who her brother was now—her big brother who could do no wrong, whom she used to follow everywhere like Mary's little lamb from the nursery rhyme; the brother she used to tease about his Buddha-belly, sticking out from atop stick legs: a shaved brown coconut; the brother who'd begged her to befriend his crushes and who, when she introduced them to him, hid behind a shy smile and endearing muteness; the brother who'd sneaked up behind her and Anita, snatched the note: 'Got you...' *His eyes devouring its contents, his face going still, a faint imprint of his earlier smile visible—just...*

The brother with whom she had, that gloomy monsoon evening eleven years ago... *Don't think about that.*

She tried to read between those three lines, picture him, swinging his briefcase—did he carry one?—as he walked briskly home. To his family. *Don't go there.* To his wife: diminutive Preeti, pretty like her name. To his daughter...

A shaft of pain.

Blindly, she clicked on the X to close Internet Explorer, clicked on the Tanner document shortcut. *Load, please load.* It sprang up on the screen with a little ping like a sigh and Shirin immersed herself in it.

She was eating a sandwich at her desk while browsing through her email when she heard Madhu's voice—clear as the bell heralding devotees to the temple on the banks of the Varuna River—just above her right shoulder, punctuated with laughter: 'I know you want a cricket team,

Shirin, but let's see how you feel after you have moaned and groaned and given birth to one!'

And in a flash, she was twenty-five years younger, sitting cross-legged on the front stoop, feeling the gentle breeze rustle the coconut-tree fronds and caress her face...

It was a hot muggy day in May, during the summer holidays. Shirin had stormed in after playing cricket with the neighbourhood kids, her clothes muddy, hair a tangled mess.

'What's cooking, Madhu? I could smell it in the fields and had to come home, even though we were winning...'

Madhu turned from the stove, glanced at Shirin and launched into a tirade. 'Look at the state of you! What will your mother say if she sees you like this? You are not a little girl anymore. How can you walk around with your hair loose and your clothes... Pah! Your clothes! Is that a tear in your salwar?'

'It was already there.' Shirin didn't want Madhu dwelling too deeply on her ripped clothes. 'I'm hungry.'

Madhu melted, a reluctant smile tugging at the corners of her mouth. 'I'm frying sweet-potato chips. After you've washed and changed you can have some. Where are Anita and Deepak?'

'Still playing. I was drawn home by this wonderful smell. I told you before, but you weren't listening...'

Madhu laughed, the last of her frown disappearing as she made to swat at Shirin with the slotted spoon she was using to scoop up the chips. Shirin ducked and ran to the bathroom, but not before she had nicked a handful of chips, Madhu yelling, 'Your hands are dirty. Wait till you've washed...' at her retreating back.

Afterwards, with the sweet potato warm in her full stomach, Shirin closed her eyes as Madhu's gentle fingers massaged coconut oil into her hair and tenderly undid the knots.

'Madhu,' she asked, 'did you ever want children?'

Madhu's hands stopped working Shirin's hair. Her voice when it came was soft. 'You, Deepak and Anita are like my children.'

'I know,' Shirin said, impatiently. 'But did you not want any of your own?'

'I had a baby once...'

Shirin was intrigued. She had never given a thought to Madhu's past before she came to live with them. She turned to look at Madhu. Madhu hated Shirin moving her head while she was combing her hair. It was one of the rules Shirin never broke as she got a thump on her head for her troubles. But now, Madhu didn't even notice. She was gazing somewhere into the distance, far beyond the fields, farther even, it seemed to Shirin, than Beerakka's house at the edge of the village. Her eyes were shiny with unshed tears, and this, more than anything, gave Shirin pause.

A heartbeat later she whispered, 'I'm sorry, Madhu. I shouldn't have asked...'

'Why are you crying, silly girl?' Madhu reached down and gently wiped the reciprocal tears from Shirin's cheeks. 'It's okay. I have you now.' Madhu smiled. It seemed to Shirin that the smile made her look even sadder than

when she had been crying. 'Now turn round and let me
finish plaiting your hair. I don't have all the time in the
world, you know...'

'What happened to your baby?' Shirin wanted to ask.
'Where is it? Is it a boy or a girl?' The words tumbled over
themselves in their hurry to pop out of her mouth, but
she bit her tongue hard, tasted the salty tang of blood. She
did not want to make Madhu cry again.

'So,' Madhu said after a while, 'how many children do
you want to have, Madam?'

'Six,' answered Shirin promptly. She had given it much
thought. 'Two sets of twins, then a girl and a boy.'

'Oh, I see...' Madhu's voice was normal again—no sadness underlying it, only a hint of laughter. 'And who will
look after all these children, then?'

'You, of course,' Shirin said at once. Then, hesitantly,
'Won't you?'

Madhu laughed out loud, making Shirin inordinately
pleased that she was happy again. 'Do you know that
there is a way of telling how many children you are going
to have?'

'Really?'

'Don't wriggle. If you keep moving your head, I won't
show you.'

Shirin sat still as the statues of the Holy Family re-
siding in the altar, hardly daring to breathe until Madhu
finished with her plaits. Then, unable to contain her excitement any longer, she jumped up and down in front of
Madhu, 'Tell me! Tell me!'

'Give me your right palm.'

Shirin held both out for Madhu to peruse.

'My! How you're growing, Shirin! Look—your palm is almost as big as mine.'

'Madhu, tell me how many children I'm going to have.'

'See this line here? It is your life line. You are going to have a long life—ninety at least. And this one is for wealth. You are going to be very well off...'

'Madhu! Children... I want to know... Ooh, that tickles...'

'Okay, okay. It's these lines here. Hmm... Let's see. One, two, three, four. You are going to have four children!'

'Only four?' Shirin was disappointed.

And that was when Madhu, laughing, asked Shirin to try and give birth to one child first...

The phone at her desk trilled, bringing her back to the present. Shirin ignored it. The memory, long forgotten and yet retained by her subconscious as clearly as if it were yesterday, made the sandwich sit leaden in her stomach. Madhu's face, eyes glistening with tears, swam before her. Shirin's stomach heaved. The sandwich made its way up her throat and she got to the bathroom just in time. She retched long after the contents of her stomach had been dumped, trying to dislodge the memories, trying to purge the past and at the same time wishing she was back in the days before.

Before. One little word. So conveniently wiping away so much.

If only it were that easy...

Shirin shook her head, giving herself the pep talk that had gotten her through the last few years. She pulled on the mask of accomplished, confident businesswoman that she hoped people saw when they looked at her and opened the cubicle door only to find her colleague—aka gossip queen—Anne's face reflected back at her from the mirror.

'Are you okay? I heard you, you know...' Anne mimed being sick. 'Is there something you are not telling us?' Anne's eyes twinkled and she did something, which must have been meant to convey mischief, with her eyebrows.

'Huh?' Shirin washed her face and hands. She desperately wanted to brush her teeth, get the awful taste out of her mouth. Did she have mints in her purse? She ought to buy some and keep them there.

Anne was still trying to get to the bottom of things. 'So, are you, you know...' She indicated her stomach and rocked her hands together.

What on earth did she mean? And then, all at once, realisation dawned, cold and heavy in the pit of her recently emptied stomach. *If only you knew, Anne...*

'I have the stomach bug. Twenty-four-hour thingy, I hope.' Her voice sounded surprisingly normal, thank goodness. 'Will take the afternoon off, I think...'

'You do that. I'll let Kate know.' The look of pity on Anne's face was far worse than her solicitousness.

'Thanks, Anne,' Shirin mumbled, grabbing her bag from her desk and running out of the office before she stumbled into anyone else—or, worse, burst into tears.

CHAPTER EIGHT
Puffed-Up Puris and
Gluey Bhaji

'Bye, Madhu.' Reena allowed herself to be swept into Madhu's embrace. Madhu was as over the top with her affections as Jacinta was reserved.

Jacinta's goodbye had been a squeeze of Reena's hand. She had pushed a wayward strand of hair out of Reena's face, looked into her eyes and said, 'Come back to visit your Mai soon, you hear?'

Then Reena had sought out Madhu, only to be squashed against her bosom, inhaling the smell of oil and spices that clung to Madhu's clothes. 'Look after yourself,' Madhu said, 'and come for Christmas. I'll make Nevri and Tukdis.' Nevri and Tukdis were Reena's favourites out of all the Kuswar—the sweetmeats made especially at Christmas.

'Hurry up, Reena, the rickshaw's waiting,' Preeti called.

Gypsy howled. Chinnu came up to Reena, mewling, and rubbed herself against Reena's legs.

She looked up at Madhu. 'I'm sorry for the hurt this caused,' she whispered, opening her notebook to the photograph. 'Do you want it?' *Please say I can keep it, Madhu.*

Plan A had not worked. After that eventful afternoon when she found out who Shirin was, she had not been able to wangle time alone with Madhu. Plan B was a washout. Now only Plan C remained and for that to work, she needed the photograph—once she'd managed to find Aunt Anita, that is. And she would. No task was too hard for Reena Diaz, Super Sleuth.

'Oh, Rinu, you didn't hurt me,' Madhu smiled tenderly through tear-bright eyes. 'It was nice to finally talk about her. I don't need her picture. I have her here with me always.' She pointed to her heart. 'You keep it.'

'Thank you,' Reena said, giving her another hug, 'Madhu, why...' One final attempt at Plan A.

'Shh…' Madhu placed a finger gently on Reena's lips. She bent down and whispered in Reena's ear, 'Don't worry too much about Shirin. One day, soon, she'll be back. I know it here.' And once again she pointed at her heart.

'Reena!' Preeti called, sending Gypsy into a paroxysm of barks.

'Go,' Madhu said with a gentle nudge.

Before she turned the corner, Reena looked back at the house—at Jacinta standing by the front door and Madhu on the steps in front of the kitchen—and waved as hard as she could.

※　※　※

Bangalore was just the same as usual: busy, bustling and unnaturally hot for the time of year. They arrived on Sunday morning and Reena's mum spent all day in bed, curled up with the air conditioner on full blast. Her dad, after having breakfast (puri bhaji which Preeti had ordered from the restaurant across the potholed road from their apartment complex—the puris: puffed brown balloons which went *poof* when Reena stuck her finger in them; the bhaji: wet gluey potatoes that smelled and tasted like paste), announced that he was going to work.

'On a Sunday?' Preeti asked with a half-hearted pout, knowing even as she said it that he would go anyway.

'I have been away for so long,' Deepak was already at the computer checking his emails, 'and I am at meetings all day tomorrow, so I will have no time to catch up on all the bits that need doing.' He talked while he typed, his fingers flying over the keys.

'Did you at least eat breakfast properly?'

'Of course I did.' He shut down the computer, stood, stretched. 'That break was good. Catching up with everyone was fun. Ma looks better than last time, don't you think?'

'Yes. She seems to be finally getting over your da's death.'

'But the journey back... God, those ghats are a nightmare.'

'I know. They'll never repair those roads, Deepak. That bus bumped its way over every single ditch it could possibly go through. I didn't get a wink of sleep and my back is aching so much.'

'How is your leg?' Her father's voice was gentle.

'That hurts too.'

One of her mother's legs was slightly shorter than the other—a birth defect—and ached whenever it was subjected to strain.

'Put your feet up today,' Deepak said, as he hefted the bag he carried to the office over his shoulder. 'Bye then, Preeti.' And to Reena, 'You, too, princess. Have a good day. Finish any homework that needs doing.'

'Bye,' Reena mumbled, chasing the bhaji on her plate with a piece of puri. She had not been able to look her father in the eye since she had found out about Shirin. She kept thinking she would talk to him, ask him what had really happened: why he did not acknowledge one sister while he fawned over the other. But the time was never right. Or, if she were true to herself, she was not brave enough. What if there wasn't a good enough explanation and the father she adored was really at fault? She'd rather live with the doubt.

She finished her breakfast and washed her hands. 'I am going downstairs to the playground for a bit, Mum,' she announced, opening the door to her parents' bedroom where her mother was sprawled on the bed, curtains drawn, pillow over her eyes.

'Aren't you tired, Rinu? Don't you want to sleep for a bit?' The pillow came off as Preeti regarded her daughter critically.

'No, I'm fine.'

'You're bored here, aren't you?' Her mother's voice was gentle.

She kicked the doorpost with her feet. 'A little.'

'Why don't you knock on number 36, see if the girl who lives there wants to play? She looks about your age.'

As if it were that easy. The girl from number 36 had never so much as acknowledged Reena, had always looked right through her.

'I'm fine, Mum.' She flashed a brilliant smile at her mother.

Preeti looked like she was about to say something else.

'Bye, Mum,' Reena said, to pre-empt any other soul-searching questions. Her mother looked so tired, lying there with her bad foot elevated by pillows. Reena did not want her to worry and not be able to rest.

Preeti's eyes searched Reena's face. 'Okay, then, wake me when you're home,' Preeti pulled the pillow back down.

Reena shut the door softly, flew across the landing to Mrs. Gupta's flat and rang the doorbell.

Please, God. Let Murli open the door. If he does, I promise to go to church the next three Sundays in a row.

Mrs. Gupta opened the door. She was wearing a flower-print housecoat. Her hair was swept up in a towel. She looked none too happy to see Reena.

I am not coming to church next week, Reena announced to God in her head.

'Oh, Reena you are back.' Mrs. Gupta's thin smile looked like a grimace, especially with her hair pulled back so severely her skin stretched into ugly, taut lines. 'Is there something you want?'

'My ball fell in the swimming pool, and I can't swim and my mum is sleeping and I can't find the man who cleans the pool. If Murli could help...' Reena made up on the spot.

She could feel her face turning crimson as the blood rushed to it. *Please, God, let Mrs. Gupta not realise eleven is a bit too old to play with a ball.* She wished the ground would open up and swallow her. She, Super Sleuth, should be able to come up with better excuses, *relevant* excuses. Why on earth had she been so impulsive? She had not thought that it might be too early, that it was Sunday. She had not thought anything at all. She had just wanted to see her friend.

Mrs. Gupta was looking at her like she was a cockroach she had found scuttling around her kitchen. How could Murli put up with her? She was about to apologise and slink away when Mrs. Gupta screeched, 'Murli!'

Thank you, God. Sorry for renouncing you so quickly. I promise I'll go to church religiously, even attend Sunday school, prayed Reena, making peace.

Murli came hurrying to the door, as string-bean-like as ever, wearing his usual white mundu, a dishcloth slung over his right shoulder. His face lit up when he saw Reena. Then it sobered into an expression of solicitous humility in Mrs. Gupta's presence.

'Reena here, Mrs. Diaz's daughter, you know, from next door...' Mrs. Gupta said, yawning. Murli nodded vigorously. 'She needs help rescuing her ball. Come back soon, mind; you've all the washing up from breakfast to do.' Mrs. Gupta yawned again and banged the door shut, ignoring Reena's effusive thank yous. Her flimsy excuse had worked!

'Reena,' Murli grinned happily when they were sitting on the steps leading to the swimming pool. 'Did you get back this morning? How was the holiday?'

The sun shone on the clean blue expanse, making the water sparkle like the gold in her mother's jewellery box. The flowers in the neat beds that flanked the pool created a picture-perfect multihued contrast. In the playground, two girls sat on the swings, chatting, their bare feet sketching figures in the mud. A gentle breeze caressed Reena's face as she sat in the shade of the decorative palm trees. It was so different to rainy, unpolished Taipur, and yet she loved that place too and it had hurt to leave. But now, as she looked at Murli's thin, animated face, for the first time since she had said goodbye to her grandmother and to Madhu, she was glad to be back.

'It was good, Murli.' One of the girls said something to the other and she threw back her head and laughed—a silvery sound like wind chimes.

'Why don't you go talk to them? Come on, I'll come with you.'

She shook her head. If they saw Murli, they'd laugh and point. They must think her a freak, sitting talking to a servant. Well, tough, she thought. 'I discovered something there, Murli. In Taipur.'

'Discovered something?'

She took the photograph from its hiding place in her notebook—which was beginning to look a bit worn, much like a proper detective's—and handed it to Murli.

Murli squinted as he studied the picture. 'Oh, that's your dad when he was little, isn't it? He hasn't changed much. And that's your Aunty Anita. If anything, she's be-come more beautiful. Who's the other girl?' He looked up at Reena, a question in his eyes. 'She looks like you.'

'I know,' Reena said softly.

'Who is she?'

'She's my dad's sister.'

'I didn't know he had another sister.'

The girls had finished swinging. They stood up in uni-son, brushed the dust off their skirts and walked off, hand in hand, in the opposite direction to where Murli and Reena were sitting.

'Neither did I. He never talks about her. Nobody does. It's like she never existed.'

'But... why?' Murli looked at the photograph again, as if searching for clues, for something he'd missed.

'That's what I'd like to know, too,' Reena whispered.

CHAPTER NINE
Cow-Dung Pastes and Gram-Flour Baths

The house was cold, uninviting. The stale smell of the curry they had had the night before hit Shirin as she opened the front door, causing her stomach to turn again. She sprinted to the bathroom, retched some more and ran the bath while she brushed, scrutinising her face in the mirror. Her eyes, dark circles underlining them, looked too big in her sunken face. Lipstick was peeling off lips that she had wished, growing up, would pout more—like Anita's. Her cheeks were hollow and the double chin she'd hoped would disappear was as prominent as ever. Only her hair shone, luxurious and buoyant, thanks to Madhu massaging it with coconut oil warm from the charcoal hearth used to cook conjee, morning and night, no matter how busy she was. She had worn it long all her life. Except the once…
Her mother's face stony as she crumpled the note, tore it into a million little pieces, picked up the scissors. Deepak's face grave. Anita's drawn, tearful. Her fearless sister for once in her life cowering behind Madhu. Madhu, palms joined, pleading. And her hair, her beautiful hair, her one redeeming feature,

strewn around the courtyard, dark against the red mud, stray strands flying in the breeze, Rex bounding up, sniffing it and ambling away disappointed that it wasn't edible…

Madhu would tut at her complexion if she saw it now: 'How could you let it go, Shirin? After all that care I took to make your skin glow. After all the countless gram-flour baths, all those pastes made from cow dung, tulsi leaves and herbs that I applied to your face every single day without fail.'

When Shirin first heard Madhu say this, she was shocked. 'You put cow dung on my face?'

'Every day religiously until you were three. Why else do you think your skin is so clear? No pimples, nothing. And it wasn't an easy job, either. Collecting fresh cow dung, finding the herbs, making the paste, applying it, waiting for it to dry and making sure you wouldn't rub it off. Do you think I put so much effort into Anita?' She didn't say Deepak. There was no need. He had the great fortune of being a boy, not a girl being groomed for marriage from the day she was born. Madhu smiled fondly at Shirin. 'It paid off, though. Look at your complexion.' She took Shirin's hand, led her to the mirrored door on the Godrej wardrobe and, in a voice filled with pride, said, 'It glows.'

Shirin looked at the pudgy, dark-skinned girl staring back at her and wished she could see what Madhu obviously saw.

'Anita's is better,' she had whispered.

'Anita is fair,' Madhu had said in a tone which brooked no argument, 'but she doesn't have your flawless complexion.'

Something of hers better than Anita's! Even though Shirin didn't quite believe Madhu—Madhu was inclined to be partial to her—when she looked back at her reflection, she found that the girl in the mirror really *did* glow.

Shirin shook her head to clear the bathroom mirror of the reflections of her childhood self and of Madhu; sweet Madhu. She wished she could rid her heart of the ache as easily, the longing to have Madhu wrap her in her arms, to whisper in her ears that everything would be all right.

This last week had been an emotional rollercoaster, the days leading up to this one taking their toll on her. Revisiting memories, like reuniting with old, much-loved friends ignited in her a yearning, a hunger which only Madhu's cooking, the feel of Madhu's arms, Jacinta's forgiving smile, seeing Reena, would satiate.

And the googling. Her brother. So close she could touch him. Why had she done that? Perhaps Vinod was right. Perhaps after all these years she was ready. To go back. But was it right? Would she be doing the right thing by *her*? *Reena...* Shirin sat down, suddenly weary. She rested her head against the door, closed her eyes. The faint tang of vomit mixed in with Mr Muscle tickled her nostrils, made her want to sneeze. Pungent. Brittle. Like... *No...* The sound of chappals hitting feet as they approached. Slap. Slap. Slappety-slap. *No. Please, no.* They reared up at her, mocking. The Eyes...

She used to see them so often in the beginning. She had fled halfway round the world, away from everything she knew, all that was familiar, and they had followed right along. The first few months in the UK, she had sprayed the apartment with tubes and tubes of Glade, to rid it of the smell that seemed to haunt her. She stopped going to bed, choosing instead to stay in the living room and watch mind-numbing television reruns, volume turned up loud to drown out the sound of chappals: thwack, thwack, thwack; the hoarse, noisy breaths: harsh, incessant; and the visions of eyes that followed her everywhere. There had been nights when Vinod had stayed up with her, and others when he had awakened in the early hours of the morning to try and persuade her to come to bed, only to find her fast asleep on the sofa, the TV chattering away in the background. He had started carrying her to their bedroom. (She still wondered how he'd managed that; even if she was then the thinnest she had ever been.) She'd got used to waking up in her own bed, even though she'd fallen asleep on the sofa, and gradually the nightmare had retreated, though it had never gone away completely. Moving to this house had helped.

She remembered when they first came to view it. It was a new construction, a three-bedroom house, 'Perfect for a young couple looking to start a family,' the estate agent had said. Shirin had walked through the rooms, sparkling new and fresh. 'And this room is just the right size for the nursery,' the estate agent had announced, and for a split second, Shirin had gazed into a future filled with children and love and laughter, instead of dwelling on the past and all that had gone before. She had looked up at Vinod then, seen his face break into a joyous smile. He'd crossed the room in three long strides and enveloped her in a bear hug.

'What?' she'd asked, feeling claustrophobic and pushing against his chest.

'You smiled. A proper, genuine, smile,' he'd replied, releasing her, beaming.

'So, what do you think?' the estate agent had asked.

Vinod had looked at her, waiting. And she had nodded slowly, standing in the room she already thought of as the nursery and realising with wonder that the sudden light feeling in her chest was hope.

Hope. One small word that fooled you into believing you could make dreams that you had no business wanting come true, that one day your home would reverberate with laughter, noise and children's harmless mischief, that somehow you would not be punished for your mistakes, that you would escape unscathed...

That's enough. There was no point dwelling on things she couldn't change. Her stomach rumbled loudly reminding her that she needed some sustenance and making her glad she was at home, alone where nobody could hear it. Resolutely she walked past the closed doors of the two empty bedrooms, down the stairs and into her big, airy, deafeningly silent kitchen and put the kettle on.

❉ ❉ ❉

Clutching the mug—Christmas present from Kate: *You will always be my friend; you know too much*—in one hand, the receiver in the other, she dialled Kate's number. 'Are you free to talk?'

Kate's voice, sounding rushed: 'Give me five minutes.'

She called back in exactly five minutes. 'I'm in the smokers' corner. It stinks. Are you all right? Anne told me you weren't feeling well. Was it seeing Jenny?' Kate asked, without pausing to take a breath.

Shirin heard bursts of laughter, a distant shout. She pictured Kate, sitting on the bench furthest from the door, legs stretched out and crossed at the ankles, phone pressed to her ear, her brows puckered in concern. 'Partly.' And, in a rush, 'Kate... I cannot live like this any longer. I want to go home.'

'You're serious?'

'Yes,' Shirin whispered.

A pause and then Kate, sounding tentative, 'You said you're not welcome...'

'I did. I'm not welcome.'

'Are you sure? Perhaps it's all water under the bridge now.'

Sweet Kate. Always looking for the silver lining. 'None of them have made contact, Kate.'

'Well, then.' Snatches of someone whistling as she waited for Kate to speak, 'Do you really think it is a good idea, Shirin? You are happy now, very different from the girl I knew once, afraid of her own shadow. The memories are coming back and *you* own *them* rather than the other way round. Why go back, destroy what you have built, the person you have become?'

❋ ❋ ❋

'Jenny returned to work today. She brought pictures of her baby. A little girl. Mia. Very cute,' Shirin said.

They were sitting side by side on the sofa watching television. Not touching.

Vinod turned to look at her. She stared resolutely at the screen.

'That must have been hard,' Vinod said.

'Twelve people were killed when a car bomb exploded in Kandahar,' the news presenter announced, his face expressionless, his voice a monotone.

'Worse things happen all the time,' Shirin wanted to say. 'I left the office at lunch time. I was sick with longing. Literally,' she wanted to say. But she couldn't find the words.

Vinod extended a hand towards her, wanting to touch her, to offer comfort the only way he knew how.

Don't, she thought. *Please don't.*

He heard her unspoken words. His hand dropped to his side, palm bunched into a fist. The pain in his eyes mirrored hers. She suddenly, desperately wanted to make him smile.

'Did you have those blue-green soda bottles with marble stoppers in Bangalore when you were growing up?' she asked.

'Yes. Why?' He turned, stared at her. 'Have you been remembering...?'

She nodded. 'All the time now. Anything sets me off. Even the picture of a Stella Artois bottle.'

Vinod smiled. It made him look years younger. 'It reminded you of the soda bottles?'

'Uh-huh. What would the nuns have to say about that?'

Vinod chuckled; a joyous gurgling sound from deep within him, like the rainwater stream in Ananthanna's field when it pushed against the makeshift dam she, Deepak and Anita had made with stones and sticks and mud.

'I... I googled them up today.'

Vinod's hand snaked along the sofa. 'Who?'

'I found Deepak. Well, not really. Three lines about him. Senior Software Engineer, Hewlett Packard, Hosur Road.'

Vinod looked at her, held her gaze. 'The healing process is working its magic,' he said softly.

A watery smile. 'Do you think they will have forgiven me, Vinod?'

Vinod, sounding impatient, 'You did nothing wrong.'

He had repeated that sentence to her so many times over the years. Why couldn't she believe him? The Eyes loomed large. Accusing.

'The past cannot stay hidden forever, Shonu.' Vinod said, softly, 'Reena will find out one day, ask questions.'

Reena. Shirin wanted to reach out, protect her from the truth.

'Did you get an email address for Deepak?' Vinod asked.

'No.'

'Maybe you should. Contact him.'

'They may not...' *want anything to do with me.* 'Nothing has changed.'

'Time. It works its magic, Shonu.' Vinod smiled softly. 'Look at us. Last year, hell, even last month, we wouldn't have been discussing this...'

She hadn't been able to talk about the past with Vinod, despite extensive counselling, and it had lain between them. A gulf as wide as the distance between India and the UK.

'Even a mention of India on TV, and you would change the channel... Before, you definitely wouldn't have googled them...'

No.

'You are ready. Find out if they are.'

'Kate thinks I should leave it.'

'She means well, but she doesn't realise just how much you miss them, miss her... Reena.' And softly, 'She has the right to know you, Shonu.'

Her heart jumped. Panic? Hope? 'I just want to see her, is all. I don't want her to know...'

Vinod banged the table with his fist. 'It wasn't your fault. You did nothing wrong. That's the truth. Tell her the truth. It's about time they all accepted it.'

I left her. I came here. How do I explain to an eleven-year-old why I did what I did? She stared at the TV. Dust. Desert. Devastation.

'I'm sorry...' Vinod's voice. Soft. Abashed.

She looked up at him, at his greying hair, his eyes ringed with tiredness. 'No. I am.'

'Stop blaming yourself, Shonu.'

I left her. No amount of counselling had rid her of the guilt. She nodded. 'Yes.'

Vinod flexed the hand that rested casually on the sofa behind her. The tips of his fingers rested lightly on the nape of her neck, raising goosebumps. 'Come to bed,' he said.

CHAPTER TEN
Maggi Noodles and Bournvita

OCTOBER

Plan C: Find Aunt Anita and ask her about Aunt Shirin.

Progress so far: Found Aunt Anita's number in the phone book. Tried calling but it's either been engaged or busy or gone unanswered. Will keep trying. Hitch: The only time this detective can use the phone undisturbed is when parents are not around, which amounts to a very tiny window of time when Mum is gossiping with neighbour.

Other avenues explored: This is how Aunt Shirin might look now. Sketch drawn based on the photograph and taking into account the time that has passed between then and now. Hitch: This detective is skilled at detection but not as skilled at drawing, hence the picture is not very realistic. This detective imagines subject to be a cross between Kareena Kapoor and Aishwarya Rai, her two favourite Bollywood leading ladies. Golden Rule: DO NOT get emotionally involved with the subject. Hitch:

Detective already emotionally involved. Subject is her hitherto unknown aunt.

Aunt Anita called just after Reena had got home from school. Reena, having tried calling Aunt Anita while surreptitiously checking that her mum was still outside chatting, was having her usual snack of Maggi Noodles and Bournvita while musing over the lack of progress in her first proper case as Detective Reena Diaz, Super Sleuth.

She worried every time she called Aunt Anita's number as to what she would say if she actually answered the phone. 'Um, ah, I was wondering, where is your sister? Why don't any of you mention her? What has she done?' Aunt Anita was fun, approachable—more like a glamorous older sister than an aunt. Even so… how would she react if Reena suddenly questioned her about an aunt she wasn't supposed to know existed, whom they had all wiped so completely from their lives? And then, Reena chastised herself, would a *real* detective worry so? A *real* detective would have marched straight to Deepak with the evidence of his lie—the picture—and demanded to know the truth. The problem with this mystery was that it was too close for comfort. She couldn't imagine Nancy Drew or for that matter, even Poirot or Miss Marple—now that she was eleven, she had permission to read Agatha Christie, 'As long as the books don't give you nightmares,'—landing such a complicated case: The case of the Mystery Aunt (she had since changed the name from the rather long initial one) as their debut. She would have been better off solving a safe, neat murder mystery that didn't involve any of her family even remotely. She wouldn't have been worried then, felt that worm of unease uncoil in her stomach when she heard Aunt Anita's number ring. She would have just marched right on, interrogating suspects, examining clues, honing in on the murderer.

She was having a second helping of masala Maggi noodles to cheer up and chase away dark thoughts of never finding her aunt Shirin—her mother had cooked the noodles just the way she liked, with plenty of potatoes, capsicum, peas and tomato chilli sauce—while simultaneously drinking her Bournvita in great big gulps, when the phone rang.

She managed a 'Hello,' while swallowing a mouthful of hot chocolate, burning her tongue and throat in the process.

'Reena? Is that you? You sound so grown-up!'

Aunt Anita! The worm of unease became a serpent.

'Um… ah…' *Super Sleuths are never lost for words. What is wrong with you?*

'Where's your mum?' Aunt Anita sounded odd.

Ask her about Aunt Shirin. 'She's outside gossiping with Mrs. Gupta as usual. Are you returning my call?'

'Your call? Princess, I really need to talk to your mum…'

Oh no. Busted. What if Aunt Anita told Preeti she was returning her call? Her mother's chagrin— 'Do you know how expensive STD calls are? We trusted you, Rinu…' *Courage, Super Sleuth.*

'Could you get her for me? Tell her it's urgent.' Aunt Anita sniffed loudly. She really did sound odd, like she had a bad cold.

Ask her now. Reena sprinted to the front door, opened it wide, yelled, 'Mum! Aunt Anita on the phone for you,' and went back to her noodles, eating to drown the serpent. *Chicken. Your one chance and you waste it.*

'Don't you like Maggi anymore?' Preeti asked as she picked up the receiver, eyeing Reena's full plate.

'This is my second helping,' Reena mumbled, staring at her plate to avoid having to look at Preeti.

'Oh, Rinu! Will you have any space left for dinner?' And then, into the receiver, 'Hello? Anu, what's the matter? *What?*'

Oh no. I'm in for it.

'It's okay, Anu. Really, it's fine. You come here. Yes, I'll talk to him.'

Her mum, ashen-faced, holding on to the arm of the sofa and lowering herself down like an old woman. *Something's wrong.* 'Mum, what's happened?' Reena asked, fork halfway to her mouth.

'Shh...' Preeti mouthed at her, and into the phone, 'Don't you worry about him. You come here, Anu. As soon as you can. Tomorrow? Yes. Book the ticket now. Take care. Yes, I'll talk to him. He'll be fine. We'll see you tomorrow.' Her voice soft, very gentle. The same tone she used when Reena had one of her nightmares and needed soothing.

Preeti stared at the receiver for a few moments and then gently laid it down on the table. Slowly, she walked across the living room to the front door, made sure it was closed and locked it for good measure. And before Reena could ask the question forming on her lips, she said, 'I don't want Mrs. Gupta getting wind of this.'

'Getting wind of what?' Reena asked.

'Your Aunt Anita is coming tomorrow. She's getting a divorce, Rinu.'

'What?' Aunt Anita actually coming here? *Part 1 of Plan C—a success*, she thought, and immediately felt guilty as she watched her mother collapse onto the sofa and cover her face with her hands, as her mother's words sank in. *Aunt Anita getting a divorce?*

'I should have called her. Can't remember the last time I spoke to her,' her mother said. 'I need to talk to your dad.'

'He's not going to be pleased.'

'Yes.' Her mother sounded defeated. And then she squared her shoulders, stood and picked up the receiver, her fingers flying over the buttons as she dialled.

'Hello, Deepak?' she walked to the bedroom, mouthing 'You eat' to Reena. Reena stared at her plate of noodles, her appetite gone. In the bedroom, she heard her mother's voice, soothing, as she talked Deepak into accepting his delinquent sister into his home: 'I know, Deepak, but she's very upset. She needs the comfort of family…'

What about your other sister? Who does she have?

Her mother walked back in, 'Right. I have to get the guest bedroom sorted, wash the sheets, but first… You look as bad as I feel, Rinu. We need cheering up.' She disappeared into the kitchen, reappearing with a box of mithai: soan papdi, laddoos, halwa and pedas. They flopped on the sofa, pigging out on the sweets and watching the local news.

'Shh… Listen. Did they say Mangalore? Put the volume up, Rinu. Oh no, fights between the Hindus and Muslims in Mangalore. Ten people killed…'

Reena looked at her mother. Preeti's hair was loose, in soft waves around her neck and shoulders. She looked worn out. There were lines around her eyes that Reena hadn't noticed before.

'This is near Taipur, Rinu.' In a whisper.

'Oh! Mai was saying there's trouble brewing in Taipur as well, wasn't she?'

'It's scary. I hope they don't start on the Catholics next,' Preeti said just as the key turned in the lock and Deepak arrived.

Preeti went up to Deepak, cupped his stubbly cheek in the palm of her hand. 'Come and have dinner first. I've made your favourite mutton curry. Then we'll talk.'

Afterwards, when they had finished the mutton, the pulao and plump, juicy rasagullas, and after they had worried about the Hindu-Muslim unrest in Mangalore, Deepak leaned back wearily in his chair. 'What is happening to my family, Preeti?'

Preeti reached across and laid her hand on Deepak's. 'She sounded so distressed, Deepak. So unlike herself.'

The sniffling. Aunt Anita didn't have a cold. She had been crying.

'Divorce. How could she even think about it? After everything that's happened…' Deepak ran his fingers through his hair.

An image of Mrs. Gupta, her button eyes bulging, ranting on about the pathetic decline of Indian morals flashed before her eyes. The cloying scent of rasagullas mixed with the spicy smell of congealing mutton curry rose to her nostrils, making her uncomfortably aware of her heavy stomach, too full of pulao and mithai and noodles.

'I didn't know anything was wrong. Last time I spoke to her, she and Uttam seemed so happy and were planning so many things together. Mind you, that was a year ago...' Preeti sighed. 'I should have called her. But you know how it is; you blink and a year's flown by...'

'This will be the last straw for Ma... She's already so fragile...Whatever happens, we should try and keep it from her. Reena, when you talk to Mai, not a word, okay? Don't even mention that Aunt Anita is staying with us.'

'Okay.' Reena nodded her assent vigorously.

Preeti laid a hand on his arm. 'Deepak, Anu's in a state. She's turned to you for comfort. Be nice to her. No lectures about how she's destroying the family name—promise?'

'I'll try.' Deepak looked sheepish.

Preeti's voice, tentative: 'Family name, honour... It doesn't matter as much as you seem to think it does, Deepak. People will talk for a bit, and then forget, move on to the next thing...'

Bang. Deepak brought his hand down on the table, hard, making the dishes clatter, the congealing curry spill. 'It does to me. To Ma. In Taipur, it is a big deal. We, the Diaz family, are a big deal. *You* know that, Preeti. We cannot allow anything to sully our name. Not a whisper of a rumour. Nothing. As it is, Anu caused enough talk, insisting on marrying Uttam, upsetting Ma, reducing her to half of what she was, leaving her open to insults and barbs. Anita took after Ma, they said. Da married beneath him, they said. Do you know what it did to Ma, being voted out of the parish council committee when Anu married Uttam? She doesn't show it, just holds her head up high. But I know… I know… And now…' He laid his elbows on the table and cradled his head in his hands. 'Oh, God, what a mess...'

From where she was sitting, Reena could see the top of her father's head, and it shocked her to find a little bald patch around his crown. 'What does it mean to marry beneath you?' she asked.

Her dad looked up at her, eyes narrowed, and for a moment she thought he was going to fob her off. Then, he shook his head as if to clear it. 'You are growing up; you need to know,' he said, almost to himself. 'Preeti? Shall we tell her Mai's story?'

Her mother nodded.

'Come, sit here,' her dad said, patting the chair beside him. 'Your Mai's father was an alcoholic, her mother a shrew. Her family was the laughing stock of the whole village. Her father used to drink and sleep on the street. When she was ten, a bus ran over him. Her mother was so grief-stricken that she went mad, literally lost her mind. Your Mai had to grow up in a convent.' Her dad paused to take a breath.

Poor Mai, thought Reena. To lose her parents like that when she was just a year younger than Reena; to be sent to live in a convent, of all places!

'The nuns kept bees and used to sell honey, the sweetest honey in all of Mangalore,' continued her dad with a faraway look in his eyes. 'Your Ab saw your Mai when he went to buy honey and fell in love with her. His parents were not happy with his choice as his family was one of the oldest and most revered in Taipur. They wanted him to marry a girl from a good family and not Mai. They thought he was marrying beneath himself—you understand?' Her father's eyes met hers. She nodded.

'For your Mai, this was the best thing that had ever happened in her life. She had found respectability. She vowed that she would never do anything that would sully the name of Taipur Diaz; that her family would be the pillars of society.' Her dad smiled gently at her. 'And that is why status is so very important to your Mai.'

This close up, Reena could see the dark circles under his eyes. 'And why is it so important to you, Dad?'

'I love your Mai,' he said simply. 'I do not want to see her hurt. She has suffered enough in her life. If status is what matters to her, then status is what I will strive for.'

Her dad sometimes spoke like a character in a book, thought Reena.

Preeti reached across and stroked Deepak's arm. 'Ma won't find out about Anita wanting a divorce, Deepak. This is Bangalore, not Taipur. News doesn't get around as quickly. And these legal proceedings, they take so long anyway. It will be a couple of years before they are divorced. Anything can happen by then. They may decide not to get divorced at all.'

Deepak looked up. 'You think? Maybe once she has calmed down...'

'When she comes here I'll have a chat with her, find out if she still loves Uttam. She must do. It must have been a lovers' tiff, strong words exchanged. The word *divorce* would have been bandied about. You know how fiery Anita is, how proud. Things must have ballooned out of proportion...' When her mother put it like that, Reena could almost believe the situation wasn't as bad as it seemed.

Her father seemed to think so too. He reached across and gave her mother a hug. With his other arm he pulled Reena close.

'I am lucky to have you, you know,' he murmured.

'You are,' smiled Preeti, 'Well, there's a lot to be done before she arrives. Spare room to be made ready, sheets to be washed, excuses to be thought of to give nosy Nupur next door before she starts spreading rumours. Bedtime for all, I think.'

As Reena walked to her room, she heard her dad whisper, 'Thank you, Preeti. You are so special.' She turned just in time to see her mother blush before she disappeared into her dad's bear hug. At least, she thought, her mum and dad were not in danger of divorcing any time soon.

UPDATE: Aunt Anita's love marriage caused a huge furore. But *she* wasn't expelled from the family, *she* wasn't forgotten. So what did Shirin do that was even worse than marrying a Hindu? (NOTE: Word 'furore' which sounds like something a lion would make, copied from the new *Thesaurus*—eleventh birthday present. Eugene Ma'am, this detective's English teacher, who's always urging this detective to use different, better words, will be pleasantly surprised when she slips this word into her next essay.)

Plan C: Find Aunt Anita and ask her about Aunt Shirin. Find Aunt Anita—Achieved. (She's coming here!) Ask about Aunt Shirin: See below.

Next Stage(s): Show Aunt Anita the picture and ask her about Aunt Shirin. Find cause of rift and try to fix it. Reunite Aunt Shirin with family, <u>especially niece</u> who was instrumental in bringing about the reunion. Hitch: Aunt Anita may not be in the mood to answer questions, on account of wanting to divorce Uncle Uttam. Note: Proceed with caution taking into account Aunt Anita's fragile emotional state.

She dreamt of a little girl in pigtails with mournful eyes and a face that Reena shared. The girl hovered in a corner, scared, covering her ears with the palms of her hands, as a couple argued relentlessly beside her. The couple was Aunt Anita and Uncle Uttam and they were shouting at each other, hurling insults. Suddenly, Aunt Anita turned and the girl realised it was not Aunt Anita at all, but a monster with gleaming eyes and a mouth that breathed fire. The girl screamed and screamed...

'Shh... Reena, it's okay. I'm here. It's all right, sweetheart...' She was being enveloped in her mother's arms; a warm, safe haven, soft as cotton candy. Her mother smelled of the sandalwood talcum powder she smothered herself in after her shower every night. Her hair was loose, messy. The bindi that she had worn last night and forgotten to remove was awry on her forehead. She was wearing her favourite housecoat, a canary yellow one with faded blue flowers. Reena snuggled deeper into her arms. She wished she could stay there forever, but already she didn't fit as neatly as she had the last time she had had a nightmare, and at the thought, the sobs which had died down to hiccups started afresh.

'Shh... Rinu, it's all right, shh...'

'Mum,' between hiccups, 'will you sleep here tonight?'

'Of course, sweetheart. I'm here, right next to you, okay? Shall I sing you a lullaby?'

'No,' Reena interjected quickly.

She felt her mother grin as she settled down beside her. 'Surely I can't be that bad? When you were a baby you quite liked my lullabies'

Reena smiled despite her tears. 'I used to fall asleep as quickly as possible just to escape having to listen to your singing efforts.'

'That settles it then,' her mother laughed, 'Sa Re Ga Ma...'

'Preeti, stop that,' shouted Deepak from the other room. 'Can't a man get some peace in his own house, without having to endure his tuneless wife break into song in the middle of the night?'

'That's it. You've hurt my feelings, you two. From now on, even if you beg me to sing, I won't.'

'There is a God!' sang Deepak. 'Goodnight.'

Reena's sobs dissolved into giggles and she fell asleep in the warm cocoon of her mother's embrace.

The next afternoon, Bangalore experienced freak thunderstorms which caused havoc in the city and perplexed the weathermen.

And Aunt Anita arrived.

CHAPTER ELEVEN
Blue-Tinged Shadow

'Shirin, do you have a minute? Marie wants a word.' Kate was businesslike, preoccupied.

'Yes, of course.' A shiver of apprehension tickled Shirin's spine. Marie was Kate's boss, the deputy head of Utilities, the division they all worked for. She was the one who had handled the issue with Ian.

'Come to the boardroom when you are ready.' With a little smile and a wink meant to reassure her, Kate was gone.

Was this because she had rushed home after lunch yesterday, taken the afternoon off? It couldn't be. She had emailed the Tanner document to Kate first thing this morning. If Kate was annoyed she would have told Shirin herself. She was upfront in dealing with her team. And Marie wouldn't be involved in something as trivial as this, would she? *Why* was Marie involved?

Shirin smoothed her shirt to rid it of doughnut crumbs, tried futilely to rub away the jam stain in the shape of North America on the right knee of her black trousers, picked up a notebook and pencil and made her way to the boardroom.

'You in trouble, then?' Rob asked as she passed his desk, grinning vampire-like as he bit into an obscenely shiny apple. 'I'll keep my fingers crossed.'

'He fancies you, you know,' Kate had said to her once.

'Who—Rob?' she'd asked, a surprised giggled erupting. They were sitting in a café, having a late lunch, celebrating a release that had gone particularly well. The smell of coffee wafted, rich, warm, and Shirin was assaulted by a sudden memory: she and her mother by the roadside shack near Mangalore Bus Station, the man pouring hot sloshing coffee from a great height into their two tiny tumblers. She had swallowed hers in two gulps. It was very sweet and very hot and had scalded her tongue. She had yelped, jumping up and down, gasping and fanning her open mouth with her hands and her mother had said, 'You look just like Rex,' and laughed—that rare magical waterfall of a laugh.

'Haven't you seen the way he looks at you? Don't you notice these things, Shirin?' Kate had asked, genuinely curious. 'Don't you ever see a man and go, "Ooh, I fancy you"? Aren't you ever tempted? You and Vinod have been together so long… Back when Dave and I were an item, there were times when I…'

She'd thought of the tingle she got sometimes when someone looked at her a certain way; when she caught a glimpse of eyes, bespectacled and serious; the feelings a certain smell—lemony musk—aroused in her… and the guilt that engulfed her almost immediately. The impulse, so deeply embedded from childhood to rush to confession, the desire for absolution—even though she hadn't been to church in years. 'I am, sometimes.'

'Thank goodness,' Kate had breathed, grinning, 'You are human after all.' And then, her expression serious, 'Would you… you know, leave Vinod? If someone came along, swept you off your feet?'

She'd thought of a different time, a different girl. Younger. Before. The fantasies she'd had, of Chandru the coconut picker, of the boatmen with their gleaming bodies, of Prince Charming whisking her off into the sunset. And then she'd thought of Vinod. His kind face. That smile. 'I couldn't do it, Kate. Not to Vinod.'

'Yes. But you wouldn't be thinking rationally, would you, in the throes of passion? You wouldn't be thinking of Vinod at all…' Kate had persisted.

Wet bodies flattened against the wall, standing side by side, not quite touching. The rain; a wavy curtain in the flickering half light of lamps. The drum roll of thunder. The power cut. Darkness thick as tamarind paste. Their breath punctuating the heady silence: in out, in out, in unison. A burst of laughter, a snatch of conversation drifting toward them on the mango-scented breeze. His face illuminated in a sudden flash of lightning. Very close. 'Run away with me.' Guilt. Shame. Vinod. *Vinod washing her ever so gently that terrible evening, his tears falling like rain…* 'I love Vinod, Kate.'

'I know,' Kate had smiled softly. 'And anyway, Vinod's a hundred times better looking than Rob.'

Kate and Marie were already seated when she entered, heads together, poring over one of the many sheets of paper spread haphazardly along the length of the table, designed to seat at least twelve.

'Hello, Marie, Kate,' she said.

The bank of windows behind them framed cherry-blossom trees in glorious bloom; a furious burst of pink and white. Snatches of conversation from colleagues on their way to lunch drifted in.

'Shirin,' Marie stood and reached across the table to clasp Shirin's hand.

The tinny music heralding the lunch van followed by the customary two cheery honks on the horn sounded. Chairs scraped and desks were pushed aside as people ran downstairs to bag their favourite sandwich.

'You're looking well.' Marie's smile, behind her designer spectacles was stern.

The shiver of apprehension ballooned. Was this something to do with the rumour of redundancies whispering through the company? Was she going first? *I've worked so hard to get here. This is my identity; who I am now.* Out loud, 'Thank you. And you look great. As always.'

That earned a proper smile. Even Marie—cropped grey hair, no-nonsense suit and uncompromising expression—was susceptible to compliments.

'Now. I'll get right down to business. You know Jay's leaving next month?'

Shirin nodded.

'And that he was handling the CMS account, which is very critical to us?'

'Yes,' Shirin agreed. *I'll fight like hell to keep my job.* She flashed a sidelong glance at Kate. Kate, head bent, copiously studying her notes, hair a red-gold curtain. *Kate, what's going on?*

'Well, I've talked to Kate—obviously—and to John Watts, whom you were reporting to briefly last November, and to a few of your colleagues. They have nothing but praise for you. All this I find very encouraging.' Marie looked at Shirin over the top of her glasses, which had slid down to her nose, and Shirin was reminded of her mother putting down her newspaper and looking at her in much the same way one rainy Sunday afternoon aeons ago: 'Have you been reading those books that clueless illiterate Duja in charge of the lending library lets you borrow?' 'No, Ma.' 'Then what put you in mind of devils possessing nuns to take over the church?' 'I'm sorry, Ma.' 'You should be; it's blasphemy.' Jacinta picking up the *Udayavani*, its pages rustling, hiding her face; had there been a hint of a smile on her mother's stern visage?

Why on earth was she thinking of her mother now?

'I have also taken the liberty of looking through your performance appraisals and talking to your staff manager,' Marie continued, 'and he agrees with me and Kate here, that you are ready for more responsibility and that you'll handle it well.'

What? Had she heard right? Out of the corner of her eyes, Shirin saw Kate smiling.

'So, we would like you to take over Jay's team and manage the CMS project.' A long pause during which

Marie looked straight at Shirin. 'As you might be aware, it is an all-male team. Kate assures me that you will be fine, that there has been no repeat...'

Ian's accusation slunk into the room; hung there. A blue-tinged shadow. And Shirin was transported back nine years to a room just like this one in the Goodge Street office: Ian standing in one corner, she in the other, Kate beside her, Marie facing all of them. Marie, looking into Shirin's eyes, as if she could read her mind: 'Now, Shirin. With your permission, Kate has told me a bit about what happened to you. I can understand where you're coming from.' Marie had paused, turned her attention to Ian. 'Ian, I can see where you're coming from, too. If someone cringed every time they came near me, if they ducked away from me when I tried to talk to them, acted for all the world as if I was going to harass them, I would be frustrated and angry too. And it would affect the quality of my work.' Another pause. 'Shirin, you are hardworking, diligent. No one has issue with your work. But you will be working as part of a team and there will be men in your team, as explained in the contract you signed when you joined CST Solutions. I cannot have this issue every time you have to work with a member of the opposite sex.' Shirin had wilted under her gaze. 'And as for you, Ian, I'm sorry you've had to go through this. I'm moving you to John's team with immediate effect.' Marie had smiled at Ian then, a slight relaxation of her facial muscles, 'I have reason to believe that you've been angling for this for a while.' A nod at Shirin, 'Can I speak to you privately for a minute?' After Ian and Kate had left, she'd said, her gaze boring into Shirin, 'Kate mentioned that you've had counselling before. I would suggest that you take a few weeks off work, go back for more intensive counselling sessions to deal with this issue you seem to have with certain men.'

Now, Shirin cleared her throat. 'I apologised to Ian after.' It was Ian's eyes that had repelled her: hooded, empty, too close for comfort; his breath when he leaned close, pungent like the smell that populated her nightmares.

Marie nodded, her strict countenance softening. 'I know.' Shirin's heart constricted at Marie's expression: an expression she'd seen so often on a much-beloved face. How could this heavyset white woman remind her so of her slender mother?

'So, are you ready to take on Jay's team, then?' Marie asked, the beginnings of a smile curling her lips upward.

Ian's accusation, the spectre of the Eyes, slunk away, to be replaced by relief. Joy even. 'Yes. Thank you very much.' A quick glance at Kate who was grinning from ear to ear. 'Thanks, Kate.'

Marie reached across, took Shirin's hand, held it in both of hers. 'Prove yourself, Shirin. Show us what you can do.'

Rob was in the process of biting into a doorstep BLT, mouth wide open, reminiscent of the baby python that had slunk into Ananthanna's chicken coop, the chicken squawking plaintively from between its fangs before disappearing into its belly. 'Been sacked yet?' he asked between munches.

'Unfortunately no.' She couldn't keep the smile from her voice.

'Despite all the things I said when Marie asked me about you?' He shook his head in mock bewilderment and smiled, giving her a glimpse of half-chewed tomato. 'Congratulations!'

'Thanks, Rob. Any of those left in the van?'

'Nope. Only the mangy salad ones.'

Shirin pulled a face.

'Why don't you go to Marks, get yourself a decent sandwich and some cakes for us lot who helped you up by putting in a good word?' Rob rubbed his stomach. 'I feel like dessert.'

Once at her desk, she called Vinod, knowing he would be on his lunch break. 'I've been put in charge of Jay's team, managing CMS, that account I told you about.'

'Good for you, Shonu.' She heard the smile in his voice. She pictured him leaning back in his chair, the grin softening his features, transforming his face.

'Marie called me in to tell me. She's the one who handled the whole thing with Ian. I thought I was going to be sacked...'

'Did she bring Ian up?' Shirin pictured him pulling at his belt, trying to tuck the beginnings of a paunch in: a recently acquired habit.

'She had to. I am in charge of an all-male team.'

'Way to go, Shonu,' Quiet pride in his voice.

'She reminded me of Ma.'

'Who did?'

'Marie.'

'Oh...' And then, Vinod being Vinod, 'Good. That's a good thing, Shonu. Let the memories come.'

And like a dam burst open, a memory spilled out, insinuating itself to the fore of her mind: She's four years old. It's too hot to wear any clothes. She follows the example of the Fernandes twins and runs around naked. Afterwards, her mother's wrath: 'Shame on you! Running around nude like that... Don't you know you are a girl?' The palms of Jacinta's hands bunched into fists, her eyes cold and hard like the granite in the Panambur quarry. Shirin is puzzled. Why is her mother asking such a silly question? Of course she knows she's a girl. That's why Madhu clothes her in dresses and churidars—not shorts like the Fernandes twins. That's why she has to wear the heavy gold earrings her grandmother gifted her with when she was born even though they hurt her lobes. She's about to open her mouth to ask why, but Madhu, hovering anxiously behind Jacinta, catches Shirin's eyes and shakes her head—*No.*

Later, after Jacinta metes out punishment (two sharp beatings on her bare stick-insect legs with the tender branch from the hibiscus plant), after she has cried out her tears and been fed and fussed over by Madhu, she turns around in Madhu's lap so as to face her and, her eyes still wet with remembered agony, whispers, 'Why was she so angry?'

Madhu pats her head gently. 'You are a girl, Shirin. Girls don't run around naked.'

'Why?'

'They just don't.'

'Shirin, are you there?' Vinod's voice in her ear, grounding her in the present.

'Yes.'

'This morning, I was rushing; I didn't get a chance...' He paused and she knew what was coming. 'Have you thought any more about contacting them?'

Softly, 'Yes.'

'I'm sure there's a way to find their email addresses in this day and age. Perhaps you could ring Deepak's employer. He's with HP now, did you say?'

'What about confidentiality?'

'Surely if you explained... Or even just called HP and asked to speak to him.'

Was it possible? She pictured herself, after saying goodbye to Vinod, dialling HP. Waiting for the heartbeat of static, the pause indicating a transatlantic connection. 'Hello?' An Indian voice imitating an American accent. 'Can I speak to Deepak Diaz, please?' *My brother.* 'Do you have his extension number?' The receptionist with her fake accent: pish pish, in Madhu's lingo. 'No, sorry; I seem to have misplaced it.' 'Hold on a minute,' the receptionist's bored voice tinged with annoyance echoing down the line. A pause. Muzak bridging the distance, punctuated by static. And then... Her brother's deep voice—reminding Shirin every time she heard it of the shock they'd all had when out of the blue, the angelic voice of his childhood, the pride of the choir, the favourite of the nuns, had transformed to this. 'Hello? Who's this?' What would she say? That she couldn't stay away any longer. That she had to come back. That she had to see her. Could she? Drop this bombshell on her brother, sitting in his office, on an ordinary workday, in the middle of an ordinary week. 'I want to come home. I want to end this. I've had enough.' Could she?

'Shonu?' Vinod's voice.

What if he doesn't want to speak to me? What if he discon-nects the call on recognising my voice? 'Yes?'

'We'll celebrate this evening.'

'Huh?'

'Your promotion.' And then, 'Are you okay?'

'I'm fine.'

'Sure?'

'Yes.'

'Okay, then. I'll see you later. Love you.'

'Bye.'

She disconnected the call, stared at the phone. Could she? Carefully, she placed the phone in her purse. And googled Hewlett-Packard Global Soft Limited, clicked on the 'Contact' tab once the page came up, stared at the phone number. So easy. Her phone peeked from her handbag, beckoning. On the screen in front of her, the number glowed. Below it was printed, in small let-ters, *9:00 a.m.—6:00 p.m. Monday—Friday (IST)*. She checked her watch. Quarter to two. Which made it 6:15 p.m. in India. She sighed, not sure if it was disappoint-ment she felt.

'Congratulations, *manager*.' Kate was at her desk, giving her a quick hug. 'What say we go to the pub for a quick drink after work? Will Vinod mind? We won't stay long.'

'I'm sure that's fine. I'll tell him I'll be late.'

'What are you looking at?' Kate peered at the computer. 'Hewlett Packard. Not thinking of leaving us in the lurch?'

'My brother works there.'

'Oh.' Kate's eyes wide, a question in them.

'I'll fill you in this evening. Right now I'm off to get cakes for Rob over there.' She raised her voice at this last bit. Rob looked up, mouthed 'Cheers' and winked.

'Ooh. Not that I'm suggesting anything, but coffee and walnut cake is my particular favourite. And I did miss lunch...' Kate laughed.

The phone number. Deepak. Her promotion. She stood, her legs wobbly from all the excitement. As she picked up her car keys and handbag, Shirin pictured Madhu's response to her promotion. Madhu would cup Shirin's face in her palms and, her eyes glowing with pride, whisper, 'Well done, Shirin, I always knew you could do it. My girl...'

Why couldn't she fathom Jacinta's reaction? Why, when she tried to picture Jacinta, to trace her features from memory, did she only see the expression in her mother's eyes the last time she saw her?

✳ ✳ ✳

The pub was crowded, but Shirin managed to bag a table by the window overlooking the high street while Kate went to get their drinks. She took off her jacket and settled into her seat, the capacious high-backed chair engulfing her. She loved being in pubs: the crunch of salt-and-vinegar crisps; the frothy smell of beer mingling with the aroma of chips, onion rings and tart sweet ketchup; the conversations flowing and ebbing; the murmur of the sports commentator on TV accompanied every once in a while by a loud collective cheer or groan—all instilling in her a sense of camaraderie. Here, in this most English of institutions, she could pretend, briefly, that she belonged. That she was not forever floating, straddling two personalities and two worlds—the one she ached for, that she had had to leave behind; and the one she found herself in, the world she would always be in debt of, as it had accepted her, broken as she was, and had allowed her to heal, to make something of herself—so that sometimes, in the dead of night, she woke screaming silently, not sure who she was anymore, lost even to herself.

She closed her eyes briefly, the stress and excitement of the day catching up. And a name came to her, as if it had been hovering in the forefront of her memory, waiting for her to retrieve it. Sinha. Uttam Sinha.

She sat up, looked to the bar to see if she could spot Kate. She saw Kate's distinctive hair, her camel jacket amongst the crush at the bar. She was deep in conversation with a tall man wearing a suit and tie, his head bent towards Kate as he listened to what she was saying. Dark hair. Glasses. Kate's type. Good for her.

At the next table, across from her, a very young couple shared a chair. She sat on his lap, her head on his shoulder. His head rested on hers. Her eyes were closed. A half smiled played on her face. She looked so… content. And for a brief moment, Shirin ached to be her, this girl with her uncluttered life. No complicated history. No messy past. A man who so obviously adored her. Her whole life ahead of her, glimmering with possibilities… *I wish I'd grown up here. White-skinned. Not having to worry about what people might think or say; not having to heft the burden of obligation, of duty; not having to honour the family name…*

A memory: skipping school on the day of the Kannada test for which she hadn't prepared, lying flat among the branches of the trees in the orchard surrounding the school, inhaling the fruity breeze, munching on raw mangoes and spying on her classmates, feeling only slightly guilty as they were called forward, one by one and hit with a ruler…

And another: the river sparkling in the sunlight, a golden blue, the boat undulating gently with the waves; St. Mary's island shimmering in the distance, a dark haze against silvery clouds and pink-tinged sky; the picnic basket containing dosas, idlis, ambades and fresh jamun courtesy of Jilly Bai snug against their sun-warmed feet, Anita laughing at something she'd said…

No, she couldn't imagine swapping her childhood for a different one. She had been happy then. Before she grew up. Before…

Shirin settled back onto her chair and looked away from the couple, out the window. Taipur. Home. Anita.

Anita Sinha. Didn't sound right. She would google it. To-morrow. And should she call Deepak? Not yet. Not just yet...

She had been looking out the window without really seeing anything, but now her attention was captured by a teenage girl, Asian, standing by the bus stop opposite the pub. She looked about fourteen, her school uniform peeking out from under her navy-blue dress coat. She stood hunched against the chilly evening breeze, her hands working busily on a mobile phone, headphones in her ears, hair falling over her face. Every once in a while she looked up, sneaked sideways glances, and Shirin, following her gaze, found she was checking out a tall Asian boy lounging against the British Heart Foundation shop awning, scowling at his shoes. Shirin smiled, her heart going out to the girl. *Go on, talk to him if you fancy him.* A tall blonde girl wearing the same uniform crept up behind the Asian girl, put her arms around her. She squealed, looked up, laughed. She was very pretty when she smiled. The blonde girl pointed to the boy, nudged her friend. She blushed. The blonde started striding towards the boy, pulling her reluctant, blushing friend along. The boy slouched, scowling, oblivious.

'Whew. What a crush. *Everyone's* decided to have a quick after-work drink this evening.' Kate sank onto the chair beside her, depositing their drinks and a saucer of spiced peanuts.

'Who was the lucky man, then?'

'Nothing escapes you, does it?' Kate laughed.

'Did you get his number?'

'What do you think?' Kate grinned and opened out her palm. A number was scribbled in her messy scrawl across it.

'That will rub out. Here.' Shirin rummaged around in her purse for a pen and a sheet of paper.

'I didn't know I would meet someone when I went to get the drinks, did I? If I did, I would have gone armed with a notebook and a tad more make up. His name is Callum. Does IT support for DCS. He seemed very nice.'

Across the street, the blonde was talking to the Asian boy, nudging her shy friend to join in. As Shirin watched, the Asian girl looked up, across the road and through the pub window, right at her.

'Do you know her?' Kate asked.

'Who?'

'That girl you're watching? You're not the only one who's observant you know.'

'No, no.' Shirin pulled her gaze away.

'So, ma'am, how does it feel to be manager?' Kate mimicked holding a mic in front of Shirin's mouth.

'Good, thank you. Especially as I haven't started doing the job yet.'

Kate burst out laughing, squeezed Shirin's arm. 'I'm pleased for you, Shirin. You are just the person for the job. It took all my willpower to keep it under wraps when Jay recommended you. Had to run it by Marie first…' She leaned back, took a long swig of her pint of lager. 'Ah. I needed that.' And, smiling up at Shirin, 'Go on then;

spill the beans. Why were you looking up your brother's company this afternoon?'

'Vinod suggested I call his workplace, ask to speak to him.'

Kate sat up. 'Do you want to?'

'What if he doesn't want to speak to me?' With Kate, she could voice her doubts.

'If you ask me, I think you should let it be. Why leave yourself open to hurt again?' She leaned forward, looking into Shirin's eyes, 'Look at you: strong, confident woman. Manager. Is there any point in going back?'

'I miss her, Kate. I miss Reena.'

Kate followed her gaze out the grimy pub window. The girl was walking down the street away from her, flanked by the blonde on one side and the Asian boy loping along on the other. He bent towards her, whispered something in her ear and she threw her head back and laughed.

'I... I think I've finally forgiven myself for what I did. I can see that, in the circumstances, I was justified. What the counsellor, Vinod and you tried to tell me all this while is beginning to make sense. I'm not saying all my choices were right; I am still guilty about... Reena. But at the time, the person I was... I understand now... That's why the memories don't hurt as much, why I am able to entertain them.'

Kate nodded once. 'Do you think after all this time they're still...?'

'I don't know...' Shirin stared at her drink as if it held all the answers. 'I think I'd like to contact Anita first.'

She paused, taking a sip of her drink before continuing. 'Anita... She's...' she scrabbled around for the right phrase to describe what she wanted to say. *Anita asking, 'Why did you do it, Deepak? Why did you give the note to Ma? It was Shirin's.' Shirin sitting shell-shocked on the front stoop, the breeze cold on her bare neck, naked without its curtain of hair. Madhu sniffing violently as she swept the courtyard clean, her body bent like a question mark, the hair she'd spent hours massaging now nothing but a pool of dark strands hugging the trunks of the coconut trees.*

As usual, Kate understood without her having to say it. 'I know. The bond between sisters. With a brother it's not the same, is it?'

'I looked up to Deepak, was in awe of him.' *Deepak's voice: 'The Diaz family is Taipur's most respected and has been for generations. Loving a Muslim. Don't you realise the scandal it would cause? The disgrace...'* 'But with Anu it was different. We would get into all sorts of scrapes. "We're partners in crime," she used to say, having picked up the phrase from one of my books...' Her little sister. Her confidante. 'She's not judgemental; at least she wasn't when...' She used to know every little thing about Anita, once upon a time. *Why, Anu, why have you stayed away?* 'When Mijju Aunty ran away with the butcher—a huge scandal in our sedate village—Anu said, "I would, too, if I was married to Rigu Uncle."'

Kate laughed. 'I like your sister.'

'You two would get along like a house on fire. You remind me, in many ways, of her...' She tried to picture, in a rosy future of the happily-ever-after kind, the three of them: Kate and Anita and her, sharing a drink and chatting and laughing. She couldn't. The image just wouldn't form.

'I was this close to calling Deepak today, Kate. Only the fact that it was after office hours in India stopped me.' *And... the fact that I was afraid. Deepak's face the last time she saw him: 'I wish to God it hadn't happened this way, Shirin.'*

'Do you have a number for Anita?'

'No. But just now, as I was waiting for you, I remembered the name of her boyfriend. Husband now, I suppose. If she married him.' *Did you, Anu? After what I did, loving a Hindu, marrying one, would have been way down the 'creating a scandal and disgracing the family' list...* 'I'll try finding her. If not, I'll bite the bullet. Call Deepak.'

Kate leaned across, laid a hand on her arm. 'If you're sure that's what you want.'

'I don't want to burden Reena with the truth, Kate.' *Reena.* 'I don't want to disrupt her life. I just... I want to see her, that's all.' The Eyes loomed, large, menacing. With all her will, she wished them away. And they went. A first. Disappearing when she wanted them to. She was ready to face up to her past. As ready as she would ever be.

CHAPTER TWELVE

Sunglasses in the Rain

Murli was waiting for Reena by the bus stop, holding an umbrella open as she got off the school bus. 'Ooh, look at Reena's friend,' she heard one of the boys in the back smirk. 'Boyfriend more like,' grinned another.

'Shut up!' she yelled, lugging her bag behind her, bouncing it off the steps—something her mother had warned her repeatedly *not* to do. *What do you care? He's your friend and he's got you an umbrella,* she thought, trying to ignore the chants of 'Boyfriend! Boyfriend!' as the bus pulled away.

'Here, give it to me,' Murli said, spitting the paan he had been chewing into the bushes by the front gate with a loud 'thoo'. He hefted her bag onto his back and opened the gate for her, while holding the umbrella with the other hand and waving hello at the security guard.

'What are you doing here, Murli? Does Mrs. Gupta know?'

'She thinks I'm in the kitchen preparing chole for dinner.' He gave her a paan-stained grin which did not quite reach his eyes.

'What's the matter, Murli?'

'Oh, Rinu, there's a great drought in my village. People are dying. The price of rice and pulses has rocketed. There is no water anywhere. And here, people are complaining about the rain...' Words tumbled out of Murli's mouth in a rush, as if he had been forcibly holding them in.

'Your family?'

'They are okay for now. Because of the money I send them, they can to afford to buy food, despite the exorbitant prices...' Murli's agonised gaze met Reena's. 'You know what kills me? The amount of food that Mrs. Gupta wastes, so casually, without a second thought... What wouldn't my people give for a few bites of the biryani she ordered me to throw away yesterday because she said it smelt...'

'I know...' Reena whispered, helplessly. She reached out and took Murli's arm, slick from the rain.

'What am I doing here, Reena? Why am I dancing to the tunes of that old hag?'

'You are saving your family,' Reena said gently.

They were beside the swimming pool. The water, the same dark blue as the eyeliner Reena's mum sometimes wore, danced a rippling tune, revelling in the rain. Murli stopped abruptly. 'Look—that would save my entire village, just that water over there.' He sniffed, turned to her, smiled weakly. 'Look at your face. I have scared you! It's okay, Reena. I am fine. It is just... so hard to be here, surrounded by luxury when I know my family is suffering...'

'You don't live in luxury! You are relegated to sleep in the little store room behind the kitchen with the cock-

roaches and rats and are at the mercy of Mrs. Gupta,'
Reena was indignant.

'It's five-star accommodation compared to a mud hut,
Rinu. And stale biryani is much better than no food at
all,' Murli said softly. He took a deep breath and then, in
a false bright voice, said, 'Enough sad stories for one day.
Did you know your aunt Anita arrived this morning? I
helped carry her bags up.'

'Oh! I forgot she was coming.'

How could she have forgotten?

That morning, she woke to busyness, the nightmare
niggling at the back of her head. Her mother had already
been up for hours, tidying, dusting, washing, getting the
spare room ready.

When Reena arrived at school, Anupama accused her
of copying her homework. Pandit Sir, the maths teacher,
made her stand up in front of the whole class for half an
hour because she was caught giggling. It was so unfair!
Raji, who sat directly behind her, had cracked the joke.
It hadn't even been funny. She had giggled just to join in.
Singh Ma'am, the biology teacher, sprung a surprise test
on them, which Reena was sure she would fail, as her mind
went blank and she couldn't remember a thing. Amidst all
this upheaval, Aunt Anita's arrival clean escaped her mind.

'She was wearing dark sunglasses. Sunglasses, when it's
raining! Occurred to me that she might have been crying...' Murli looked questioningly at Reena.

Reena was tempted, sorely, to tell Murli about Aunt
Anita's possible divorce, if only to get his mind off his

own problems. But she had promised to keep it a secret. 'Oh, Murli, you know how stylish she is. Perhaps wearing sunglasses in the rain is the latest fashion trend,' she made up on the spot. She was getting good at lying under pressure. But she needed to work on her excuses...

Thankfully, Murli seemed to be taken in. 'You can never tell what these high-class people find fashionable,' he muttered, shaking his head. 'Ah, perhaps she's acting in a movie. All Bollywood actresses wear sunglasses when they don't want to be recognised.'

Reena nodded her agreement, pleased to see Murli animated again, almost back to his normal self.

'She's so pretty; I thought she was an actress the first time I saw her. It's a short leap from modelling to acting, you know,' Murli said knowledgeably, as though he was an expert on the subject. 'So, you never know, we might be seeing her face plastered all over the city soon...' He stopped suddenly, stared at Reena, 'Maybe that's why she's here, for a shoot...'

'I'll find out, Murli,' Reena whispered, as though she and Murli were colluding in a great secret.

Murli deposited Reena's school bag in front of her door. 'Please do. I should get her autograph for my daughter. She'll be thrilled...' Murli's grin dimmed at the thought of his daughter.

'Are you going to be okay?' Reena asked tentatively.

Murli nodded vigorously. 'I'll be fine. I just wanted to chat to someone, is all... You cheered me up. You always do. I better sneak into the house before *she* finds out I haven't even started on the chole.'

'Thank you for carrying my bag, Murli, and for the umbrella.'

'Oh, that! It's nothing.' He winked. 'Maybe you can find out from your Aunt Anita about your other aunt?'

Murli had stumbled on Plan C?

'You know. The missing one. The one from the picture,' Murli continued

Her missing aunt. The girl in pigtails from her nightmare rose before Reena's eyes. She closed them. She felt Murli's cold fingers, wet from the rain, on her shoulder. 'It's okay. I'm sure there's some simple explanation,' he said gently.

'Yes.' She remembered the look on her dad's face when she asked him how many siblings he had, the way Mai had gone still on the sofa. 'I'm sure there is.'

'Find out if your Aunt Anita is appearing in a movie. And tell me...' Murli's grin was his old one. Only the lines around his eyes spoke of his worry, his fear.

'Your family is going to be fine, Murli. I'll pray for them.'

His face softened. 'God listens to children's prayers, you know.'

'I know.'

'Now I really must be going. You have fun with your film-star aunt.' He flashed his yellow teeth in a smile and was gone.

The house smelt of frying spices and the promise of a feast. Reena found her mother and Aunt Anita on the balcony. They sat side by side on reclining cane chairs under a canopy of bed sheets which her mother had hung out to dry, sheltered from the rain that was whipping the gulmohars into a frenzy and turning the begonia beds to muddy slush.

'I don't know where it all went wrong, Preeti,' Aunt Anita was saying. She looked as glamorous as ever. Her face, Reena was glad to note, even though she knew she was being silly, was not that of the monster from her nightmare. Her head was resting on a cushion. Her eyes were closed. Tears squeezed out from beneath the lids and ran down her ivory-complexioned, heart-shaped face.

Reena cleared her throat. 'Hello, Aunty. Mum, I'm home'

Her mum and Aunt Anita hurriedly sat up, Aunt Anita furtively wiping her face.

'Reena!' Her aunt held her slender arms out for a hug. 'My goodness, how you've grown!'

Aunt Anita smelt wonderful, as usual: fruity, almost edible. Being hugged by her was like entering a different, more exotic world.

'I haven't prepared your snack, Rinu,' said Preeti, standing. 'I'll do it now. You stay here and chat to your aunt. I'll call you when it's ready.'

Reena went to sit in the chair her mother had just vacated, catching a spray of water from the windswept branches of the jacaranda tree just beyond the balcony. She had a sudden vision of the cracked fields of Murli's drought-ridden village, parched and crying out for rain.

Aunt Anita took a sip of her tea which was on the little table between them, and put on her sunglasses.

'How was school, Reena?'

'As usual, Aunty—boring.'

'Boring?' Anita giggled, and Reena was pleased that she had made her laugh. 'I used to find it boring, too. I hated it, in fact.'

'But Mai said you were very good at your studies.'

'Perhaps that's why I found it boring.' She turned to look at Reena, and Reena found two miniatures of herself staring at her from Aunt Anita's shades. The nightmare niggled again. 'You must be very bright, too. After all, you are your father's daughter!'

'Was Dad very clever?'

'He was—and extremely mischievous.' Anita giggled again, remembering.

'Mischievous? Dad?'

'Deepak loved all creepy crawlies, the slimier the better. Once he caught a huge frog and put it on Sister Shanthi's desk...'

'Did he?'

'Uh-huh. The terrified frog jumped everywhere, creating havoc. Ma was summoned to meet with the nuns. The priest was called in. Pompous old Father Sequiera. Deepak was suspended from school for a week. He had to go for confession every day, and it was decided that he would be a special altar boy from then on, permanently under Father Sequiera's watchful eye...'

Try as she might, Reena couldn't reconcile her quiet, serious father with the naughty little boy from this story. No wonder her father had a lot to reminisce and laugh about during his visits to Taipur.

'Ma was told by the nuns that her son was going to be a rowdy when he grew up, one of those good-for-nothing drunks who hang around the village. Deepak went into hiding. Madhu only managed to find him late that night, cowering behind the rack where she hung her clothes.'

'What happened then?' Reena worried for the little boy her dad had been, fearing what was to come.

'Ma had cooled off a bit by then, but he got a good thrashing with broomsticks anyway. They hurt like hell, let me tell you.' Anita winced at the remembered pain.

'And?' Reena prompted.

'Deepak regretted the incident, only because he had to be an altar boy for the rest of his school life. No more nodding off or chatting in church. And from then on, the nuns picked on him all the time, especially Sister Shanthi. They weren't very holy, those nuns. We couldn't wait to escape to college. I am glad Deepak didn't send you to a convent school. But then he wouldn't, not after what we went through...'

Anita sighed and settled back into her chair, closing her eyes. She was getting sad again.

'I never wanted kids but now... I wish...' she whispered, almost to herself.

Reena panicked. She was not used to dealing with these quick mood swings. Why was her mum not calling her for a snack? How could she stop her aunt from start-ing to cry again?

And then, almost from nowhere, a thought came into her head and, without thinking, she said it out loud.

'What about Aunt Shirin? What was she like as a child?'

Her aunt jerked and stiffened like the crows on pylons being electrocuted during a thunderstorm. She turned to stare at Reena. Reena could feel her eyes boring into her from behind the sunglasses.

Aunt Anita opened her mouth slowly, and seemed sur-prised when words came out.

'How do you know about Shirin?' she asked.

CHAPTER THIRTEEN
Untouchable Prince Charming

Shirin ran to the bus stop, barely noticing the spitting rain. There was one other person waiting: an older lady wielding an umbrella. As Shirin approached, she looked at her watch. 'If you're after the 114, it's late. It was due two minutes ago.' Her voice was tremulous with age.

'Oh, good. I thought I had missed it.'

'They are always late, these buses,' the woman clucked, peering up at Shirin from under thick grey eyebrows. 'You are not one of the regulars, are you?'

'No, I drive usually. My car has gone in for a service.' She leaned against the pole displaying bus timings and information. *Loud hoarse breaths just behind her, whistling between her shoulder blades, raising goosebumps. Pungent. Hoarse. No.* She whipped round. Nothing. No one. Deep breaths. Calm.

'They cost a fortune these days, don't they?' the old lady was saying.

'I'm sorry?' Shirin grimaced. And then nodded as she realised the woman was talking about her car. 'Yes. Oh, yes.'

'You should get one of these.' The woman waved her bus pass. 'You young people will have to pay of course, but not as much as you shell out for your car, what with fuel and MOTs and tax discs and whatnot.' She paused, squinting up the road. 'Is that the 114?'

'Yes. Here it comes. After you...'

The bus was empty. Thank goodness. No noisy breaths. No sound of chappals. Shirin chose a window seat near the back and watched the world trundle by.

The rain had stopped and the clouds had shifted slightly allowing stray rays of sun to infiltrate the grey morning and brighten it somewhat. A few leaves were already starting to change colour. A bit early, Shirin thought, it being barely the beginning of October.

It had been late October when she and Vinod arrived in the UK. All she remembered about those first few weeks was walking. Once Vinod went to work, she would leave the flat they were renting and walk for miles. She walked to escape the bare walls, the silence, the empty eyes that haunted her. She walked until she could feel no longer. She walked to escape herself.

One overcast morning she opened her mouth to let a sob escape and tasted the English rain. It did not have the earthy, rich taste of freshly churned mud that she had been expecting. It did not have the spicy, slightly bitter scent you get when you tear a mango leaf in two—the aroma she associated with the monsoons. English rain smelt and tasted of nothing at all. It had none of the fury, the passion of the monsoons. Instead, it was weak; half-hearted. She spent the rest of her walk distracted: part of her resenting the English rain for being nothing like the monsoons; the other half rejoicing.

Over the next few weeks, she began to notice other things, to pay attention to this new world she found herself in. Everything was different—the trees, the weather, the people, the food. There was more order, less mess. There was no overcrowding, no constant blaring of horns. There were no smells.

Autumn had set in and Shirin found she liked crunching on a multihued bed of foliage—a carpet laid out just for her, canopied by trees with leaves all the colours of the rainbow—and not having to worry about snakes. She liked the way a ray of mild autumn sun infiltrating the thick cluster of trees caught a reddish orange leaf swirling in the wind and transformed it golden yellow. She liked that it wasn't a leaf she recognised, that she could name or associate with her past...

The bus chugged to a halt and the older woman from the bus stop shuffled out. As the bus pulled away, the woman looked up. Her eyes met Shirin's and she smiled, waved goodbye. The moment of recognition, the brief connection, made Shirin inordinately pleased.

By the time she got off at her stop, the clouds had been chased away by the sun. She pulled sunglasses out of her handbag and began the brisk walk across the park to the office. In the far corner a low wall separated the children's playground from the dog-walkers' section. On it perched two little girls giggling as they shared a secret; heads close together, bare legs dangling, the skirts of their summer dresses dancing, looking for all the world like Shirin and her best friend Pramila, half a lifetime ago.

Pramila: timid, dark, plain, born in the wake of a handsome older brother. Pramila, whose house bordered the convent, who lived, literally, in the nuns' shadow.

Pramila with whom Shirin fantasised—sitting on the uneven compound wall of their empty school in the evenings after they had both finished their homework—of being beautiful. In their dreams, they were princesses: fair-complexioned, slim, gorgeous. They would each find a prince, who would rescue them from drudgery and shower them with kisses, who would carry them away into the sunset.

Pramila, in whom Shirin confided her crush on coconut-picking Chandru, he of the gleaming chocolate limbs and rippling muscles, he of the cheeky grin reserved especially for her: 'I will marry him, run away from home and live happily ever after.' Pramila, her plain face worried: 'You will be an outcast, Shirin. Your family will disown you.' Shirin, repeating the lines she had read in many a romance novel, heard in many a Bollywood movie: 'I will bear the disgrace, for I have found my Prince Charming, my one true love.' 'But he's an untouchable, Shirin.' 'He's my Untouchable Prince Charming, then. Only I am allowed to touch him.'

In her mind's eye, Shirin saw the two girls, one dark as mustard seeds, the other watermelon-shaped, both misfits with eager-to-please expressions permanently etched on their faces, just starting to grow breasts and become aware of boys, sitting side by side on the cracked cement wall, painting glorious futures for themselves. How naive she and Pramila had been! They hadn't realised that, as in every fairy tale, there would be a price to pay for securing Prince Charming. In her fantasy about Chandru, she had blithely accepted the cost of being an outcast as fee. And now, she was one. *Be careful what you wish for.*

The office was abuzz with news of the upcoming charity ball that CST Solutions held annually with its partners and clients. Shirin had paid the requisite amount each year but managed to get out of attending, and as far as she was concerned, this year wasn't going to be any different.

Kate was perched on her desk going through her collection of pens when she approached with a mug of coffee. 'You've got quite a selection here,' she remarked.

Shirin smiled. 'What do you want from me, woman?'

'Come to the ball, Shirin.' And, while Shirin was still rooting for an excuse, 'I won't take no for an answer. Now that you're manager, you've got to set an example.' And, while Shirin fumbled, 'The theme is "Multiculturalism".'

'There's a theme?'

'Wear a sari, Shirin. Everyone's dressing up.'

'I...'

'You have got one?'

'Yes,' Shirin lied. Why? 'Kate, I...'

'Good. Andrew's wearing a kilt. I'll wear something suitably Irish; I have a shamrock T-Shirt, will match it with a skirt or something...'

'Kate...'

'You'll have fun. Live a little, Shirin.'

'That's not fair...'

Kate put one hand on each of Shirin's shoulders, looked into her eyes. 'Shirin, you're my friend and I love you. I've been meaning to say this to you for ages.' Kate took a deep breath. 'Shirin. It's been eleven years. You cannot hide away forever. And much as it pains me to say this, you may not be here next year. This time next year you'll be with your family, having fun in the sun, your friend Kate a vague memory.'

I wish, Shirin thought as she smiled along with Kate at the fantasy. 'You would be right there having fun along with me.'

'Come to the party, Shirin. You'll enjoy it, I promise.'

Sometimes, Kate reminded Shirin of a bulldozer, albeit a well-meaning one, squashing anything that showed the least bit of resistance briskly into shape. She was looking expectantly at Shirin now, eyebrows puckered, green eyes bright. 'Go on; say you'll come.'

'I'll come.'

Kate squealed, jumped off the desk, put her arms round Shirin. 'You won't regret it.'

Justine, who was walking past, asked, 'What's all the commotion about?'

'Shirin has agreed to come to the charity ball. But, ooh, she plays hard to get. Poor Vinod. She must have put him through hell and back before she agreed to marry him.' And with a wink at her, Kate was gone.

She would need to buy a sari, Shirin thought as she took a sip of her coffee. It was lukewarm. Bittersweet. Like the memory of the trip to Chennai to buy saris for her wedding. She and Jacinta setting out at dawn to catch the express bus from Mirakatte to the train station in Mangalore. Madhu bustling around packing the food she had spent most of the night cooking: idlis, melt-in-the-mouth soft, wrapped in muslin; pudina chutney flecked with mustard seeds; tender coconut, cardamom seed and jaggery stuffing oozing out of thick patholis wrapped in banana leaves; parothas; egg curry. Madhu pulling Shirin into a tight embrace so close Shirin could feel her hot spiced breath on her cheeks. Jacinta telling Pedru Ab, proprietor of the 'Medical Store' that sold liquor, whom they passed on the way to Mirakatte trying to gingerly step over the drunk sprawled across the entrance to his shop, 'We're going to Chennai to buy saris for Shirin's wedding.' The pride in her mother's voice blooming in Shirin's chest. Mangalore Train Station: Crowds pushing, elbows digging into Shirin's arms, shoulders, stomach. The reek of sweat and unwashed bodies. Scents of Bru coffee, samosas, seera and upma from the canteen permeating the stale air. Beggars circulating, jostling the crowd: 'Amma, enu thinnilla, enadru kodi.' Jacinta hugging her handbag and the tiny pink train tickets close to her chest. The train pulling into the platform with a shudder and a sigh. Everyone lunging to find their compartments, a spare seat. Jacinta yelling, 'Second Class, S2, Shirin,' above the crush of people separating them. Shirin finding their seats and holding on to them, arms spread out, while waiting for her mother. Jacinta's face in the window peering in: glasses awry, hair escaping bun, worried eyes lighting up when they saw Shirin, face transformed by her rare smile.

Her mother's smile. The gift of at last being able to picture it again made tears smart as Shirin walked to the coffee machine to get a fresh cup. How could she have forgotten the way Jacinta's smile could soften her whole face? And that day, that particular smile had been reserved just for her.

Jacinta and Shirin had sat across from each other, silent for the most part as the train ate up the miles to Chennai, watching crows disperse in droves from telephone lines scared by the train's piercing whistle; pretending not to notice labourers unashamedly hitch up their lungis and defecate on the railway tracks; watching as the sun's rays lost some of their fire, as they slanted lukewarm through the dirt-encrusted window, creating patterns in the grime, as dusk painted the rows of emerald fields and dancing coconut trees grey, as the sun dipped into the sea, draining the sky of colour. They had shared in silence the food Madhu had packed, listening to the chatter of the family next to them, exchanging smiles when the children argued and the harassed mother threatened to throw them out of the train. And as twinkling yellow lights relieved the black outside every once in a while, they had climbed up to their narrow berths, top bunks facing each other. Shirin had watched as her mother fingered the beads and murmured the rosary, as she tucked it back into her sari blouse after, as she adjusted her handbag masquerading as a pillow under her neck, as she pulled the pallu over her eyes. Just before she closed her eyes, she had turned, met Shirin's gaze. 'Goodnight,' she'd whispered with a little smile. Shirin had realised then that this was what she had been waiting for, and she had allowed her own heavy lids to close, had fallen asleep to the steady rocking of the train punctuated by shrill whistles, oblivious to the whispers and giggles of the children in the bunks below packed two to a narrow berth: the head of one circling the feet of the other; to snatches of conversation as people walked by and the occasional howl of pain as they bumped heads on the bunks; to noise and bustle as the train pulled into a station; to vendors hawking their goods at all hours of the night, 'Fresh Oranges,' 'Halwa,' 'Chai.'

All her life she'd angled for her mother's approval. She'd tried so hard. Especially after Deepak betrayed her with the note. The shock when she found it in her maths notebook when she came in from break: *I love the way you flick your hair back when you're concentrating, the way your face looks in profile framed by all that beautiful hair. I love the way your smile lights up your face. I love you. Tariq.* Tariq, the studious, bespectacled boy who sat behind her in class, who always came first to her second in the end-of-year exams. Was this note really meant for her: dumpy, bookish Shirin? Or was this all an elaborate joke? Heart thudding, she had turned round, met his gaze: big brown eyes staring intensely at her from behind square black frames. He'd smiled at her then, a soft, shy smile. And she'd turned back to her book, to the note, face flaming, hands trembling and a warm sweet feeling coursing down her insides.

Afterwards, her mother flings away the scissors, her cold eyes flashing. 'No daughter of mine behaves like this. Gallivanting with Muslims.' That word. And she is five again, scared and ashamed, the sour taste of bimblis in her mouth. 'I am disappointed in you. Ashamed of you. Behaving like a whore. And—' a contemptuous glance at Anita, peeking from behind Madhu's left shoulder, '—corrupting your younger sister with it. You will go to confession tomorrow, both of you. And Shirin, you will only go back to college till the end of this week, just so he can see you like this. This... boy. How could you? Next week onwards, you will go to PPC College in Pelam. Remember, I am watching you. If I get word of you behaving like this again, I will disown you. You will be dead to me... You will not bring disgrace to our family. Is that understood? I said, is that understood?'

Shirin finished her coffee, shook her head, tried to clear her mind. But the memories kept coming, persistent.

College the next day, the sniggers, the jeers: 'Turned into a boy overnight?' The look on Tariq's face, the note awaiting her in maths class: 'I am sorry.' She had passed the note back. He had run up to her after class, 'Shirin—wait.' She had hurried away; turned just in time to see Deepak's arm swing back, make contact with Tariq's jaw...

She had tried so much harder after that, to be the good daughter, to do her mother's bidding. She had tried...

She hadn't expected to bump into him again at uni...
Enough... She opened Outlook, flicked through her mail.
Nothing urgent. A couple of documents to be handed in
by the end of the week. Issues that may have cropped up
during testing, to be sorted. No issues yet. Good. She was
taking over Jay's team on Monday. Then, she would have
no time to breathe. But until then... She opened Explorer, googled 'Anita Sinha', clicked on the first entry: Anita
Sinha, Model, Face of India. Leading Modelling Agency.
Linked with Bollywood.

And found *her* Anu staring back at her from the screen.

CHAPTER FOURTEEN
Film-Star Aunt

'Reena, how do you know about Shirin?'

Aunt Anita leaned forward, her fingers trembling as she picked up her cup of tea gingerly from the table.

'I found a picture of her, with you and my dad, when you were about my age.' Her sleuthing notebook was under her pillow, the photograph nestling within it.

'Where?' Aunt Anita shifted in her chair. 'I thought all the photos were destroyed.'

'It was tucked behind one of the pictures in an old photo album in Taipur. I think Madhu saved it.'

'That photo must have somehow escaped being burnt. That was the fate of all Shirin's other photos.'

Time to put Part 2 of Plan C into action. 'What did she do that was so bad?'

Aunt Anita stilled. She was silent for so long that Reena, who had been holding her breath, let it out, convinced she was not going to answer. She swatted at the mosquitoes that had started buzzing, looking for human flesh to feast on. Darkness had set in early, due to the storm, bypassing the twilight that Reena loved.

Her aunt spoke then, so quietly that Reena had to lean forward in her chair to hear. 'It's best to leave the past alone, Rinu.'

'But surely you must miss her. Don't you ever feel like contacting her, seeing her, knowing how she is? If I had a sister...' She stopped, realising that she had done the very thing she had not wanted to do. Her aunt was crying silently, huge tears running down her cheeks from behind her sunglasses.

'Of course I miss her. She was my confidante, my protector, my best friend. If I did something wrong, she took the blame. She couldn't bear the thought of me being hurt. I'd give anything to talk to her now, when I am going through this—this thing with Uttam...' She shut her mouth with her fist, as though afraid she'd said too much.

'Then how can you live your life, not knowing where she is, how she is?'

So softly that Reena had to strain to hear, 'Because I am a coward.'

What did Aunt Anita mean, *Coward*? Daring, fearless Aunt Anita, who defied her mother to marry a Hindu... Why was she afraid to contact Aunt Shirin? Who was she afraid of?

'Sometimes, it is easier to leave things as they are, rather than to fight, go against the flow...' Aunt Anita was saying, still in a whisper.

Fight whom? Go against whom?

'She used to say I was the brave one... I have yet to meet anyone as courageous as her, doing what she did...' Aunt Anita continued, still in a whisper.

Aha. A clue. Whatever Aunt Shirin did, Aunt Anita thought it courageous. It didn't make sense though. None of it did. If Aunt Anita didn't agree with what had been done to Aunt Shirin, if she thought what Aunt Shirin had done was courageous, then why hadn't she *done something*? Why continue to pretend Aunt Shirin didn't exist?

She identified with this newfound aunt of hers. She knew what it was to be invisible, to have people look right through her like she didn't exist. 'What did she do anyway that is so awful that none of you even acknowledge her? And if you don't agree with what happened, why don't you contact her? You are an adult. You can do anything. Who are you afraid of?'

'Shh...'

Reena hadn't realised she had been yelling. It was as if, by defending her aunt, the girl in the photograph, she was defending herself.

'Do your mum and dad know that you know about Shirin?' Aunt Anita continued, not seeming to mind Reena's outburst.

Reena shook her head, *no*.

'You of all people finding it...' Her aunt wore the same funny half smile Reena had glimpsed on Madhu's face. What did it mean? Aunt Anita reached across and squeezed her arm. 'I can't imagine what you must have thought when you found out, how you must have felt...' She stopped. 'Wait a minute; how did you know that that girl in the picture was Shirin?'

'I asked Madhu.'

'What did she tell you?' Aunt Anita's eyes bored into Reena's.

'She told me what Aunt Shirin was like as a child.' The words 'Aunt Shirin' stuck in her throat as she said them out loud. They sounded clumsy, artificial. Aunt Anita was waiting, her face tense. Why? What was it she didn't want Reena to know? 'Nothing much else,' Reena continued. 'Madhu said it was not her place.'

Aunt Anita visibly relaxed. 'Darling Madhu.'

'What is it you are all hiding? Why this conspiracy, this...?' Reena stopped, frustrated. She wanted to throw something. She wanted to yell so loud her mother stopped whatever she was doing and came to rescue her.

Aunt Anita reached across and, with her finger, tipped Reena's face so her eyes met hers. 'I wish I could explain...'

Reena looked away. Why didn't Aunt Anita explain, then? Why didn't anyone tell her anything? She bit her tongue to keep from voicing her anger out loud.

Aunt Anita let go of Reena's face and leaned back in her chair, resting her head on the cushion.

The storm had finally abated. Night had set in, and lights around the pool had come on, bathing everything in an eerie glow. Men were returning home from work. They shouted greetings as they passed each other briefly on the way to their families. Women had started cooking dinner, and aromas of chapattis baking, of spices sizzling in oil floated up to Reena, making her stomach growl. Disjointed snatches of conversation from neighbouring flats reached her ears and she tried to make sense of the chatter, to stop her mind dwelling on her spat with Aunt Anita. Her mother had obviously used the snack as an excuse to give Reena and Aunt Anita some time together. Or maybe she had just wanted some time to herself, a break from having to console Anita. *Oh, Mum, I hope I haven't made everything worse,* Reena thought.

'About cutting Shirin out of our lives,' Aunt Anita's voice was just audible above the noisy song of the crickets. 'It was a long time ago. A decision was made. I... I wish...'

'You two look so grim. What have you been talking about?' Preeti stood in the doorway, an indulgent smile on her face.

Oh no, Mum—bad timing, thought Reena. What had Aunt Anita been about to say?

As usual, Preeti did not wait for a reply. 'Come on in,' she said, 'or the mosquitoes will have a field day.'

❊ ❊ ❊

Progress so far: This detective confronted Aunt Anita boldly about Aunt Shirin. Aunt Anita didn't reveal much, on account of her fragile emotional state, except to say that she thought what Aunt Shirin did was <u>courageous.</u>

Plan D: Work on Aunt Anita.

This time it was Aunt Anita who was waiting for Reena as she got off the school bus. She was perched on the little mound of mud just outside the gates to Reena's apartment complex, clad in skinny jeans, a figure-hugging T-shirt and high heels. Her legs were crossed, displaying ridiculously slim ankles, and she was reading a book. Whatever she was going through, Aunt Anita always dressed with care. It mattered very much to her how she looked, the image she projected, she had told Reena once, laughing. 'Silly, really, but that is how I am. I always feel better when I know I look good.' She was wearing those ridiculous film-star sunglasses again, but today they did not look out of place. It was a scorcher. Even at half past five in the evening, the sun shone down relentlessly, perhaps to make up for the fact that the previous day it had been eclipsed by the storm.

As the bus pulled up, the driver, seeing her aunt, let out a low long whistle. Reena caught the older boys staring, their mouths open, at this vision of loveliness sprouting from a mound of mud.

'Who is she, Reena?' they called out as she started down the steps and her aunt closed her book and stood, revealing endlessly long legs. She had had to endure a whole day of teasing from them about her 'boyfriend' and now they were being sweet as gulab jamuns.

'Is she a film actress? A model? Do we know her?'

Reena ignored them, but Aunt Anita caught some of their questions. She grinned and waved as the bus pulled away, more slowly than usual. The bus driver and the boys beamed like monkeys. Reena noticed that the security guard had turned his chair so he faced Aunt Anita. He was grinning too, something he never did, not for Reena at least. Across the road, a collection of men had gathered, hiking up their lungis, patting their hair in place, ostensibly to buy beedies off the little shop, but really to stare at Aunt Anita. That shop had never seen so many customers at this time of day. Aunt Anita lazily lifted one arm in salute to the ogling men. They laughed with delight and hitched their lungis up even higher.

'Why didn't you tell them I was a model?' Aunt Anita laughed.

'Didn't want to,' Reena mumbled, not in the best of moods after the name-calling she had endured all day, but glad her aunt was happier today. The attention Aunt Anita got from men always lifted her spirits. Personally, Reena thought it would annoy her after a while, having men stare at her all the time. But what did *she* know? She had never experienced it, except by proxy when she was with her aunt.

'So how was your day?' Aunt Anita asked Reena, waving at the security guard with two fingers like the film actresses did on TV. The security guard shone and swivelled his chair to follow their progress, as they walked down the steps, past the pool and towards their block of flats.

'Okay,' she mumbled. She had ignored everyone, but having to pretend that it didn't hurt had cost her. Divya had joined in as well and that had hurt most of all. She knew why Divya had done it of course—to be one of the crowd. Suddenly she understood what Aunt Anita had meant when she said that sometimes it was easier to go along with something rather than take a stand. Reena hoped she, Super Sleuth Reena Diaz, was different— more courageous, *not* a coward.

'Shall we sit here for a bit?'

Aunt Anita indicated the shady spot by the pool where Reena and Murli sat sometimes.

'Okay.'

Reena dropped her bag and flopped down. She shut her eyes against the sun and focused on the blurry 'cell figures' dancing across her closed eyelids. She was going to take a stand for Aunt Shirin, she promised herself.

Super Sleuth Reena Diaz: Not afraid of anything or anyone.

'You were right, you know. What you said. About Shirin... A wise little thing you are... And brave. Like her.'

Reena opened her eyes and stared at her aunt. *How did she know what I was thinking?* Her aunt was playing with her book, her beautifully polished nails the pale pink of prawn shells against the sand-coloured book edge. Based on her aunt's reaction the previous day, Reena hadn't expected her to bring Aunt Shirin up again. She had spent her time at school, especially during Kannada class, thinking up ways to pursue Plan D: How best to ask her aunt about Shirin without antagonising her? And now, Plan D was looking to be a success with precious little effort on her part. Either the art of detection was very easy or she was extremely good at it...

'I've been thinking about it all day. Perhaps it's time.' An odd note crept into Aunt Anita's voice. 'And you...' For the first time since she'd mentioned Shirin, her aunt looked right at her, still thinking aloud. 'You're old enough to understand; well, not fully perhaps...'

Stop treating me like a child. Of course I'm old enough,
Reena screamed in her head.

'I really ought to talk to Deepak… Try once more.'
Aunt Anita said.

No, thought Reena, her father's face and the blatant
lie he'd told her swimming before her eyes: *'You know I've
just got the one sister, your Aunt Anita.'* Somehow she knew
that if her dad got wind of this, the photograph would
be confiscated, the topic banned, and they would all go
back to pretending Aunt Shirin had never existed. *Please,
Aunt Anita, please don't.* She didn't dare say it out loud
in case her aunt, perversely, went straight to her dad. In
her experience, especially since finding the photograph,
adults were not to be trusted. And—hang on a minute;
Aunt Anita had said, 'Try once more.' Did this mean she
had tried before and failed? Was it her dad Aunt Anita
was afraid of? How could that be? Her dad adored Aunt
Anita. He had been true to his word and had not lectured
her about her impending divorce.

Her aunt was still thinking out loud, 'But will Deepak…? He can be so…'

Yes, it was her dad. Had the rift, Shirin being disowned,
been something to do with him? *No, please let it not.*

Aunt Anita glanced at Reena, nodded her head, having
reached some sort of decision. 'At the very least, you deserve to know about Shirin. And I'm aching to talk about
her. What was it you wanted to know?'

If what she was thinking was right, if it implicated her
dad in some way, should she find Aunt Shirin? Or forget she

existed like the rest of them and 'go with the flow' as Aunt
Anita had said. Divya calling her a freak, teasing her about
her boyfriend. *No, I am not like that. I refuse to be a coward.*

Aunt Anita cleared her throat and Reena realised she
was waiting. 'Everything. How she was, what she liked,
her hobbies. I want to get to know her. She is my aunt
too.' *Detectives cannot afford to shy away from the truth, no
matter how much it hurts.*

Aunt Anita closed her eyes. 'I kept her letters, you
know...'

'She wrote to you?' Reena sat up, her voice shrill.

Aunt Anita nodded. 'Not after... You know... Before,
when I was away, doing my pre-university course.'

'Oh...' Reena digested this information. There were
letters, written by Shirin herself! What else would she
find? And would her aunt let her...

'I read them when I miss her desperately, when I ache
to see her, talk to her.'

Reena nodded, not wanting to open her mouth lest
the question that was on the tip of her tongue popped
out involuntarily.

'I have them with me now. You can borrow them if
you like. Get a feel for the person Shirin was...'

At last, a breakthrough! Despite her worries about her
dad being involved, Reena found herself behaving the
way men did around Aunt Anita—grinning like an idiot,
unable to stop.

Progress so far: There are letters—actual letters that
Aunt Shirin wrote! Aunt Anita has promised to lend them

to this detective to read. Plan D galloping ahead at full speed.

This detective thinks, based on something Aunt Anita said, that the person Aunt Anita is afraid of, who is perhaps stopping her from contacting Aunt Shirin, is her brother Deepak, this detective's dad. This detective hopes that this is not the case as, despite everything, she does adore her dad. He has his faults, like his lecturing about status and family name, but he is the one who sneaks her chocolate when she is up late studying for exams and who still even now lets her sit on his lap sometimes and rests his chin on her shoulder where it tickles.

This case is too close for comfort and this detective is tempted to stop, but she is going to continue, as would all good detectives. <u>Do not let emotions get in the way of truth</u>.

Next Steps: Find clues in the letters as to the cause of rift.

CHAPTER FIFTEEN
Rickety Old Rickshaw

'Anita! Anu...' Shirin called, before she could stop herself. She was in Wembley, shopping for saris.

The woman turned and Shirin's heart sank. Of course it wasn't Anita. What was she thinking? Perhaps it was seeing her picture on the computer—that gorgeous smile, that heart-stopping face: The Face of India. How she would have teased her! How they would have laughed! *Ooh, Anu, Face of India now, are you?* And: *You married Uttam, became a model, both of which Ma was opposed to. Did she let you? Has she changed that much? Did she not launch into her usual, 'No daughter of mine will swan around half naked in front of strangers. No daughter of mine will marry a Hindu...?' Perhaps she did try to stop you, but you did it anyway. Good for you.* And: *Anu, why did you change your name to Sinha? I remember that time Michu Aunty got married, became Michu Machado, how you swore never to do that, to give up your identity so easily, take on someone else's. You were adamant. And you always kept promises, even ones made to yourself. So what happened? What changed?* And: *Anu, why have you stayed away? I thought you, of all people, would understand...*

'I'm sorry. I thought you were someone else...' she mumbled, not quite meeting the woman's eyes.

'That's okay. Happens all the time.'

'Does it?' Shirin looked up, surprised.

'No,' laughed the woman.

It does to me, Shirin wanted to say. Every so often, she saw someone who looked achingly familiar, and before rational thought set in, her heart leaped, making her hope for one brief moment that it was a member of her family come to find her, to bestow forgiveness, to take her home...

Once, she had seen a woman standing at a crowded bus stop in her rear-view mirror and something about her—perhaps it was the way she stood, stooping slightly, or the way wispy curls escaped her bun—convinced Shirin it was Madhu. It had been during the early years in the UK, when hope still flared. She ended up giving the woman—a Sri Lankan who could speak very little English but was determined to communicate, pleased that Shirin appeared to have recognised her—a lift to her destination, a one-bedroom flat in a block of council houses in Kenton. 'You meet me Sri Lanka,' she insisted. Shirin didn't have the heart to tell her she had never been to Sri Lanka. 'Come have tea,' the woman said when Shirin dropped her off outside her block of flats. Shirin squeezed her hand and left, amid reassurances that she would visit another time.

And she had. She'd been shopping in Kenton, almost a year later, when an ungovernable impulse made Shirin decide to visit her—this stranger she had accosted at a bus stop. She drove to the block of flats, walked up the two flights of stairs, the poky stairwell stinking of urine and littered with Burger King wrappers and beer cans, and knocked on number 22—the doorbell was broken—remembering the way the woman had held on to her hand, pointing upwards in the general direction of her flat. 'I live number 22. Come, have tea.'

Nobody had answered. Shirin had checked her watch. It was 7:00 p.m., a time when most people were home. She'd knocked again, louder this time. She was just turning to go when the door to number 20 opened and a black woman poked her head round the door.

'If you're after Tushara, she's moved.'

'Oh,' Shirin had said, momentarily at a loss as to what to do next. 'Where to, do you know?'

'No. Kept herself to herself she did.'

'Thank you for your help,' Shirin had smiled at the woman and turned to go.

'She couldn't speak no English, didn't know nobody. Not like the other Asians here, with their aunts and uncles and cousins all crammed into one tiny flat, you know what I'm saying? You the only one come lookin' for her.' She had looked curiously at Shirin. 'What was it you wanted?'

'Oh, nothing important. I gave her a lift once and she invited me in. I was busy then, said I'd come another time'

'Too late now, darlin'.'

Too late... Shirin thanked the neighbour and made her way down the stairs, trying to picture the Sri Lankan

woman—Tushara her neighbour had called her. She re-
called a small lady with a closed smile, wispy hair escaping
her bun, her joy at being recognised, the intense loneli-
ness coming off her in waves. But when Shirin tried to
picture her face, all she could see were Madhu's familiar,
much-beloved features, seared in her mind like a worn,
much-used map.

She had never approached anyone else again, no matter how familiar they looked, except just now, when irrational impulse had hijacked sense.

'I'm Malini, by the way,' said Anita's look-a-like, for-
mally extending a hand.

'Shirin.'

'Nice to meet you, Shirin. Bet you will laugh about
this with Anita when you see her next...'

If I see her... Shirin surreptitiously crossed her fingers.
She thought of the email, even now making its way to
Anita's inbox. She had clicked on Anita's picture, found
a little bio for her, an email address in the contact details section, and before she could change her mind, had
sent her an email. Had she seen it yet? Anita, laughing at
something, saying to someone, Uttam perhaps, 'Give me
a minute, I'll just check my email.' And there, nestling
among the spam and the agency circulars, From Shirin.
Vaz @cstsolutions.org.uk: Hi Anu, It's me. I'd like to talk.
If you would, too, email me back. Love, Shirin, xxxx.

She had thought and thought about what to write, had
composed a long letter filling Anita in on all that had
happened during her eleven years away—nothing much

when she got right down to it, her life these last few years
spent wanting, aching, missing—asking Anita question
upon question about everything she had missed, was still
missing. And in the end, she had deleted it all, had written just those three sentences and run the email by Kate,
who had said it was 'just right'. Was Anita opening it just
now, as Shirin went about addressing strangers by her
sister's name? Would she reply? What if she didn't? 'Ah,
Shirin, don't think that way,' Kate had said.

A memory: Shirin is five years old. She wakes to Jacinta's sobs. Her mother's nightie is wet with sweat and
she is breathing very fast as though she's been running
for miles between sobs. Shirin panics. She's never seen
her mother cry before. A frantic, dishevelled Madhu runs
to wake Ananthanna next door. The neighbourhood dogs
howl. Deepak sleeps, little snores escaping from between
pursed lips. Madhu wipes Jacinta's forehead with a muslin
cloth, 'It's all right, ma'am. Ananthanna is coming with
a rickshaw. Hang on.' Ananthanna and his wife lead a
hobbling Jacinta gently out the door. And Jacinta is swallowed by the night.

Questions circle Shirin's head, chasing sleep from weary eyes: Is her mother going to heaven? Will they only be
able to visit her in the cemetery, stare at a wooden cross
adorning a mound of mud and imagine it to be her, like
they did old Mr D'Cunho? She closes her eyes tight, trying
to shut out a world which makes no sense at all, a world
where Madhu is the calm one and her mother the hysterical one, a world which turns upside down while Deepak

sleeps and her grandparents snore. When she opens them again it is morning. Beside her, Deepak stirs. Sun slants in through the iron bars of the window, creating patterns on the wall. Sun shining this bright only means one thing. Deepak smiles. 'No mass today.' He rubs the sleep out of his eyes. 'Why?' And then, taking in the rumpled bed sheets and empty space beside him, 'Where's Ma? Has she gone to church alone?' Shirin puts a finger to her brother's lips and asks him to follow her into the courtyard. They squat under the guava tree, on the sweet-smelling bed of leaves and, with a mere tremble of her upper lip, Shirin says, 'Ma is going to die. We'll have to visit her in the cemetery. We are going to have to be very brave.'

Madhu comes looking for them. 'Didn't you hear me calling? Why are you hiding? Don't you two want breakfast? I've made Sajjige Roti, and tamarind chutney to go with it.' She peers closely at them, 'Have you been crying?' Shirin tries to smile but her mouth won't do her bidding. 'Is Ma going to die?' Deepak asks. Madhu bends down, scoops them both up in her arms. 'Of course not, silly boy.' 'I'm not silly, she is. She told me Ma is not coming back.' Deepak buries his head in Madhu's shoulder. 'Don't you worry about your mother.' Madhu's voice is tender, 'She's going to be fine.'

For the first time in her life, Shirin does not believe her.

Later, she sits on the little mound of earth by the mango tree where their compound ends and Ananthanna's begins, from where if she looks really hard she can see the road and anyone turning into the little clearing that widens into the path leading to their house. She draws faces in the mud with a twig, Rex dancing circles around her, messing her sketches. She listens intently for the sound of an auto rickshaw signalling her mother's arrival home— hope triumphing over the knowledge that weighs heavy in her chest: something bad has happened to her Ma. She watches the postman arrive on his bike, the menagerie of neighbourhood dogs keeping pace, kicking up dust, trying to nip at his ankles. He props his bike beside the bush by the clearing and, picking up a packet of blue envelopes— stamps peeking out—makes his way down the path, half whistling, half humming a Kannada blockbuster tune. He comes to a halt beside the mound where she is sitting. She refuses to look at his face, unreasonably angry with him for having turned up instead of her mother, staring instead at his long thin legs, clad in the khaki postman uniform, which is now the dark brown colour of mud. He's wearing Bata chappals with blue straps, one of them held together by a large safety pin. His feet are dirty and one of his toenails is missing. His long legs fold, bending gracefully into a V shape, and suddenly she's looking into his gaunt, bespectacled face. His hair is wet, and when he smiles, his eyes crinkle, creating a busy network of lines along the sides of his face. 'Hello there, little one, who are you waiting for?' Rex, who's been barking furiously, stops at the sound of the postman's voice and tries to lick his face. Shirin bursts into tears, 'My ma is going to die.' 'It can't be possible! Who told you that?' The postman rocks back and forth on his haunches, looking completely at ease in what has to be a very uncomfortable squatting position. His eyes are kind. 'You don't think she'll die?' 'I don't think God will let her! How can He allow a pretty girl like you to be orphaned?' Shirin smiles for the first time that day, a warm feeling settling in her heart. No one has called her pretty before. People sigh when they look at her and say to Jacinta: 'Good thing Walter's in the Gulf. This one will need plenty of dowry,' which makes frown lines appear on her mother's forehead.

An auto rickshaw pulls up. And Shirin is running, pigtails flying, praying, 'Please let it be my ma. Please, Mother Mary. I will be a good girl, I promise.' Ananthanna gets out of the auto. Alone. Tears prick Shirin's eyes. Ananthanna smiles when he sees her. 'Shirin, go tell everyone the baby's been born. Mother and baby are doing fine. The nuns said to visit in the afternoon.' And Shirin, bent double from trying to catch her breath, her hair flying in all directions, laughs until tears track dusty streaks down her face.

It had made sense all at once, Shirin remembered, smiling at her naive five-year-old self as she walked up and down Ealing Road trying to work up the nerve to enter one of the myriad sari shops lining the street. She saw her childhood self standing on the path, Timothy the postman laughing along with her. 'I knew my ma was going to have a baby. I touched her stomach and felt the baby kick. I want a girl and Deepak wants a boy. Oh, I forgot to ask Ananthanna if I've got a brother or sister.

If it's a brother, my grandmother will be happy.' 'Why?' 'Well, boys are always better, aren't they?' 'Rubbish. I think girls as kind as you are worth a million. Look how you worry about your ma. Boys don't do that.' 'Don't you worry about *your* ma?' And Timothy the postman had thrown his head back and laughed, his nose crinkling in a fascinating way, 'You're a sharp one, you are.'

A shiver traversed Shirin's spine. She was aware of goosebumps sprouting on her arms, the creepy feeling of being watched...

She realised that she was standing in front of 'Krishna Saris', that while she had been lost in the past she had been grinning at the unnaturally thin blonde mannequins decked in gold-flecked maroon saris, bindis and high heels, reclining coolly in the shop window flanked by kurta-draped dark-haired male counterparts. What was that reflection in the window? Was it... She blinked, tried to think clearly, keep panic at bay. The reflection moved, took shape. *No*. She half turned; poised to run. One of the shop assistants peered around the mannequins, checking her out, apparently trying to decide whether she was crazy or just a too-keen window shopper. Their eyes met. The shop assistant withdrew. The next minute, she was at the door. How could Shirin have mistaken this slim, efficient-looking Asian girl clad in a sky-blue ghagra for the spectre from her nightmares? 'Excuse me, ma'am; is there something wrong with our display?'

'Oh no, no, I was just looking.'

'Do you want to come in? We have saris, churidars and salwar kameezes, lehngas, chaniya cholis...'

She couldn't turn away now. Once inside, the familiar, nostalgic smell of new fabric, whisper-soft silk, transported her back eleven years to another world.

'Are you looking for anything in particular?'

'No thanks, just browsing.'

The shop assistant got the message and left her alone. Kishore Kumar crooned 'Meri Sapnon Ki Rani Kab Ayegi Thu' via the speakers and Shirin remembered the driver of the rickety old rickshaw that had conveyed them to the hospital to visit Ma. He had been singing a Kannada song at the top of his voice, the rickshaw dancing in tune thanks to the many ruts in the road. 'Raj Kumar film,' he had announced grinning, displaying rotting teeth, sickly yellow gums…

Shirin squashed onto her grandmother's enormous lap, being tossed up to the flimsy roof of the auto every time the rickshaw hit a pothole. The hospital: square corners, right angles, no familiar orange 'Mangalore Tiles' on the roof; smelling of the bitter tonic Shirin was forced to drink when she was ill, mixed with the phenol the cleaner had used to scrub the floors. Her terror reflected in her brother's eyes. Shirin worrying if this was all a trick, sucking at the clean handkerchief Madhu had tucked in her pocket. Maybe they wouldn't get to see their mother at all. Maybe this was the place where they sent naughty children. Nuns swarming everywhere, one leading them down an endless corridor to a long room filled with mothers and newborn babies, the babies sounding just like kittens. Shirin, peering out from behind her grandmother's sari, spotting her mother at the far end. Her mother: wearing a strange gown and cradling a comma-shaped bundle in her arms. Shirin running, her footsteps echoing on the granite floor. Deepak following suit, ignoring their grandparents' admonishments. Jacinta patting Shirin's head and Deepak's with her free hand. Shirin noticing nothing but the bundle her mother was holding: tiny, with a scrunched-up face the size of Shirin's palm. Shirin reaching out a tentative finger and gently rubbing the baby's cheek: downy, like moss. The baby mewling, miniature palms bunched into fists punching the air. Warmth spreading through Shirin. 'Is it a girl?' Not really caring anymore what sex it was. Jacinta nodding, yes. Her grandmother sighing, sinking heavily onto Jacinta's bed, 'Not another girl!' Shirin clapping her hands, jumping up and down, 'Deepak, what did I tell you? God answered my prayers.' Her grandmother mumbling, 'Wish He'd answered mine.' And Anita, as if wanting to locate the source of all the noise, opening her eyes and looking right at Shirin, her tiny face flooding red as she started to yell, a huge cry for such a little thing.

And Shirin had loved her sister, completely and unconditionally from then on, despite the fact that her grandmother chose that moment to say, 'At least this one is fairer than Shirin. This one is going to be pretty. Takes after our side of the family...' And the comparisons began.

She realised she was holding an emerald sari up to her cheek, as if the feel of it would transport her to monsoon-drenched fields sparkling in humid, after-the-rains sun; as if it would bring back the tart, spicy taste of raw mangoes soaked in rock salt—the mangoes just this colour: a dark, heavy green. It was the colour of the churidar she had worn to Anita's christening, the colour splashed across the first picture her sister made for her, the colour of the guavas in the tree in the courtyard before they ripened in the sun, the colour that Shirin most associated with home...

'What did you buy?' Vinod asked when she returned, laden with carrier bags.

'Wait and see,' she replied.

'Tease...' Vinod said, swatting at her with his *Financial Times*.

❃ ❃ ❃

'You can come in now,' Shirin called, eyes shut tight against her reflection in the bedroom mirror.

She had not wanted Vinod to be present while she donned a sari for the first time in eleven years. What if she had forgotten how to wear it? Once she'd put on the blouse and underskirt, she unwrapped the sari—the emerald of the Arabian sea at Pelam beach, placid after being whipped to a frenzy by the monsoons; the gold green of the Varuna River on a humid, rain-parched morning.

For a few minutes, Shirin simply sat on the bed in her blouse and underskirt, caressing the smooth silk of the new sari, revelling in its familiar feel. When she did start to dress, she heard Madhu's voice, telling her exactly what to do: 'This is the side that you tuck into your stomach. Now do the pleats. Gently does it, don't mess up the folds...'

When she'd finished, she looked up and found herself gazing at a girl from the past—a girl she had thought was lost forever. Images trotted in front of her, one after the other in quick succession. She closed her eyes, sat on the edge of the bed and called out to Vinod.

When she heard him come into the room, she stood, opened her eyes.

'You look beautiful,' Vinod's voice was soft with awe. 'Saris suit you. I had forgotten just how much. And this colour, it's perfect...' He came up behind her, put his arms around her. Shirin watched her reflection flinch, saw the quick flash of hurt in Vinod's eyes before they both ironed out their features. Vinod did not move away to give her space as he would have done once. Instead, he waited. And gradually, she leaned back, relaxed into his embrace.

'Why did I agree to do this, Vinod?'

'Because it was either a sari or a corset?'

She laughed. 'Seriously...'

Vinod bent down, whispered in her hair, 'You'll be fine, Shonu. You needed to do this sometime. '

'I...'

'You'll have fun.'

'Do I really look okay?'

'Are you fishing for compliments?'

She smiled, looked at herself critically in the mirror. 'Do you know what would go wonderfully with this sari?'

'What?'

'My gold.' And for a brief moment, as was so often the case these days, she was transported. To Canara

Bank, Taipur's only bank. Smelling of money, gold and old secrets—a dank, wet smell. Jacinta, wringing hands in front of the portly, sweaty bank manager: her stoic mother nervous! 'I would like to get my gold out of the safety-deposit box, what with my girls now approaching marriageable age.' Gold twinkling up at them in myriad shapes: bangles, bracelets, necklaces, earrings; tucked into her mother's underskirt and transported carefully home. Gold, padlocked in the Godrej wardrobe next to the altar, the key in a knot at the end of Jacinta's sari, with her at all times. 'For when you get married, Shirin. Gold as part of your dowry.' 'Where is it, do you think?' She wouldn't look at Vinod.

'Gathering dust in some vault in Bangalore, I expect. It was registered in my father's name, at his bank. When we left, I couldn't...' He paused, waited until her gaze met his in the mirror. 'Do you resent having had to leave everything behind? You could have had your pick of saris, instead of having to buy a new one...'

'Of course not! A small price to pay, in the circumstances...' She couldn't believe they were having this conversation, now, after skirting the topic for so many years. She paused. Should she? Yes. 'Do you...? Resent it?'

He looked at her, 'The truth?'

She watched their reflection: she in a sari, caught in a strange eleven-year limbo; he in his usual present-day uniform of stripy shirt and black trousers; his arms wrapped around her, her head resting on his chest. 'Yes.'

'Sometimes I do.'

'Oh.'

He caught the flash of guilt in her eyes before she could mask it. 'Shonu. It wasn't your fault. None of it.'

Eyes. Empty. Accusing. A mother's wails. A mother's anger.

'I don't even know why I thought of the gold.'

'I'm glad you did.' Vinod gently released her from his embrace and went to the wardrobe. 'When you told me you had to wear a sari, I got you this.'

He held her palms in his and deposited a little box in them. She opened it with tremulous fingers and discovered a thin gold necklace nestling on scarlet velvet, a little heart-shaped pendant that had the letters S and V engraved. *Frolicking waves kissing a duet of initials encased within a heart: T loves S. The roaring of the sea loud in her ears. The roaring of desire loud in her body.* Where had she gone, that young girl? Why was she thinking of that now, when her husband had just given her a gift?

'Shall I put it on for you?' Vinod asked.

She nodded, unable to speak.

She watched as he tenderly secured the clasp, his touch the merest whisper on her skin.

He looked up, asked, 'What do you think?'

She fingered the little heart, ran her thumb over their entwined initials. 'It's perfect.'

❃ ❃ ❃

'Shirin, you look great in your sari! Even more beautiful if that is possible. Come, let me introduce you to everyone.'

Kate looked gorgeous in her outfit, the green of her shirt bringing out the green in her eyes, her hairdo making her look very elegant. When Shirin told her so, she laughed. 'Have you met Jyoti? She's from PricewaterhouseCoopers, who do our accounts. Jyoti, this is Shirin, one of the most valued members of my team.'

Before she could thank Kate, she had disappeared amongst the crush of people and Shirin found herself facing a smiling older woman wearing a marigold sari with saffron flowers set in a gold border and absolutely dripping with jewellery. She reminded Shirin very much of Aunt Winnie.

'Busy, isn't it?' she said. 'Have you got a drink? No? Come with me.'

Afterwards, armed with drinks and canapés, they found a relatively quiet corner to sit and chat. Jyoti was from North India originally but had lived in the UK for nearly thirty years. 'This is my home now,' she said. 'My relatives in India have passed on. The kids are settled here. What about you? Do you go back often?'

Shirin took a big gulp of her drink. 'Not as much as I would like.'

'Do you have any family here?'

'No, they are all in India.' *Please don't ask me any more questions.*

Jyoti reached across and patted Shirin's knee, her myriad bangles jingling with the movement. 'Beti, don't get me wrong. I am telling you this as an aunt...'

Oh, God, has she guessed? Did I give something away?

'...since you have no relatives here, nobody to give you advice. And men, they are useless in such matters.'

Shirin carefully laid her glass down on the low table beside her. She crossed her hands on her lap to stop them trembling.

Jyoti touched the thin necklace Shirin wore, light reflecting off the gold rings adorning her every finger. 'This is well and good and with churidars it would be perfect. Did your husband give it to you?'

Shirin nodded, relief flooding as realisation dawned.

'You felt you had to wear it, so as not to hurt his feelings. I understand.'

Shirin grinned widely. She knew exactly what Jyoti was going to say next.

'Your sari, Beti, it is so grand. What it needs is gold. Lots of it. Not this flimsy little necklace. No offense, mind.'

'None taken,' laughed Shirin, reaching for her drink. Her first impression had been right. Jyoti was very much like Aunt Winnie. Being in her company was like being among the aunts back home.

CHAPTER SIXTEEN
Chats on the Veranda at Twilight

'They are in chronological order. That means...'

'I know what it means.' Eagerly, Reena took the precious parcel from Aunt Anita's hands—a sheaf of worn blue envelopes, held together by a rubber band.

'I don't know if you'll understand some of the things she...'

'Aunty! I'm eleven!'

'I know...' Aunt Anita's eyes twinkled. 'Look after them. They mean a lot to me.'

'I will.' And, with a quick peck on her aunt's cool cheek, 'Thank you.'

Hiding the letters in her history textbook, Reena went to her room and closed the door. Once inside, she gingerly pulled out the rubber band and opened the first letter. Shirin had a neat, slightly sloping script. Reena tried to picture the young woman she imagined Shirin to be, writing it. She couldn't. She lay on her stomach on her bed and began to read.

Progress so far: This detective is in possession of letters Shirin wrote to Anita when Anita was away at college.

This detective assumes Shirin was around twenty-two? <u>Check this.</u> She has a cursive handwriting that would have made Eugene Ma'am, this detective's English teacher, very pleased.

Some extracts from the first letter, which this detective has carefully chosen as they might provide clues into what happened some time—a year?—later:

1) This extract shows that the subject misses her sister and brother who are both away at college:

Anu, if you are missing home, I can assure you, you are not missing much. Everything is pretty much the same here, just as you left it, except that it's not as vibrant, not as lively without you around. I miss your voice, the mischievous glint in your eyes, the way laughter bursts out from inside you like a waterfall. I miss Deepak with his practical jokes, his loud laugh, and his boundless appetite. It is quiet here without the two of you.

Do you remember the evening before you left, how we sat on the veranda watching the rain pouring down in frenzy? The coconut trees in the front courtyard swayed wildly. Little streams formed in the paddy fields, churning the freshly dug soil ready for sowing into a muddy mess until all we could see were fields of water. In Ananthanna's field, women bent double against the rain and sang as they sowed paddy saplings, their makeshift cane shelters making them look like giant question marks. They sang a haunting melody and from where we sat, sheltered and warm, drinking hot tumblers of sweet tea, we could just hear it. Do you remember how happy we were to just sit there in companionable silence? I miss that.

Yesterday, I sat on the veranda again, when I got back from college. I sat there with my accounts book, ostensibly to study, but really to daydream. I sat till the day started to wane and the setting sun swathed the sky in many shades of pink and the crickets started their nightly orchestra. Madhu came out and collected my plate. She had made bhel puri for me, with potatoes and green peas and chaat masala—just the way you like it. Are you jealous? She chided me for sitting outside in the dusk. 'The mosquitoes will have a nice juicy feast,' she scolded. 'Come on in.' 'In a minute, Madhu,' I mumbled, feigning interest in my notebook. 'Don't act like you are studying. It's dark. You can't see a thing,' she said. I was glad she couldn't see me blushing. She switched on the veranda light and went back in. The light bathed me in a warm, rosy glow and attracted the flies. I watched the more intrepid of them get too close to the light and die with a buzz and a sigh. I wondered what you and Deepak were doing.

NOTE: Look up meaning of the word intrepid.

> Intrepid (adj.) fearless; daring; bold: as in—Reena Diaz was an intrepid sleuth. [This detective plans to impress Eugene Ma'am, her English teacher, when she uses the word in class tomorrow. This detective has been trying to copy the extracts in Shirin's cursive style, and she has to admit, her handwriting is already much improved.]

2) She envies her sister her freedom:

> Anu, are you missing home? Or are you enjoying the freedom, savouring the joys of being on your own—of not having to get up for mass, or say the rosary every night, no nuns and no guilt trips, no confessions and long sermons.
>
> I can imagine what your argument will be. You still have to get up for class, share a room with a stranger, and stick to hostel rules. But you are away from home! On your own! You can talk to boys without the whole village knowing and telling Ma you are running wild. You can stay out till late, or stay up all night if you want to. You can have midnight feasts. You can dance in the rain without the village gossips starting rumours. You can paint the town red. You can have a boyfriend. Will you? You must have a long line of admirers to pick from already. Knowing you, though, you will choose someone different, someone unique. Have you found him? Who is he?
>
> NOTE: Did Shirin get so tired of the rigid, unyielding routine of home that she rebelled (like this detective feels like doing sometimes) and did something so drastic that it caused her to be wiped out of her family's lives forever?

3) News of what's happening at home:

> Anyway, the whole point of this letter was to tell you that Da is coming home for good. You should see Ma. She can't stop smiling. I mean, you know Ma. She's so aloof most of the time. Anyway, she's walking around with this permanent, goofy grin on her face now.

> NOTE: Da coming home caused something, perhaps? Did she and Da clash? <u>Find out.</u>

4) This detective thinks this extract is the most important clue:

> At the rate at which Ma is hunting proposals for me, I should be married soon, and living with my in-laws this time next year. That is her plan, anyway. But someone has to agree to marry me first...

> You know, Ma is starting to get so worried that, for her sake, I wish someone *would* marry me, even if the chances of that happening seem remote, what with prospective grooms complaining about my weight, my complexion, my hips, you name it...

> On the other hand, all those dreams I had of falling in love—what of them?

> NOTE: Based on this extract, this detective concludes that perhaps Shirin ran away—eloped

with someone highly unsuitable. But to ban her
from their lives, pretend she never existed… Isn't
that too dear a price, too harsh a punishment?
And this detective comes again to the fact that
Anita married a Hindu and was spared. So, why
not Shirin? Because she was the eldest, perhaps?
Find out.

Reena lay on the bed for a long time, staring at Shirin's
gently sloping, precise script. She lay there until the shadows in her room lengthened and her mother knocked on
her door yelling, 'Dinner's ready!'

She gently folded the letter and kept it aside, beside the
others. Then she left her room to join her family, feeling
a little removed from them, like she was watching them
from a distance, like she was part of another girl, one they
had all shunned…

CHAPTER SEVENTEEN
Parcels from the Gulf

Shirin came into work groggy. After the party, she had lain awake, her thoughts keeping time to Vinod's rhythmic snores. *Will she reply? What if she doesn't?*

Sometime during the long night, as the black behind the curtains lightened to deep grey, Vinod woke up. 'Shonu, there's nothing to be gained from worrying so.' His voice was tinged with annoyance, thick with sleep. 'I promise you, when you go into work tomorrow—today,' he'd said after a bleary-eyed appraisal of the bedside clock, 'there'll be mail from her. Sleep. Please.' He'd put his arm around her, pulled her close and after a bit she had relaxed into his embrace. She had fallen asleep with him spooning her, startling awake to the alarm clock and golden light—dazzling like the jewellery Jyoti had worn the previous night—spilling in through the gap in the curtains and dancing on the pillows, on Vinod's stubbly face.

Kate was right; why on earth am I subjecting myself to this? With trembling fingers, she clicked on her office Outlook. There were plenty of emails awaiting her but not the one she wanted. *Oh, Anu, I wish... for so many things: to see you, touch you, to listen to your voice...* She immersed herself in work, finishing the test plans requiring her attention, preparing handover documents for Rob who was going to be taking over her job when she took over Jay's. Kate walked past a couple of times, looking questioningly at her. Both times, she gave her a thumbs-down. Vinod didn't call. Shirin had asked him not to, saying *she* would call *him* with news, if any.

Just before lunch she checked again. *For the last time*, she told herself. Nothing. The office felt claustrophobic all of a sudden. She sent Kate a message via Intranet: Going to Tesco, need anything? A reply pinged back, almost at once: No, babe. You get some fresh air.

Lovely Kate.

She picked up a basket and headed straight for aisle 11, which housed the sandwiches and crisps. *Why were you expecting her to reply? Fool.* Aisle 11 was festooned with red-and-green streamers, bursting with offers and packed with biscuit tins, boxes of chocolate, mince pies, crackers, grinning Santas with wobbly heads. The legend below aisle 11 read 'Seasonal Goods'. 'But it's only October!' She didn't realise she had said it out loud. The Asian man stacking the top shelves peered down at her from behind thick lenses, 'What were you looking for, ma'am?' The ladder he was balancing on wobbled precariously.

'Sandwiches. Don't worry, I'll...'

'They're in aisle 22,' he smiled, squinted, 'Are you from Sri Lanka?'

'India.'

'I'm from Bangladesh.' He grinned, displaying yellow teeth, brown cavities. 'We're neighbours back home.'

Shirin nodded, smiling distractedly, her attention arrested by a bag of dry-roasted cashew nuts. The cashew tree in the courtyard—emerald leaves dotted with ripe buttery fruit: a tropical Christmas tree awash with golden baubles; knobbly cashew nuts sprouting off the ends of the pear-shaped fruit like inverted question marks.

'You go back often?'

Shirin's mind flashed to Jyoti, her Aunt Winnie lookalike at the previous night's charity ball, who'd asked the same question. When Shirin was leaving, Jyoti had taken her hand, opened it palm up and pressed a piece of paper containing her phone number into it. 'There is a well of sadness within you, isn't there, Beti?' Shirin had blinked, unable to say anything. Was it that obvious? 'Call me. Anytime you want to talk.' She'd hugged Shirin hard. Sweat mixed with the same overbearing flowery perfume her mother wore. Shirin had closed her eyes, breathed it in.

'Not as often as I'd like,' she said now.

The Bangladeshi man nodded vigorously, setting the ladder to rocking again. 'I know. Tickets too expensive.'

He waited for Shirin to say something and when she didn't, 'Walk straight down. Sandwiches at the very end.'

'Thank you.'

'You're welcome.' Another flash of rotting teeth and the man went back to loading his shelves.

Christmas stuff out already, Shirin mused, putting the cashew nuts into her basket, imagining biting into a ripe cashew, the juice running down her chin. She wasn't ready for Christmas. She was never ready for Christmas. The holidays stretched endlessly with no work to occupy Vinod and her, to take their mind off what was missing from their lives. The cold kept them housebound; gloomy dark days spent lounging round the house eavesdropping on other people's merrymaking made them crabby. Even Vinod, who was normally so calm, so even-tempered, lapsed into a dark moodiness that Shirin knew not to cross.

It had got better with time. Now, when people asked, 'What are you doing for Christmas?' she could manage a smile and say, 'Oh, having a quiet one, just me and Vinod.' And, 'Lucky you,' they'd say, face contorting in a grimace. 'We're having the entire family, the whole she-bang. Mum will get drunk; Dad will have an argument with Uncle Peter. What wouldn't I give for a quiet one!' And Shirin would think: *Be careful what you wish for.*

The first winter in the UK was the hardest.

Shirin, who almost all her life had walked to morning mass in the watery light of dawn and for whom the sun rose after communion when the crows began their daily chorus, amber rays slanting in through the windows of the ancient church and creating wonderfully distracting patterns on the pulpit; for whom twilight was bath time, and dusk rosary time; this, night eating into day and the sun never really shining all winter, was a new phenomenon.

Winter brought Christmas and, with it, memories of holidays: of long days spent playing in the fields and splashing in the stream when it got too hot; of rows of red chillies drying in the sun; of Rex the Third snoozing on the mat, his nose twitching; of once-a-year visiting relatives laughing lazily on the stoop, sharing paan and gossip; of Jacinta's rare open-mouthed laughter; of Kuswar wars between Taipur's leading cooks—Madhu, Mrs. Fernandes and Lenny Bai: 'She made only nine varieties this year.' 'Her nevris don't have cardamom in them.' 'Not enough sugar in her kokkisam.' 'Green burfis! Who would want to eat such a thing?'; of crib competitions— the cribs fashioned from mud and silt, the bed for baby Jesus made from mango leaves, the guava standing in for a Christmas evergreen—judged by Father Sequiera and his loyal band of altar boys; of best hens fattened, pork cooking, mutlis steaming and the promise of a feast.

That first Christmas, Vinod bought a tree, baubles and a Santa suit. He went over the top with the decorations and their rented flat, which had looked empty before and too big for the two of them, was now so packed with wreaths and holly and mistletoe that they kept tripping over the stuff. He arrived from work one day with a copy of *Delia's Christmas* and spent many evenings trying out different recipes. He bought board games and videos, books and Christmas CDs. He filled their silent flat with so much chatter that Shirin felt herself drowning in it; it crowded out her thoughts, which was no bad thing. They spent the holidays faking smiles at each other, trying not to guess at each other's thoughts while avoiding their own. They tried to go out as much as possible, dressed like snowmen in myriad different layers, neophytes as they were to the freezing cold. They attempted to ice-skate. They spoke of safe things, of nothing at all, while what they were missing, what they had left behind, sat between them: a yawning abyss.

On Christmas day, Vinod asked her if she wanted to go to church. She shook her head *no*, not looking at him, afraid of what he would see in her eyes. He cooked Christmas dinner, setting off the smoke alarm and almost burning the flat down, staining Delia's pristine white cookbook an irrevocable charred brown. He served Christmas dinner in the Santa suit and the sight of his brown skin peeking out from beneath the cheery white wig made Shirin cry, the tears that kept coming making the turkey seem salty, so that afterwards she could never eat turkey without remembering the time she had seasoned it with tears.

Shirin walked to the park. It was warm for October and she didn't fancy eating at her desk, waiting for the ping to indicate a new email had arrived. She found a nice patch of grass devoid of dog mess, emptied out her lunch, spread the Tesco carrier bag on the grass and sat down. She opened the bag of nuts, popped one in her mouth. An explosion of honey sweetness. They weren't dry-roasted, they were candied. The nutty syrupiness reminded her of Nevris and her attempt to make them, their second Christmas in the UK...

She had started her software course that September and they had finished for the holidays. It was a particularly miserable day, windy with the icy rain that chills to the bone. For want of anything better to do, she decided to try out the new Asian grocery store that had opened in Kingsbury. She was debating between the Balti Mix (Hot and Spicy) and the Bombay mix (Mild and Fruity) when she spotted the jaggery sitting next to the pack of cardamom seeds and, on an impulse, made up her mind. She bought cashew nuts, maida, ghee and freshly grated coconut from the freezer section. Then she went home and cooked.

She defrosted the coconut and fried it gently in ghee adding a cup of sugar at the last minute. She crushed the cardamom seeds and pounded the jaggery. She fried the cashew nuts, chopped them finely and added them to the mixture. She mixed the maida with ghee and salt and made the dough. She rolled it out into circles like she was making very thin puris and put some of the mixture in the middle. Then she folded the ends into a half-moon crescent and sealed them with milk. She did not think as she worked. And even though she followed by rote everything she had seen Madhu do countless times, she did not allow Madhu's voice to seep into her thoughts, to dictate the recipe out loud to her in her head. Not even when she realised she did not have the special Nevri shaper to make the distinctive twirls while sealing and had to make do with a fork did she dwell on what Madhu would have said—though the thought hovered.

When she started deep frying the Nevris—far too many for the two of them—the sun-soaked, honey-sweet scent of countless lazy Christmases filled their newly purchased central-heated sterile house. And even before she took a bite of a Nevri and tasted regret, she knew that this had been a mistake. 'What's cooking?' Vinod had asked eagerly that evening, sniffing as he entered. 'Oh, an experiment gone wrong,' she'd replied, shivering inside her coat, fleece, turtleneck jumper and vest. Despite running the extractor fan full blast and opening all the windows, the scent of home lingered. It had permeated the house, seeping into everything, reaching out from the past, refusing to let go. 'Smells heavenly. It might not be to your exacting standards but I'm sure I'll like it, *Madame*,' Vinod had grinned, executing a mock bow. An aftertaste of regret lurked in her throat. She'd swallowed it down. 'You won't like it. Trust me. Shall we go out to dinner? I fancy—' *anything that doesn't remind me of home* '—Italian,' knowing it was Vinod's favourite. 'Your wish is my pleasure, *Madame*. Let's go.' And that was the end of her spell of Kuswar cooking...

'What are you doing?'

Shirin pushed her book away from her eyes, shaded them with her hands and squinted up at the owner of the little voice that she was sure had just addressed her. She found herself staring at a vision in a red-and-yellow-striped dress, with wavy white-blond hair that shone like a halo in the sun.

'Let me guess,' she said, sitting up. 'Your name is Angel?'

'No, it isn't,' the little girl giggled. 'You're funny.'

'Well, you looked just like an angel standing above me in your pretty dress and matching sandals.'

'They don't match! Look, the sandals have green flowers on them. And no stripes.' The little girl put her hands on her hips and looked critically at Shirin, 'You *are* funny,' she reiterated with more conviction. 'What were you doing when I saw you?'

In all her thirty four years, Shirin had not had to explain her actions to a six-year-old before. 'It's a lovely day, so I decided to have my lunch at the park.'

'But you weren't having lunch.'

'No,' Shirin conceded. 'After I finished, I had some time left before going back to work, so I decided to have a nap.'

'With a book on your face?' the little girl giggled.

'Well, I agree that that must have looked weird.'

'It did.'

'Where's your mum?'

The angel flopped down on the grass beside Shirin, a sigh escaping from between puckered lips in a whistle of exasperation. 'She's so slow, not fast like me. She's coming.'

Shirin nodded. 'She knows you're here?'

The angel plucked a dandelion, closed her eyes and blew hard. 'Uh-huh...'

'Did you make a wish?'

'What?'

'You're supposed to make a wish when you blow.'

A laugh as precious as sunshine on a winter's day burst through the little girl's mouth. 'You *are* funny. I'm off school today. It's an insect day.'

'Insect day?'

'Yes, when teachers have to go to school and children don't.' A giggle. Like the gurgling sound of a stream that had burst its banks in the monsoons.

'You must enjoy school, I'm sure.' Shirin smiled. 'School is fun.'

'No it isn't.'

'Abigail...' The angel turned. A tall woman came running up, panting, and scooped her up in her arms.

A familiar yearning spread through Shirin.

The woman buried her face in her daughter's hair. 'I thought I'd lost you. How many times have I told you not to wander off and talk to strangers? I was worried sick.' The woman tore her gaze away from her daughter and turned to Shirin. 'I'm sorry if she bothered you.'

'No bother. I enjoyed talking to her.'

'She says school's fun,' Abigail pointed at Shirin, making a face.

'Of course it is,' Shirin and the woman said in unison, and then started to laugh.

Abigail, belatedly shy, wrapped chubby arms round her mother and burrowed her white-blond head in the crook of her mother's neck.

'How many do *you* have?' the woman asked Shirin.

'I'm sorry?' It took a second for the penny to drop and then she couldn't hide her dismay.

'Sorry, I just assumed...' the woman looked flustered. 'It's just... what you said about school... I'm sorry...' She gently untied her daughter's arms from around her neck and stood her down before turning to walk away.

'Wait,' Abigail turned to Shirin, held her dress out and twirled. 'Do you like my new dress?'

'It's beautiful,' Shirin managed. 'A lovely dress for a lovely girl.'

Abigail giggled. 'Bye,' she said, putting her little hand in her mother's. 'She thought I was called Angel,' Shirin heard her say as she skipped in step beside her mum, her voice sweet as syrup-filled jalebis.

Shirin watched them until they reached the children's play area and Abigail disappeared up the slide. Then she stood, brushed down her suit, gathered her book and walked slowly back to the office, trying to ignore the yearning that had ballooned into an all-consuming craving. She tried to focus on safer things: the issue that had cropped up during integration testing that stubbornly refused to be fixed. Work. Emails. Emails… *You've survived all these years without a word from them. What's so different now?*

Abigail swam before her eyes, persistent: 'Do you like my new dress?'

How does it feel to have your little girl wrap her arms around you, bury her head in your shoulder? How does it feel to hear her say, 'I love you, Mummy'?

Think of safe things. Abigail twirling, 'Do you like my new dress?'

She thought of new clothes, the crisp foreign smell of them, Madhu's eyes lighting up at the word 'foreign', of treasured parcels from Walter arriving twice a year; once in May and once just before Christmas, of Shirin going with Madhu to the post office, signing on the little square next to her mother's name, 'JACINTA DIAZ' in the cursive style Sister Shanthi had made sure they all perfected, her tongue sticking out, the Reynolds ball pen which Timothy the postman had given her feeling unfamiliar and thicker somehow, used as she was to HB pencils. The exotic parcel had occupied pride of place next to the altar on top of the old wooden wardrobe which housed the good tablecloth and serving dishes, the red glow from the little bulb in front of the Holy Family illuminating the dull brown wrapping to deep russet, inviting Shirin, Deepak and Anita to rip it open and take a peek at the goodies inside. The three of them would sit at the edge of the front courtyard, their legs dangling down into the stream below, looking across the fields to the path beyond and willing Jacinta to appear. When they spotted her, a colourful dot in the distance manoeuvring down the rocky path to the bridge across the first stream, they would run, 'Ma! Ma! The parcel's here.' Jacinta's stern face would relax into a soft smile as they hurled themselves at her, barefoot and muddy. The contents of the parcel were always the same: a letter for Jacinta—a thick one—resting on top, which she touched reverently and hugged to herself, closing her eyes; clothes for Shirin, Deepak and Anita, neatly folded, crisp and shiny, feeling and smelling different to the clothes in Raju's shop. And the best part: Kit Kats, tucked away behind the clothes and letter, nestling beside a couple of tins of Kraft cheese and just starting to melt. They would have a finger each. The fourth finger, they divided into three parts. There was always a scuffle as to who got the biggest, which Jacinta resolved with a stern, 'Do you realise how lucky you are? Look around you. There are people starving. If you fight one more time, I am going to give the Kit Kats to Laxmi's children who do not even have a decent roof over their heads.' That would shut them up, and they would go outside and argue in secret.

They hardly, if ever, thought of Walter, the man behind the parcels. A pleasant, mild-mannered man who visited every alternate summer, a bit older each time. Once he was gone, promptly forgotten. Remembered briefly, gratefully, when the parcels arrived. Cursed heartily the last Friday of each month when they were forced to write a letter each—Jacinta insisted it had to be at least a page long—detailing their progress at school, their achievements: 'Dearest Daddy, I came seventh in class in the mid-term exams. Sister Shanthi praised me for singing nicely in the choir. A python got into Beerakka's chicken coop and ate all seven of the chickens she was fattening for Mari Habba. Nagappa caught it. It was very long, longer than Ananthanna's field even. But it fit in a gunny bag (where it vomited two of the chickens, Nagappa said). I won the high jump. With lots of love, Craving your blessings, Shirin.'

Her father. A stranger.

A headache loomed. One of the bad ones, pressing against her skull. As she made herself a cup of coffee—strong, black—to take to her desk, Shirin tried to picture him. Walter. The soft-spoken man who stayed for the summer every two years; whose presence guaranteed feast food—chicken sukka, pork bafat, pickled sardines, mackerel fry, mutli, panpole—every single day; who made her mother smile, hum and even blush a couple of times; the man who tickled Shirin till she begged him to stop, who allowed Deepak to beat him at cards, who sat Anita on his lap and read Bible verses to her while she bunched his sparse hair with rubber bands and decorated it with aboli flowers. He drank at least five litres of water a day—Shirin had counted once—and lost it all in perspiration which permanently beaded his face and arms. He wore only a lungi and no shirt, had springy, curly hair on his chest which Shirin, Deepak and Anita had tried to straighten while he slept by weighting each hair down with pebbles, and a potbelly larger than a pregnant woman's that he let them bounce and slide on. He snored when he slept, even louder than Grandpa and Grandma used to, and sometimes he sputtered to a stop, his mouth open, and Shirin worried he was dead. He had hair growing out of his nostrils and dimples that merged onto his double chin.

However hard she tried, Shirin couldn't quite remember his face. She tasted the familiar bittersweet tang of regret at the back of her throat. She swallowed it down, relegated the sudden yearning to see her father—to pluck him out of her past and look at him, memorise his features until they were branded in her brain as insurance against ever forgetting them again—to that secret corner of her heart which housed other yearnings, other regrets: a corner of her heart that was forever expanding.

Her father had accompanied her to Bangalore for her wedding and neither of them had known what to say to each other. If only she had known then that this was the last chance she had to get to know him, the last time she would see him...

Unless...

She went back home someday.

Despite her promise to herself, she checked Outlook once more. And, once more, there were plenty of emails requiring her attention but not the one she was looking for.

CHAPTER EIGHTEEN
Hand Stretched to Infinity

'Rinu, you look tired. How was your day?'
'I got told off for daydreaming during the Kannada lesson.'

Aunt Anita giggled, the sound like temple bells. 'I hated Kannada too. The grammar...'

'I know, so much to remember! What about you? What did you do?'

Reena and Aunt Anita were walking back to the apartment. Her aunt had been waiting for her outside the gate to their apartment block again, sitting as usual on the mound of mud, wearing a salwar kameez, the kind that film actresses wore, with a short, pale green sequinned top and matching, flared trousers which showed off her long legs and thin waist to perfection.

She could get used to being picked up at the gate, Reena decided, but not to being accosted at school by the older boys and asked question after question about Aunt Anita. The fact that she was married and almost twenty years older than them did nothing to dent their enthusiasm. Even Raj, whom she had thought was a decent sort, and whom she secretly had a crush on, seemed besotted by Aunt Anita.

She had decided that being accosted by the boys was worse than the name-calling and teasing. The girls in her class, Divya included, were annoyed that the boys were paying her so much attention and they were even cattier to her than before.

The bus driver had slowed down dramatically when he spotted Aunt Anita waiting for Reena at the entrance to the apartment block; usually he took off before Reena had time to get off the last step, but today he took his time. The boys had started whistling as romantic Hindi film music started blaring suddenly out of speakers that Reena had not even known existed in the bus. The driver combed his sparse oily hair in the mirror above the steering wheel as Reena climbed off and then turned to flash Aunt Anita a smile that was even oilier. The queue for bidis at the little hut across the road was longer than the previous day, and the customers, instead of facing the shop, were staring at Aunt Anita with grins so wide they looked like performing monkeys.

When Reena and Aunt Anita turned to walk inside there was a chorus of groans from the men and boys. Aunt Anita laughed and waved the bus away to a wild crescendo of cheers. The bus driver's off-key rendition of Hindi film music faded into the distance.

'We went shopping,' Aunt Anita said, 'to a mall. I think it's only been a couple of years since I last visited Banga-lore, but, my God, the difference! This city is booming! Malls and flyovers popping up all over the place.'

Reena smiled, pleased to see Aunt Anita so animated. She was not depressed all the time anymore. She had stopped wearing sunglasses constantly. Staying with them seemed to be doing her good.

'We had a great time,' Aunt Anita continued, 'I bought some clothes. Your mother got pillow covers, of all things. Then we ate at one of those exclusive eateries inside the mall, where it costs three times the price outside. We each had a masala dosa and some tea. That came up to four hundred rupees! It's all these rich young software engineers that are making all the difference: the nouveau riche with their nuclear families; the pampered society wife, the spoilt children.' She stopped, suddenly realising what she had said, and blushed. 'Not you of course. You are the exception to the rule.' She reached across and cupped Reena's cheek in her palm. 'So, have you been reading Shirin's letters? What do you think?'

They were by the pool. The sky, a brilliant cloudless blue, was reflected in its depths. The water shimmered and sparkled like the sequins in her mother's best ghagra choli. In the distance, beyond the flats, Reena could just make out the top of a banyan tree, the branches swaying slightly in the mild breeze. As she watched, a V-shaped formation of birds flew past, regally swooping across the horizon like a hand stretched out to infinity. She closed her eyes.

'Reena?'

She heard the question in her aunt's voice.

'I... I read the first letter.' The words she really wanted to ask were at the tip of her tongue. *Why? Why shun her? What did she do that was so bad? Did she marry someone unsuitable?*

Was that it? But so did you. Why was she punished and not you?
But she was afraid her aunt would get annoyed and ask for
the letters back. So she cleared her throat and said instead,
'They are in English.' *Super Sleuth, where's your courage?*

Her aunt smiled. 'That's your Mai's fault. She made
sure we wrote our letters in English—to Da, to each other. "We pay so much money to send you to English medium school, you might as well practise it," she used to
say when we grumbled.'

'I am getting a sense of who she was. Thank you for
sharing the letters, for sharing *your* Shirin with me.'

Aunt Anita beamed. It was like the sun breaking
through clouds after a monsoon shower. And Reena suddenly understood why men went weak-kneed and crazy
for her aunt, why they fell under her spell.

'You're welcome, sweetie. It's nice to talk about her
with someone after all this time.'

'That's exactly what Madhu said!' A pause while she gathered up courage. *I am not going to let Aunt Shirin remain
invisible anymore.* 'Aunt Shirin... She seems so nice, so kind.
I cannot imagine her doing anything to warrant all of you
shunning her; her own mother pretending she never existed.'

Aunt Anita flinched. 'Please, Reena. Just leave it—okay?'
Don't push it, Reena, don't. 'Why?'

Aunt Anita pinched the bridge of her nose, closed her
eyes. 'I... It will cause hurt all round.' She cupped Reena's
face in her palm. 'Look at me.' Her voice was soft. 'Read
the letters; get to know Shirin. Leave the rest be. It's mad-
dening, I know. But it's for the best.'

Not what you said before. Are all adults so fickle or just you? Reena looked away, up at the sky. The birds were gone. The sky seemed bereft. 'I *hate* being a child. Every-one talks down to you...' Rogue tears pricked at her eyes.

'Reena...'

She picked up her satchel and dragged it up the stairs. She stormed into the flat, ignored Preeti: 'Rinu, guess what, I packed you the rava dosa from Sukh Sagar.'; ran to her room and banged the door shut.

'What's the matter with her?' she heard a perplexed Preeti ask.

'She got told off for daydreaming during her Kannada lesson,' Aunt Anita lied effortlessly. She was, Reena noted with grim pleasure, panting from trying to catch up with her.

All the adults in her life seemed skilled at lying, Reena seethed. She lay on her bed and stared up at the ceiling, picturing a lonely girl who yearned to fall in love, sitting on the veranda in Taipur, missing her siblings. She lay there until she could no longer ignore the hungry calls of her stomach, and when her mother banged on her door for the third time: 'Come on out, Rinu; Mr Shastri is not worth it. You'll feel better after eating your dosa,' she went to the dining table and devoured her snack while studi-ously avoiding Aunt Anita's eye.

Afterwards, while her mother was in the kitchen wash-ing up, she flopped onto the sofa beside her aunt who was flicking through channels.

'There's nothing good to watch at this time, is there, Reena?' Aunt Anita said.

'I'm sorry I lost my temper,' Reena mumbled, staring at the TV. 'And I wasn't being fair to you. You are one of the few adults who treat me as an equal. Well, most of the time anyway.'

Aunt Anita laughed. 'You are something, you know that?'

'You're not angry with me?'

'Why? For showing some spirit? ' She reached across and tousled Reena's hair. 'You're a niece to be proud of, that's for sure.'

Reena blushed, feeling unworthy. 'Do you regret giving me the letters?' *Now why on earth did you ask that? Serve you right if she takes them back.*

'No. And I won't ask for them back, don't you worry, until you have read them all. I'd like you to get to know the person Shirin was before...' A pause. Aunt Anita stared past the television at something only she could see.

Whew, Reena thought. *Golden rule of detection: Think before you speak.* If she had taken the letters, where would Super Sleuth Reena Diaz be?

'When you meet Shirin,' Aunt Anita met Reena's gaze, held it, 'and one day you will, she'll say the same thing I bet. That you're a...' she looked away, 'a niece to be proud of.'

Why? Why had Aunt Anita looked so discomfited when she said that last bit? Why couldn't she meet her eye?

❊ ❊ ❊

That evening after dinner, instead of watching a Hindi movie with her mother and aunt, Reena excused herself saying she had a maths test the next day, lying as easily as the rest of her family. Perhaps it ran in the blood. Once in her room, she locked the door, reached for the bundle of letters, opened the next one and started to read.

Letter 2: Extracts:

1. In this extract, subject guesses about Uttam.

   Anu, this Uttam you keep mentioning in your letter, is he in your class? He sounds very interesting. And you seem to really like him. And respect him. I don't think you've ever really respected a boy before. They tend to make a nuisance of themselves around you. So, is Uttam just a friend or something more, perhaps?

   NOTE: When she was younger, did subject yearn to be a detective as well? She would have been good at it. Perhaps she found something she shouldn't have and that was the reason she was shunned? This detective hopes that is not the case. If this detective discovers the cause of rift, <u>will she be shunned too?</u>

2. Aha, Eureka, Abracadabra. THE CLUE.

   In your letter, you asked me about my postgraduate college, how I am finding it, and if it is any good. It is. I enjoy it. And, Anu, you'll never believe this: Tariq is here, doing an MS in Electronics and Communications.

I thought, after everything that happened, he would not want anything to do with me. But...

The first morning, after induction, I was in the canteen eating chattambades and catching tantalising glimpses of the sea shimmering beyond the teachers' mess when a familiar voice, very close, whispered, 'Hello.' I turned and found myself looking into his eyes, those beautiful brown eyes I had only ever thought I'd see in my dreams. 'Your hair's grown back,' he said.

NOTE: Shirin says, 'After what happened, he would not want anything...' What happened? Something to do with her hair? And *who is this Tariq of the beautiful brown eyes?*

3. This detective knows now why Aunt Anita gave her the letters to read. They contain the explanation, the clues to what happened. She meant for this detective to find out; she recognised the potential in this detective.

He loves me, Anu. He loves me. Still. Despite everything.

We were sitting on the rocks behind the Hindu temple, watching the tiny specks that pass for boats bobbing gently up and down at the point where the sky meets the sea. On the beach, a lone vendor selling baby cucumbers liberally coated with chilli powder and chaat masala did brisk business. The sea breeze raised goosebumps on my skin as the faded curtain of dusk fell on the golds and the orangey-reds and the pinks: the sun's last act. And he leaned towards me, his spicy breath warm on my cheek, and told me he loved me. He asked me to run away with him.

And I did run. The coward that I am, I ran like hell to catch the last bus home. (I know, I swore. Don't tell Sister Maya.)

NOTE: So she didn't run away with him. Not this time. Why does she need to <u>run away</u> with him? Mai does not approve perhaps. But why? Tariq. The name sounds Muslim. Aha. Marrying a Muslim is worse somehow than marrying a Hindu. Perhaps that was it. Eloping with a Muslim is far worse than marrying a high-born Brahmin, even today…

NOTE 2: Shirin keeps referring to something that happened before. What happened?

4. Even though this extract makes this detective want to shake the subject, hard, (Golden rule of detection: Do <u>not</u> allow personal feelings to get in the way of detection—so not the hallmark of a good detective), a picture is beginning to form:

In other news, Aunt Winnie came over yesterday with a proposal for me. Boy is from Bangalore.

Wealthy family. Has one older brother who refuses to get married: first love gone sour put him off for life according to Aunt Winnie. Ma was very excited about the proposal: 'From Bangalore, really? Wait till the parish committee hears about it!' (you know what she's like). She's worried about the older brother and kept asking Aunt Winnie all sorts of questions about him. Aunt Winnie harrumphed and said, 'If you want to be like that, Jessie...' Ma placated Aunt Winnie with jackfruit and paan and gave her one of those horrible CVs she made containing all relevant information about me—my vital statistics, my qualifications, my hobbies—to pass on to them. She also included that unflattering picture of me, taken in Benny's studio when I turned nineteen.

Remember?

Remember how Ma decided when, after a year of rigorous groom-hunting I was still on the marriage market and no one had shown the slightest interest in me, that what was missing was a full-length photograph. She was convinced that once she circulated a picture along with the CV, offers for my hand would pour in. Poor Ma!

Do you remember how she and Madhu deliberated for a long time on which sari I was to wear, launching into a detailed discussion on the colour that would suit me best, make me look relatively lighter skinned? Finally they decided on that orange sari with pink flowers and gold border that I absolutely loathe. Madhu altered the sari blouse so it would fit me. Ma painted my lips with that bright-red lipstick (the one you called 'tart gear') and plastered talcum powder on my face. I kept my head down the entire way to the studio, refusing to look at all the many people we encountered, and to all of whom Madhu proudly announced that I was going to have my picture taken in preparation for my wedding.

Benny kept asking me to stand up straight and then when I did, he asked me to bend slightly. He was not happy with my smile, complaining that I showed too many teeth or no teeth at all. The picture that he and Ma finally agreed upon is horrendous. You know the one. Ma bought around 50 copies of it.

Anyway, that is the picture which is going to the suitor in Bangalore along with the CV in which Ma has listed my weight five kilos lighter than I really am and my height two inches taller. She has also declared that I am 'wheat-complexioned'. I have never understood that expression. If she said I was the colour of coconut husks at least that would be nearer the truth. She has bragged about how well I cook (does appreciating Madhu's food count as cooking?) and how I am the best singer in the choir (I haven't sung in the choir since I was ten). She's said I can dance Bharatanatyam (do the few lessons I took at school with you, but dropped out because I had two left feet, qualify?) and that I can play the guitar (again, does interest but no ability count?).

You know, Anu, even if—and it's a big if—someone does agree to marry me (why would they when there are hundreds of more beautiful, lighter-skinned, thinner girls out there?), by the time I explain away all the many embellishments to my CV, he will run miles.

I know what you will say: 'Run away.' I know that's what you would do. But, Anu, I'm not you. Although, when Tariq catches up with me after class, his breath fogging up his glasses and offers his sweet smile and his hands to carry my books; when we sit in the library, heads bent, almost touching and I find it hard to concentrate on balancing accounts, distracted by the droplets of sweat beading the hair on his bare arms, wanting to touch them; those times I so wish I was you: impulsive, 'devil may care' courageous.

I have to go. Rosary time. Yes, I can picture your gleeful grin. Reply when you can. I am counting down the days to Christmas when you, Deepak and Da will be here and the house will feel like home again.

NOTE: This detective feels frustrated with Aunt Shirin. If she was in her shoes, she would have run away and not subjected herself to all this humiliation and this business of arranged marriages when she had a perfectly good suitor who loved her. So what if he was unsuitable? So what if her family was opposed to him?

This detective feels she is honing in on the reason for the rift—something to do with subject's marriage. It is an exciting feeling, being this close to the truth, and yet somehow scary as well. Perhaps all great detectives feel this way?

CHAPTER NINETEEN
A Good Match

She called him as she was leaving the office. 'No reply.'
'There can be a number of reasons for that, Shonu. It's her work ID, isn't it? Well, she may be off sick, away on a shoot with no access to her email, on holiday...' He didn't pause to take a breath as he rattled off the reasons. He must have been thinking them up all day when she didn't call.

'Did you think she wouldn't?'

'No! I hoped she would.' A pause. And then, 'You can always call Deepak. Or we could go back, just turn up, shock them.'

Briefly, she entertained the fantasy. Her mother's face. Anger, regret, shame. 'Not yet.' *I need to see the counsellor again, get closure.*

'Soon, then.' And, softly, 'Shonu, it may be something as simple as Anita not having had the time to check her emails as yet...'

'Hmm...'

His voice gentle: 'I'm leaving work now. See you at home.'

'Bye.'

Kate came up behind her as she disconnected the call, helmet on, keys dangling from her index finger.

'You came by bike?'

'Yup. You want to ride pillion?'

'No, thanks.' She managed a smile.

Kate put her arm around her. 'She might just be busy. If she had a day like the one I just had, she may not have had a chance to check her emails.'

'It's not like they've been falling over themselves to get in touch these past few years. I'll live.'

The elevator doors pinged open.

'Sure I can't give you a lift home? Much faster than your old banger.'

'Kate! How dare you? It's my pride and joy.'

'Doesn't detract from the fact. It's still an old banger...'

Shirin couldn't help it. She laughed.

As she got into her old banger, Kate, sweet Kate, said, 'There's still tomorrow. It might be waiting for you when you come in.'

Shirin blew her a kiss.

❋ ❋ ❋

'Shall we go away this Christmas?' she asked.

Vinod turned from where he lay on the sofa reading *The Economist*, one eye on the television: BBC News 24, the flat-faced presenter churning out one awful disaster after another.

When he'd got home from work, he had tried to bring up Anita and the email but she had stopped him. 'I don't want to talk about it.' Her standard reaction to anything that hurt too much to contemplate. *Relegate it to a corner of your mind. Don't talk about it until it manifests itself in nightmares and even then, try and ignore it.* 'But, Shonu, you have to talk, let it out. You were getting better...' His mouth had set in a grim line. She had opened a bottle of wine, taken a long swig. 'Please, Vinod.'

'I can't read your mind, Shonu,' he'd said once, in the middle of an argument when she'd shut down, blanked him out. 'I don't know what goes on in there.' He'd jabbed a finger at her forehead. She had thought he was going to hit her. Afterwards he had held her, and she had sat stiffly in his arms and listened to his sobs, endured his apologies. 'I love you,' he had said. *Love, what love? What do we have together, Vinod? Our bond—one horrific incident that still casts its shadow, maligning everything.*

And now they were sitting in the living room, watching television, eavesdropping on other people's tragedies.

He gave her a bemused smile. 'Where exactly did you have in mind?'

Shirin shrugged. She hadn't thought that far.

'We could just go home.' He was looking at her, waiting for a reaction.

'Oh, Vinod,' Weary. And, softly, 'Do you get homesick?' *Why had they never talked about this?*

'Of course I get homesick. I miss them.'

Because it hurt too much.

His voice harsh as he continued, 'God, do you think it's been easy turning my back on my whole life before you?' And as she started to speak, 'Don't you dare apologise. We never talk about this. Well, we are now and I am telling you how I feel.' He took a gasping breath, 'That doesn't mean I am not happy. With you. I am, but the two things need not be mutually exclusive, as you well know.'

She apologised anyway. 'I'm sorry.'

Vinod clicked his tongue. 'Not your fault. If I wanted to, I would go.'

'Why don't you go, then?' Her voice loud, grating.

'When I return home, I will do so with you. You are my wife and I am proud of you. I am not going to hide you away like a guilty secret.'

She understood. It would be a betrayal of her if he went back on his own. It would look like he was tacitly admitting her culpability. 'No pressure on me, then.' Why was she being like this, so sarcastic, when all he was doing was speaking his mind, finally, after years of skirting the truth? She was hurt. She had not realised this was how he felt. If she was to be completely honest, she had not been thinking about him at all; it had all been about her. Her feelings, her shame, her guilt. 'I'm going to go see the counsellor again. And then we'll go back. Together.' She looked up at him.

His voice gentle, 'I'm happy here, Shonu. With you.' He closed *The Economist*, sat up and moved closer to where she was sitting on the armchair, hugging her legs with both arms, head resting on her knees. Madhu's favourite squatting position. Madhu sitting in the kitchen, beside the hand grinder, nursing a tumbler of tea, smiling at her... *I need you, Madhu. I need you now.*

'But visiting the counsellor is a great idea.' And then, 'What about Switzerland?'

'Huh?'

'You wanted to go away at Christmas?'

The secret to their marriage: don't talk about things that matter. Talk about something else instead. Like a holiday they both knew they wouldn't take. She knew she should talk to him, now that they were finally airing things in the open, eleven years too late. But instead, she played along, relieved. 'We could rent a chalet. Hibernate. Perhaps even learn to ski...'

That made him smile and she was inordinately pleased. 'Really?' The twinkle in his eyes that she absolutely loved. 'Do you remember what you said after we went ice-skating that last time?'

'I didn't say anything. It was you, complaining about the cold, complaining about falling, the pain in your knees, your back. You're just too old for this sort of thing...'

'Oh, I am, am I?' He reached across and with one finger traced a line under her arm where she was the most ticklish.

'Hey, not fair. You always resort to underhand means to win an argument.'

'I didn't know we were arguing.' In one fluid motion, he had gathered her in his arms. She stiffened. 'Eh, Shonu?' he whispered in her ear. Slowly, she relaxed against him. 'I know why you want to go away this Christmas...'

'Stop whispering in my ear. It tickles.' She turned to face him. 'Why?'

'So you can get out of attending Jane and Neil's party.'

She buried her face in his jumper. 'How did you know?' she laughed and it came out all muffled.

Every year, Vinod's boss Neil and his wife Jane hosted a posh Christmas party. And every year, when all the guests were seated at the table, Jane turned to Shirin and asked, her eyes shining in anticipation, 'So tell us again, how did you and Vinod meet?' like the answer was Shirin's best party trick.

Where did she begin? How did she tell these people who couldn't fathom a relationship without having known the person first, been in love with them, about how things really worked in India, how you grew up watching your mother squirrel away bits and pieces of gold: 'for your dowry' and you knew what was coming; how the village matrons started sizing you up as soon as you turned fifteen, shaking their heads and muttering ominously, 'This one will need a lot of prayers'?

If she was really honest, she would say it all began with the note, the summer she turned eighteen...

That summer, Jacinta embarked on her most important task as the mother of an Indian girl.

Finding a good match for the eldest daughter was vital. If the eldest set a good example by marrying into a decent Mangalorean Catholic family, then chances were that proposals for the siblings would follow suit. If the eldest daughter did something foolish—like married outside the community, or fell in love, with a Hindu or, God forbid, a Muslim—the siblings would in all probability not get married at all, as no self-respecting suitor would associate with, let alone marry into, a disgraced family.

Shirin had her first marriage 'interview' a few months after she switched colleges. Her hair had started to grow back and was now shoulder-length, just fitting into a neat plait. Tariq visited her regularly in her dreams, his intense eyes lighting up when he saw her, his hands caressing her face, his lips meeting hers… She always woke when she got to this part, hot and flustered, and spent the rest of the night fantasising about what would happen next, her body aching, arching, wanting… Anita had reported that Tariq had returned to college a week after Shirin left, his arm in a cast, his jaw bruised, left eye swollen, and that he kept well away from Deepak. Once, when Deepak was ill, he had approached Anita, whose school was next door to the college, and asked how Shirin was doing. Anita had walked away without replying, knowing that Deepak's friends were watching…

The suitor's name, Jacinta informed Shirin, was Anil. Anil and his family arrived an hour and a half later than they were supposed to. Shirin waited, feeling the sweat trickle down her back and pool around her armpits. She was sure it would leave tell-tale marks on her sari blouse. The unfamiliar jewellery that her mother had insisted she wore itched. The many gold bangles made a sound if she so much as lifted a finger.

Anil's mother grilled Shirin for the best part of an hour. 'Bit dusky, aren't you? And on the heavy side…

What is your weight? Do you dance, cook, sing? Do you wear contact lenses? What is that mark on your skin?' Every blemish was questioned, examined and commented upon. Anil hardly spoke except to agree with his mother: 'Yes, she is big-boned. Yes, it would be handy if she knew how to sew. Yes, it's a shame she can't cook North Indian food. Yes, she shouldn't have cut her hair; it looked better long, like in the photo attached to her CV. Yes, in her CV she said she was skilled at Bharatanatyam.' And finally, when Shirin thought she could stand the litany of her imperfections no longer, it was over and they were saying their goodbyes. As Shirin turned to go inside, Anil's mother called out, 'Don't be disheartened if we don't get back to you. Anil has five more girls lined up.' *Good luck to them,* Shirin thought.

After they had left and Shirin had changed, she went to Madhu, who was washing clothes by the well. Madhu held Shirin, her hands dripping suds all over Shirin's face and blending with her tears: a salty, soap flavoured cocktail. She rocked Shirin back and forth like she had when she was a child, the clothes lying forgotten and forlorn on the washing stone, gently pushing Shirin's hair which was escaping the confines of the plait away from her face with wet hands, 'Shh, it's okay, Shirin. They were horrible people. Not everyone is like that.'

When she came back in the house, Jacinta, who was reading the *Udayavani* in her housecoat as she was wont to do in the evenings, peered up at her from above her spectacles. 'Come here, Shirin. Sit by me.'

Shirin sat on the cool cement floor beside Jacinta's cane chair. 'You did well,' Jacinta whispered. Shirin wondered if she'd heard right. The heaviness in her heart eased the slightest bit. The tube light flickered, died. 'Low voltage, again,' grumbled Jacinta as she always did when this happened, 'How are we supposed to do anything after dusk, if there is either low voltage or no power?'

Outside, crickets kept up their nightly song, frogs croaked and rain drummed on the tiles. Dogs howled and old Ananthanna walked home drunk, teetering precariously on the little mud lane between the fields and managing to maintain his balance—just—unaware that he was getting completely soaked. He shouted insults to his wife, who had been dead ten years, loud enough for the whole neighbourhood to hear. His voice carried over the rain, strident and vitriolic. He would stand there, shouting in the rain until his harassed daughter-in-law ventured out into the muddy fields with an umbrella and coaxed him home.

In the dark, Jacinta's hand found Shirin's, squeezed, and settled there. Shirin accepted it like a gift, and they sat like that until Madhu came in from the kitchen carrying lit candles and grumbling about the government and how there was never any power in the villages and if there was no electricity how was she supposed to grind the rice and lentils for dosas now that ma'am had insisted she use the mixer and had given the hand grinder to Muthakka.

The whole cumbersome process of arranging her marriage, more gruelling than the worst job interview: the hunt for eligible bachelors, the visit from the suitor and his parents, the interrogation, the wait for the results, to find out if she'd passed scrutiny, won their approval—did get better after that, perhaps because Shirin learnt not to take the rejections, the hurtful comments, the emphasis on her many imperfections, too much to heart. What hurt was to see Jacinta waiting on tenterhooks after a prospective groom had been to see Shirin, hope mingling with worry on her usually unreadable face and then, after each rejection, the hope draining out to be replaced by a drawn, haggard expression—until the next proposal. What hurt was to overhear the village gossips say, within Jacinta's earshot, 'If only Anita had been the eldest, she would have been snapped up by now,' or, 'How old is Shirin now? Oh... In danger of becoming an old maid...' And, 'Soon, Anita will be of marriageable age. She will have a long line of suitors no doubt, and poor Jacinta will still have Shirin on her hands. If only Shirin had a lighter complexion, if only she were thinner...'

What hurt was the unavoidable fact that she was not the daughter her proud, beautiful mother deserved.

Gradually, the proposals dwindled and the lines on her mother's face multiplied. Shirin waited for her Knight in Shining Armour, knowing that it was fantasy—who would want her anyway? *Tariq.*

Tariq. His beautiful tawny-gold eyes. Those full lips that she so wanted to kiss. She had given up hope of ever seeing him again—and he had turned up at her university. Every morning, she said goodbye to her mother's displeasure and dumpy Shirin who couldn't snag a suitor and climbed aboard the 'Sugama' bus that would take her to college. As the bus turned the corner, she pushed and elbowed her way through the heaving, sweaty crowd, her face in people's armpits as they struggled to hold on when the bus juddered over potholes, catching a glimpse of the bespectacled face waiting patiently for her in the shade of the banyan tree by the bus stop. She would stagger off the steps and see his face light up at the sight of her, and she was transformed; she was Shirin, delicate swan, beautiful princess. They would walk up to the main building together, he carrying her books for her, and part at the entrance to go to their respective classes. They met up at break and shared a tea in the canteen, and her lips touching the tumbler after he'd sipped from it felt as intimate as a kiss. They would skip the canteen altogether at lunch, and walk to the sea. They would sit, side by side, not quite touching, and sketch their initials in the sand, boldly entwined, and it always felt like the worst kind of betrayal to hunt for them the next day and find fresh white sand, unsullied, to realise the waves had erased this evidence of their love. He held her hand sometimes, as they walked back to college from the beach, letting go just as they left the cover of trees and came onto the road, and she was left wanting more, so much more. She desired him. She had certainly wanted him to kiss her that evening when they'd sheltered from the rain by the electronics lab, darkness caused by the power cut a cover, their breath punctuating the silence. She had seen his face illuminated by a flash of lightning, very close. *Kiss me, please*, she had thought, inching her face closer, shocked by her brazenness. *Crush me against you. I want to be held, touched all over. I want to know what it feels like.*

But when it came right down to it, could she brave being disowned by her mother, bringing disgrace to her family for Tariq? No. Not after what happened with the note… 'You are the eldest. You are required to set an example. The eyes of the whole village are on you. If you step one toe out of line, you are not only ruining your future but hers as well.' Her mother had yelled that horrible evening, her eyes flashing, one finger pointing at Anita. 'Look at her. Do you want to destroy her? Think, Shirin, think,' her voice softening suddenly, 'with your head, not your heart.' Her hand reaching out, gently caressing Shirin's shorn head, her bare neck. Had there been tears flashing in her mother's eyes?

What would her mother do if she found out about Tariq now? *No.* Shirin was so careful. Her college was far enough away. Deepak and Anita were away at college in different states. And her mother was preoccupied with fixing her marriage.

The passion from the romantic novels is not for me. I will learn to love the man who marries me, duty-bound, until duty becomes truth. And one day, when my children are old enough, I will let them choose, will vicariously participate in their passion as they fall in love. No arranged marriages, no forced humiliations for my children, she told herself every night, as she prayed for a good proposal to come, for a suitor to say yes to marrying her, so the worry could be wiped off her mother's face, so she could see her mother's rare open-mouthed smile again.

And then one day Aunt Winnie—one of the many 'aunts' who weren't related—arrived with news of a prospective groom. She knew someone who knew someone who had heard about this family—Mangalorean Catholics settled in Bangalore, own business, two sons—who were looking for a well-brought-up Mangalorean Catholic girl for their younger son. He was called Vinod.

'The older son. Where's his wife from?' Jacinta asked as she heaped rice and two fat pieces of fried pomfret onto Aunt Winnie's plate.

'He's not married.'

'*He's not?* Why?' Jacinta sounded shocked.

Aunt Winnie prised the fish off the bone and divided the rice into several little mounds, topping each with a piece of fish. 'He doesn't want to, it seems. Some love affair gone wrong when he was younger, after which he swore never to get married. And now, the younger son is of marriageable age and the parents are not prepared to wait for Prem to change his mind any longer.' She squidged each mound into a ball and popped one in her mouth, closing her eyes as she chewed. 'Hmm. This is nice,' she said, 'If you ever want rid of Madhu, I'll take her.'

'Can't the parents put their foot down, insist on him getting married?'

Aunt Winnie gaped, mid-chew. 'Jacinta, he's thirty-five!'

'So? If it was Deepak, I'd…' Jacinta paused, brow crinkling. 'I don't know, Winnie, I'm not sure about this family…'

Aunt Winnie put the last ball of fish and rice into her mouth, munched, spat out a stray pin-bone. She poured the tumbler of water onto her plate, washing her hand. Shirin watched the fish bones swim in the dirty yellow water. Aunt Winnie looked over at Shirin and Jacinta's eyes followed. Shirin blushed as the two women surveyed her, top to bottom, taking in her many imperfections. 'It's not like you have a choice, Jessie,' Aunt Winnie said at last.

Jacinta chose a light-pink sari with a sky-blue border. 'Pink suits you, Shirin. It makes you look less dusky.' As with all the previous suitors' visits, Madhu cooked all day, concocting pakoras and sweetmeats, the lovely aromas making Shirin hungry despite the butterflies in her stomach. At five o'clock, Nagappa's son announced breathlessly, 'They are here. They have come in a huge Ambassador car!'

At least they were punctual, unlike many of the other families who had come to see her.

Right on cue, the dogs started barking. Shirin, face pressed against the window bars, sneaked a peek. Vinod was tall, with a kind face, Shirin thought. The stool she was standing on, on her tiptoes, wobbled, the end of her sari caught on her feet and she almost lost her balance on the window bars, but managed to right herself, just in time to see Jacinta, looking gorgeous in a vermilion sari, graciously welcoming Vinod's parents. And Vinod was looking right at *her*, at Shirin. He grinned. Shirin blushed and looked away. The stool wobbled again and this time she jumped down quickly and righted her sari, with trembling fingers that wouldn't do her bidding. Vinod's face filled her mind—his kind eyes, and that smile. Had he liked her, or had she ruined it already?

She heard Jacinta say, 'She's in her room,' and then call out, 'Shirin!' in a high-pitched tingle of a voice quite unlike her usual firm one. Shirin took a deep breath and stepped out, head down, praying she wouldn't trip.

Afterwards, she went over it again and again in her head. She had managed to offer everyone tea without spilling any, though her hands were shaking as she handed Vinod his tumbler and she was sure he noticed. She thought she'd suitably answered his parents' many questions. She was too shy to meet Vinod's eyes again.

A couple of weeks went by, with Jacinta on tenterhooks the whole time. Then, one evening, when they were reciting the rosary before supper, the dogs started barking furiously outside. Jacinta stopped praying and waited—something she never normally did. Rosary time was sacred. No distractions, however urgent, were entertained. There was a knock on the door. They all looked at each other. Nobody visited this late at night unless it was bad news. Before Jacinta could open the door, they heard Aunt Winnie's familiar voice, 'It's only me. I am sorry I came so late, but I just heard.'

Jacinta opened the door, steady and calm as usual, only her eyes betraying her anxiety. Before the door was fully open, Aunt Winnie had managed to squeeze her substantial girth inside, and was dancing around the room, clapping her hands and squealing like a schoolgirl. 'They said yes, Jacinta, they said yes! There's going to be a wedding here soon. All your worries are over. Shirin is getting married.'

It was when Shirin heard her name that it hit her, and she had to sit down as she was suddenly finding it hard to breathe, as if it was she who had been dancing around the room and not Aunt Winnie. Vinod, the man with the kind eyes and the nice smile, had said yes.

Her mother was saying, 'He's not the most handsome of men…'

'What do you mean, Jacinta? First you worry that she will never get married and then when someone agrees, you find fault. Does it matter? They live in Bangalore. They have their own business. And with Shirin…'

Shirin knew Aunt Winnie had been about to say, '… you can't be picky; it's not as if she has had twenty offers for her hand.' She was grateful Aunt Winnie stopped when she did. Some of the other aunts wouldn't have.

'And his brother. I would have liked to have seen him.'

'He had to stay behind, look after the business. With a family-run business, everyone can't just traipse away leaving it unattended, you know. Anyway, you will have plenty of opportunity to see him. They have invited you over next week.'

'What? Really? It's happening so fast.' And her mother smiled. One of those rare open-mouthed smiles Shirin treasured.

Had she heard right? Was she going to Bangalore next week to Vinod's house? She would diet all week, eat nothing. She would not have any supper after rosary even though Madhu had made chicken sukka and spicy fried squid because her Da, Anita and Deepak were all home for the holidays. She still couldn't believe it. She, dumpy, dark-complexioned Shirin, was no longer destined to be an Old Maid. She was getting married...

❊ ❊ ❊

Over the years, living in the UK, Shirin had learnt many things. When they first met her, most people asked, 'Where are you from originally?' Her accent was a dead giveaway.

Once they got to know her a bit, the women always asked, 'How did you and your husband meet?'

Shirin learnt to say, 'Through mutual friends'—the answer she gave Jane every year when she asked the same question of her at the Christmas table, after the champagne toast and pulling of the crackers, in front of all the guests.

Every year Jane waited, hoping Shirin would say more; reveal what she had said the first time, when she didn't know any better. 'We had an arranged marriage.' Afterwards, there was silence. Silverware had stopped clinking. People had stared at her, the paper hats on their heads clashing with their party clothes. The woman on Shirin's left had broken the silence, reaching across and touching Shirin lightly on the arm. 'Oh, my darling. We're so sorry for you.'

She had sneaked a glance at Vinod sitting at the other end of the table. He'd given her a little smile.

'We're happy together,' she'd said with more conviction than she felt. Happiness, of a sort. Achieved at great cost.

❅ ❅ ❅

Shirin dreamt of the third suitor who had come to see her. He asked question after question. 'You have big hips. Do they run in the family?' 'Do you wear contact lenses?' 'What is that scar on your knee?' The suitor was short, squat and he stank. The sour, rank stench of alcohol. He loomed above her, shouting out the questions, not waiting for her answers. She clapped her hands on her ears; she shook her head from side to side. He kept on going. She woke up screaming, 'Stop. Please Stop.' And she was in Vinod's arms, being enveloped by his familiar smell: sweat and a hint of musk. 'Shh... Shonu. It's okay.' And she thought, as she faded into sleep, *The right suitor picked me.* The Eyes pounced from behind closed eyelids. 'Boo.' It was a long night.

There was no email from Anita the next morning. She told herself she hadn't been expecting it. She told herself it was okay. She told herself it had been a bad idea to try and contact them anyway. She thought of Vinod, homesick but staying here, with her. She called her counsellor and booked an appointment—she got one for the next day; there had been a cancellation. She thought of *her. Reena.* And the ache that was always there ballooned, all-consuming.

Running. Bare feet flying on blistering tarmac. Horns blaring. The damning screech of brakes. Chaos. Waking up in hospital groggy, haunted by Eyes. My baby. Where's my baby?

And as Rob approached her desk with news of a major issue that needed immediate attention, she made up her mind. *I'll call Deepak. I need to see her.*

CHAPTER TWENTY
Navarathna Super Deluxe

'Mum, I don't want to have an arranged marriage,' Reena announced the next morning at breakfast. She had spent the previous night tossing and turning, nightmares about having her picture taken, her CV bandied about and her parents worrying about getting her married haranguing her. And, she figured, if she prepared her parents now, they wouldn't disown her later, if she ended up choosing someone they didn't like. *Stop thinking like that. For one, you don't know for sure if that's what happened. And, two, your mum*—a quick glance at Preeti who was adding bruised cardamom pods and thumb-sized pieces of cinnamon bark and ginger to the pot of tea boiling on the stove—*is not like Mai, obsessed with status. Your mum has refused to employ a servant despite repeated barbs from Mrs. Gupta and her posh—or so she thinks—friends. She will stand up to your dad if he insists on arranging your marriage.*

Her dad had already left for work. Aunt Anita was reading the celebrity news supplement of the *Bangalore Times* while munching on a piece of toast. On hearing

Reena's statement, she stopped mid-crunch and stared. Reena refused to catch her eye.

Preeti laughed, set Reena's glass of milk next to her plate and cupped her face in her hands. 'What's brought this on, eh?' She bent down and kissed the tip of Reena's nose. 'Do you like some boy, is that it?'

'*No*,' Reena said, pulling away, disgusted.

'You have many years to go yet before even thinking of marriage, Rinu. And anyway, your dad and I had an arranged marriage. And it's worked out fine. See.'

'But I don't want to.' She still would not meet Aunt Anita's eye.

'Okay, okay, baba. But you have to finish your studies first, get into a good college. Then, you think of marriage, yes?'

'Oh, Mum!' *Why had she ever brought this up?*

'It is some boy, I am sure,' she heard her mother whisper to Aunt Anita as she washed her hands and went to find her satchel. Her mother had never caught on that her 'whisper' was louder than her normal talking voice. 'My baby has a crush. She's growing up!'

Aunt Anita murmured something in reply.

'Bye, Mum, Bye, Aunt Anita,' Reena said, lugging her bag behind her.

'Wait. I'll walk you to the bus.' Aunt Anita stood, the newspaper rustling as she tossed it aside.

Oh, God, thought Reena, *I should have kept my mouth shut.* Even though this was a great opportunity to pursue Plan D, she did not want to talk to Aunt Anita right now. She knew her aunt had twigged onto the real reason for her making that statement at breakfast, and she did not want her confiscating the letters before she had had a chance to read all of them and copy out the bits she thought relevant. She thundered down the stairs, Aunt Anita keeping pace with difficulty.

'I didn't have any idea her letters would affect you so, Reena,' her aunt said when she finally caught up with her, panting. 'How many have you read?'

'I read the second one last night. I just...'

'Will you be okay reading the others?'

This is what she had been afraid of. 'I'll be fine.' *Why hadn't she just kept mum?* 'I won't read them late at night, that's all.'

'That's what you were doing yesterday? What about your maths test?'

'There isn't any.'

A slow smile spread across Aunt Anita's face. 'Devious. Hmm...' In the next instant, she was serious. 'Reena, arranged marriages are not all bad. Your parents love you. They will make sure they choose someone right for you...'

Reena let out an exasperated snort. 'Aunty, I...'

But Aunt Anita was no longer looking at her. Her gaze was fixed in the distance, somewhere beyond the banyan tree. Reena spotted her school bus turning off the main road into the street leading to her block of flats. 'My bus...' she began.

'I had a love marriage.' Aunt Anita's voice was soft. 'And look where it got me.'

Reena couldn't resist asking, 'Why did they shun Shirin and not you?'

Pain fled Aunt Anita's eyes, to be replaced by incomprehension. 'What do you mean?'

'I assumed, from the letters, that she eloped…'

A bark of startled laughter escaped Aunt Anita's open mouth. 'Shirin would never have run away to get married. Not her.'

First rule of detection: Don't jump to conclusions. 'Then what…'

'Your bus, Reena.'

Second rule: Don't push it. Wait for the right time and then pounce. The right time is *not* when the subject being interrogated spies the perfect getaway—the bus taking detective to school. Not for the first time, this detective wishes she wasn't constrained by the constant unbearable trials of childhood, school being the worst.

IMPORTANT UPDATE: Shirin *did not run away*. But did she still marry someone unsuitable? Tariq? Aunt Anita very cleverly did not say. Perhaps next letter provides clue? Read it this evening. [An explanatory note—This detective is writing this during her Kannada lesson, this notebook fitting comfortably inside the gigantic Kannada textbook. This detective didn't dare bring the letters to school, though she was sorely tempted because a) Aunt Anita asked her particularly to take care of them and b) what if nosy Naina found them?]

❄ ❄ ❄

She knew from the cheer that rocked the bus that Aunt Anita was waiting for her, even before she looked out the window. Aunt Anita stood at the bottom of the steps, her arms open wide. An invitation. Reena stepped into them. Aunt Anita twirled as if they were a couple in a ballroom. The boys hooted and cheered.

'Have you made up with Uncle Uttam?' Reena asked.

For a brief moment Aunt Anita's face fell. Then she resumed her dancing, Reena still cocooned in her arms. Even though she was flushed with embarrassment, Reena had to admit it felt nice.

'Why are you so happy, Aunt Anu?' she couldn't help but ask.

'Oh, just an email I received,' Aunt Anita's voice: too casual. As though if she said anything more it would explode with joy.

'And? From?'

With her finger, Aunt Anita tapped the tip of Reena's nose. 'Curious, are we?' And then, the joy bursting through, 'It's all such a coincidence, Reena.'

'What?'

'I'll tell you. Soon. I promise. As soon as I get a reply.'

'Oh, Aunty, that's not fair…'

'I know.' And with a kiss on the tip of her nose, 'You have to learn to be patient.'

'I hate adults. Always giving advice. Never sticking to…' Huffing, she stormed to her room for the second time in two consecutive days, shut the door and, ignoring her mother: 'What's the matter now?!' opened Shirin's third—hefty—letter.

A thought occurred to her as she read, 'Dearest Anu,' and she stopped short. The reason for Aunt Anita's mysterious joy. It wasn't the obvious: Uncle Uttam calling to make up. So… could it be? She tried to recall precisely what Aunt Anita had said. Something about a) an email and b) a coincidence. Was it possible that the email was from Aunt Shirin? What was it Aunt Anita had said? 'I'll tell you as soon as I get a reply.' Was she waiting on Aunt Shirin's permission to tell her, Reena, all? Or was Reena jumping the gun? *I'll try and get it out of Aunt Anita.* Heart thudding with excitement, she walked to the door of her room. Voices. Her mother: 'Hormones kicking in, that's what it is.' No. She was better off staying in her room. *I hope she replies now, if it is her, and I'm sure it is. Who else could it be?*

IMPORTANT NOTE: This detective thinks there has been a breakthrough in the case. <u>That Shirin has corresponded with Anita via email.</u> Watch this space.

Extracts from letter 3:

1) Subject breaks up with Tariq:

> Anu, it was wonderful to see you at Christmas. You have changed, you know. You have gained a new sophistication and that makes you seem more beautiful somehow—if that is possible. I saw a different side to you this time. I saw you in love. Throughout your holiday (how odd that from now on, your childhood home is a place you come to on holiday!), you looked a little lost, as if you had misplaced something and were looking for it.

I am glad you were there when Aunt Winnie came with the amazing news that Vinod has agreed to marry me. Did you see Ma's face light up? I've never seen her so happy, so relieved. For that reason above all else, I am pleased to be marrying Vinod.

The night before you left, when you urged me to run away with Tariq—'Follow your heart for once, Shirin!'—I couldn't reply. 'You're too sensible, too duty-bound,' you said, exasperated by my silence. I've always been more eloquent on paper than in person, so I'll try and explain now. I think I love Tariq, but I'm not in love with him, the way you are with Uttam. (Yes, I pinched that line from one of my books, but it does explain how I feel. I've had plenty of time to analyse my feelings, especially after seeing you, hearing you talk about your Uttam.) That is why I will not run away with Tariq. When the rejections from suitors were coming in droves, I was tempted to take up Tariq's offer. And then, I asked myself, would it be worth being disowned by my family, causing scandal, being responsible for you not having any suitors because you belonged to a disgraced family? Could I live with the guilt? And would it be fair on Tariq if I ran away with him not so much because I loved him but because of my situation?

The day after it all got confirmed and Ma sat me down and told me I could finish my degree after marriage if Vinod wanted me to, but for now I was stopping college and concentrating on preparations for the wedding, I saw Tariq for the last time. He knew our story had a time limit, a predestined ending. He had always known. We were standing under the banyan tree by the bus stop. He touched my hand as the bus came and the conductor hopped off with an ear-splitting whistle. 'Be happy,' he said. I watched him through the back window: the branches of the banyan tree sweeping the ground around him, his arm raised, palm outwards as if in surrender, until the bus turned a corner, the conductor muttering something in Tulu about foolish young love as I sniffed and accepted my ticket.

I miss him.

NOTES: A thought just occurred to this detective: a possibility which might just be the truth and explain Mai's shunning of Shirin. A possibility that this detective does not want to contemplate as she has grown to like Shirin. Very much. But a good detective considers *everything*. So here goes: Did Shirin find love—Aunt Anita and Uncle Uttam kind of love—after her marriage, with someone *other than her husband*? Or perhaps she discovered that she missed Tariq too much and ran away with him *after marriage?*

2) This extract describes Shirin's first visit to her future in-laws' house:

We set off in Navarathna Travels—*Super Deluxe*—the Friday after you left. Madhu cooked jackfruit poli and patholi; Ma bought chakulis, halwa, holige and chikki from Best Bakery in Pelam: gifts for the future in-laws. We said the rosary and then Valli came in his rickshaw and took us to the bus stop in Mirakatte. Madhu held me close and whispered in my ear, 'It will be okay,' her breath tickling my cheek. As we waited for the bus, everybody in Taipur gathered to wish us luck. And I mean everybody. At half past nine in the night! Normally they would have been in bed, snoring. I suppose it is a big event, someone from Taipur marrying into the city. When the bus finally arrived, forty-five minutes late—all the well-wishers having settled down for an impromptu picnic right there in the mud, with cashew feni from the arrack shop and egg bhurji, masala puri and chilli-coated deep-fried sardines from the cart by Sanjeev medicals—we found our seats, Ma stowed our bag overhead and we sat down. But the bus didn't move. We waited. Finally, the bus driver turned, yelling down the aisle to us, waking snoozing passengers, 'There are people outside waiting to wave goodbye.' I swear,

Anu, it was like we were going to the moon. Anyway, Ma pushed the curtains aside, pressed her face to the window, waved. The whole village waved back. Then, and only then, did we set off, to the kind of merry cheer only capable of people drunk on cashew liquor.

Once we left Taipur behind, Ma patted my hand. 'Sleep,' she said. 'You don't want bags under your eyes tomorrow.' She closed her eyes and was snoring in two ticks. I looked out at the silhouettes of coconut trees, the twinkling lights punctuating the darkness, the silvery wink of shadowy rivers rippling in moonlight and I wondered what the morrow would bring.

We reached Majestic bus station at dawn. Ma shook me awake. For a moment, I wondered where I was. Then I looked out the window, saw the rows and rows of buses; beggar boys darting among them jangling tin cups of coins, identical haggard expressions on their faces; women sweeping dusty platforms, sari ends tucked into hips; hawkers peddling wares—and I knew. We took the number 276 bus from Majestic to Malleshwaram and an auto from there to Vinod's house. His house is on the corner, at the junction of two dusty, unpaved streets. There are houses on all sides and a makeshift temple—a deity carved into a brick wall, hidden by wilting garlands of flowers attracting bees and flies—opposite. Boys play gulli danda and lagori on the road; dogs and cows wander; an old lady sells peanuts in tiny paper cones, '*Piping hot, one rupee only*'; a drunk staggers along, singing off tune at the top of his voice, the boys giving him a wide berth; a man sits just outside the gate to Vinod's house, aligning spokes on a bicycle tyre, a mountain of similar tyres, rubber deflated like lips caught in a permanent sneer, stacked beside him.

As our rickshaw pulled up, the boys dispersed, the drunk urinated into the ditch beside the road next to the temple, and we were surrounded, as if from nowhere, by an army of beggars—a stick-thin woman with a bedraggled child on her waist, an old man limping, a young boy, hair sticking up, shirt torn, arms extended, eyes pleading: *Amma, enadru kodi*. Vinod's father came rushing out wearing only a lungi and vest. He opened the gate, pulled us inside, waving at the beggars, 'Shoo! Shoo!'

Vinod's house has a small front courtyard, three-quarters cemented, with a washing stone and tap on one side. The tiny uncemented part serves as garden: a chikku tree, a lime tree, aboli plants. Vinod's mother welcomed us in, showed us the bathroom, urged us to freshen up. 'Then you can have breakfast and some rest. In the afternoon, all the relatives are coming to see you.' There was no sign of Vinod. As if she had heard my thoughts, Vinod's mother said, 'Vinod and Prem have gone to the factory. They'll be back for lunch.'

Their house is not as big as ours, but Ma said, after breakfast as we lay side by side on the hard bed in the unfamiliar room and tried to hear our voices above the din from outside echoing through the thin walls—an argument; children's laughter; vendors' shouts, '*Fresh vegetables, bhendi, bhaji, tendli*", '*Ripe thothapuri mangoes*' ,'*Juicy lychees*'; bhajans blaring from someone's tape-recorder—that by city standards it is huge and is worth a lot of money. 'And it is going to be your house soon, if all goes well,' Ma brushed my hair away from my face and looked at me with an expression of such tenderness, I squirreled it away in my heart to cherish when I need soothing.

I woke to Ma pulling on my shoulder, whispering urgently, 'Shirin, time to dress. The relatives have come.' I wore the orange sari; allowed Ma to pile my hair up into a bun; put kajal on my eyes. (It itches. How do you put up with it? I had to fight the urge to rub my eyes the whole time it was on.) I dutifully smiled at all the relatives, answered their many questions, tried not to notice their assessing glances, their nudges to each other when they thought we weren't looking. Then Vinod arrived. With his brother Prem.

Vinod. What can I say? I hardly got to see him much, surrounded as I was by his many relatives. But after lunch, I looked up, sought him out and found him looking right at me. He smiled. That smile, Anu. It lights up his face. Transforms him. I blushed. I was too shy to look at him again.

There was just one thing that made me uneasy. While we were eating, I felt hot breath on my sari blouse, my back. I turned. Prem was walking away. He half turned, smirked, but did not meet my gaze. I swear he was right behind me, very close. Why? I did not see him again. It was like he'd disappeared. His parents did not mention him or comment on his absence. Neither did Vinod. But then, the house was chock-full of relatives. Perhaps that was the reason. Still, it was odd. If Deepak disappeared in the middle of a family gathering, Ma would notice, surely. Or at least one of us would. But it was as if Prem vanished into thin air. I might be making a mountain out of a molehill, but one thing is for certain: I am not sure of Prem. He's furtive; doesn't meet anybody's eye. And there's something about him...

I told Ma that later, in the evening, as we finally sank onto our seats in the Navarathna Super

Deluxe for the journey home. Worry lines appeared around her eyes. 'I know. I wasn't sure of him, either. But the rest of the family seems nice.' She turned to me, held my face in her hands, looked into my eyes. I mean, this is Ma, Anu. She has never done this to me before—at least, not that I remember. 'You are marrying Vinod,' she said. 'And, Shirin, I talked with him today, a lot. I wouldn't want my daughter to marry just anyone.' Yes. She said that. 'He's kind. A nice boy. He will look after you.' And I thought: I have done the right thing, not running away with Tariq. It hurts, Anu, to think about him, but I'm sure it will get better with time. He appears in my dreams and I wake up guilty that I am thinking of him when I am marrying Vinod. I will Vinod's kind face to appear in my dreams instead. It hasn't happened as yet. But soon, perhaps.

NOTES: This detective's hand aches from copying out this extract. She was sorely tempted to shorten it, but dedication is the hallmark of a good detective and so she persevered. Also, this extract raises another possibility: Vinod's brother, Prem. Shirin is unsure of him. Does he have anything to do with what happened? Find out.

Also, on a personal note, this detective thinks Shirin is such a lemon. Why would anyone give

up a man who loves them and subject themselves
to this? This detective wants to grab Shirin, shake
some sense into her.

Reena took a long time to fall asleep that night, her mind
full of questions and possibilities. Aunt Anita had maintained her unusually ecstatic mood all through dinner.
Reena managed to corner her just before she went to bed,
on the pretext of saying goodnight. Like all good detectives, she went straight for the jugular, carefully watching
Aunt Anita's reaction. 'The email was from Aunt Shirin,
wasn't it?'

Aunt Anita laughed, a gushing waterfall. 'You really are
something, Miss Reena Diaz. Goodnight.'

'Oh, Aunty…'

'And short-tempered with it. You'll know tomorrow. If
there is a reply.' She folded her hands as if in prayer. 'Let's
hope so. Sweet Dreams.'

When Reena finally fell asleep she dreamt. Of marriages and love and furtive men who would not meet one's
eye. Of trips to a part of Bangalore alien to her and yet
strangely familiar, populated with beggar boys and deities
peeking from behind fading garlands. Of a girl with pigtails and a face that Reena shared, who played hopscotch
on the road kicking up clouds of dust and who begged
Reena to please, please, bring her home…

CHAPTER TWENTY-ONE
Dog-Eared Diary

Mid-afternoon, just as she was in the middle of fixing another code five (extremely urgent) issue which had brought testing to a standstill—the day seemed to be filled with code fives—a message popped up on her screen with a ping. A smiley face. 'You've got mail.' She ignored it, distracted, her mind on the problem before her. It was only after she had sorted it out and testing had resumed that she checked her Outlook. And there it was.

From Anita_Sinha@FaceofIndia.com. Subject: Oh, my God, I cannot believe it!!!

She laughed out loud. Typical Anita. *Neither can I, Anu.* She clicked on it. A long letter. From her sister, who hated writing, who thought writing letters was a waste of time spent living: 'Come, let's go pick water lilies. Press them on a page and send them to Da instead of writing to him. He'll like that.'

Her heart singing, she started to read:

Dearest Shirin,

I cannot believe it! It's you. After all these years. Imagine my surprise when, after a long break—I have been off work, long story, will explain later— decided to check my mail on the off chance there was something from Uttam. Okay, there it is. I can't go two sentences without bringing him up...

Shirin grinned. It was like talking to her sister; her letter just as messy as her thoughts, jumping all over the place. Her Anu hadn't changed one bit.

Uttam and I have split up. I am staying at Deepak's for now.

Staying at Deepak's? Shirin's heart jumped.

It's been a week since we split up and I have almost forgotten what we argued about. It was a bad one. We both said things we shouldn't have. I was hoping he would call me, ask me to come back. I miss him, Shirin. There I go again, slipping so easily into little-sister mode, offloading my problems on you. Shirin, I've missed you so much. I have so many things to tell you. But most of all, I want to say sorry. I'm sorry, Shirin, for abandoning you. For not keeping in touch, for going along with Ma and Deepak, for shunning you. I still talk to you, you know, mostly, I have to admit, when the going gets tough. At night, into my pillow, I talk, imagining it to be you. Uttam caught me once. He laughed. He doesn't understand this bond between sisters. It's been so hard without you, like missing a limb. But it must be a thousand times worse for you. I didn't have to leave everyone and everything I loved behind. And that after everything you'd been through... When I reached this new low in my life with Uttam, I came to Deepak, even though I knew he didn't approve. I wanted the comfort of

family. You didn't have that. At your darkest time, the time
when you needed us most, we reneged. I am sorry. I struck
a deal. My seventeen pieces of silver were Uttam. I wanted
him. You were the price I paid. Ironical, isn't it, that now
I've split up with him, I get an email from you?

Shirin, I have something to confess, to get off my chest
before writing anything further. And I will understand
if I never get another email from you, if, after hearing
what I have to say, you decide never to contact me, talk
to me again. Here goes: Shirin, I used you. Shamelessly.
I announced I was marrying Uttam, just after everything
happened with you... I timed it just right. After what
happened with you, what I was doing didn't seem quite so
bad in Ma's eyes. It didn't have the same devastating im-
pact as it would have done before... And of course I bargained. I wanted to get in touch with you, not go along
with them. But it was you or Uttam... And I chose him.

I did one thing, though, my little rebellion. I changed
my name to Sinha. I did not want to be associated with
the Taipur Diazes any more. Stuff their status and their
standing in Taipur society...

All these years, one thought has been hounding me.
If it had been you in my situation, you would <u>not</u> have
done the same, made the choice I did. Chosen your love
over your sister. You were always the bigger person, Shirin. Shouldering the blame when I did something wrong.
Carrying my crosses for me.

Over the years, I've wanted to get in touch countless
times. And every time, Ma's face swam before me, distort-

ed, truly ugly as she snipped off your beautiful hair, that hair I have always admired and envied. And I became, once again, that girl cowering behind Madhu, that girl who couldn't stand up for her sister... What if I got in touch and you didn't want to talk to me? I could understand after what I did.

I brought it up with Deepak once. You'd been gone six years and the pain of losing you had morphed into a dull ache. I was flying to London on a shoot and I was determined to look you up, bring you home...

You were here, Anu? So close.

Deepak blustered and pontificated with his, 'People in Taipur have been looking up to the Diaz family for generations,' and, 'I will not allow the family name to be sullied even though you tried your best with Uttam. When are you going to have a child? People are talking...' I lost my temper. 'We are living in the twenty-first century, not the middle ages!' I yelled. 'How can you live with what we've done, Deepak? I'm finding her and bringing her back.' 'Reena,' was all he said. 'Think of what this would do to her. She is happy, settled. It's what Shirin wanted.' There was vulnerability in his face, and fear. He loves her, Shirin, more than he's loved anyone, more even than his love of status and family name. For all his faults, he's a good dad. You chose well.

I didn't come to London in the end. The shoot got cancelled. I think I was glad I didn't have to make the choice, didn't have to be proactive. I could preserve the status quo but still console myself if I tried.

You once told me you admired my 'devil may care' courage. What courage does it take to barter your sister for your love? What courage does it take to come up with excuses not to do the one thing that would make a difference? You are the brave one, Shirin, the truly courageous one. Taking all that happened on the chin. Doing what you had to for Reena.

In your email, you said, 'If you want to talk...' It should be the other way around. I cannot believe you still want to talk to me. After what I did. Thank you.

Shirin, your email, it came in the wake of me being grilled by an eleven-year-old on how I could possibly abandon my sister, how I could wipe her out of my life. Yes, I am talking about Reena. She's grown into a lovely young girl—mature, sensible, kind. When I look at her, I feel broody. I who have always maintained I am not maternal. She's been asking me about you. She found that photograph of us taken on your twelfth birthday, the one where we had to pose in Ashok's studio for what felt like hours and I started to cry and had to be consoled by promise of mango ice cream after—if I smiled. Remember? Madhu had saved it. Reena doesn't know much, only that you are her aunt. She's angry on your behalf with all of us. As she should be. What we did, are still doing, is disgraceful. I gave her the letters you wrote to me while I was away at college. Hope that is okay. I wanted her to get to know you first, before easing her into...

She looks just like you.

Shall I tell her?

Shirin, I have so much more to say. But I will end for now with this: Come home. This has gone on long enough. Ma and Deepak can be talked around. Please come home.

Lots and lots of love (remember how we used to sign off letters to Da this way? Only Ma made us add, 'Craving your blessings.' Bleugh.).

Anu xxx

'Shirin.' She was vaguely aware of arms around her. Kate. She pointed to the screen. 'Read,' she mouthed.

'Are you sure?'

'Yes.'

Afterwards, Kate locked Shirin's computer. 'Come outside for a bit.' Kate led her to the smokers' corner. 'Hay fever,' Shirin explained, sniffing, to Jane, Justine and Rob who were blowing smoke rings and laughing about something. In silent agreement, she and Kate chose the bench furthest from the door, tucked into the rose bushes. 'Hay fever in October? What was I thinking?'

'You weren't. Sod it. They weren't listening anyway. Here. Have a good cry,' Kate said, handing Shirin a pack of Kleenex.

Shirin blew her nose, crumpled the tissue in her fingers. 'She's found out about me. She's angry on my behalf.' Through her tears she smiled. And then she was laughing, so hard she had to gasp for breath.

Kate laughed along with her.

'When I think of going home,' she said, sniffing, 'I think of my mother…' Her ma's face. Closed. Turning away. *You are dead to me.* A memory: reading her mother's diary, hungrily lapping up her mother's words, the cold seeping in through the floorboards and settling in her bones...

Just before her marriage, when she was preparing to leave her childhood home, Shirin discovered her mother's diary—a worn hardbound notebook, a posy of faded pink carnations adorning the front with 'JACINTA MACHADO' written in bold capitals below—lurking among her mother's best saris at the back of the Godrej wardrobe. It felt like a gift, at an emotional time. Shirin had had no idea that her mother kept diaries. At last, an insight into her mother's mind. Without pausing to question whether what she was doing was right, Shirin packed the diary.

She didn't have time to read it. Preparations for her wedding were under way; there was so much to do. She couldn't read it immediately after her wedding either. But she hid it among her belongings, savouring this secret from home, looking at her mother's handwriting, conjuring her up when homesickness threatened; and waited for the right moment to read it. It never came. Events took over and after *it* happened, Shirin was too depressed to care or even remember that she had something of her mother's.

And then one gloomy, drizzle-soaked autumn morning, their first week in the UK, Shirin was pacing aimlessly between cardboard boxes that Vinod was in the process of unpacking, when she saw something disturbingly familiar poking out of one of them. Curious, she pulled it out. And found herself staring at her mother's busy, untidy handwriting, so unlike Jacinta's calm, reserved exterior. She stopped pacing, plonked herself down on the chilly wooden floor, and, one finger unconsciously caressing the pages her mother had once touched, where her aloof mother had poured out her feelings, she started to read.

That overcast wintry day, sitting among the cardboard boxes which were all she and Vinod had of the past they had left behind, with her mother's diary on her lap, something had unfurled in the cold emptiness that had settled within Shirin since *it* happened. She had been wanted. Her mother had wanted her. This diary was proof. Her mother's voice described the joy she felt on discovering she was pregnant, her excitement on having a sibling for Deepak, but stopped right before Shirin's birth. She'd flicked through the few remaining pages, feeling cheated, wanting to read more, to find out how her mother had felt when she was born: a girl; dark-skinned; plump.

'How could she do what she did, Kate?' Jacinta's face the last time she'd seen her swam before her eyes. That day, after reading the diary, she'd tucked it carefully back into the box, feeling bereft, chilled to the bone. She'd put on another coat, pulled the hood over her head, left the apartment and walked, as she had done every day since she and Vinod arrived in the UK, as if the very act of walking would erase her mistakes and the recent past... 'For a long time, I could not forgive myself for what I did. But she's my mother... Mothers forgive, don't they? If Reena had been in my situation, God forbid, I would have believed her, been there for her...'

'Shirin...'

'One day, when I was about eight I think, Ma took the three of us by bus to Mangalore. I got off at the wrong stop. As the bus pulled away with her in it and me standing outside, I saw her face. And I carried her expression of pure panic with me for days, savouring it, like a gift. That was the first time I knew, *really* knew that my ma loved me...' She paused, took a breath. 'All my life I've tried to please her, to be worthy of her. When I married the man she chose for me, I thought I had succeeded. She was happy, proud even. Of me. And then...' Her mother's face. Wounded. Ashamed.

'This is about Reena, too, Shirin.' Kate's voice was soft.

'Oh, Kate. Why do you think I did what I did? That horrible choice I made. It is about Reena, but it is and always has been about Ma... How can I ask Reena to invite me into her life, to accept me, if my own mother cannot forgive me?'

❊ ❊ ❊

She forwarded Vinod Anita's email and he called right back.

'You read it?' she asked.

'Yes.' Joy in his voice, dancing down the phone line.

'Anita said she looks just like me.'

'She's beautiful, then.' And, a heartbeat later, 'We can go home now, Shonu.'

Chappals hitting feet. Like slaps. Hard. Urgent. Fetid rank breaths. Gaining. A pair of eyes, empty, menacing.

She willed them away. They went. Vinod's face puckered in pain: 'I miss them.'

She took a deep breath. 'Yes. Once Anu has talked to Ma and Deepak and Preeti. And prepared Reena.'

'Sounds to me like she's already made up her mind about you. She's on your side, giving her aunt a piece of her mind.'

She laughed along with Vinod, identifying the emotion ballooning in her chest as pride. 'Yes. That she is.'

CHAPTER TWENTY-TWO
Destined for Greatness

'So, is she starring in a film, then, your aunt?' Murli asked, grinning. Since Aunt Anita's arrival, Reena'd hardly had time to see him, but now they were sitting in their usual spot by the pool, Murli having escaped his chores for a few minutes.

It was a sunny Saturday. Birds chirped, women gossiped, sitting or standing hunched in little groups outside their flats. Chattering monkeys in bold gangs of twos and threes hopped from the roof of one building to the other, trying to enter flats through windows left inadvertently open, drawn by the promise of food, scents of cooking. One sat right across from Reena, black lips on a hairy brown face stretched in a smirk, munching on a chapatti, feeding bits to the baby straddled across its stomach. The two girls were on the swings again, actually swinging this time, heads thrown back, pig-tails flying. Upstairs in their flat, Reena's dad worked. Aunt Anita and Preeti were shopping. They had asked if Reena wanted to come but she'd declined, saying she'd rather read a book. 'Just like your Aunt Shirin,' Aunt Anita had whispered in her ear, and, 'No reply yet.' The fact that she said the two together: Aunt Shirin and reply, in the same sentence, Reena took to be confirmation that the email had been from Aunt Shirin. It was only a matter of time before Reena found out the truth. 'She'll be back soon. I know it,' Madhu had said last month. Reena's heart jumped at the thought of meeting this mythical person she had grown to like and even perhaps love, without ever having met her... The girl from her dream rose before her eyes. *Bring me home, please.* She blinked.

'Reena?'

Murli was waiting for a reply. What had they been talking about? 'The sunglasses were just a fad. She's not acting in any movie, as far as I know.'

Murli looked disappointed. 'Oh, well, I will get her autograph for my daughter, just in case.'

'How are things in your village?'

Murli smiled again, a wide grin. 'The monsoons arrived on Wednesday. Not a moment too late. It hasn't stopped raining since. See, your prayers worked.'

'I'm glad.'

The girls stopped swinging, jumped off.

'So how long is she staying, then? Your aunt?'

'A while, I think. She wants a break from everything.'

Murli nodded. 'These posh people like your aunt, they tire easily. Not used to hard work, see,' he said wisely.

Reena threw a pebble in the pool and they both watched it ripple.

'So did you find out any more about your missing aunt?'

Missing aunt. 'Don't call her that, Murli. It... sends shivers down my spine. Her name is Shirin.'

'Shirin.' Murli rolled the word around on his tongue, dragging it into three syllables. 'Unusual name.'

Should she tell him about the letters? She had been carrying the secret around too long. 'Aunt Anita gave me letters to read.'

'Letters?'

'Aunt Shirin wrote to her.' Calling her 'Aunt Shirin' still felt odd. 'Before it all happened. Whatever it was that happened to make them wipe her out of their lives.' She looked up to the open window of her flat, lowered her voice to a whisper. 'Aunt Anita won't tell me what happened. Says it's for the best. *I hate it.*' Reena pulled out clumps of grass from beside where she was sitting, flung them hard. They did not go far like the pebble, just flopped down weakly next to her outstretched hand.

The girls came and sat by the pool close to where Reena and Murli were sitting. They started whispering something, their heads close together.

'Every family has secrets, Reena,' Murli's voice was soft, 'and they're there for a reason.'

'What could she possibly have done...?'

'Maybe you should listen to what everyone says. Perhaps unearthing this will do more harm than good.'

'Oh, Murli, not you too.' Reena stood up, started stomping towards the stairs.

'Wait.' He caught up with her, held her hand. 'I'm just saying... You might get hurt, Reena. Have you thought that they might all be protecting you?'

She stared at him, puzzled. 'Why do you think that, Murli?'

'I don't know.' He chewed his bottom lip. 'I just thought it could be a reason, is all. Don't look so worried. When did all this happen, with your aunt, with... Shirin?'

What was it Madhu had said? 'Eleven years ago.'

'Before you were born then.'

'When I was a baby. I just turned eleven, Murli.'

For a brief moment, something flitted across Murli's face: an expression she had never seen before. Then it was gone.

'Anyway, it's nothing to do with you. Forget what I said. I have to go back. *She'll* be wanting her food.'

She glanced towards the pool. The girls were watching them curiously. When she met their gaze, they looked away. *I am Super Sleuth Reena Diaz. I refuse to be invisible anymore.* She retraced her steps, started walking towards them. She turned once and saw Murli give her a thumbs up and flash his yellow-toothed grin before dashing up the stairs. *The worst they'll do is ignore you. Well, Aunt Shirin has been ignored for eleven years. You can do this, Super Sleuth.*

'Hi,' she said, as she drew level with them. 'I'm Reena. I live at number 26.'

Two pairs of brown eyes staring at her.

She kept her smile fixed.

Then, 'That's your flat isn't it?' said one of the girls, just as a monkey sneaked in through the open window.

'Uh-oh,' Reena said. 'Mum did ask Dad to keep the windows closed.'

The girls laughed, and patted the space beside them. 'Come, sit. We watched you skim that pebble before. Can you teach us how?'

She spent the rest of the morning playing with the girls, Geeta and Gowri. She taught them how to skim stones, and after, they invited her back to their flat to meet other girls from the complex, including the snooty one from number 36, who wasn't snooty at all, only short-sighted and too vain to wear glasses. It turned out that her new friends were in awe of her friendship with Murli, that *they* had been afraid to talk to *her,* had thought *she* was superior. How could she have got so many things wrong? She mused as she walked home, unable to ignore her growling stomach any longer. On Monday, she resolved, she would talk to Divya; march right up to her and ask her if she wanted to be friends again. Perhaps Divya was afraid to take the first step and wanted Reena to instigate the conversation. She had caught Divya looking her way a few times, but she had always looked away when Reena met her gaze. *I do not want to ignore her for eleven years like my family have done with Aunt Shirin,* she thought. She felt courageous, different, brimming with energy. Was this how it felt to be a grown-up?

❋ ❋ ❋

Reena sat in the kitchen watching her mum grind red chillies, coriander seeds, cumin seeds, turmeric and vinegar to a paste in the new mixer she'd purchased in the Diwali sales.

Her dad had locked himself in the bedroom; he was on an important conference call. Aunt Anita was having her hour-long cleansing and creaming session in the bathroom. There was still no reply—Aunt Anita had checked once when she returned from the shopping trip, and once before she went to have her bath. Reena knew Aunt Anita was disappointed. The euphoria of the day before had gradually dissipated and the sunglasses had reappeared.

Reena hugged the secret of her new friends close, but now that the buzz of talking to them, playing with them, had settled, Murli's comment played on her mind.

'I got such fresh mackerel from that Arun in the Mangalore shop, Rinu. He always saves the best ones for me. They must have been caught just this morning,' Preeti said as she marinated the mackerel pieces in the red paste making sure they were completely covered and no skin peeked through. 'I bet you, today, my fish fry will be better than Madhu's.'

The warning Murli had given that morning had made Reena alternately worried and scared. Whatever had happened with Aunt Shirin had happened eleven years ago, right around the time she was born. Why had she not thought of this before? What sort of a detective was she?

Progress so far: Murli (this detective's friend and confidante: think Doctor Watson to Sherlock Holmes) thinks that the reason nobody is willing to say anything about the rift is because they are protecting this detective. Could this be the case?

Reena stopped writing and sighed deeply. Her mother looked up, 'What's the matter, Rinu?'

'Mum, why am I an only child? Why don't I have any siblings?' She had always asked for more siblings; it had never before occurred to her to ask why she was an only child.

Her mother came up to her, squatted in front of her, 'Look at me,' she said. Reena recoiled from the vinegary smell on her mother's hands. The spices made her eyes water. Her mother yelled, 'Wait!' ran to the kitchen tap as fast as her limp would allow, washed her hands, dried them on her salwar bottoms and pulled Reena onto her lap, cradling her in her arms. 'Don't cry, Rinu. Whatever is the matter? Why this question all of a sudden?'

She was tempted to curl up in her mother's arms and forget about everything: Aunt Shirin, Murli's words. Murli's words. Reena sniffed, buried her face in her mother's shoulder.

Her mother patted her back gently, then pulled her up. 'Come with me.' She led her to the full-length mirror in the guest bedroom—Aunt Anita's room—as the main bedroom was out of bounds; they could hear Deepak pacing behind the door, snatches of what he was saying: '...ready for testing... first week of November...' Reena sneaked a glance at the bathroom. Still safely locked. She could hear the shower running. What had got into her?

'There. Look at you. Do you see what I see?'

Reena squinted, blinked. Where was her mother going with this? She saw a plump, dark-skinned girl almost as tall as her petite mother. She saw another girl, one in pigtails and old-fashioned churidars, wanting Tariq of the beautiful eyes but willing to marry anyone if it made her mother happy.

Preeti cupped her face with her palm, traced her features with her fingers. 'You are perfect, Rinu. Our special miracle. And not only are you beautiful outside, you are also loving, kind. You have a beautiful heart.' Preeti pulled Reena close into a tight embrace and Reena was enveloped once more in her mother's smell: sandalwood talcum powder, sweat, spices. She sneezed. Preeti held her tighter, whispered, 'Ever since I was little, my dream was to get married, have lots of children. Then God gave me you. Just you. And in you, he gave me everything I had ever hoped for in a child. You were... you *are* perfect. You were enough.' She looked at Reena quizzically, making sure she was fine. 'Are you okay now?'

No, Mum. I want to know how I am connected with Aunt Shirin's banishment. She nodded.

'It's the start of puberty. That's what's causing all these mood swings,' her mother said, smiling fondly at her. 'I have to go cook. Your poor dad needs some sustenance after that phone call that's been going on forever. Day off, he says. What day off? By the way, don't you have any homework to do?' A twinkle in her eyes.

'I'm just going...' As Reena passed the bathroom, it opened. Aunt Anita emerged in a cloud of steam, a towel wrapped around her head, her face devoid of makeup. 'Still no reply,' she mouthed when she saw Reena. She looked stunning. Like a film star—the steamed-up bathroom her stage.

Reena sat on her bed and took out Aunt Shirin's next letter—a thick one. She wondered would things have been different if Shirin had had someone like Preeti for her ma. She thought of Mai, frail frame resting against the front door of the house in Taipur, looking into her eyes, 'Come back to visit your Mai soon, you hear?' and felt guilty. She sighed, crossed her legs, leaned against the pillows and began to read.

Extract from letter 4:

This letter is composed of solely one extract in which Shirin describes preparations for her wedding:

And so, the wedding date is set. Ma is busy writing out invitations. We have to personally deliver them to every single guest, she tells me, even if they live on the other side of Mangalore. I still cannot fully believe it, Anu—that I am getting married to a man I hardly know. I look at it, written down here, and I think, surely not. And of all the many suitors, I am glad it is Vinod who's said yes. Not that I got to talk to him or anything, but the fleeting impression of him that I had was a favourable one. I don't know how I'll feel the next time I see him, at the engagement—*my engagement*—next month. It's all happening so fast.

Ma is going about doing a million things at once with a fervour I have not seen in a long time. She is so wound up. Even having Da home doesn't seem to help. Guess organising a wedding does that to you. I try to keep out of the way as much as possible, but when she does corner me, I get a big lecture on how I should be happy and grateful, how my long face and moping is driving her to distraction. Then, when she runs out of steam, I get handed a list of things which are so urgent that they had to be done yesterday.

I would like to explain to her that I want to be happy. And in some ways I am. But then I realise that in a couple of months, in seventy days to be exact, I am going to have to leave my home and this village that I love and go live in the city. And what I've seen of Bangalore, I haven't been too impressed. Where are the coconut trees bowing allegiance to the wind, the wide open spaces, the verdant green fields?

I am to say goodbye to my parents and relatives, to my brother and sister, and go and live with this new family, none of whom I know. I have to follow their rules, do things their way. I have to ask their permission to visit my own parents. And Bangalore is not easily accessible. It is eight hours away by bus. There is no train connection and flights are too expensive. It won't be easy for all of you to come and see me.

And I have one secret concern, which worries me constantly: I am told I will learn to love Vinod.

I am told love will come, it will happen over time. But what if it doesn't? What if I cannot love Vinod?

And Tariq. He still visits me in my dreams. And I wake up guilty, feeling I have betrayed Vinod. And this is my other big worry: what if he haunts my dreams *after* I am married? What then?

And then there is Prem. I know I am stupid to worry about this man; he's Vinod's brother, what would he do? But the feeling I got when I saw him... And Ma feels the same. I overheard her talking to Aunt Winnie the other day. 'Winnie,' she said, 'this family, are they all what they seem?' 'Why do you ask?' Aunt Winnie said. I pictured her putting her hands on her hips like she does when she's annoyed. I was pressed against the wall in the dining room, the shadows hiding me. 'That Prem...' Ma said. Aunt Winnie clicked her tongue, 'Jessie, you are never happy unless there is something to worry about. And I don't know what you've got against that poor boy. I looked into the family and they seem all right. There is nothing there... ' 'It's just...' Ma hesitated. I pressed my ear closer. 'I don't want to give her away without knowing what I'm getting her into.' 'You know what she's getting into,' Aunt Winnie huffed, 'and it's not as if you've got a lot of choice.' That shut Ma up.

On a brighter note, Madhu has started preparations for the engagement. It will be held in the newly built hall adjacent to the church. Smells of cooking fill the house as she grinds masala and makes marinades and grates coconuts. Our freezer is already full and now she is stocking Nagappa's. Ma did mention that she was happy to hire the Konkan caterers who do the food for all local weddings and engagements. You can imagine what Madhu had to say to that!

Ma has booked rooms in the new hotel in Mirakatte for Vinod and his family to stay when they come for the engagement. They will be coming to us for breakfast before the ceremony and then we'll all go together to the church.

The wedding is taking place in Bangalore. Vinod's family has offered to organise the church and the hall for the reception and find caterers to do the food. Ma accepted gratefully as she doesn't know Bangalore at all well. Of course, she plans to travel there a couple of times before the wedding to confirm everything is to her liking. Vinod and his family have refused dowry, which is one worry off her mind. But this has made her all the more determined to have a very grand wedding, long distance notwithstanding.

The plan is that I travel to the city two nights before the wedding with Da, so I am well rested and ready for the ceremony. Vinod's family has promised to find a place for me and Da to stay. Madhu says this confirms what a wonderful, generous family they are. 'No dowry and now all this help with the wedding as well. You are so lucky, Shirin. What other family would do this?' Ma and the rest of the wedding party (that includes you and Deepak though I wish you were coming with me) will leave Taipur by hired coach the night before the wedding. I get butterflies in my stomach just thinking about it all.

Ma has insisted I wear a gown for the wedding instead of the traditional white sari. It is being made by the best dressmaker in Dommur; you know the one, 'Outfits for all Occasions' opposite the bus stop—run by the lady who learned to sew in Thailand. Ma took me there yesterday to choose the design. Between the dressmaker and her, they decided on something that will make me look thin. I know you'll want to know how the gown looks so I'll try to describe what I remember. It is the palest ivory white, with pearl beads hand-sewn around the neck, which is V-shaped. It has transparent lace sleeves and an extremely long train. I don't remember much else. I was too busy sucking in my stomach while the dressmaker was doing the fitting and the measuring. I plan to go on a diet, lose the stomach by the time the wedding comes around. *My wedding!* I meant to start the diet last week, but what with Madhu cooking for the engagement, the smells... The fitting session went on forever. I was out of breath by the end of it all, and happily agreed when Ma suggested the Masala Dosa at the little hotel opposite. I will start the diet tomorrow.

Yesterday, when we returned home after selecting the gown, Ma summoned me into the dining room. I stepped back in surprise as the entire dining table was covered with gold; rows and rows of velvet jewellery boxes in all sorts of colours, open and displaying their twinkling treasures: earrings and necklaces, bangles, bracelets and rings.

'Sit down, Shirin,' Ma looked very grave. 'This is the gold I have kept aside for you over the years.'

I nodded, awed.

'The gold will be given to you at the wedding reception in full view of all the guests, just before the ceremony where you change into your sado. Vinod's family have refused any dowry, which is magnanimous of them, but I want to make sure everyone knows that *your family* is not stingy, that we are giving *Vinod's family* gold (and a lot of it too), in lieu of dowry.' She allowed herself a small smile and added, 'Your mother-in-law has already bought the sado, the sari you will be wearing for the reception. Aunt Winnie tells me it cost Rs 15000. That will show all the relatives what a well-to-do family you are marrying into!'

I've decided I will spend my last few weeks as an unmarried woman visiting all the places in Taipur that I love and committing them to memory, while I still belong here. After my marriage, I will be an outsider visiting only during holidays or feast days—like you.

This past week, I walked to the very end of the village, to the River Varuna, with its border of coconut trees which bow down gracefully as if to drink from its water. I watched the rows and rows of chappals left by devotees outside the Hindu temple and wondered if the homeless boys who sometimes steal our chickens ever steal them, and if they do, are they punished, and if so by whom? I watched the Hindus pray with heartfelt devotion to the God of the river, and emerge from the temple munching Prasad, red Kumkum smearing their foreheads. I looked at all these people, every one of them sure of where they were headed and what they wanted, and wished I had but one ounce of their certainty about my future.

I went to the beach. I walked up to Nemar, past the big field where the Aaatas are held, and took the bus from Nemar to Doohe. Do you remember how Madhu used to take us to the beach when we were little? We would play in the sand all day, our sustenance the little picnic comprising of bhajis, masala vadais and hot sweet tea in a thermos packed lovingly by Madhu.

I managed to squeeze into the extremely crowded bus (why are buses to Doohe always so crowded?) and held on for dear life as it jolted and shuddered through the many potholes in the barely tarred road. I got off at my stop, and breathed in the salty tang of sea. 'Fresh mackerel, sardines, fat juicy prawns, crabs and squid. Come and buy, ma'am,' the fisherwomen sitting in the shelter of thali bonda trees shouted after me. I walked past them towards the wide turquoise expanse, to the wall of haphazardly placed granite rocks that the people living by the sea in their little huts have built as protection from the floods that besiege them on stormy monsoon nights. I sat on one of the rocks, looked out to the ends of the earth, and, for the first time in ages, felt at peace.

Then I took the bus back home into chaos, the kind only a household preparing for the first marriage to grace its portals in twenty-three years can generate.

NOTES: Another hefty extract. Lots of exercise for this detective's hand muscles. But it does provide an insight into the subject's mind and provides proof to back up this detective's hunch: Prem. Both Shirin and Mai are wary of him. <u>Find out more</u>.

Reena lay in bed, the letter beside her, and stared at the ceiling. It wasn't really the white she'd always assumed it to be, but a very pale yellow. Plaster was peeling off in places, and there were a couple of cobwebs. No lizards like the ones in Taipur, busily skirting around the dark wooden beams looking for insects.

Shirin's words written so long ago swirled around inside Reena's head. Whatever happened to alienate Shirin from her family had happened after her marriage...

Reena had a sudden irrational urge to reach back in time and meet Shirin, warn her. Shirin had had a sense of foreboding about her marriage. She had felt uneasy. She had been proved right...

Update on breakthrough: The email Aunt Anita was waiting for (which this detective has deduced must be from Aunt Shirin) has not arrived as yet. *Watch this space.*

What now? Reena thought as she tucked her casebook under her pillow. She felt restless, anxious. The day had been such a roller-coaster. On the one hand, there had been the high of making friends; on the other, Murli's words, which had shifted something in her head, made her question things she had taken for granted, raised doubts like cobras uncoiling, ready to strike. She wanted to do something. She wanted the email to arrive. She wanted desperately to see Aunt Shirin, to put a face to this girl, woman from the letters. Did she manage to love Vinod? Or did she end up loving someone else? Reena was fed up with only questions and no answers, fed up with waiting, fed up with being fobbed off because she was a 'child'. She checked the clock on the wall. Not quite lunch time. She did not want to leave her room. She could hear Aunt Anita and her mum laughing as they watched a comedy show while they waited for her dad to finish his call. She stared bleary-eyed at the wall, and then her gaze slid, as if of its own volition, to the bedside table where the letters lay. Inviting. Beguiling. She picked up the fifth letter, the last. A thin one, unlike the others. She read it. Read it again. And, with trembling fingers, pulled out her casebook.

Extract from the last letter:

> This detective's hand is shaking as she writes this, hence the appalling handwriting. She does not want to record this, but a good detective does not hold anything back, even if the evidence is incriminating. So, here goes:

> Anu, you must have heard by now. Do not panic. It's not as bad as it sounds. I know it's hard and your mind is not in it, but do please try and concentrate on your studies and exams. This is it. The finals. Your scores will determine whether

you get the university you want. As hard as it is, do try and focus on your studies.

Deepak is fine. He's recovering well. It was such a shock though. Ma was beside herself when she got the phone call. I have never seen her lose control like that and I hope I never will again. She went at once. He's at Manipal and they are taking very good care of him. By the time you come, he should be right as rain. Except of course… 'That is why the royal family insist on having an heir and a spare,' he joked, after it sank in. You know how he is. Ma was tight-lipped, shaken. Her only son. No hope of carrying on the family name, the long line of Taipur Diazes. 'I should never have agreed to let you have that motorbike,' she kept repeating. 'It's okay, Ma, I'm all right,' he said. 'How will I ever get you married now?' she asked, anguish colouring her voice. And the thought of his marriage reminded her of mine, looming on the horizon, just a few weeks away, and all the things that still needed to be done. 'You and Madhu stay here with him; I have to go meet the priest, organise the banns,' she said and was off.

NOTE: Does this mean what this detective thinks it means?

A commotion in the living room. Now what? She ignored it, went to the sink at the corner of her room. What did this have to do with Aunt Shirin? Was her dad involved? Was *she*? How? Murli's words came to her: 'Perhaps they are protecting you.' Why had Aunt Anita given her this letter? Because it contained clues to the rift? Knowing Aunt Anita, it was quite possible she had forgotten it was there, just given Reena the whole lot, unthinking. Her head ached with the weight of the questions circulating inside it. What else would she discover before all this was over? How many more lies?

She splashed water on her face, glared at the girl in the mirror: dishevelled hair, bloodshot eyes, frown like thunder. A blink. And then: a girl in pigtails parroting, 'Bring me home, please.'

Screeches from the living room. Curiosity won. How long could she hide in her room anyway? She would have to face them all sometime. Traitors. She opened her door and was greeted by the sight of Preeti holding Anita close to her, saying over and over, 'I knew it. I told you, didn't I?' Tears ran down both their cheeks, but they were smiling.

'Your Uncle Uttam called,' Preeti announced, catching sight of her standing in the doorway to her bedroom. 'He's missed Aunt Anu. He's coming here.'

My uncle? Is he really? Are any of you even related to me? All those lectures her parents—*her parents?*—had given her about being honest, truthful at all times. And now…

Anita sniffed. 'We still have a lot of talk about, many issues to resolve…'

'But they love each other and don't really want a divorce,' Preeti finished for her.

'I'm sorry to have to ask this, but why didn't he call earlier?' Her dad—*dad?*—was standing in the doorway to his bedroom, mobile phone in hand.

'I was the one who said we should get a divorce. He didn't want to have to beg. He was waiting for me to call.' Aunt Anita's voice was pregnant with joy.

'But he couldn't wait anymore and he decided to call anyway and tell her how much he loved her and to hell with his pride... I do love happy endings.' Preeti rubbed her hands gleefully. 'So, let's celebrate. Reena, get dressed. We're going out.'

'I don't want to.'

'Oh, Rinu, why?' Preeti flicked a quick glance in Aunt Anita's direction. Aunt Anita was staring at the phone in her hands, foolish grin wide on her face, oblivious. 'Are you okay, sweetie? You don't look well.' She walked up to Reena, put a hand on her forehead. 'No fever.'

Reena melted, losing herself in her mother's arms, her familiar comforting embrace.

'Shh... Rinu, don't cry. You're not yourself today. What's the matter?'

'Headache,' Reena sniffed. *Coward.*

'Here darling, I'll tuck you into bed, get you a glass of warm milk and a crocin. You'll feel better after you've had a rest.'

She gave in gratefully to her mother's ministrations, the crocin making her drowsy, so she did not have to think, to give in to the thoughts crowding her head, demanding attention. She slept fitfully, on and off, blissful dreamless sleep, and woke in the late afternoon, mellow marigold rays dancing rose patterns on the milky walls, the smell of cooking: chicken sautéing in yogurt and spices, onions frying, basmati rice browning in ghee wafting in through the barely open door, with her mother's voice clear in her head: her mother standing beside her in front of the mirror in Aunt Anita's room, 'Look at you. Our special miracle.'

A possible explanation for latest development based on last letter: doctors often get it wrong. This detective has reached the conclusion (based on solid evidence: her mother's words) that she was a miracle baby, the one who confounded expectations, who arrived against all odds, who left the doctors speechless. This detective concludes that she is, therefore, destined for greatness.

CHAPTER TWENTY-THREE

Mrs. Vaz

'The Richardsons are moving. They've put their house up for sale. Three-hundred-thousand-pound asking price. Not bad, eh?' Vinod said. 'They bought theirs around the same time as us, didn't they?'

'They moved in at Christmas,' Shirin called from the kitchen where she was washing the dishes, yellow gloves flecked with sudsy bubbles. She looked out the kitchen window over at the Richardsons' garden where laundry in various shades of white flapped in late October wind, cherry trees devoid of blossom stark against a dull charcoal sky.

It had been October when she and Vinod had moved in, and she'd spent hours standing at this very window, staring at the garden bereft of flowers, hardly able to believe that this was all hers. This house. This garden. To do with what she liked...

The spring after their first winter in England when, like the sprouting buds, Shirin had walked her way into a tentative new persona through the icy pavements of Harrow, Vinod, who'd noticed the change in her but had not said anything, showing it instead in the spring in his step, the slight relaxing of the worry lines around his eyes, had said, 'Shall we look for a house?'

'Why?' She'd asked without thinking.

Vinod had lost it then, banging the wall in frustration, earning a yell from the neighbours, American students: 'Hey, watch it man!'

'Shonu, we're not going back. This is home now,' he'd said, guilt sprouting, anger spent.

She'd smiled, even though she knew he knew it was fake. 'Yes, let's look for a house.'

And then, when the estate agent showed them *the* house and with it dangled the promise of a family...

Their first proper home together. Children. Noise. Laughter...

The first thing Shirin had bought for the new house was a cot for the nursery. She had gone into town for some groceries and was walking past Mothercare when she saw it. It was a sturdy wooden cot, not fancy; in fact quite practical—but it caught her eye. She could see her baby lying in it, blinking up at her, and then when it was older, holding on to the bars and pulling itself up to standing. The fledgling hope that had taken root in her heart when the estate agent first showed her the house had sprouted wings when they moved in. She had been determined to fill the void in her heart with the sound of her children's laughter...

Shirin sighed as she dried the dishes, put them away. She wondered where the cot was. Vinod must have discreetly disposed of it. Or perhaps it was still in the loft.

Why was she thinking of it now? How had musing about the Richardsons led to this?

Rob and Helen had moved in at Christmas, a toddler and a baby in tow. The baby's wails had reverberated through the thin walls, kept Shirin awake all night, reminding her of another baby, no longer hers. She'd waited impatiently for Vinod to wake. 'Let's make a baby, now,' she'd said when his eyes fluttered open. 'Are you sure?' Vinod had asked, rubbing the sleep from his eyes. 'Yes.' She'd held his gaze. He'd reached up with his hand, tried to cup her face. She'd flinched, moved away. 'But, Shonu,' he'd said, the hurt stark in his eyes, 'you don't like to be touched. By me.' And there it was: the crux of the problem—which even a year and a bit of counselling had been unable to solve.

She'd visited the Richardsons bearing gifts for the children, wine, a poinsettia and a card bearing the legend 'New Home' for Rob and Helen. She'd held the baby, looked into his rheumy blue eyes and ached for another baby: huge brown eyes, wispy hair. She had ruffled the toddler's hair, said to Helen, 'We're going to start a family.' How liberating it had felt, to put her ache, her deepest wish into words, to have Helen nod in agreement. 'They'll grow up together while we sit and chat over cups of tea.' As if it was that easy; as if it would happen and soon; as if, by the very act of putting her wish into words, she had set it in motion. She'd returned home determined.

The actual creating the children part, however, was not easy. She flinched whenever Vinod touched her and it hurt to see how much that hurt him. 'I don't want to do this if you are not comfortable with it, Shonu,' he said, repeatedly. 'I want to do it,' she insisted, willing her mind to focus on babies: on whisper-soft cheeks; grubby faces; dimpled, toothless grins. But her body froze instinctively every time he tried to touch her, however much she wished it otherwise. 'Open your eyes,' Vinod said softly. 'Look at me.' And that first time, he talked her through it in his soft, soothing voice, telling her again and again that he loved her, holding her gaze, making sure she knew it was him. It got easier after that, and as long as she looked into his eyes, it was all right. There were times when his eyes were superseded by the empty ones of her nightmare and she screamed and screamed. Those times, Vinod held her in his arms. He whispered in her ear, 'Shh... It's over... It's all right.'

It got better with time. And it got worse every month when, like clockwork, her period arrived. After three long years, they consulted fertility experts who found nothing wrong with either of them; no reason as to why they couldn't conceive. 'Keep trying,' they urged cheerily. And so, armed with new ways of calculating ovulation dates, and a new sliver of hope, Shirin and Vinod tried again. And again. They went back and paid for treatments. 'There is no reason why you cannot conceive,' was all the experts would say.

Vinod mentioned adoption once. She'd looked at him wordlessly then. They both knew that they couldn't afford to have their past put under scrutiny. It was best left behind. Put to bed along with any hopes of having children. 'Why do you stay with me?' She'd asked him. The question that she'd always wanted to ask but had not dared to as she was too afraid of his answer. There was a loud crash. She had looked up startled. The remains of dinner lay scattered on the carpet, interspersed with the shattered remains of Vinod's plate. He had looked at her, eyes wild. 'It wasn't your fault, Shonu. When will you stop beating yourself up for what happened? If anyone is to blame, it is me. If only I'd come earlier that day... I promised in my wedding vows to honour and protect you. I failed...' She had wanted so much to comfort him, ease away his anger, his pain. She knew he wished more than anything for her to touch him of her own accord, hold him in her arms. It was the one thing she couldn't do. 'I love you, Shonu. That is why I stay with you. Not out of duty, as you seem to think. Not because I have to. I love you regardless of whether we have children or not. So don't ask me this question again. Don't insult me.' Shirin had nodded, unable to speak or look away.

The Richardsons' toddler, James, was a strapping thirteen now—headphones an extension of his ears. The baby, Reece, was ten. Shirin had kept her distance when the family she'd longed for never happened, embarrassed at having opened herself up to Helen. She told herself she was busy with the software course and soon after, her job. She saw Helen and the kids in the garden sometimes, in the summer. She waved, busied herself with tasks she hadn't noticed she had to do. Like the family she'd wanted, the chats over cups of tea did not materialise.

Thinking of James and Reece made her think of Reena—Reena grilling Anita about her, of her reply to Anita's email, sent last thing before she left work for the weekend.

Dearest Anu,

Thank you for your lovely email. I know how you hate writing letters. I wasn't expecting a reply and your email—it was a gift.

Anu, I have so much to say I don't know where to begin. I miss our chats. Remember how we used to sit chatting on the veranda at twilight with Rex the Third running circles around our legs, scents of dinner wafting from the kitchen and Madhu nagging for us to come in? I miss seeing your face light up as you describe something, your chin resting on your knees. Do you still do that?

Anu, about Uttam, if he doesn't call, why don't you call him, seeing as how you feel?

I want to come home, Anu. I want to see Reena and you and Madhu, darling Madhu—has she changed much?—and Deepak and Da and Ma. But Ma, does she want to see me?

And about telling Reena; I'd like to wait until I know for sure about Ma.

Love and kisses to Reena (does she like to be hugged and kissed or is she too old for that now? Oh, I have so many questions).

She had written, 'I envy you your access to Reena.' And deleted the line. Kate had agreed, 'Yeah, babe. I think you should. Delete it.' She had ended the email there.

Vinod came into the kitchen as she was putting the last dish away and started rummaging in the cupboards. 'There's nothing to eat in this house.'

'There's nothing you want you mean. There's plenty of fruit.'

'Oh, fruit,' Vinod pulled a face, 'I feel like crisps, or Bombay mix, perhaps.'

'Chuda. Remember our engagement, when that whole pack of chuda exploded on Uncle Bathu's face?'

Vinod turned to her, eyes lighting up. 'I remember.'

'You should have seen Madhu's face. How annoyed she was. "Useless drunk," she kept muttering furiously as she cleaned up. She didn't want anyone hijacking my day.' She paused, watching Vinod open a bag of yogurt-coated raisins and pop one into his mouth. 'We haven't talked about any of this, have we?'

'No. You didn't want to...' Vinod chewed, made a face. 'What are these?'

'Healthy snacks,' Shirin giggled. 'I do want to talk about it now. I want to remember everything.'

'Good. The healing process.' He flashed a cheeky smile.

'Oh, will you stop... By the way, I saw the counsellor today. She said what is holding me back is fear of rejection.' The counsellor's gentle face; her watery-blue gaze like the reflection of sky on sea on a clear day: 'You are ready emotionally, Shirin, but the little girl in you still wants to please her mother.'

'Well, of course. I could have told you that for free.'

She laughed. 'I thought you liked her.'

'I do.' His voice hollow from where he was rummaging inside the cupboards. 'So, I was thinking, asking price of two hundred and seventy-five thousand. The Richardsons have a garage. We don't. So...'

'Hang on, Vinod. What's this about?'

'Us moving back. We are, aren't we?'

His head framed by the cupboards. His eyes on hers.

'Ma... She hasn't forgiven me.'

Bang. Vinod brought his hand down on the kitchen counter making the plates jump. 'My parents haven't forgiven me either. For walking away. With you. My new bride. For turning my back on them. In their time of need.' His eyes, burning vessels of pain. 'You say you are tired of living like this. So am I. *So am I!*'

She went up to him. He moved away. She stopped, shocked. She was always the one who moved away, the one who flinched from his touch. For the first time she understood how it was for him, how it had always been. Since...

'I have waited, Shonu. Patiently. But even I have my limits...'

'We've built this life out of nothing...' she began, 'and if we give it up before we're sure... What if it's not what we think it is? We've been away eleven years, Vinod. Things have changed.'

He would not look at her. His words reverberated in her head. 'You say you are tired of living like this. So am I.'

He cleared his throat. 'Before all this... you were saying?'

'Huh?'

'Our engagement?'

And they were back on safe ground. Doing what they did best. The golden rules governing their relationship:

Avoid talking about things that cause friction. Pretend nothing happened. Change the topic. She closed her eyes, not wanting to look at Vinod's face, see the hurt still swimming in his eyes. Her mind helpfully supplied the memory. Her engagement. The excitement. The nervousness. The fear. 'I couldn't sleep for days preceding it. And the day before, I couldn't keep still, imagining the worst. What if your bus got stuck in the ghats and you were late? What if you had an accident? What if...'

She had paced the front courtyard, getting in the way of the men putting up the marquee: 'Left a bit. No. Right. Hold it up, Vincy, it's falling. Out of the way, Shirin.' Up and down she'd paced, with Rex the Third providing her company, tongue wagging, thinking this was a special kind of game. Up and down. So nervous. Trying to escape the thoughts crowding her head: *What if Vinod thinks I look too fat in my engagement sari? What if he changes his mind, does not want to go ahead with the wedding? What will Ma do? The disgrace...*

'Stop that; you're giving me a headache,' Madhu had shouted from the kitchen. 'If you want something to do, go to Nagappa's and bring me the chicken stored in their freezer. Oh, and the coconut.'

'And you don't start,' Madhu had yelled at Rex the Third who'd started barking. She was frantically grinding rice and lentils for the dosas and idlis to be served at breakfast to Shirin's in-laws-to-be.

Rex the Third ignored Madhu, went up to the tamarind tree and stood guard, growling. Baby's head bobbed into view as she climbed up the hill: sweat beading greying hair, lips sucked in, dimples peeking. Rex barked louder. 'Shh, Rex, it's only Baby,' Shirin said, scratching the itchy spot under his neck, soothing him.

Baby, despite her name, was in her thirties. She was Jacinta's favourite fisherwoman and always made sure she gave Jacinta a couple more fish for her money. She had helped out at the house a couple of times: once when Madhu was ill, and again the summer Jacinta's mango trees had surprised her with a windfall, each branch weighed down with the fruit. Jacinta must have asked her to come and help Madhu with the preparations and cooking for the morrow, Shirin surmised.

'Did I hear you say Baby?' Madhu screamed from the kitchen.

Baby grinned at Shirin, 'So, ma'am, getting engaged are you? Do you remember when you decided to teach me English?' She pronounced it 'Hinglish'. Shirin blushed, recalling how she had chased Baby round the fields with a stick for refusing to learn the alphabet beyond 'A,B,C', how when Jacinta caught wind of this, Baby had lied, covering for her.

'What is Baby doing here? Rex, shoo her away. Good dog,' Madhu bellowed. She viewed Baby as a competitor, vying for a place in Jacinta's family and in her affections.

Undaunted, Baby headed for the kitchen. Shirin followed, glad for this respite from her thoughts. 'You need any help?' Baby asked Madhu, while vigorously chewing paan.

Madhu tucked a strand of hair behind her ear and wiped the sweat off her brow with the pallu of her sari. 'Shirin, tell her no.'

'Well, I'm here if you need me.' Baby squatted down on the step outside the kitchen door and patted Rex the Third who had stopped barking and come up to her, tail wagging, tongue hanging out.

'That dog is useless. If a burglar came to steal chickens, he would go and lick his face instead of barking,' Madhu muttered, furiously grinding the rice into a paste. 'Since you're just sitting there doing nothing, you might as well help me. Spit the paan out first.'

Baby stayed over, both she and Madhu working late into the night finishing the pork and chicken curries, adjusting the salt in the boti, making tendli bhaji with fresh cashew nuts (kindly donated by Lenny Bai) and honey-sweet tender coconut flesh. And the next morning they stood side by side in the kitchen, busily frying dosas, having formed an uneasy alliance.

'They're here,' Nagappa's son announced, hopping on one foot, waiting eagerly to see how many rupees Jacinta would press into his open palms. He grinned with delight when he saw the three ten-rupee notes and skipped away, pleased with himself.

Vinod looked different in his suit and tie. Formal. His hair was slicked down, flattened in a side parting. Shirin almost fell off the stool in her room, where she was standing looking out of the window as before, when she tried to get a closer look. As Vinod passed under the window, he looked straight up at her, as if he had been expecting her all along, and smiled. Her heart stopped beating for a full minute.

'You were looking for me, weren't you?' she asked Vinod now, lightly teasing, testing the waters.

'No. I was looking at the sky, checking for rain.' Vinod met her gaze, smiled. Apologetic. 'And I saw this heavenly pair of eyes peeking through window bars right at me.'

Eyes. Prem.

Vinod's brother, Prem, had walked in behind him. He caught Vinod's smile and looked up too. Shirin jumped off the stool in fright. In Bangalore, Prem had avoided looking at her and at Jacinta. Now she knew why. Vinod's brother had dark, empty eyes, devoid of all emotion. He scared her.

'I didn't know,' Vinod said. 'You should have told me.'

'I hardly knew you, Vinod. How could I, a stranger, complain about your brother to you?'

'Oh, Shonu,' His voice aching. 'If only...'

She'd stayed in her room while Vinod and his family ate. After breakfast, as they were leaving, Shirin had peeped out the window and caught Vinod looking up discreetly, searching for her as he walked past.

'You were looking for me,' Shirin teased.

'I wasn't.'

'Liar.'

His brother had looked up too, and even though she was standing back, even though she was sure he couldn't see her, it felt like his empty eyes were looking right at her. She had a sudden urge to tell her mother to stop the engagement, cancel the wedding. In all her worries until this moment, she had imagined Vinod calling the wedding off, not the other way round. Never the other way round. But now Prem...

'Really? You considered doing that?' Vinod asked.

She nodded.

'It would have been best in the circumstances, perhaps.' Vinod sounded crushed.

She stood on tiptoes and, forcing herself to swallow the fear that inhibited her from touching him, lightly brushed his lips with hers. 'Don't say that.'

'If you had a chance to do it all again, to go back to that point in time, would you stop the engagement?'

All that she'd lost. All that she ached for. All she had now: this man. Who had stood by her through it all. 'Don't ask me that. It's not fair,' she whispered.

It was the thought of Jacinta that had stopped her, the thought of the effort her ma had put into organising her engagement, the relief her ma had felt at finally finding Shirin a groom, the crushing disappointment if she reneged. She'd thought of all the people waiting at the church. She'd thought of Vinod, his smile, his kind eyes. She'd thought then that it was too late. To stop the engagement. To retreat. And for what? Just because Vinod's brother gave her the creeps?

She had shrugged off her doubts and kept her mouth shut as her mother and Madhu dressed her in the rose-petal-pink sari, as they did her hair and looped flowers through it, as they piled jewellery on her. The face staring back at her from the mirror was pale, eyes huge, dark. Madhu had leant close, whispered, 'Look at you. My baby. All grown-up. Beautiful.' Tears had sparkled in her eyes. Jacinta had met Shirin's gaze in the mirror and flashed a small, satisfied smile.

At the church, as her mother helped her out of Uncle Ron's Ambassador car (specially hired for the short distance that Shirin would normally have walked—'You can't walk! Not on your engagement day!'), Vinod, who was talking to someone, his back to her, turned. Their eyes met. His face lit up. He reached her in two long strides, took her hand in his and squeezed gently. That was enough to quell her doubts. She wanted to marry this man.

'Madhu's food was a huge success. After lunch, Jacinta led Vinod away to introduce him to all the Diaz relatives and well-wishers. Shirin was leaning back in her chair, fingering her ring—*I am engaged*—her eyes following Vinod as he mingled with her people, when she felt hot breath on her shoulder, making the hairs on her neck stand up, raising goosebumps. She turned, and found herself looking into soulless eyes—his face too close, his breath hot on her face. His grin a leer. He held out his hand for her to shake. 'Congratulations, Voniye.' She recoiled, fear spearing her stomach, wanting to yell for help, suddenly all alone in this crowded room, not finding her voice. 'Prem,' her future father-in-law—his arm a clamp on Prem's shoulder—led him away.

'I didn't know,' Vinod said, leaning against the cupboard and closing his eyes. 'Da never told me. We talked

to Prem before. He promised not to drink, make a scene.'
He paused. Then, 'He could be quite charming when he
was sober. Although by the time of our wedding, he hardly ever was. Oh, Shonu, I should never have married you,
put you in danger like that.'

'Vinod…'

'But I thought, we all did, that he would never… and
I had had enough of having my life held back because of
my brother…' He rubbed a hand wearily across his face,
looked at her, 'And I wanted you, ever since I saw your
huge eyes peeking out from between those bars that first
time, I wanted you…'

*And me, when you put your hand in mine, I wanted you,
too.* Why couldn't she say it, make him feel better, remove
that haunted look from his eyes? 'Vinod, it happened.'

'Yes.' Vinod sounded defeated. 'It did.' And then,
'Shonu, you're right. No point giving all this up.' He
waved his hands around to indicate the house.

'It's just… Here we are both liked, respected… If we
went back, and were treated like outcasts… If we were
shunned…Especially you, for no fault of yours… I
couldn't bear it, Vinod…'

He came up to her then and, with his finger, traced her
features. She willed herself not to flinch, to move away, as
was her instinct. 'Yes. I know,' he said.

She took a deep breath, looked into his eyes. 'I'm sorry.
All these years, I've been so absorbed in my own pain. I
had no idea… Have you been very unhappy?'

'I am happy with you.'

Not really an answer. She persisted. 'Your parents...
What you said…'

'Oh, Shonu, if they had needed me, really needed me,
I would have stayed with them, no matter what. But it
wasn't me they wanted...'

She took another deep breath. 'Vinod, about what you
asked. I...'

'Shh... You were right. I wasn't being fair, asking you
to choose...'

But he was hurt. She could tell.

All that night, Vinod's question played in her head. *If
you had known then, what you know now, would you have
stopped the engagement? Would you?*

Her infatuation with Tariq, her dream of finding love
like Anita had with Uttam, her doubts of whether she
would learn to love Vinod... They had all dissipated
when Vinod's hand had found hers, when his face had
lit up in a smile at the sight of her. After the engagement,
after what happened with Prem, she had had nightmares.
Every night she woke up screaming, and Madhu held
her, like she had when she was little, soothed her, joked
with her, 'Soon, you'll be doing this to your own child.'
Her own child. She wanted to create one. With Vinod.
And the words that were building up in her head, that
were threatening to spill out of her mouth, 'I can't. I can't
marry him. I am afraid of his brother,' stilled. She wanted
Vinod. After all, she was marrying him, not his brother.
And perhaps she had imagined it all; perhaps because of
her dislike of Prem she had imbibed his actions with men-

ace. After all, what had he done really? Just held his hand out to congratulate her. So he had come a bit too close. So what? She was making too much of what had happened. And so she assuaged herself, calmed her fears and did nothing.

If you had known then, what you know now, would you have stopped the engagement? Would you?

I should have, by rights, Vinod. Even back then, I had an inkling, a premonition. But there was Ma, running around organising last-minute details, that rare smile now a permanent fixture, her voice proud as she declared to all and sundry, 'They have two cars. A big house right in the centre of the city. And their own business. What more could I ask for?' and the words died in my mouth.

If you had known then, what you know now, would you have stopped the engagement? Would you?

Perhaps... Vinod washing her ever so gently that horrible evening, his tears falling like rain... Reena... *I don't know, Vinod. The thing is, I don't know.*

Vinod moved onto his back, jostling her arm. She looked down at him, at the impossibly long eyelashes curling on his cheeks; his face less lined in repose, the mole peeking from under his left nostril. And she saw herself as the naïve young girl she had been, counting down the hours the night before her wedding, worrying about spending the rest of her nights with a man she barely knew, worrying about the brother-in-law who scared her...

Shirin spent her last night as a virgin in a cramped bed in a little room in a convent in Bangalore. Her da snored in the next room, lost to the world. Jacinta, Madhu, Anita, Deepak and the rest of the wedding party, which comprised practically the entire village of Taipur, would arrive the next morning. The church ceremony was at four o'clock and the reception would go on late into the night.

She couldn't sleep for worrying: How would she look in her gown? Would Vinod hold her hand like he had at the engagement? Would his face light up on seeing her? And Prem. He would be the best man, surely. How would that go? All the apprehensions about him came flooding back. Those strange empty eyes. Her heart thudded loud against her chest. To calm herself, she pictured Vinod: his kind eyes, his smile. Her husband tomorrow! This time tomorrow, she would be in bed with him beside her. A tingle, a shiver of anticipation. Would she be able to please Vinod? Or would he be disappointed? Her fleshy body. What would he think? Would it hurt? She felt an ache deep inside as she imagined him holding her in his arms, kissing her, taking off her clothes...

She alternated between hope and despair, fear and a strange fevered excitement. She worried about so many things, but she did not worry about the actual wedding itself, whether it would go smoothly. She just assumed it would.

And on her wedding morning, she woke to a downpour the likes of which Bangalore had not seen in years.

Vinod stirred beside her, 'The wedding. All those premonitions. Did you want to call it off then?'

She looked into his eyes, deep black flecked with brown, like the night sky just before dawn. Both of them lying side by side pretending to be asleep, thinking of the same thing. How many times over the past decade had they done this?

Their wedding. The sky midnight blue and weeping on what was predicted to be a sunny day; an incessant, unseasonal assault dousing Bangalore. The bus full of relatives stuck in the ghats due to flooding. The clap of thunder like the voice of God intervening when the priest asked, 'Do you, Shirin, take Vinod as your lawfully wedded husband?' Shirin's 'I do,' encored by a flash of lightning that lit up the church and stole the power, smothering them in darkness. A hush settling in the church heaving with people in their wedding finery. No rustle of silk, no clink of gold. The only sound that of rain whipping the sloping roof. And then, old Richa Uncle's voice booming, 'Stop this wedding. It is a sham. God has spoken.'

Voices, all at once, whispering, shouting to be heard, building to a crescendo, inhabiting the darkness, drowning out the rain. The priest's voice trying for control, 'A mass is on. Please stop.' A candle flickering, the face of a nun hovering above it. Then, the sweet voices of the nuns rising in song, overriding the rabble. 'Heavenly Father, send thy blessing.' The congregation joining in; song reaching up to the rafters of the church, sending the crows sheltering there a squawking: fluttering shadows silhouetted in dazzling light as the power came on. Eyes blinking in the sudden harsh brightness, mouths open in refrain. Shirin's gaze resting on her mother's face—worried, drawn, on this, her wedding day. Her mother's face.

Vinod's eyes searching hers in the dark: *Did you want to call it off?*

'No,' she said. 'Did you?'

The rain had reduced to a mere drizzle when they stepped out of church, a married couple. Traffic was moving outside the church grounds again, not as many horns blaring. Vinod had put his hand in hers and squeezed. His head bent close, his lips just brushing her ear, raising goosebumps, arousing desire, 'Congratulations, Mrs. Vaz.'

'Not then, not now. Not once in all these years.' He pulled her close and after a bit, she settled into his embrace.

'What about your parents?' she asked. 'Were they worried about what happened, what Uncle Richa said?'

She could feel his heart beating under his night shirt. She snuggled in closer, breathing in the musky scent of him. 'I think they were relieved that it was the rain and Uncle Richa who misbehaved and not Prem.'

Prem had appeared from nowhere, clasped Vinod's hand. 'Congrats, brother,' he had smirked. Vinod's smile froze. 'You've been drinking,' he whispered. 'Tell me something new,' Prem laughed. He came and stood next to Shirin, tucked her hand in his arm, motioned to the photographer, 'A picture with my Voni.' She tried not to recoil from his touch, the alcoholic fumes on his breath. Vinod's dad came up then, led Prem away. Shirin relaxed. 'Sorry,' Vinod whispered. 'It's okay,' she whispered back, even though it wasn't. And they both switched on smiles for the next lot of well-wishers coming forward to congratulate them.

'I cannot imagine how it must have been for you, Shirin, saying goodbye to your family, coming home with us,' Vinod said softly.

She was glad they were finally talking about all this, even though it had been eleven years in coming. 'It was nerve-wracking,' she said, remembering...

When the car stopped in a cloud of dust, outside the gates of Vinod's home, *her* new home, Shirin felt claustrophobic. She was missing her parents, brother, sister and Madhu, to whom she had bid goodbye, and was worrying about the night to come. She had travelled with Vinod, his father and mother. Prem was nowhere to be seen, and for this, Shirin was glad.

Cows, stray dogs and people milled around even at this time of night, some of them fast asleep on rags which passed for mattresses beside the gutter by the side of the street, snoring without a care in the world, one hand busy, even in sleep, squatting flies. The ones who were awake looked curiously at her, decked in her bridal sado and dripping with jewellery, and as she got out of the car, approached, begging for alms. 'Amma, Amma, I haven't eaten all day. Give me a few paise, Amma. God will bless you always.'

'Go away. Shoo!' Vinod's father muttered, closing the gates.

Vinod's mother was already opening the front door. 'Wait,' she said as Vinod made to lead Shirin inside. She retrieved a stainless-steel thali filled with rice grains from where she must have left it, behind the front door, before she left for her son's wedding. 'You have to step on this as you come into our house. It's supposed to bring good luck.'

Afterwards, Shirin and Vinod had to kneel in front of the altar, which took pride of place in the living room, and pray for a long and happy married life. When it was over, Vinod led Shirin into their bedroom.

Shirin was shaking with nerves. Vinod must have sensed this. Once inside, he locked the door behind him and turning to her, smiled shyly, 'I am new to this too. And, like you, I am extremely nervous.'

Shirin laughed, slightly hysterically.

Gently, Vinod walked up to where she was standing, backed up against the wall. He led her to the bed. She looked at him, not knowing what to do, what was expected of her. She knew what was coming of course. She just didn't know how to get from *now* to *then*. Should she take off her clothes? Wouldn't it look wanton? She was not comfortable with her body, with its excess flesh in the wrong places. And with Vinod watching...

He smiled softly. 'Sit down,' he said. 'How do you wear your hair when you sleep?'

'Loose,' she whispered.

'Then let me help you get rid of these.' He touched the flowers in her hair.

'Oh...' She had forgotten about them. 'Thank you.' She was overcome with shyness and something else: a thrill of excitement; a sliver of desire, as he tenderly touched her hair, gently removing all the pins and flowers. With great care, so as not to hurt her, he worked her plait loose. His touch was so soft, so deliciously alien.

'You've got beautiful hair. It's so thick,' he said, running his fingers down her hair, his voice a caress.

Desire intensified, became want and longing. She closed her eyes. 'It feels so light. I had forgotten how heavy the flowers were,' she whispered.

'Do you want to go to the bathroom and change from that sari?' Vinod asked.

Trembling, she nodded.

She was very shy to come out in her nightdress, and hesitated for a long time behind the door of the bathroom.

When she did step out, Vinod smiled at her. 'You are beautiful,' he said softly.

Nobody had ever called her beautiful before, not the way he did, like he meant it.

'Really?' she wanted to ask, but couldn't form the words. By the time she was able to speak, he was in the bathroom.

Shirin waited for him, perched on the edge of the bed. Her tiredness had fled, to be replaced by a tingly anticipation. She had read all about what would happen next in one of the forbidden books from the library, but worried that she would be found wanting in some way. She had dieted before the wedding but she was still overweight. Vinod had said she was beautiful but would he still find her so with no clothes on? What about that ugly scar on her left thigh, the scabs on her knees?

Her stomach dipped as the bathroom latch turned and Vinod came out in his pyjamas. She couldn't look at him. She felt the springs sag as he sat beside her on the bed. He smelled fresh; of Liril soap and something else, something musky. Shirin's heart was beating so loudly she was sure he could hear it. Gently he placed his hand on top of Shirin's, sending shivers down her spine. She had read about this feeling too. She closed her eyes.

'I know, Shirin. I am exhausted too.'

Shirin's eyes flew open. Did he think she was tired? No.

'Shall we lie down, maybe just hold each other and get used to each other tonight? I have waited this long for you. I don't mind waiting a little longer.'

No. No. You've got the wrong end of the stick, thought Shirin. But how could she say it out loud without appearing loose, like one of *those* women?

She lay still in Vinod's unfamiliar arms until his breathing steadied and she was sure he had fallen asleep. Then she turned and looked at him: this stranger who was now her husband. His mouth was slightly open and soft little sighs escaped it. How could he sleep? Didn't he desire her? *She* desired him. Her whole body was tingling, aching. Lying in his arms was torture. 'You are beautiful,' he had said. 'I have waited this long for you.' Then why hadn't he pulled off her nightie and devoured her, like the heroes did in books and movies?

Why hadn't he kissed her?

CHAPTER TWENTY-FOUR
Girl in Pigtails

A unt Anita confronted Deepak at dinner that evening. She came to the table *sans* sunglasses and winked at Reena as she sat down, and Reena knew then. She had received a reply.

'Aunty…' Reena began.

A finger to her lips, 'Shh…'

She complimented Preeti on the mackerel fry and laughed at something Deepak said even though it wasn't remotely funny. Deepak leaned back in his chair, chewed his mouthful and regarded his sister quizzically. 'I know Uttam called and things are fine between the two of you. But there's something else, isn't there? What are you not telling us, Anu?'

Aunt Anita laughed, 'I'll tell you, then. I got an email, after eleven years, from someone I was instructed to forget.'

A shocked silence around the table. *I was right. The email was from Aunt Shirin.* Reena watched her father's face flood red, his eyes settle first on Reena (was that fear she saw in them?)—the same expression echoed in her mother's gaze, huge eyes in a face drained of colour—and then turn to her aunt. Her father opened his mouth a couple of times before he found his voice, 'Anu, what is the meaning of this? How dare you bring this up in *my* house, at *my* table?'

'She contacted me, Deepak,' her aunt's voice soft. Gentle even. 'She wants to come back.'

Spot On, Super Sleuth.

'No.' *Bang.* Deepak's hand on the table, spilling the rice, overturning the glasses. Water spilling onto the tablecloth, the stain seeping dark red, like blood. Her dad's panicked glance on her again. 'Reena, go to your room.'

'Deepak, she...' Aunt Anita said.

'Reena, I said, *go to your room!*' Her dad yelling, voice laced with dread. Why? That sinking feeling she had had when she read the last letter, which she had tried to dispel and almost succeeded, returned.

'She knows about Shirin,' Aunt Anita said.

Her parents turned to her as one, their eyes wide. 'What? How?' barked her dad.

'Deepak.' Her mother's hand on his arm, trying to calm him. Her mother's face white, pinched.

'I found a photograph when we visited Taipur last month.' Reena whispered.

'What photograph? I thought they had all been destroyed.' Her dad's voice gruff.

'It was of the three of you when you were my age. It was hidden behind one of the other pictures.'

Deepak and Preeti exchanged glances. 'What do you know about Shirin?'

'She doesn't know anything, Deepak. Just that she was our sibling. And I showed her some letters Shirin wrote me,' Aunt Anita said.

Why were her parents so afraid? What didn't they want her to know?

'Deepak, you cannot hide it from her forever...' Aunt Anita said.

Murli's words echoing in her head, 'Perhaps they are all protecting you.' She felt tired suddenly, scared. She wanted her mum.

'I will if I have to.' Her dad lowering himself onto a chair like an old man, cradling his head in his hands.

As if she'd read Reena's mind, her mother came up to her, put her arm round her, led her to her room, tucked her into bed. Her mother's face pale as she bent close, her kiss laced with fear. *Mum, why are you and Dad so afraid of Aunt Shirin? What is it you are hiding from me?* And in the next instant, *I don't want to know. I'd rather not know.* And, *Super Sleuth, where's your courage?* The words of Shirin's last letter floated before her: 'No one to carry on the family name, the long line of Taipur Diazes.' Who was she then? Who was Reena Diaz, Super Sleuth? *Who am I, Mum?*

Raised voices filtering in from the dining room, the argument still going strong. Her dad's voice: 'Do you know what this will do to Ma?' Aunt Anita's, trembling with indignation, 'All you care about is Ma and her blasted status in bloody Taipur society... I talked to Ma.'

A startled pause, and then, her dad, 'What?'

'When Shirin's email came, I called Ma. I... I wanted to know how she felt.'

'And?'

'Ma is weary, Deepak. She doesn't care about status as much as she used to. She is getting old and she... she wants Shirin back. "What use this status," she said, "when I miss her so?" Those were her exact words. She said she tried to tell you this when you went to Taipur in September.'

'She might have...' Her dad's voice defensive.

'I know it's hard, Deepak, given the circumstances,' Aunt Anita's voice was gentle. 'Have you once thought about what Shirin went through, is still going through?'

Her dad, defeated: 'She didn't want Reena to know. She was adamant. Why this sudden change of heart?'

Her aunt's voice, soft: 'She just wants to come home, Deepak.'

She didn't want me to know what? The bed creaking as her mother settled in beside her, holding her close, her spiced breath warm on Reena's cheek. The casebook under her pillow, a hard damning lump. *Super Sleuth, what have you unearthed?*

❄   ❄   ❄

The phone rang, shrill, demanding, refusing to stop, dragging Reena out of a sleep populated by visions of a girl in pigtails playing hopscotch, who, when the dust cleared, and her face—Reena's—was revealed, parroted, 'They're protecting you,' like a robot. The argument between her dad and Aunt Anita had continued late into the night.

Reena had drifted in and out of slumber, anchored by her mother's arms, raised voices filtering into her dreams, turning them into nightmares. She wondered when they'd stopped arguing, called it a night, gone to bed. She blinked at the bedside clock. 3:25 a.m. Reena heard her parents' bedroom door open, her father curse as he stubbed his toe on the door stopper, his voice thick with sleep, 'Hello?' And then, louder, shot through with panic, 'Madhu?'

Reena sat up, wide awake. Her mother was already at the door, going to Deepak. Madhu? Why was Madhu calling and not Mai? Why was she calling in the middle of the night? Madhu had never called, ever. She didn't know their number. She was illiterate, she couldn't read.

She heard Aunt Anita's door creak open, the soft swish of her nightgown sweeping the floor. 'Deepak, what…'

On jelly legs, she walked to where her mother and Aunt Anita clustered around her dad at the phone, and her mother, face drawn, eyes wide with worry, put her arm around her, pulled her close.

'What riots?' Her father yelled. 'Riots! In Taipur?'

Slowly Deepak put the phone down and sank into the chair Preeti had pulled out for him. He ran his hand through his hair.

'What happened?' Aunt Anita asked the question Reena had been afraid to.

'There were riots in Taipur. It started off as a harmless fight between college boys and escalated into violence as these things do, with Hindus and Muslims blaming each other.'

'It's been building up. There've been lots of little incidents, petty fights between the Hindus and Muslims. When we were there last month we witnessed one in front of Aashirwad...' Her mum wrung her hands.

'Never mind that. Why is Madhu calling now? Is Ma...?' Anita interjected.

'They set fire to buildings, burnt down buses in Mirakatte. The parish council from the church intervened, trying to make peace. So last night, they burnt down the church hall while the parish meeting was in progress. Old Mr D'Sa is the only one who succumbed. Ma is seriously injured. She's in hospital. One of the nuns looked up our number and dialled it for Madhu.' Deepak's voice was shaky, disbelieving.

He stopped, as if afraid to continue. He looked first at Preeti, then Anita and finally his gaze settled on Reena. He looked at her for a long time, and then he looked down at his hands.

Then, so quietly that it was just a whisper, he said, 'She's delirious. She keeps saying one word over and over.'

'What, Deepak?' Aunt Anita's voice was harsh with worry.

'Shirin. She's asking for Shirin.'

In the silence that ensued, Reena watched an intrepid ant make its way across the dining table carrying a grain of basmati rice twice its size on its back.

'Coincidence,' Aunt Anita whispered, her eyes on Deepak. 'Karma, as the Hindus say.'

Silently, her dad handed Aunt Anita the phone. Aunt Anita's hands shook as she took it from him. 'Her number... It was in her email.'

A pause as she looked Shirin's number up, dialled and put the phone to her ear. A pause that felt like eternity. *Pick up, Aunt Shirin. Please.* Aunt Shirin jolted out of sleep by her phone ringing. Her sister's voice inhabiting the darkness of her snug bedroom after eleven years of silence. 'Come home.' The girl in pigtails from her dream swam before Reena's eyes: 'Bring me home, please.'

'Hello,' Aunt Anita's voice wobbled. 'Vinod? Is that you? This is Anita. Yes, it is me. Ma is not well. Can I speak to Shirin? Shirin! It really is you...'

CHAPTER TWENTY-FIVE
A Daughter's Duty

Saturday. The Eyes. They were everywhere. Stalking her. Like in the early days after.

A headache had gradually crept up on her, dull at first, now throbbing. It loomed like a bad omen behind her eyelids, threatening nightmares. She had managed to fight it off with paracetamol and ibuprofen. She couldn't any longer.

'I am going to bed,' she said.

'That bad?' Vinod asked.

She nodded, barely able to keep her eyes open. Once in bed, the duvet pulled up to her chin, she succumbed, heavy eyelids shutting closed.

Pain bloomed red flowers on a field of white, where a pair of empty accusing eyes danced, holding court, telling a story...

The morning after her wedding, Shirin woke to sunlight streaming in through unfamiliar, mosquito-netted windows, pink curtains waving; in a bed far too big for her and smelling of man: musky with a lemony tang; draped in strange blankets—and still a virgin. She looked

up: flaky white ceiling, red blades of a Bajaj fan dron-
ing lazily. No lizards draped precariously across wooden
beams. No being shaken awake by Madhu from depths
of slumber, with a cheery, 'Time for mass.' She wondered
if the coach had reached Taipur yet, with dawn arriving
orangey rose over the tops of the coconut trees, or if it was
stuck somewhere in the ghats. She wondered if her family was thinking of her, if they were missing her. A snap-
shot of Madhu: lipstick smeared across her face, holding
Shirin close, body racking with sobs, loath to let her go.
'Look after her,' she'd said to Vinod, wagging a trembling
finger at him, 'Heart of gold, she's got. Heart of gold...'

Heated voices raised in argument filtered in through the
thin walls. Vinod... Was that really Vinod's voice? 'Couldn't
you at least have stayed off the drink on my wedding day?'

Shirin sat up, pulling the blanket around her, con-
scious of her flimsy nightgown even though the door to
the bedroom was closed and there was no one to see her.

A feminine voice murmured something. Her mother-
in-law? Then, 'You scared her. I hadn't been wedded two
minutes and you had to make a scene. What the hell am
I supposed to tell her? That I hid the fact that I have an
alcoholic for a brother, that I have been hiding it, protecting *you* all my life...?'

Now she knew. The empty eyes—only filled by alcohol. She bunched the sheets in her fists.

'Vinod...' Her father-in-law's voice.

'And now you slink in, dead drunk. Her first morning
with us. What am I supposed to say? How am I supposed

to explain?' The edge of pain in Vinod's voice made Shirin want to hold him, to console him, to do the things they hadn't the previous night.

'I will take him out. Don't you worry...' Her father-in-law again.

'We should have told them upfront. She'll think I trapped her into marrying me...' Vinod, *her husband*, was worried about lying to her. He cared about what she thought. He cared.

'She'll think no such thing. You are a catch for them. No dowry, wealthy...'

'Ma, don't start. I want to leave here, begin anew.'

'Please, putha...'

'Like we agreed, we will stay here a month. Then we are moving out.' The proprietary use of 'we'. Shirin's heart bloomed. Just her and Vinod in a little house of their own. In time, maybe children... Vinod's voice, soft: 'I can't take this anymore, Ma. Lying to everyone. Especially her, I don't want to deceive her...'

'Not married a day and already she has such a hold over you.'

'She's my *wife*, Ma...' His wife. A warmth spread through Shirin. His wife. Then why hadn't he kissed her, made love to her?

Sounds of dragging. Loud cursing. Slurred. Prem. The gate opening. A car starting. Silence. Then, footsteps. Halting outside the bedroom door. Shirin lay back down, pulled the blanket up over her head. The bedroom door opened softly, the latch turned, the bed sagged beside her.

His smell: woody, spicy; pervading her senses. Would he hold her? Would he kiss her? Make love to her? The tingle of anticipation, the desire, the ache. She felt him turn. The bed complained, creaked. And then, nothing... Slowly she pulled down the sheet, opened her eyes. He was leaning on one elbow, looking down at her. As she watched, with one finger, he traced her features. So gentle. Hardly a touch. More a whisper-soft caress. On her eyes, her nose, her mouth. Her gaze locked with his. Desire exploding in her breasts, her lower body. Her mouth opening in a small moan, an involuntary sigh.

An ear-splitting crash invaded their intimate silence, stilled the finger on her lips. She wanted to flick her tongue out, pull his finger into her mouth, suck on it. The crashing sound continued: a stainless-steel tumbler falling, rolling round and round on the floor until it stilled. Other sounds filtered in. The rattling of the front gate. Dogs barking. Vendors yelling. Footsteps sounded; loud, deliberate. They hovered near the closed door of their bedroom, stopped. A strident knock. 'Vinod, Shetty Uncle is here. He couldn't attend the wedding yesterday. Wants to wish you well.' Footsteps moving away. Sounds from the living room. A man's voice.

Vinod retrieved his finger leaving Shirin bereft, cold. She wanted to pull the blanket back up. She wanted to pull Vinod down, on top of her, to ease the longing, to fill that suddenly empty part of her. Instead she smiled shyly up at him. Oh, why was she so timid?

'Time to get up,' he whispered. He bent down. Shirin's heart caught in her throat. Was he going to kiss her? He did: a feather-soft kiss on her eyebrow. She swallowed her disappointment and got up to face her first day as the new daughter-in-law.

Her mother-in-law cornered her as she stumbled to the bathroom, while Vinod was making small talk with Shetty Uncle.

'I have waited all my life for a daughter to help with the chores,' she announced. 'From tomorrow, I expect you to wake at six thirty and help me with breakfast.'

Shirin nodded meekly. Her mother-in-law still blocked the entry to the bathroom. 'Now, after you have brushed, come and make tea for our guest and help with the lunch preparations.'

'Yes,' said Shirin, and only then did her mother-in-law move.

After Shetty Uncle left, Vinod announced that he had to pop into work for a while. 'This is what happens when you have your own business. Never a moment's rest.' His voice hardened as he said the last bit.

That afternoon, she accompanied her mother-in-law to the dry cleaner's. As she hopped along to match her mother-in-law's stride, Shirin was assaulted by thoughts of home. What were they doing at this very moment? Were they eating lunch, munching on fat red rice soaked in mackerel curry with sweet squash bhaji and brine-soaked lime pickle? Were they missing her?

Walking back, laden with bags, Shirin felt someone hovering over her right shoulder. 'Voniye, let me carry that for you,' a voice said. She looked up. Prem. She had not felt uneasy when he came up behind her and she didn't now. He took the bags from her, not meeting her gaze. No pungent tang as he stepped close. 'Why aren't you at work?' her mother-in-law asked, smiling. 'Just got back. Vinod is coming with Da.' He sounded normal. Slightly diffident. Very different from the leering Prem who scared her.

Why had she been so scared of him? He was okay, really, she decided as he regaled them with jokes all the way home. Teasing his ma. Laughing at himself.

When they reached home, he held the door open for her: 'See you later, Voniye, I am going out.' He returned half an hour later with boxes of soan papdi and laddoos. 'For the lovely women of the house,' he said, grinning.

As she helped her mother-in-law roll chapattis for dinner, Shirin mused about her brother-in-law. To think she'd actually gone so far as to consider calling off the wedding because of her irrational fear of Prem! Yes, he had a drink problem. So? Richa Uncle, Mini Aunty, her cousin Ronnie all had drink problems. Her mum and Madhu had always accused her of an overactive imagination, worrying that there were ghosts lurking in the toilet, convinced there was a dead body in the courtyard that time during a power cut when she stumbled on a coconut frond... She watched her mother-in-law place the perfect circle of chapatti dough right onto the flames, watched it puff up and rise, the charred sweet smell enveloping her.

This unease, this fear of Prem was irrational, all in her head.

That evening, after she'd bathed, she lavishly applied the body cream that smelt deliciously edible (wedding gift from Anita), and waited eagerly for Vinod to consummate their marriage. He held her in his arms gently as if she was something precious—when what she had wanted was for him to crush her roughly against his body—and, instead of kissing her, said, 'I have a confession to make.'

She waited, looking up at him, wanting him to do so many things to her, wanting them *now*.

'I lied to you. By omission. My brother Prem... he's an alcoholic. That's why he's not married, even though he's older. I am sorry. I should have told you earlier, but I... when I saw your eyes peeking down at me from between the bars of the window, Shirin... your beautiful eyes... I... I couldn't find the words...'

Her beautiful eyes. How could he say these lovely things and not make love to her? He kissed first her left eyebrow and then her right. Why didn't he kiss her mouth? She wanted to know how it felt. She wanted to see if he tasted like he smelt: spicy, of woodsmoke.

'I am sorry. Does it bother you that I lied?'

She shook her head. She couldn't think straight. His presence, being in his arms, was so distracting. Why were they wasting time talking about Prem? As if he'd read her mind, Vinod smiled tenderly at her. 'You are my special miracle, Shirin.' He traced his fingers lightly down Shirin's face and all thoughts fled her mind. 'Shonu. Can I call you Shonu?'

She nodded, unable to speak. Was this it? Was he going to...?

Vinod bent down and kissed her on the lips. It was better than all her fantasies; more pleasurable than she had imagined. She had to restrain herself from throwing herself at him and begging him to have his way with her. After, he casually ran his fingers down her throat, raising goosebumps, stopping just above her breasts. *Please.* She moaned so loudly that he had to shush her. She was so embarrassed that she couldn't look at him. 'Shonu,' he said softly, and even though her eyes were tightly shut, she could tell from his voice that he was smiling. 'My little tigress.'

She blushed. She felt his fingers trace her profile.

'Have you ever been in love?' he asked.

Tariq. 'No.'

'Did you want to?'

'Run away with me, Shirin,' he had said. 'Yes. I fantasised about Prince Charming whisking me away into the sunset.'

'Oh.' A pause while his fingers stopped just short of stroking her breasts, making her want to arch to meet his touch. 'Were you disappointed that you had an arranged marriage?'

'A bit...'

'Oh...'

'Until I realised that instead of coming on a horse, my Prince Charming came with his parents and asked my mother's permission to whisk me away. He was a gentleman, my Prince Charming, with impeccable manners...' How had she known what to say? She was normally mute around him, so full of longing that no words came out.

He bent down and kissed her again, for longer this time. 'I cannot believe you are mine,' He said, 'Tell me about you. I want to know everything.'

I want you to make love to me. I want to know how it feels to be loved. Her wantonness worried her. Was she wrong to want her husband? Was it sinful to lust after him? Why did he not want her? Was there something wrong with her? Did she have body odour? She couldn't possibly. She had checked. And he was holding her close, kissing her eyebrows, her nose. He wouldn't if she had BO. Maybe she was too hairy. But she had waxed before the wedding. Perhaps she did not have enough hair. It couldn't be that. He hadn't even undressed her. Maybe it was her weight. She must be repulsive to him. But he kept saying she was beautiful...

It was flattering that he wanted to know about her life, and so she told him. Talking about home made her forget her shyness, how tongue-tied she felt around him. She told him about the nuns and the priests, Madhu, Jacinta and Walter, Anita, Deepak and Rex the Third. He listened and he laughed. He looked deep into her eyes (as she had always wanted him to) and played with her hair. He kissed her once more and then again. But he did not make love to her.

The next morning she stirred awake when Vinod eased himself softly off the bed. She was getting used to his solid presence beside her. 'Go back to sleep,' he whispered, bending down to kiss her nose, his stubble, which had sprouted as if by magic overnight, tickling her cheek, causing an involuntary giggle. 'No,' she whispered back, 'I'm getting up too.'

She helped her mother-in-law make breakfast, waved goodbye to Vinod soon after, feeling bereft. There was no sign of Prem. He must have left earlier.

After she'd cleaned the breakfast dishes, her mother-in-law asked her to go to the market: 'You remember how to get to the dry-cleaner's? Good. The market is the first right after. Here's a list. Get me these things. You might as well start as you mean to go along.'

Shirin walked down the crowded, dirty street, getting lost only a couple of times. The stench of rotting vegetables, the noise of flies buzzing and people haggling reached her before the market came into view. The sun beat down mercilessly, plastering her hair to her head. Her underskirt was wet with sweat. Her sari blouse stuck to her back and fat droplets collected in the nape of her neck.

By the side of the main road were vendors: some sitting on mats, others not bothering with mats and squatting cross-legged on the dusty mud, all heralding their wares: fresh vegetables, fish, bangles, hair clips. She was fingering the wilting bunches of spinach bhaji, trying to choose the freshest one, when she had the strangest sensation of being watched. She shrugged it off at first. So many people were pushing past, pressing into her. Carts equipped with little gas stoves jostled for space, selling egg bhurji, biryani, chaat: the smells permeating the air, attracting flies. People argued and bargained. Drunks staggered and weaved their way through the crowd. Stray dogs and cows milled. But the feeling of being watched persisted, raising goosebumps despite the sweltering heat, despite the crush. *My imagination again*, she told herself.

The pungent musky odour of rotting vegetables, fish and perspiration permeated the air, making her want to gag. She bought the bhaji, surreptitiously looking over her shoulder. A man standing in the back of an open truck piled high with juicy striped watermelons threw them down to his friend who stood, arms outstretched amongst the press, and caught them one by one, not missing.

Goosebumps. Despite the sweat beading her upper lip, saturating her sari blouse.

Piles of jackfruit, prickly green exterior yawning open to reveal the yellow fruit inside, juggled for space alongside baskets of mangoes, teetering masses of tomatoes, onions, dry red chillies and fresh green ones. Triangular flags depicting the lotus—Vote BJP—and the palm of the human hand—Vote for Congress; leftover remnants of the recent election campaign, flapped forlornly overhead. Next to the vegetable vendors sat the fisherwomen, chatting among themselves while managing to sell their fish and compete with each other at the same time. She thought she heard footsteps behind her. Thwack. Thwack. *Well, of course, there are hundreds of people here. Stop this now, Shirin.*

People piled into the road, weighed down by their wares, and the bus drivers had to honk their way at snail's pace through the throng. A cow stood still in the middle of the road, peacefully chewing cud, not caring about the build-up of buses behind, the persistent honks. Finally one of the bus conductors jumped down from the bus in front, chewing paan and shaking his head in frustration, the khaki bag hanging loosely by his side and blending with his khaki uniform; the bus tickets, a riot of blue, green and pink, peeking out. He gently gave the offending cow a nudge on her backside. Shirin stopped to watch and the footsteps she was half aware of stopped right behind her. She turned. A gaggle of women in matching bright pink churidars. She fought the impulse to run. She still had the meat to buy. Her mother-in-law would not be pleased if she went home without half the stuff: 'I thought I heard footsteps. Someone was following me.'

The cow mooed gently and swished her tail right in the conductor's face. Then it turned slowly round to look at the conductor, who was busy wiping his face with a multi-coloured checked handkerchief the size of a dinner plate, and very deliberately defecated right on the conductor's feet. Someone clapped. Shirin turned to walk towards the butcher. Thwack. Thwack. Right behind her. A whiff of something pungent. She whirled round, bumping into someone, stepping on their toes. 'Hey, watch out, you almost broke my chappal,' a woman yelled in Shirin's ear in Kannada. 'Sorry. Sorry,' Shirin mumbled.

The cow, with another swish of her tail, gracefully walked off the road and into the crush of people, who made space for it to walk past as if it were royalty, leaving the conductor holding his handkerchief and staring at the pile of cow dung adorning his feet.

Shirin was at the butcher's, trying not to gag at the reek of chicken droppings and raw meat, trying to ignore the terrible squawks of the poor chicken she had selected for that evening's supper, trying not to look at the blood slowly trickling down the drain by the side of the shop, when she felt a prickle at the back of her head. Hot breaths, rank, sour, lifting the hair off her neck. She turned, even as her heart thudded against her chest, as goosebumps played havoc on her skin. A pair of eyes. Empty. Leering.

'Ma'am, ma'am, your chicken is ready. Did you want anything else?'

'No, um, uh...' she held out the money, grabbed the change and the bag the butcher was holding out to her, and ran. She pushed through the crush of people, ignoring the annoyed yells, the 'watch outs', the dogs following her, barking. Chappals hitting feet, slap, slap, slap, right behind her. She ran through the crowded roads, clutching the shopping bag close, reciting 'Hail Marys' in her head. Hoarse breaths, loud, harsh, gaining. *No.*

The sun dipped behind a cloud and it was dark, all of a sudden. The ends of her sari caught on a stone and she tripped. Her sandal broke. Pungent breath upon her. She turned, looked into a pair of empty eyes. She screamed. A man urinating into the ditch on the opposite side of the road turned, yelled, 'Are you okay?' his voice drowned by the persistent horn of an approaching bus. She gathered the shopping and ran barefoot, sandals forgotten. She only stopped when she reached the gate to Vinod's house and she held on to the bars, bent double, trying to catch her breath.

No harsh breaths except her own panting gasps. No chappal-thwacking footsteps. No goosebumps.

'Are you okay, ma'am?' the man squatting opposite the gate beside a giant pile of tender coconuts asked. 'Do you want a drink? 50 paise only.' He handed her an opened coconut, straw sticking out.

'No, thanks.' Trying to ignore the man's crestfallen face—it was her mother-in-law's money; she didn't know if she would have to account for a tender coconut—she opened the gate and walked inside on jelly legs.

'There was no need to run, no hurry,' her mother-in-law said, a small smile on her face, holding out her hand for the shopping bag. 'What's this? This bhaji is rotting. Not fresh at all. And these tendli—my God... the chicken... only bones. Which butcher did you go to?'

The butcher. The Eyes. Shirin's legs threatened to give way.

'I'll have to come with you tomorrow, show you who to buy from...' At these words, Shirin couldn't stop herself. She put her arms around her mother-in-law and gave her a hug.

'Now, child,' her mother-in-law said, awkwardly patting Shirin's back, 'There's no need for this.' But her voice was gentler than Shirin had ever heard it. 'Come, we've work to do.'

Afterwards, they stood side by side in the kitchen, Shirin's mother-in-law grinding masala for the chicken curry in the deafeningly loud mixer and Shirin chopping onions, trying to ignore the blisters on the soles of her feet, trying not to think of cooling Boroline, of Madhu in the crowded kitchen of her childhood populated with delicious aromas, drowsy dog and Nagappa's cat trying to steal fish bones.

'Not that way; that's too big. Small pieces, like this.' Her mother-in-law peered at her, at her runny nose, at the tears falling freely down her face, which she'd tried, unsuccessfully, to rub away using her sari blouse. 'Here,' she handed Shirin a cloth.

Shirin blew her nose noisily, chopping the onions the way her mother-in-law had showed her, not sure if her tears were due to the onions, homesickness or the scare she'd had. *Don't think about that. Don't go there.*

'He was such a busy little boy, always doing something,' her mother-in-law said, as she soaked dry fish in cold water from the tap.

'Huh?'

'Vinod. You see this little wooden handle here?' She pointed to the window. 'He put that in. All on his own. When he was nine.'

As they cooked, her mother-in-law regaled her with stories of Vinod. Shirin listened, agog, tears forgotten as she tried to imagine this husband she was in awe of as a little boy. And as they sat together eating lunch—dry fish chutney, red rice, leftover fish curry, raw-jackfruit pickle—her mother-in-law started talking about Prem. 'Vinod must have told you...' Her voice was tentative. A question. Shirin nodded, mind flashing, without her wanting it to, to that morning at the market. She was sure it was Prem she'd seen. But she hadn't really seen him. Only felt his breath on her back, too close. And the Eyes. As if they didn't belong to a person at all... *Are you imagining things again? But I did see the Eyes, someone did follow me. Did they really? And you're sure it was Prem?* Prem carrying her bags, cracking jokes, bringing her sweets… Her appetite was gone. The food suddenly unappealing.

'Growing up, he didn't stand a chance,' her mother-in-law was saying, 'Vinod was better than him at everything, despite being younger. And it was our fault as well; we compared them all the time. On hindsight...' Now that she'd started talking, her mother-in-law seemed to want to keep going. *Please stop, I don't want to know.* 'And then, when he was fifteen, he fell in with this crowd. Rich boys. And he discovered alcohol. We got the priests and nuns to talk to him, took him to the rehab clinic in Kankannadi, even stayed with him for a week in the retreat centre in Potta. Nothing worked...'

'He can be so nice when he's sober. You saw yourself yesterday.' Her mother-in-law's voice was a sigh. Her hand, which rested on the table, clenched and unclenched on a handkerchief. Instinctively, Shirin reached across, put her hand on her mother-in-law's and squeezed. 'It's been hard for Vinod, you know. After he did his MBA in London,' pride in her mother-in-law's voice, 'he was offered a job there. He really wanted to take it. But he had to come back, join the family business. Prem. We can't handle him on our own when he's drunk.' A pause while her mother-in-law used the handkerchief to wipe her eyes, 'Vinod wanted to tell you before the wedding. He doesn't like to lie. We couldn't find any girl from Bangalore to marry him. Everyone here knows. Doesn't want to be associated with our family.' She was being privy to her mother-in-law's deepest secrets, Shirin realised, her darkest shame. She left her hand on her mother-in-law's until her agitation stilled. 'Shall I serve you more rice?' she asked.

It happened four days after her wedding. Shirin was all alone in the house. Vinod, Prem and her father-in-law were at the office. Her mother-in-law had gone to visit one of the neighbours who'd had a heart attack and was recovering in Manipal hospital, an hour's bus ride away. 'Vinod and them will pick me up on their way home. Will you be okay?' she'd asked of Shirin. 'Of course,' Shirin had replied, pleased to have a couple of hours' solitude.

Jacinta had called just after her mother-in-law left. Her mother, who was not a phone person, had sounded enthusiastic.

'There's some good news,' she'd gushed. Shirin had never heard her mother gush before, but there was no other word to describe it. 'Deepak's marriage is fixed. The girl's name is Preeti. She's very well educated, has done her MA. Very good family.'

Shirin smiled, saying, 'Hmm...' and, 'Ah...' at the appropriate places and counting the number of times her mother said 'very good', the way she peppered her speech with adjectives. Usually when Jacinta called, it was Shirin who had to make conversation while her mother listened. It was great to be at the listening end of her mother's rare animation. She didn't want to ask, but she did. 'Do they know about Deepak?'

'Yes.' The sigh audible in her mother's voice. 'She... Preeti... limps. It is barely noticeable. Birth defect. One leg shorter than the other. They haven't had many offers for her hand. She's a sweet girl. Thin and fair-complexioned. Not very tall. Deepak likes her very much. The family is from Mangalore. Good family. Deepak told her straight out. They were upset, of course. I think the parents didn't want to go ahead. Then Preeti piped up and said, "We can always adopt."' Her mother paused to take a breath.

'She sounds very nice,' Shirin said.

'Yes. The engagement will be here. Once the date is decided, I'll let you and Vinod know.'

Shirin felt a sudden painful rush of homesickness. She could practically smell the grass, taste Madhu's fish fry and see the hibiscus flowers swaying gently in the breeze. She ached for the easy familiarity of home.

'Oh, I almost forgot. Deepak's got a job in Bangalore. With Infosys. Very good-paying job.' Pride in her mother's voice. 'He's moving there in a few months.'

Her brother would be here, near her. 'That's wonderful!'

'You're all moving away,' her mother sighed. 'He said he'll visit home regularly.'

'Of course he will, Ma.' *Wish I could come home now, just for a bit, just to rest my head on your shoulder, to lose myself in Madhu's embrace.*

'How are you?' her mother asked

'Okay.'

Jacinta hesitated. 'You are happy, aren't you, Shirin?'

'Yes. Vinod is very nice'

'And your in-laws?'

'They are nice too.' What else could she possibly say?

'Okay then. Take care. Give my love to everyone'

'Wait...' Shirin said, but her mother had already disconnected.

There were so many questions Shirin wanted to ask, so much she wanted to tell and so much she wanted to know. If it had been Madhu on the phone, Shirin would have said, 'How are you? What did you cook for lunch? What have you made for dinner? Do you miss me? Do you fill the void I have left behind with busyness? Do you remember me when you make my favourite dishes?

'Madhu, I was brought up to believe that making a good match was my duty as a daughter and that being a good wife was my vocation. Why didn't anybody tell me how hard it would be? When I got married, I thought I had done my job, ticked all the boxes and got the certificate. But nobody prepared me for after.

'I didn't realise that I would spend lonely nights in my husband's chaste arms wondering why my marriage had not been consummated, that I would spend long days slaving to please my in-laws. You taught me to cook. But nobody taught me how to deal with my in-laws, the complicated dance I have to perform to keep everyone happy. Nobody told me what to do about my brother-in-law—

who I am pretty sure followed me to the market and spied on me—who sometimes looks at me in a way that sends shivers down my spine. Do I tell Vinod? How, when I am so shy, so tongue-tied around him? When all I can think of when I'm in his arms is why he doesn't make love to me. And what if he takes his brother's side? Dismisses my worries as fancies of imagination? After all, he's known me less than a week and his brother his whole life.'

Shirin conducted imagined conversations such as these with Madhu as she cooked, washed dishes and scrubbed clothes, when waves of homesickness caught her un-awares. She ached for the uncomplicated life she had led in her little village where everyone had known her from the time she was a babe in arms. She ached for mango trees, wide open spaces and the comfort of Madhu's arms. Instead, what she had was dust, crowds and the compli-cated feelings that Vinod's arms aroused in her.

Vinod: his kisses, the way he looked at her. Tonight would definitely be the night, she thought. Tomorrow, she would no longer be a virgin.

And now, she had Deepak's engagement to look for-ward to. A celebration. Going home. It would be such fun. Anita would be there, full of stories about college life and Uttam, her love. They would tease Deepak about Preeti and watch him blush. They would threaten to tell Preeti about all his many infatuations and crushes.

Lost in thought, she was barely aware of the front door slamming shut. She glanced at the clock. 5:15 p.m. Her mother-in-law had left at 4:30. Surely she couldn't be back so soon? Vinod was not due home till 7:00 p.m. at least. Something must have happened.

She walked to the living room quickly. When she saw that it was her brother-in-law staggering in the doorway, panic gripped her heart. She had not considered this possibility. Since that day at the market, she'd hardly seen Prem. He arrived home late at night after she and Vinod were in bed, left early in the morning. He'd stayed out of her way and she had relaxed, become complacent. *Stop it, Shirin. He's nice, he brought you sweets. It's all in your head.* But he was leering at her, definitely leering. This was the other Prem, the one who made her uneasy, scared her.

'So, Voniye,' Prem sneered, taking a step towards her, swaying on his feet, 'aren't you going to offer to make me some tea? And perhaps something more. Something you give my dear brother every night.' His words slurred. He licked his lips loudly.

She could smell the alcohol from where she was standing, at the opposite end of the living room. She started taking small steps backward toward the dining room, hoping he wouldn't notice. Did it have a door leading outside? She couldn't remember. Did any of the rooms? *Vinod, please come home now.*

'Are you running away from me, Voniye?' A smirk. Prem looked directly at her and Shirin reeled back. His eyes. Expressionless, empty, yet somehow menacing. The Eyes from the market. She had not imagined them.

As she watched, Prem locked the front door, very deliberately. Fear gripped her heart, rooting her legs to the ground, even as every instinct warned her to flee. She was trapped. Why had she not confided in Vinod her worries regarding Prem? Why had she not gone with her mother-in-law to the hospital? Why had she been so pleased at the thought of having some time alone? *Vinod, please come home.*

'Why are you doing that?' she managed to whisper.

'You belong to me really. I am the older one.'

'No.'

'He's my brother. I'm sure he won't mind if I share you just this once.' Prem was smiling.

'No. No, Prem. This is wrong.'

He advanced towards her, laughing. 'Vinod won't mind. My *younger* brother, always so perfect, always so good... He'll share. He has to. After all, he gets to have you every day. And I, the older one, have nobody. Is that fair? I ask you, *is that fair?*'

And then she was running, running for her life, running through all the rooms as fast as her legs could carry her. It was no use. He was rapidly gaining on her, no matter how hard she ran. She could hear him right behind her. His breaths harsh. His chappal-clad feet, SLAP, SLAP, SLAP, gaining relentlessly. This house was too small and too unfamiliar. There was no place to hide.

Please, God, she prayed, her breath coming in gasps, *please help. Vinod, COME HOME! Please. Now.*

He caught up with her in the kitchen. She couldn't run any further. There was nowhere to run. The kitchen had no exit, and he was blocking the only entrance. He advanced towards her, swaying on his feet. Her lips moved in prayer, to a God she had unquestioningly believed in all her life. Surely He would protect her now? Her breath came in loud sobs. Tears ran down her face without her even realising. She was trapped. There was no reasoning with this man. His intent was written all over his face: in his sneer; his maniacal laughter. He was almost upon her when she realised that God would not intervene, that it was up to her to save herself. Her hands, which were behind her back, scrabbled around in the drawers she was backed up against for a weapon, and, almost by chance, landed on the handle of a knife...

He was upon her before she could do anything with the knife, pinning her down, trapping her. His breath made her gag, her sobs escaping in huge gasps. He was laughing as he tore at her clothes, at the Salwar Kameez in the latest style her mother had bought her as part of her wedding trousseau from the new shop in Dommur. His eyes widened as he took in her lingerie, a gift from Anita. And as he started pawing at her breasts, Shirin shut her eyes tight and did what she had done a million times when she was growing up. She escaped into an imaginary world inside her head where all was well...

Afterwards, he rolled off her, grunting with pleasure. Slowly, Shirin willed herself back into the nightmare. Every part of her body hurt; the pain unimaginable, and yet nothing compared to the anguish in her heart. She was ruined. Vinod would not want her now.

And as if thinking of him had brought him to her, Shirin heard his voice.

'Open the door. Now.' Loud thuds, banging.

'Coming, little brother,' said Prem, languidly zipping up his trousers.

As if from a distance, Shirin heard Prem open the door, heard Vinod say, 'You're drunk. Where's Shonu? What's happened?' Heard him run through the rooms, Prem's laughter following him, and stop abruptly in front of her in the kitchen. Her eyes were shut tight. She would not open them. She did not want Vinod to see her like this. Ruined. Worthless.

And then, Shirin felt Vinod's touch on her face, her hands, her body as he gathered her in his arms. 'What happened, Shonu?'

Prem laughed. She flinched.

'Little brother. Perfect in every way. But cannot give it to your wife now, can you?'

'What did you do, Prem? What did you do?' She heard the anger in Vinod's voice. The anguish. He laid her down on the floor, oh so gently. She heard him stand, heard someone choking. Her eyes flew open. Vinod...

Vinod had his brother up against the wall, his hands around his brother's neck. It was Prem who was choking. Good.

'What have you done, Prem?' Vinod repeated, his voice a wail.

When Prem was blue in the face, Vinod dropped him abruptly and turned away. He started toward Shirin. A mistake. Prem lashed out at Vinod, hitting him in the shoulder. 'She wanted it.'

Vinod punched him back.

Prem retaliated with a blow to Vinod's stomach. 'She was gagging for it.'

Vinod punched Prem again, so hard that Prem reeled back from the blow but just managed to maintain his balance.

And a thought that had been hovering since this nightmare began crystallised in Shirin's head: True. What Prem was saying was true. She *had* desperately wanted it. She *had* been gagging for it. Had she brought this upon herself by wanting to lose her virginity so desperately, by wanting to consummate her marriage so much?

'Ha! She was a virgin,' Prem leered.

Vinod punched him so hard he fell to the floor.

'You couldn't even get it up enough to give it to her.' Two more punches. Vinod was sobbing now.

Prem stood up. Staggered. 'My perfect brother. Not perfect in bed, now, are you?'

As she listened to Vinod's loud, broken sobs, anger, white hot and sharp rose inside Shirin. She wanted to hurt Prem, this man who had taken so much from her. She moved to sit up and realised that she was still holding the knife. Slowly, despite the protests of her body, despite the fact that she was bleeding, she stood and with all the strength left in her, she stabbed the man who had raped her. She'd been aiming for the back of his neck. She got his left shoulder. Blood spurted, soaking her hand, red as the flesh of juicy ripe tomatoes stacked in teetering rows at the market, red as the chilli powder Madhu used to pound to a paste in the hand grinder. *Don't think of home. Not now.*

Prem roared in pain and clutched his shoulder. His hand came away covered in blood. He stared at it, shocked, and with another loud roar, advanced towards her, eyes wild. As he lunged at her, he slipped and fell forward, his head hitting the stone kitchen counter with a thud. Shirin watched in horror as his heavy breathing stilled, as his expression froze, as the blood spewed from the wound in his head. Overcoming her revulsion, she shook him, willing him to wake up, shouting, 'Prem! Prem!' over and over again. But he just lay there, his bloodshot eyes open, staring unseeingly at her...

❄ ❄ ❄

The phone rang shrilly, waking her. Nightmare. Thank God. The bedside clock blinked out the time, 23:15, in blood-red digits.

'Must be those teenagers again,' Vinod, who'd been reading *The Economist* beside her, grumbled. They had had crank calls recently from teenagers shouting swear words. He smiled down at her softly. 'Go back to sleep.'

They did not have caller ID. There was no need as hardly anyone called them on the home phone, work-related calls being directed to their mobiles.

'Leave it,' said Shirin, closing her eyes and pulling the duvet close.

But she knew he wouldn't.

Just in case...

'Hello... Hello, Anita? Anita, it really is you!'

Anita! Her Anita! It couldn't be. Her eyes flew open, met Vinod's wary ones and she knew it was. Why was she calling? What time was it in India? The dark hour before dawn. *Something's happened.*

Panic held Shirin's heart in a vice-like grip and wouldn't let go even as Vinod talked to Anita while signalling frantically to her with his eyes, even as she heard him say those dreaded words, 'What's happened?' in a tone that confirmed her worst fears.

The nightmare: the memory of her crime, fresh in her mind. A premonition.

'Yes, she's here,' Vinod's voice was grave. 'Just hold on...'

He handed the phone to her, eyes worried. As she took the receiver from him, she saw her stricken reflection staring back at her from the dressing table mirror. Why had they placed the mirror in such an awkward place? Why on earth was she thinking that now?

She listened to the static on the phone, a heartbeat before she said, 'Hello, Anita?' and heard her beloved sister's voice, five thousand miles away but sounding just as if she was beside her, after eleven long and silent years.

Vinod's hand reached hers across the tangle of bed sheets and squeezed.

'Shirin...' Anita's voice caught on a sob. 'I can't believe I'm speaking to you!'

'Anita, what's happened?'

'It's Ma. She's... she's not well. And she's been asking for you. Constantly. Can you come?'

'Is she... Is she…?' *Dying?* She couldn't say it.

'When can you come?'

'As soon as I book my ticket. Oh, Anu, why didn't you call me earlier?'

Crackly static hummed down the line, filling the awkward pause, the unsaid words. *You fool. Why on earth did you say that?*

'You know...' Anita whispered, finally.

'Yes.'

'So you *are* coming?' Anita asked, her voice shaky.

'I am. I was going to anyway.'

'I know.' Her sister's voice soft.

She was going home!

❊ ❊ ❊

'Kate.'

'Yes?'

Beloved Kate. Her best friend. Her only friend. Who knew everything about her. Her darkest secret: 'I went to kill him, Kate. I *wanted* to kill him.' 'You had reason enough, Shirin. God knows, I have thrown enough plates at Dave; it's a wonder he's still alive.' Her deepest shame: 'I could not look after my daughter, Kate. I… I ran away from her.' 'You did the best for her in the circumstances. That's not the same as running away.' Kate, who loved her despite it all. Who had broken all the rules and promised her the job right after her interview. Who had been instrumental in promoting her to manager despite the hiccup with Ian. She hated letting Kate down when she had entrusted her with the responsibility of managing a team. Shirin had worked herself and her team hard and they were set to deliver to deadline. If Shirin went now, it wouldn't be a catastrophe. The team could cope without her. She prepared to say all this, but her mouth wouldn't work, even as Kate waited for her to speak.

'Shirin,' Kate's voice was gentle. 'Are you okay?'

And still, Shirin couldn't speak.

Kate stood, came round the desk and put her arms around Shirin. 'What's the matter?'

At that, like a dam bursting, the words flowed. 'My mother, she's dying...'

Kate didn't hesitate. 'Go.' And then, meeting her gaze, 'How? When?'

'Anita called late last night.' How she had longed to say these words!

'Oh, Shirin.' Kate held her close.

'She's asking for me, Kate. Ma. She's asking for me.' Hardly able to believe it herself. 'I... I hope I get a chance to make peace.'

'You will.'

'But if they called, she must be really...What if it's too late?'

'Shirin, there's no point thinking that way. When are you planning on leaving?'

'Tonight.'

'And Anita called last night? Well, then...'

'I'm sorry, Kate.'

'Huh?'

'About work...'

'Shirin, work is the last thing you should worry about. I'm not saying we won't miss you. But we'll manage. Take as long as you like. Just go.'

'Thanks, Kate.'

'But come back, you hear?'

Shirin grinned shakily. 'I will.'

Kate's eyes sparkled with tears. 'Good luck. With Reena and everything. Take care... I'll keep my fingers crossed for your mum.'

'Thank you. Vinod will keep you posted.'

'He's not going?'

'No. His boss is not as understanding as mine. I'll miss you, Kate.'

Gently, Kate released her from her embrace. 'Me too. Call me,' she whispered, 'And now go.'

✻   ✻   ✻

'Damn that effing son of a bitch. I could kill him.'

Shirin stopped packing, looked up. Vinod's hands were bunched into fists, eyes bloodshot.

'You were right, Shonu, as always. When I asked him for leave and he said that I could go, but that he could not guarantee the job would be waiting when I got back... I was tempted to say, "Fuck you asshole, I quit." But I realised I didn't want to lose it. The job. It's my identity, who I am now...'

She nodded. 'I know.'

'I wish I was going with you. I wish I could be there for you when...' He pulled her into his arms and after a bit, she rested her head against his chest and listened to his heartbeat.

'I'll be fine.'

He stroked her hair. 'You are the bravest person I know.'

She looked up. 'Really?'

He met her gaze. 'Yes. Really.'

I'm scared, Vinod. If she's asking for me, does that mean she has forgiven me? And Reena. Does she know? And if she does, what then? What of me? She did not voice her doubts. Instead, she stood on tiptoes and, ignoring the instinct that held her back, put her hands around his neck, pulled his face down to hers and kissed him. And right there, among her clothes, half in and half out of the open suitcase, she gave herself to him. All of her. No holding back. No flinching. To this man who had stood by her, who had stayed with her through those dark, dark days and nightmare-populated nights after. And who was still here with her, a barren woman who couldn't give him the one thing he desperately wanted... What sane Indian man would do that?

Afterwards, 'Where was this temptress hiding all these years?' he teased, and she heard the smile in his voice. She raised herself up on one elbow, her breasts brushing the springy, curly hair on his chest, his spent member growing under her gaze. She looked in his eyes and said the one thing she knew he wanted to hear, but which she found so hard to say: 'I love you, Vinod.'

His eyes flashed with sudden tears and he pulled her close. 'I love you too,' he whispered. And they made love once more, she wanting to hold on to this man, her rock, before she went back into the world that had shunned her, her eyes wide open and holding his as he moved deep inside her.

❄ ❄ ❄

Heathrow Terminal Three was a bustling throng of people, all shapes, sizes and races, all pulling huge trolleys overflowing with luggage, all in a hurry. Shirin and Vinod made their way to the Air India check-in desk.

Here time slowed. It was as if they had left the airport behind, like they were in India already. Women in saris and churidars, children and grandparents in tow, milled around, straying from the queue. In the corner, a Sikh family squatted in a row and ate chapattis and aloo sabji from stainless-steel tiffin boxes.

Once her luggage was checked in, Vinod walked her to the security desk. He was not usually demonstrative in public. Their Indian upbringing saw to that. But now, he pulled her close and kissed her on the lips, surprising both of them. 'Shonu...' he whispered, 'I will miss you. Look after yourself. And call me.'

'I will.' She could not let go.

'I love you.' His eyes were soft, his face creased from the effort it took to hide his worry.

Shirin nodded and pulled away before she admitted she was scared or burst into tears. 'Bye.'

She waved until she could no longer see him, until he had disappeared in the swarm of people, until his face swam before her eyes. Why was she doing this, going back, risking rejection? She was happy with Vinod; she had a wonderful friend in Kate and a job she loved. And then she thought of her mother, in pain and asking for her. *I am not coming back because you want me to. I am coming back because I want to. I have had enough of hiding away, punishing myself, colluding with you and your blasted pride. I refuse to be shunned. I want my daughter to know me. My daughter. Reena…* Briskly she made her way towards the departure gate, clutching her handbag tightly for support. When she reached the gate and saw the words, 'Flight AI 105 to Bangalore' scrolling on the monitor, she sank down into a chair, feeling lightheaded all of a sudden.

It was happening. She was so near home that she could smell the rich, earthy odour of rain-drenched mud, hear the distant roar of the sea. So near that she could almost touch the beads of sweat glistening on top of Madhu's upper lip as she cleaned, scaled and prepared the fish for dinner.

After eleven long years, she was, finally, going home…

CHAPTER TWENTY-SIX
Dark Silhouettes

'She's coming as soon as she can,' Aunt Anita announced after she'd disconnected the call. Tears were streaming down her face, but she didn't seem aware of them. 'She sounds just as she used to: gentle, soft, slightly hesitant... God, I can't believe I just spoke to her.'

They went by car. Deepak drove, Preeti beside him. Reena sat in the back with Aunt Anita. Outside, dark silhouettes whizzed past, their headlights briefly relieving the absolute black of night. Reena imagined the car eating up the distance between Bangalore and Taipur, desperate to reach Mai, to take her loved ones to her, to alleviate her pain. She pressed her face against the cool glass pane of the window, cocooned in air-conditioned comfort, and looked at the lights shining from the isolated little huts they passed, and imagined the ordinary lives that were being lived inside.

She's coming home. Aunt Shirin is finally coming home. What's going on in her mind right now? What is she feeling?

What am I going to find out?

Don't think about that.

Lights twinkled in the darkness just ahead. Coaches, Lorries and cars had pulled into the muddy field beside a little shop making brisk business selling tea, coffee, beedies and snacks. A small shack beside it passed for a toilet.

Deepak pulled up next to a coach which declared boldly in capitals, 'Durgamba Express', and in smaller letters, 'Bangalore to Mangalore, Kundapur, Mumbai', across the front and sides. It was packed full of weary travellers, some of them fast asleep, their mouths open, heads resting against the window, the turmeric glow from headlights playing hide and seek with the shadows on their faces.

'Time for a break,' Deepak said, his voice determinedly cheery.

No one moved. Reena looked at the coach looming above. A child's face was pressed against the glass pane of the window opposite. Curious eyes framed by curly hair peered down at her. The boy smiled, revealing yellow cavity-ridden teeth. Reena shivered.

'Come on, I need a coffee,' her dad said and they all slowly piled out of the car.

The rest of the journey was quiet, uneventful. They were each lost in their own thoughts. Reena managed to doze off a couple of times. The silence was broken by Aunt Anita when they neared Mirakatte.

'Oh, my God!' she exclaimed, clamping a hand on her mouth.

In the open space where the weekly market congregated were the charred remains of what had once been a bus. The market was deserted. There was nobody about, which was unusual for this time of the morning. Even the rickshaws which stood in a line, waiting for passengers beside the main bus stop were abandoned. There were no rickshaw drivers milling around and gossiping while smoking beedies, their lungis hitched onto their waists, or trying to persuade people laden with bags to hire them instead of taking the bus. The butcher's shop and the little grocer's shop by the corner were shut. The 'Medical Store' was shut too. Mirakatte looked like a ghost town.

'This is worse than I thought,' Preeti said, just as a rock came out of nowhere and hit the back of the car.

'Speed up,' Anita urged and before they knew it they were driving over the bumpy pipes in front of the gates of the ancient hospital, put there to deter the stray cows from wandering in, where Reena had got her foot stuck and sprained her ankle once, when she was little.

'Whew. I never thought Taipur would get dangerous. I always imagined it to be the safest place in the world.' Aunt Anita sounded distressed.

'Everything changes. And nothing is ever as it should be,' Deepak said tiredly, sounding like a weary old man as he got out of the car.

The hospital, thankfully, was just the same, busy and humming with activity. It smelt the same, too: of bitter medicine and raw fear.

'They wouldn't dare do anything to us. We treat any-one who needs medical attention here—Hindus, Muslims and Catholics alike. And they know it. They need this hospital. They need us. All the wards are full because of the riots, and we've had to send the really bad ones to the big hospital in Manipal.' The nun who was taking them to see Jacinta spoke so fast that Reena's tired mind had to work extra hard to keep up. 'This can't continue. It will stop, sooner or later. The Bishop arrived yesterday and he's been trying to reach a peaceful agreement with the Hindus and Muslims.'

She paused outside a closed door.

'Now, I must warn you, she doesn't look too good. She has had some severe second-degree burns. But she's responding well to treatment and should be able to go home soon.'

The nun opened the door and announced cheerily, 'Jacinta Bai, look who's come to visit!'

It was a cramped room, with hardly enough space for all of them. Madhu sat hunched beside the bed, wearing the faded sari she lived in. Her hair had completely escaped her bun and was everywhere. There were more lines on her face than there had been the last time Reena had seen her, just a month ago. Her eyes were red-rimmed and puffy. She had been crying.

Jacinta looked tiny in the huge bed. She wore a loose housecoat. There were welts and blisters on every bit of exposed skin. Her face was swollen and red. She opened her eyes with difficulty when they came in. She looked at each of them in turn, her gaze finally settling on Reena.

Her lips moved.

'What is it, Ma?' Deepak asked gently.

'Shirin.' Her whisper was loud in the quiet room. She beckoned to Reena with her eyes.

Reena walked towards her, slowly. Madhu moved away, making space for Reena beside Jacinta. With great effort, Jacinta opened the fingers of her palm. Reena understood what she wanted. She laid her hand on Jacinta's swollen one. Jacinta's skin was feverish, hot. Slowly Jacinta closed her fingers around Reena's hand.

'Mai,' Reena's voice was soft. She hoped it didn't betray the anguish she felt at seeing her grandmother like this. Did this happen because she had been angry with her Mai? Had she caused this somehow?

'Shirin...'

'She's not Shirin, Ma. She's Reena, our daughter,' Deepak said gently.

'Shirin's daughter, Reena...' Jacinta nodded slowly, every movement an effort, her gaze tender as it rested on Reena.

'No, Mai,' Reena started to protest but stopped when she saw the same expression mirrored on the face of every other person in the room. It was the expression she'd sported the time her mother caught her with an adult magazine. None of them would look at her. It was as if some secret they had all been privy to had been inadvertently exposed...

CHAPTER TWENTY-SEVEN
Spilt Coffee

'Ma'am, please could you step out of the queue; I need to look at your passport.'

Shirin felt a stab of alarm. Why had they singled her out? What had they found?

'Your passport, ma'am. Can I have it please?'

As the official flicked through her passport, flashing a glance at her to compare her face to the one in the photograph, her panicked mind reached back to the dreary weekend morning, their second winter in the UK, when, after a particularly bad night of being harangued by nightmares—Prem's face, his accusatory eyes—she'd asked Vinod, 'In India, do I have a criminal record?'

Vinod. She wanted him now. By her side. To sort this out, whatever it was. She fingered the phone in her purse. Should she?

That winter morning so long ago—suddenly crystal clear in her mind—Vinod had looked up, startled at her question. In her mind's eye, she saw the *Financial Times* spread out around him, the orange pages strangely obscene on the pristine white duvet. 'No, Shonu. You don't have a criminal record. Not in India. Not anywhere. I can't believe you've lived all this while with this fear. My parents bribed the police. If you give the police a large enough sum of money, Shonu, they will turn a blind eye to anything... And anyway, that stab wound...' Shirin had flinched then. Coffee had sloshed, a drop falling on the *Financial Times*, brown stain leaching through flimsy orange paper onto the snowy duvet. Shirin had closed her eyes. Blood had seeped in behind closed eyelids. Her hands touched Prem's shoulder, his head, tried to stem the flow, came away bright red, sodden. 'Shonu, you didn't kill him.' Vinod's voice in her ear, soft, tender. She didn't deserve it. She pulled away. 'Shonu, there wasn't even a formal police report. I checked. To find out if we were implicated in any way, before I applied for visas to come here.' *I don't deserve the pristine, untainted pages on my passport. Nothing changes the fact that I stabbed him. I committed the crime. It was me. If I hadn't stabbed him, he wouldn't have fallen. Hit his head. Those empty eyes, unseeing...*

'Here, ma'am, you can go.' The official handed her back the passport, flashed a smile.

She nodded at the man. Eyes the palest shade of blue, like the sea at dawn. 'Thank you, sir.'

She arrived at gate 25, found a seat by the glass window looking out onto the tarmac and stared unseeingly at the giant wing of the plane that was going to take her home.

'It was the same that other time too,' Vinod had said that day.

That gave her pause. 'What other time?'

Vinod had swallowed, not meeting her eyes. Guilty. 'It was when Prem was a teenager. He had been out with his gang. Those rich boys that got him into all this. They got drunk. The next day, the parents of one of the girls turned up at our door, accusing my brother of rape, demanding that he marry their daughter. They threatened to go to the police. My parents begged and pleaded, and in the end paid them off...'

Shirin was shocked. 'So he had done it before?'

Vinod was having trouble working his throat. 'Just that once, Shonu. He was sixteen. My parents kept a strict eye on him from then on. He couldn't give up the alcohol, but he stayed away from the girls. He was all right. Until... I should have known he had it in him all along. I should have known that the brother I felt sorry for was a monster underneath. I should have known...' Vinod had bunched the duvet, hard. 'I was going to kill him that day, Shonu. I would have...'

'Do you blame me?' Shirin had stared at her coffee, looking at the dark drown dregs and seeing something else.

'Blame you? Why? Shonu, I blame myself. Every single day. Did he do that to you to get his own back at me? Why didn't I notice his absence at work and leave for home earlier? If only I had got home earlier, I could have stopped it, stopped you having to go through...'

'Did you believe what he said?' She still couldn't look at him.

'What? All that nonsense about you wanting it?' He reached out and touched her face gently. She cringed. His hand dropped away. And on his face comprehension dawned. 'Is that why you cannot bear to be touched by me—because you think that somehow it is your fault?'

'That's what the counsellor says,' she'd whispered. The counsellor. Thick brown hair pulled back into a ponytail. Cloudy glasses, square frames, kind eyes. *'You think what happened was punishment for wanting him so badly. You are afraid to touch him, to be touched by him, in case something bad will happen again. And, you think it's just punishment for your crime: Not being able to touch the man you love, staying away from the daughter you love, being exiled from the home you love.'*

'Look at me,' he'd urged.

He'd made sure she was looking right at him. 'No. I didn't believe anything he said, Shonu. Not for a minute.'

And that was enough. Now there was only one question left. One she had wanted to ask since their wedding night.

This time she looked straight at him. 'Didn't you want me?'

'Oh, Shonu...' Tears glistened in his eyes. 'How could you think that? Have you been thinking it all along? Did *you* believe what Prem said?'

She shook her head, entranced by his tears.

'I didn't ever explain to you why I was waiting, did I? I thought you knew. More fool me.' The tears trembled on Vinod's eyelashes and started down cheeks stubbly from a night's growth of beard. 'I wanted you so badly, Shonu. I desired you so much. Couldn't you tell?'

Again, she shook her head.

'Why do you think I held you so gingerly, so far away from me? I wanted to crush you, to devour you. And when you emitted those little moans, it took all my strength not to...' He paused, took a deep breath and looked at her, oh so tenderly. 'I wanted our first time to be right. I didn't want you to remember it as having sex with this man you had been contracted to marry. I wanted *you* to *make love* with *me*.' A pause that came out a sob. 'And he ruined it. My brother ruined it...'

The tears had created two silvery tracks on his cheeks now. Vinod cleared his throat, looked straight at her. 'He took away a lot, Shonu, but not everything. Not our future. We've still got that.'

Shirin reached across and, with her finger, caught one of Vinod's tears in her hand. It was the first time since *it* had happened that she had touched him of her own accord.

'We do,' she agreed.

❄   ❄   ❄

'Ladies and gentlemen, this is your captain speaking. In a few minutes, we will be landing at Bangalore International Airport. The local time is 5:30 a.m. and the temperature is a pleasant twenty degrees. Thank you for flying Air India. Hope to see you again soon.'

Shirin looked out the window. The plane was taxiing on land, past squat buildings that looked like they had mushroomed out of dry red mud. It was all so familiar, as if she had never been away. The plane taxied to a stop in front of a building declaring, in bold letters, 'Bangalore International Airport'. The beautiful Kannada script with its curvy voluptuous letters winked at her from billboards everywhere. She stood on unsteady legs to retrieve her cabin baggage, her vision blurred by a film of tears.

Home. Jacinta desperately ill and asking for *her*, for Shirin. Jacinta's face the last time she saw her eleven years ago. That nightmare evening. Her mother-in-law's screams. The ambulance arriving, the stretcher carrying Prem past the growing crowd of spectators munching paan and spinning yarns. Her father-in-law walking beside the stretcher, a broken man. Vinod carrying her out of the kitchen with a gentleness she didn't deserve, undressing her for the first time—oh, the irony of it— bathing the blood off her so tenderly, crying the whole time. She, dry-eyed, hounded by Prem's empty gaze. Lying in a foetal position, staring at the walls. Prem's eyes staring back. Dawn arriving, blush-pink, like the merest hint of blood sprouting from under bruised skin. And with it, Jacinta. Her mother's familiar, beloved voice: 'Where is she?' Shirin's heart rising: hope, an ache. *Please hold me, Ma. Please make all this go away.* The bed creaking. Her mother's smell enveloping her, caressing her. Her mother's hand on her arm, kiss on her cheek. *Hold me, Ma. Don't let me go. Take me away, far away. I want to go home. To coconut trees whispering in the breeze, conversing with crows. To power cuts, patholis wrapped in banana leaves, mosquitoes humming in twilight skies. To air so heavy it sighs as it waits for the monsoons. To rain drumming on tiles and ricocheting off roofs. To Boroline and the shelter of Madhu's arms. Take me home.* Jacinta's voice, weighed down with sorrow: 'What have you done, Shirin? Tell me, is it true?' Vinod's voice breaking on a sob: 'She was raped.' Jacinta, insistent, 'Tell me, Shirin, did you do what they say?' Vinod: 'They are not telling you the whole story. None of this is her fault. It's mine. I should have protected her...' Vinod crying. Jacinta, dry-eyed, waiting for Shirin's reply. Prem's eyes mocking. Shirin nodding imperceptibly. *Yes, Ma, I'm guilty as charged.* Jacinta's face. So many emotions. Pain, anger, fear, hurt and, worst of all, shame. 'How could you, Shirin? How could you do this? After everything... You have disgraced me and brought disgrace to our entire family. You are dead to me from now on. Dead.'

The heat hit her first, heavy and humid after the air-conditioned comfort of the airport. And then the noise. There were people everywhere: relatives waiting for their loved ones; bored-looking taxi drivers in their khaki uniforms and sailor hats holding plaques while chewing paan. A host of hawkers descended on her, urging her to take a taxi, to hire a coolie for her luggage. Cars honked constantly, all of them in a hurry, causing a traffic jam which a lone harassed policeman tried to direct. Drivers shouted abuse and insults at each other and at the policeman, half their bodies hanging out of the car window, one hand on the horn. It was absolute chaos and it calmed Shirin like a drug as she made her way to the domestic airport, ignoring the hawkers who continued to follow her and beg for her custom.

The domestic airport was not quite as busy this early in the morning. She couldn't believe she was here, on Indian soil, making her way to Taipur again for the first time since she had left for Bangalore two days before her wedding, a lifetime ago.

Tired-looking cleaning women wearing saris with pallus tucked into their waists mopped the floors and cleaned the toilets. Shopkeepers yawned as they opened their little kiosks selling outrageously overpriced goods. Smells of filter coffee permeated the morning air.

The airport started filling up slowly. A family comprised of parents, kids and grandparents took up the whole bench of seats opposite Shirin and beside her. The grandmother took off her flip-flops and sat cross-legged and barefoot in her chair. Then she set about patiently unknotting the end of her pallu, while talking non-stop to the other women and nagging her husband at the same time. He ignored her and fell asleep with his mouth open and started snoring, little purrs at first which gradually increased in volume.

'See,' the grandmother said with a shake of her head. 'This is what I have to put up with!'

The children who were running around in circles, their sneakers gliding smoothly on the polished mosaic floor of the airport, screeched to a halt when they saw their grandad, pointing to his open mouth and giggling while they conferred busily together.

Children. Reena. Mewling like a kitten, pressing into her...

Those dark days after... Staying in a rented flat near Vinod's office while he set about finding a buyer for his business, looked for a job in England. 'You'll like it there, Shonu. There are green fields, open spaces. Just like Taipur.' She'd flinched then. Taipur. A longing. An ache. No longer home. For Shirin, those days were a trance, an unending nightmare. She healed physically. The bruises faded. Her colour returned. But she couldn't eat. She couldn't sleep. She lay in bed, staring at the ceiling as if it held all the answers. She was haunted by eyes. Prem's empty eyes. Jacinta's filled with shame. Her mother-in-law's full of bottomless pain... In the end, despite her continued refusals, Vinod took her to a doctor. After the examination, the doctor called them in. 'Congratulations,' she beamed. 'You are going to be parents.'

Shirin blinked, came back to the present.

'Aha. No mischief, children. I know just what you are planning...' the grandmother in the seat next to her was saying to the children, wagging a finger at them. They ran away.

There was a thunderstorm the night she went into labour. Rain at her wedding, rain at the birth of her child. A clap of thunder, a mewling wail, the doctor holding up a wriggling blood-soaked bundle, 'Congratulations, you have a healthy little girl—seven pounds three ounces.' She had looked at the blood dotting squirming brown flesh and screamed and screamed, while the Eyes laughed. They had to sedate her.

A fly buzzed near her ear. Shirin swatted at it. The knot the grandmother had been fiddling with opened, revealing a treasure trove of paan, which she distributed among the other women. They all started munching busily together. The kids ran up to the mother with cries of, 'We're hungry.'

She couldn't produce milk. It just wouldn't come. She was dry as the River Varuna during the drought. Her baby cried and cried, the wails reminding her of another mother's wails the night she stabbed her son. And she had run away, run from her baby. Barefoot, through the scalding streets of Bangalore. *Running. Bare feet flying on blistering tarmac. Horns blaring. The damning screech of brakes. Chaos. Waking up in hospital groggy, haunted. My baby. Where's my baby?*

The mother opened one of the bags and took out a stainless-steel tiffin carrier. She fished around in another bag and extracted some banana leaves. She opened the tiffin carrier and took out idlis from one compartment, chutney from the other and distributed these to each child on a banana-leaf plate.

'She's fine,' Vinod had said. 'I hired a wet nurse. You rest.' 'She doesn't deserve me, Vinod,' Shirin had replied. 'I cannot look after her.' 'I will,' Vinod had said. 'How will you look after both her and me?' 'I will,' Vinod had reiterated, in the same solemn tone he had used for his wedding vows. Softly, she had voiced her greatest fear: 'Vinod, she's a constant reminder. I am afraid I will… I will hurt her like I did Prem…' His eyes, stalking her.

'You love her, Shirin.' 'I do, and that is why... she is better off without me.' And, the thing she most dreaded: 'I do not want her to look at me and read in my eyes the truth about her conception.'

She had called Deepak that night. It was raining when he and Preeti came to collect Reena, the clouds doing her weeping for her.

The family next to her started packing away their belongings. The grandfather was shaken awake, the children's hair combed. Shirin swiped at her eyes and stood, realising with a pang that her flight had been called.

As the little plane circled the skies above Mangalore, preparing to land in Bajpe Airport, Shirin pressed her nose against the glass window and looked down at the beloved landscape of her homeland. Rectangles of mud-red fields winked up at her. Rivers snaked in the valleys between hills, the perky blue water twinkling in the sunlight. As the plane swooped further down, she had her first glimpse of coconut trees, their palms fluttering in the light breeze as if they were graciously waving hello, and she was aware of hot tears sweeping down her cheeks, even as she smiled.

When she came out of Bajpe Airport, the heat hit her in a humid wave, engulfing her in a sweaty embrace. She hailed a taxi at random from the huge group of people who had lunged at her offering to carry her luggage, to drive fastest, to be the cheapest fare. As she waited for the taxi to pull up, she breathed in the sight and smell of home—the green hills in the distance; the long blades of grass wilting in the sun; the air smelling of rain-soaked mud with an undertone of something spicy; the little black-and-yellow auto rickshaws with the drivers hanging out of their seats; the tiny cottages with uneven cement walls and red-brick roofs.

'So, who are you visiting in Taipur?' the taxi driver wanted to know.

Shirin looked out of the window at the achingly familiar landscape, one she had visited in a thousand dreams. She wished the driver would leave her alone. She didn't know what to say. She didn't know how to reply without breaking down in front of this stranger.

She cleared her throat. 'My mother,' she said in what she hoped was a firm voice that discouraged further conversation.

She didn't want to close her eyes and pretend to be asleep. Then she would miss out on this, her first glimpse of her hometown after eleven long years.

'Hope she wasn't affected by the riots.'

Shirin stopped looking out of the window and focused on the driver.

'What riots?'

'You don't know about the riots in Taipur?'

'Riots, in Taipur?' Shirin repeated foolishly, unable to believe what the driver was saying.

'Hindus and Muslims have been fighting each other. I heard they burnt the parish hall of the Mother Mary of Miracles Church when the Christians tried to make peace. Mahatma Gandhi would be appalled at the state of India now. The politicians say it is peaceful. Where is the peace? Everywhere there is unrest, violence...'

They passed a little thatched hut selling snacks, framed by coconut trees. Clusters of tiny yellow bananas hung in the entrance. A stack of tender coconuts sat neatly in an upside-down V formation at the front of the shop tempting people to get a respite from the heat by drinking their honey-sweet water and eating their juicy flesh. She realised with a wrench that the little blue-green soda bottles with marble stoppers had been replaced by bottles of 7UP and Fanta.

They were driving past Kapu now and, despite the air conditioning, she opened her window to breathe in the salty, sharp scent of the sea. If she concentrated, she could even hear the gentle ebb and flow of the waves in the distance.

'Shall I switch off the air conditioning, ma'am? Do you want to leave the window open?' the driver asked.

'No, it's okay.' Shirin closed the window, wincing as the Dommur Mangalore buses sped past, dangerously close, horns blaring, in constant competition with the lorries packed with hay bales, which careened at breakneck speeds, their cargoes wobbling precariously.

And then they were driving past the jasmine hawkers, peddling their wares in little hand-woven cane baskets at the base of the bridge, past the teetering old billboard set in an empty field that declared boldly, 'Welcome to Dommur, Garden Town' ('Garden? What garden?' Shirin always thought whenever she saw this sign), and then through Dommur, past new Maruti and Hyundai showrooms displaying flashy cars that wouldn't have looked out of place in the UK, past the timber factory in Donegilu and the theatre in Mirakatte, sporting posters for the latest Shivaraj Kumar blockbuster. Fancy new buildings, each outdoing the other in extravagance, had cropped up in Mirakatte, Shirin noticed. Yet, though much of it was different, the essence of her hometown was there. Everything was so familiar, just as it had been in her dreams, her memories.

When they passed the marketplace, Shirin saw the burnt embers of the bus and her heart stilled. She noted the absence of people, the deserted feel of the place. It was a shame, a travesty.

Then they were driving past the 'Medical Store'. The driver turned left and drove down the mud path, past the haunted house and the Hindu cemetery, before stopping by the lake, alongside the clearing which opened into the path that led to the house of her childhood...

She paid the taxi driver, adding a hefty tip, for which he thanked her profusely, offering her his mobile number if she ever needed a taxi again. India really had changed for the better, mused Shirin, if taxi drivers could afford mobile phones now. She stood there, long after he had turned and driven off with a jaunty wave, remembering Deepak's promise to Jacinta one dark night, aeons ago. They were returning home after attending a wedding and Jacinta had been standing at the clearing, lighting up the path for them with a torch, asking them to watch their step. 'I don't want you falling in the stream,' she had warned.

'When I'm older, Ma, and have lots of money, I will buy you a car and build you a proper road so you can drive up to the house and show off to the neighbours,' Deepak had announced, turning back to look at Jacinta. He'd lost his footing and would have fallen into the stream had Shirin not screamed and managed to hold on to his shirt.

'Thank you, Deepak. But from now on, watch where you're going, okay?' Jacinta had said, and even though Shirin couldn't see her face, she knew Jacinta was smiling. She remembered wishing she was the one who had said those words, that she was the one who had made her aloof mother smile.

Slowly, Shirin made her way down the path toward her childhood home. In the clearing by the well sat a girl in a chair with her back to Shirin. *Reena?* The girl seemed immersed in a book. *She likes reading. Like me.* Heart thudding, Shirin leant over. Wispy tendrils, escaped from the ponytail of chaotic curls, danced on a slender neck beaded with droplets of sweat that gleamed like tears in the sunshine. The girl turned. Oval face. A pert little nose. Full cheeks dusted with golden down. Film-star lips—like Anita's. Chocolate eyes. Red-rimmed, wide with dawning recognition. *Reena*, sang her heart.

CHAPTER TWENTY-EIGHT

Grandpa Walter's Favourite Spot

'Why did Mai say that? What did she mean?' Reena asked, finally finding the courage that had evaded her ever since she read Shirin's last letter.

Mai was sleeping, her little chat having exhausted her, small moans escaping from between parched, swollen, slightly open lips. None of the other adults huddled around the tiny room would meet her eye, not even Madhu.

A nun bustled in, shooed them all out: 'The doctor is coming.' She straightened the bed sheets, placed a chipped jug of water on the table and, with a, 'Wait outside for a couple of minutes,' shut the door on them. They heard her falsely cheery voice through the thin wood of the door, 'Now, Jacinta, wakey-wakey; the doctor's coming to see if you are okay.'

The adults *still* wouldn't look at her. Was it true what Mai had said? *No. No! No! No! No!*

She had to know.

'Mum,' *(Mum?)* Reena went up to Preeti, put one hand on each of her mother's cheeks, pulled her head down gently, insistently, 'is it true, what she said?'

Preeti's guilty gaze shied away from hers.

Look at me, Mum. Please.

Preeti's eyes met Reena's, held. A gentle, tender gaze filled with all the love her mother had for her. *Her mother? Yes. Yes. Yes. Yes.* Her mother walking her up to the mirror: 'You are our special miracle.'

The doctor walked past self-importantly, shoes clicking on the mosaic floor, an entourage of nurses and a peon holding files in his wake. He entered Jacinta's room without knocking. Murmurs wafted from behind the closed door. The doctor: clipped, masculine. The nurses: high-pitched, servile. Jacinta's hoarse whisper: Shirin.

Preeti opened her arms wide, pulled Reena in. She wanted to pull away, to run as fast as her legs could carry her, away from this building smelling of the bitter medicine forced down her throat when she was ill, away from this life she found herself in, surrounded by adults who would not meet her eyes, who had lied to her all her life. But then she breathed in the familiar smell of her mother's sweat, the crushed, rustling feel of her sari, the warmth of her mother's body, and despite herself, despite her anger at her for not having answered her question, Reena relaxed in her mother's embrace, snuggled into it. The exhaustion of the previous night's journey, the excitement of contacting Shirin, the emotion of seeing a desperately unwell Mai and hearing what she had to say caught up with her in a rush. Her eyelids felt heavy, started to close.

The girl from the photograph floated before her eyes. *Are you my mother, Shirin? If so, then why, why did you give me away? Was I not good enough for you? And to think I championed you, wanted to reunite you with your family... I hate you, hate you, hate you. I hate you all. Liars. Traitors.*

She heard the door open, a swish of feet, the doctor's voice: 'I'm discharging her. There's nothing more we can do for her here. Sister Smitha will give you the list of medicines and ointments. You can buy them from here; I don't think any of the medical stores are open. If there is any change for the worse, let me know...'

'Is she...?' Her dad seemed to have finally found his voice.

'It depends. We have to wait and see. She should get better. But if a patient doesn't have the will to live, there's not much we can do. Who is this Shirin she keeps asking about?'

Reena felt her mother still. A heartbeat later, her father's voice, rusty as if it needed clearing: 'My... our sister. She's in London. Arriving tomorrow.'

'Good. Good. That might perk her up.' Footsteps receding. Silence. And then feet shuffling. Her father clearing his throat, 'Right, I'd better get this medicine, then.'

Aunt Anita: 'Is Reena...?'

Her mother's cheek against hers, eyelashes fluttering: 'Asleep.'

Madhu: 'We'd better get them both home. Ma'am and Reena.'

Then, she was floating in her father's strong arms, like she used to when she was a child. As if from afar, she heard the car door swing open, emitting that annoying whine it was prone to. She was propped up gently in the seat by her father, her body cushioned by her mother's soft shoulder, her head fitting nicely in the nook of her mother's neck. Bliss. From behind closed lids, a blurry Jacinta smiled at her and whispered, 'Shirin's daughter.' *No. No! No! No!*

When she woke, she was on the mat in the living room in Taipur, her mother snoring fitfully beside her. Her clothes clung to her body, wet from perspiration, despite the ceiling fan half-heartedly circulating hot air directly above. Mosquitoes feasted on city flesh. Outside, the nightly cricket orchestra reached a crescendo. Slowly, recollection dawned. Mai's delirious words. Her parents refusing to meet her gaze. Questions buzzed in her head like Kannada verbs. Was she, Reena, the reason Shirin had been ostracized, shunned? Murli's words: 'Perhaps they are protecting you.' Had she been conceived in disgrace? *No.*

Preeti's quiet snores beside her, the smell of the sandalwood talcum powder she applied liberally at night after her bath. There was a time—before she discovered the photograph—when she had believed unequivocally that her parents would never lie to her. How naïve she had been!

She woke again to golden light dancing on her eyelids, to voices trying to whisper, but not quite managing.

'Shh... She might wake.' Her mother's voice. *Her mother?*

'We have to tell her, Preeti,' her father's voice. Soft. Desperate.

'But Deepak... my baby...' Her mother's voice. A wail.

'I had hoped... she didn't have to know.'

I know. I am not stupid.

'There was no way you could have kept it from her forever.' Aunt Anita.

Rage. Hot. Like eating raw chillies.

'She's sensible. She'll understand...' Aunt Anita again.

Oh, stop taking me for a fool, you...bastards. No, I am the bastard. Me.

Her mother's quiet sobs.

'Here, have some tea...' Madhu.

Lying on the mat, pretending to be asleep, Reena cried softly, tears squeezing out from behind warm eyelids. She got up after her mother's sobs had died down. She brushed her hair, washed her face and went to find them. They were all clustered in the kitchen, sipping tea and talking while Madhu cooked.

'Rinu! Looks like your body needed that nice, long sleep you've had. What do you want to eat? Samosas with tamarind chutney? Raw banana curry? Conjee with buttermilk and fried salted jackfruit with coconut? Koilolis? Mutlis?'

Reena managed a smile. 'Have you been up all night cooking, Madhu? What are you celebrating?'

'Shirin's arrival of course. I can't believe she's coming. After all these years.' With her pallu, Madhu wiped away the tears of anticipation, of joy from her eyes.

'Come, sit down,' her mother beckoned.

Reena took in her swollen face, the stark need in her eyes. 'No.' And her voice breaking on a sob as she watched her mother's face crumple, 'You lied to me. All of you. I hate you, hate you, hate you and her, Shirin, most of all.'

Everyone started talking at once.

'Rinu…'

'Reena, what…'

'My whole life is a lie. When were you planning to tell me? Liars!' Reena yelled. 'Don't tell me I'm not old enough. Don't tell me I won't understand. Don't patronise me.'

'Shirin…' Jacinta called from inside.

'Rinu…' Preeti began.

'Stop fobbing me off with some half-baked lie. I understand things. I. Am. Not. A. Child.'

'You are to us…' Deepak began.

Reena turned and stomped out of the house, fuming, stepping on Gypsy's tail and causing her to yelp in protest and run around in circles, trying to lick it better. Breathless from the rage that engulfed her, Reena plonked herself down on the grass in the shade of the guava and cashew trees, angrily pulling out clumps with both fists. Gypsy stopped running and stood with her tail between her legs looking at Reena with huge betrayed mournful eyes. Reena burst into tears.

'I'm sorry. That was the wrong thing to say.'

Deepak had followed her out of the house. She buried her face in her hands and refused to look at him. Gypsy flopped on Reena's sandals, which she'd tossed aside when she squatted down.

'I know you are growing up, Reena. But as a parent that's hard to accept…'

'You are not my parent. Why don't you just come out and say it? It worked out fine, didn't it? You could not have children. That bitch didn't want me. And the family name was intact…'

SLAP. Reena cupped her smarting cheek and stared at Deepak, hurt welling up in tears she thought she'd exhausted in her eyes. Gypsy howled.

Preeti put her arms round Reena. She shrugged them off.

'I am still your father and there are still some rules, no swearing being one of them.' Deepak said, his voice sounding desperate.

'Rules for me, but none for you,' Reena whispered.

Preeti put her arms around her again and this time she sank into her mother's embrace.

Deepak took a deep breath, held out his hand, meaning to stroke her face. Reena shrank away. 'I am sorry. Yes, we lied to you. We were protecting you, Reena.'

She didn't say anything. She couldn't. She hated them, all of them, even her mother whose arms were wrapped around her. She hated her body for the comfort it derived from those arms, she hated herself for not being stronger, for not pulling away.

'Some truths are best hidden. Buried.'

Under a mountain of lies? My life is built on a foundation of lies and now I am teetering. Falling. She looked up, met Deepak's gaze, found her voice. 'Who am I? I want to know.'

Deepak took a deep breath, 'Well, here goes. The truth.'

And there, in the shade of the trees, with Preeti's arms around her, her father on the grass beside her and Gypsy fast asleep at his feet, Deepak told her the story of her parentage, of her birth and Shirin's exile, of secrets and loss and heartache. She sat there for a long time after he had stopped speaking, barely aware of the tears falling down her cheeks, not knowing if they were for Shirin or for herself, grateful of Preeti's arms around her silently offering the comfort she so desperately needed and angry at herself for wanting it.

Absently, she noted the orange anthill at the base of the jackfruit tree, and wondered if, as the Hindus believed, there was a cobra nestling inside, about to spring its venom on unsuspecting victims. She watched a saffron dragonfly land on the maroon hibiscus flowers blossoming by the well, and she imagined it a yellow pin pricking a bright-red heart.

'We're sorry, Reena, so sorry.' Deepak's voice was gentle.

Preeti cupped Reena's face in her palm and looked deep into her eyes. 'She wanted what was best for you. It must have been so hard, to give you away. I couldn't do it… but she did. Because she loved you. So very much. Her sacrifice. Our gain.' And then, softly, 'It's okay to be angry with us, with her. To hate us even. We'll understand. She will too.'

'How do you know?' Reena sniffed.

'I know.'

'We love you very much, Rinu…'

'Um... I'd like to sit here for a while. You go on in...'

Preeti and Deepak exchanged glances, undecided.

'Are you sure?' Deepak asked, finally.

She nodded.

'Rinu. It's a lot to take in. If you have any questions, ask—okay?' Deepak said.

Preeti knelt down on the grass and looked into Reena's eyes. 'And we'll answer to the best of our knowledge. No more secrets. That's a promise.'

Fat chance. I'll never believe anything you say ever again. Reena watched her parents make their way back to the house. They walked side by side, slowly, and it was as if she was looking into the future—a sudden dizzying glimpse—where the people she'd believed to be her parents were old and bent, weary with the burden that was life.

Perspiration beaded her neck, ran down her back in rivulets—like monsoon rain gushing down pipes at the sides of the house—and collected in the waist of her shorts. She felt tired. So very tired. She thought about Shirin, getting closer and closer to home, landing around now. It sent a shaft of pain right down her middle. She clutched her stomach, doubled over. Gypsy leapt up, made to lick her tears. 'Shoo, Gypsy.'

From the house, her mum—*mum?*—What else could she call her? 'Rinu, you okay?'

'Yes.' She must have been peeping through the window, keeping an eye on her.

'Shall I sit with you?'

'No.'

Preeti turning away to hide her face crumpling.

Oh, go away and leave me alone. I cannot deal with your hurt right now. I am hurting enough.

Loud shouts. Commotion. Surely Shirin couldn't be here already? *What do I say to her? What do I call her?*

It was Nagappa's grandson, dancing down the path, wearing nothing but a pair of dirty shorts too small for him. 'The riots have stopped,' he announced breathlessly.

Madhu, who had come running out of the kitchen, her apron awry, looked disappointed that it was not Shirin. She turned to Reena and her expression softened. She came up, 'Shoo, Gypsy,' put her arms around Reena, held her close. 'There, there. Have a good cry.'

'What happened, Naresh? How do you know the riots have ended?' Reena heard Deepak ask of Nagappa's grandson.

'The Bishop had talks with the Hindu and Muslim leaders. They have agreed to end the riots. They apologised… said they did not know that there were people inside the hall; they thought they were burning down an empty building.' Naresh paused to catch his breath after the long speech.

'As if…' Madhu began.

'The Bishop has asked them to apologise personally to the affected families, so they might be arriving here sometime,' Naresh finished.

'When they come here, I will give them a piece of my mind. I am a Hindu myself and know many good Muslims. It is despicable behaviour and cannot be excused,' Madhu announced, her arms still firmly encircling Reena. 'Anyway, it's all over now. You go inside, Naresh. You deserve freshly cooked samosas after that piece of good news. I'll be along in a minute.'

With her apron, Madhu wiped away the last of Reena's tears. 'Do you want some samosas, Rinu? I have made tamarind chutney to go with them. Or if you want something cool, I've made Dahi Vadais.'

'No thanks, Madhu. I'm not hungry.' And then, at the look on Madhu's face, 'I'll eat a lot at lunch, once um... Aunt...' The word rolled around on her tongue, suddenly alien. What should she call Shirin? 'Shirin is here...'

Madhu bent low, whispered in Reena's ear, 'She loves you. Very much. It will be okay. I promise.' She squeezed Reena's hand. 'Come in for a snack soon.'

Madhu hobbled in but Deepak hovered. 'Thank God for that. Taipur can try to get some semblance of normality back now,' he said, voice falsely cheery. And then, softly, kneeling beside her, 'And you? It will take you a while to get some semblance of normality back, no?'

She didn't reply.

He stretched his hand out and tentatively patted her shoulder, 'Lot to take in, isn't it?'

She shrugged his arm off. 'I am going in for a drink.'

She went to the fridge, shying away from her mum's open arms, mumbling yes to Aunt Anita's solicitous, 'Are you okay?'—*No, I'm not actually. I don't know what I'm feeling, but I do know that it's not 'Okay'*—got a bottle of ice-cold water and, armed with a chair, her casebook and an old novel she had found in one of the wardrobes (it had the words 'Taipur Circulating Library' stamped on its yellowing pages in faded blue ink), went back to her chosen spot by the well. Madhu had told her once that this was Grandpa Walter's favourite spot. He used to sit there, in the shade of the guava and cashew trees, Madhu said, with his ever-present Bible, sweat dripping down his bare chest, collecting around his ample waist and soaking into his lungi.

Gypsy came, tail wagging, nose sniffing, and plonked herself on Reena's feet. 'Move, Gypsy. You're making my legs hot.' Reena pulled her legs out from under Gypsy's warm belly and folded them beneath her. Gypsy whined a complaint and flopped back on Reena's sandals, her paws stretched out in front of her. She was hot too. Her tongue was hanging out and she seemed to be eyeing Reena's bottle of water. She made as if to lick the drops of condensation off it. Reena moved it out of her reach.

A tiny breeze ruffled the leaves of the trees every once in a while, and the shade afforded solace from the relentless heat. The air was heavy and humid. Bees droned lazily. Butterflies flitted. The empty fields baked in the sun, the mud cracked. It felt like the whole world was waiting. Waiting for Shirin.

This detective was right. Prem did have something to do with the rift. He… He… Her hands shook. She could not do it. She looked at her previous entry. 'This detective has reached the conclusion that she is destined for greatness.' And for the first time in what felt like ages, she smiled.

Prem is this detective's father and Shirin is her mother. She wrote.

Case resolved successfully.

THE END.

When she was feeling up to it, she would write everything out in detail, the whole gory tale, warts and all. Not now. Not today. She tucked her casebook beneath her bottom where it would stay safe and hidden, and opened the novel—*The Thorn Birds*—knowing she couldn't read, but wanting to try, desperately wanting to escape, at least for a bit, her own story. She did manage to read, however, instantly identifying both with Meggy Cleary's laments for her mutilated doll and with the doll itself, realising that that was how she felt: mutilated, used, betrayed. She did not hear the taxi pull up, or the sound of footsteps coming up the path. It was only when a shadow teased grey patterns on the yellow pages of her book that she turned and found herself looking at what could only be described as a vision.

The woman who stood before her was stunning—not in a film-star sort of way like Aunt Anita—but in a different, more real way. She had glowing olive skin, long black hair which cascaded in silky waves down her back and framed her oval face, huge expressive eyes which tilted upward slightly at the corners, full lips and a mouth that was designed to smile.

She carried a suitcase, which she set down beside Reena's chair. Gypsy stirred, looked up at the stranger and growled. It was not her usual throaty bark. It seemed that Gypsy, too, like Reena, had misplaced her voice.

'Hi,' smiled the stranger, holding out a hand. 'I'm Shirin. That's one of my favourite books you're reading. Like it so far?'

In the shy smile, Reena recognised the girl from the picture she had found all those weeks ago. In the shy smile, Reena recognised herself.

And, as if by magic, she found her voice again. She took Shirin's hand in hers.

Madhu was right. It was going to be all right. 'I'm Reena. And, yes, I think I'm going to like the book very much.'

CHAPTER TWENTY-NINE
Swaddled Bundle

'*R**eena*,' sang Shirin's heart. And in the next beat,
'*Does she know?*'

'Hello, I'm Reena.' She extended her hand. Perfect.
Delicate. Beautiful.

Shirin took her daughter's palm in both of hers as if in
prayer. And on this, her tears fell, unchecked. She looked
down at her daughter's perfect face and found her tears
mirrored in those beautiful eyes.

She knows.

Her baby. After the labour, after she woke from her se-
dated state, she had held the swaddled bundle that was her
daughter, and Reena had snuggled up to her and buried
her tiny head in the space between her breasts, her body a
question mark on her chest, while rain drummed on the
tiles above. Shirin had looked at her in wonder: this beautiful thing created out of something so ugly. Scrunched-
up face, wiggly arms. Toes like inverted commas. As she
watched in awe, Reena had opened her eyes and stared
right at her. And for one brief, blessed moment, lost in
the fathomless dark eyes of her newborn daughter, Shirin

had been free of the other pair of Eyes that haunted her constantly.

She opened her arms: an invitation, a plea. And Reena walked right into them. She held her daughter close; felt her heart beat a rhythm against her chest. She was tall. Her head fit snugly under Shirin's chin. Her hair smelt of sandalwood. The sun beat down on Shirin's closed lids, warming the tears still squeezing out of them. The dog, a replica of Madhu's strays, licked her sandals. Bees droned, birds chattered and water gushed over the stones in the stream below: a musical tinkle. Somewhere, someone laughed. The air smelt like a fruit orchard; the sharp tang of mango leaves mixing with the pungent tamarind and the milder cashew and guava. Smells of frying spices floated up to her nostrils. Home. Her daughter in her arms. She was home.

'Reena, come eat something.' A familiar voice, a voice she had heard so often in her dreams. And then louder, joy dancing in each syllable, 'Shirin. My Shirin.'

And then, Shirin was cocooned in the familiar warmth of Madhu's arms. Madhu smelt as she had always done, of coconut oil and spices: the scent of her childhood, of love, of refuge. Shirin took a deep, steadying breath and gave in to the exquisite, much-longed-for comfort of being mothered again, not heeding the tears that squeezed out from behind grateful eyelids and wet the front of Madhu's apron.

'You came, Shirin,' Madhu said, her voice a smile. 'Finally, you are here.'

After a long moment, Madhu held her at arm's length and examined her.

Madhu had gotten old in her absence, Shirin realised with a pang. Her hair was completely grey and as untidy as usual. It still resisted the confines of her bun. Her face was lined. But she was still the Madhu she remembered and had ached for. She was still the Madhu she loved.

'See, didn't I tell you that you would blossom into a beauty? Wasn't I right?' Madhu cupped a palm on Shirin's cheek, 'My Shirin.' Her voice was thick with pride. Her face beamed through the tears.

'Shirin...'

It was Deepak. His hair was greying prematurely. And was that a bald patch on his crown? God, what had the years done to her dashing big brother? He enclosed her in a bear hug. 'Welcome home,' he said.

She stepped back, eyed her big brother, 'Really?'

He met her gaze; his steady, 'Yes. Really.'

'I couldn't stay away any longer, Deepu,' she whispered in his ear.

And, 'I'm sorry,' he whispered back. 'I was, still am, a fool. Took everything Ma said as gospel. Should have known better.' Shirin nodded briefly. And, 'Thank you,' he said. 'Thank you. She's an absolute angel. Our pride and joy.' *And mine*, thought Shirin, sneaking a glance at Reena, unable to tear her eyes from her daughter's face.

Preeti came up: a slight woman with a sweet face and kind eyes. She looked just the same as she had done that fateful night all those years ago. 'She knows,' Preeti whispered in her ear. 'We had to tell her this morning. Something Ma said. She's taken it well.'

'My turn,' Anita said loudly, and they all laughed. She pulled Shirin into her arms for a hug. 'Shirin, how I've missed you...'

Even in the stifling heat, her sister looked and smelt delicious. As always.

'I've missed you too,' Shirin whispered into her sister's ear. And then, 'Where's Da?'

Anita's eyes dimmed and Shirin knew. It was too late.

'Come and see Ma,' Anita said, and Shirin choked on the bile that rose in her throat.

'She's been asking for you constantly.' It was Reena. She slid her hand in Shirin's as if it were the most natural thing in the world and led her inside.

The house was just as Shirin remembered. Nostalgia and memory merging into reality. The cement floor cool under her feet. The front room with its wooden bench and grandfather clock. The windowless dining room: Godrej safe, wooden wardrobe which housed the tablecloth and plates reserved for guests, the altar with the constantly burning red bulb which cast an eerie glow in the dark, cool room. Jacinta was in the tiny room off the dining room, the room which they had used for studying. This room had a window: a little hole in the wall with two wooden bars in the shape of a cross. Shirin remembered spending hours in this room ostensibly studying but in reality spying on the neighbours.

It housed a bed now and in it laid Jacinta. Shirin drew in a quick, shocked breath. A sigh. Her ma was smaller than Shirin remembered. Feeble. Her hair, which had always been pulled back into a tightly oiled bun, lay loose around her head. It was completely white. Her face was bruised and swollen.

Without warning, Shirin's mind flashed back to that terrible day when her mother had renounced her. That time, she had been the one with the bruised and swollen face...

Shirin closed her eyes briefly. When she opened them, she found Jacinta looking right at her. Her mother's eyes were twin pools of pain. Shirin had seen them like that once before and they had haunted her ever since.

'Shirin...' Jacinta held out a hand. It seemed to require all her strength to do so.

'Ma...' Shirin put her hand in her mother's frail one. She knelt down beside the bed, so she was at her mother's eye level.

Slowly, Jacinta raised her hand and rested it on Shirin's cheek. 'I am sorry, Shirin, so sorry...'

Now you're sorry. Her mother had forgiven her. Why didn't she feel better? Why did she only feel anger, sharp and hot like the point of a knife piercing tender skin?

Every word her mother spoke required great effort. 'When you were born, I made a promise to myself, to you, that whatever happened, I would be a better mother than mine had been to me. But in the end, I was worse than her, Shirin, worse...'

Jacinta's eyes were soft. She was looking at Shirin with such tenderness—the look Shirin had ached for. 'It was my pride, my blasted pride. You were hurting. You had been through so much. And yet, at the time you needed me the most, I abandoned you...' Jacinta's face crumpled. Tears slid down her cheeks and soaked into the pillow. 'That morning when I walked up to your in-laws' house, your house, people clustered in groups and pointed and whispered. It was what I had endured every day of my childhood and I could not go back. I would not. In those brief moments before I disowned you, I thought of everything I would lose otherwise: how I would never be able to get Deepak and Anita married, how the whole village would laugh at us. I thought of the shame, the disgrace, of how I would be an outcast again... I did not think of you...' Jacinta took a long, deep breath that came out a sob.

You made me an outcast instead.

Jacinta clearly had more to say and seemed to want to say it before her strength failed her. 'I, of all people, should have understood. My alcoholic father... The day we met Prem for the first time, the signs were there. A part of me knew. But I refused to pay heed.' A pause. A gasp. 'Over the years I have wanted to contact you so many times...'

'Why didn't you, Ma?' Biting out the words.

'My pride, my blasted pride.' Jacinta whispered.

Anger. White hot. Like harbouring a plateful of chillies in her stomach. 'All those years, I was aching to see Reena. And I stayed away...' She couldn't bear to look at her mother. She turned, her eyes seeking Reena. Reena met her gaze, her eyes wide, innocent, the eyelashes glittery from tears. *My daughter. My beautiful child.* She opened her mouth, but nothing came out. *Can a voice shatter from too much pain?* She cleared her throat, willed her voice to not let her down. 'I wanted nothing more than to see you grow up. But I stayed away. I thought: if my own mother cannot forgive me, how will I ever face my daughter?' She paused, gathering her thoughts. There was so much she wanted to say. And it was so important she said this right. 'I know you found out the truth today. That must have been hard. What I did… it must have felt like betrayal. What mother gives her child away? You may think—if you haven't already—that you weren't wanted. That isn't true. I loved you, Reena. I love you. So much. You were the one good thing to come out of everything that happened. When they handed you to me and you nuzzled close, trusting me so completely, trusting me to protect you, I knew then. You deserved better. You didn't deserve a mother who was so broken she couldn't give you the love you deserved. You didn't deserve to live like an outcast, in a different country, away from the land and the people you belonged with. None of what happened was your fault and you didn't deserve to carry the burden of your history for the rest of your life. You didn't deserve a mother who did what I did…'

She looked around at her family then, these people she had so longed for, assembled in this room, and the anger, the hurt finally burst out of her. 'I blamed myself for eleven years for what I did to Prem. Despite the counselling. Despite what my husband and my best friend said. I was to blame, wasn't I? My family definitely agreed. They shunned me, stayed away.' Neither Deepak nor Anita met her gaze. 'From birth I was conditioned for guilt. Being a girl was my fault. Daring to accept a note from a boy who loved me—my fault. What Prem did to me—my fault. I must have provoked him in some way. What I did to him. Unforgivable. I was guilty. I was rotten inside. The girl who consorts with boys. The girl who loves a Muslim. The girl who brings disgrace to the revered family name. And I gave away the one good thing to come out of it all. My daughter. Was it fair to ask her to live with the ignominy brought on by her horrible mother?'

None of them would look at her. Not her mother, whose tears squeezed onto the pillow, not her brother nor her sister. *The cowards*. 'And I did to my daughter what my mother had done to me. I deserted her. The irony of it.' She paused, took a breath. 'And through it all, that nightmare time, those nine long months of pregnancy, living in a fug of depression in a rented flat, the stranger I married looked after me. Not any of you. No. A man I had known for a week—at that. He believed in me. He stood by me. He convinced me that what I did was not my fault. Why didn't you?'

And still they wouldn't look at her.

'You didn't forgive me for what I did and I have craved your forgiveness all these years. Why, Ma? I was just a girl then. A girl who had left her family and all that was familiar to live with strangers. A girl who was trying so hard to please her mother by being a good wife, a good daughter-in-law, a good sister-in-law. And now you are ill, you call

me. Because you require my forgiveness. A tick in the box.'
She paused, trying to catch her breath. 'Even if you hadn't
called me home, Ma, I would have come anyway. I wasn't
ready to stay away any longer, to be in cahoots with you,
with your image of me as someone horrible, someone to be
shunned. Yes, I stabbed him. But he hurt me. He hurt me.'

Jacinta's feeble voice. 'I'm sorry.'

She couldn't bear to be near her mother. 'You took
so much from me.' She stood, turned to run and almost
bumped into Reena.

'I'm sorry.' Shirin's gaze bored into Reena.

Reena put her arms around her. Shirin stopped, her
agitation stilled. Gently she rested her head on her daughter's hair, whispered into her ear, 'I love you.'

'Shirin, you must be very hungry after that long journey,'
Madhu said, trying to ease the tension that had settled in
the room, glutinous like the bitter medicine she had been
forced to drink when she was ill. 'I have made all your favourites. Samosas, potato bondas, biryani, pork and mutli...'

Shirin managed a watery smile. 'You don't know how
long I've waited to eat your food again, Madhu. But I
need some time to myself. I need to leave...'

'Leave? You just came.' Madhu sounded panicked.

'Don't go,' said Jacinta weakly.

Shirin gently kissed the top of Reena's head, her cheeks,
the tip of her nose. 'I can't stay here. Not now. But I'll
come back, I promise.' She tipped Reena's face up with
her hand and looked into her eyes. 'This time round, I
won't let you go...'

CHAPTER THIRTY

Colossians 3:13

'She's beautiful, Vinod.' The tamarind tree sighed in the breeze that lifted the hair off the nape of her neck. Gypsy followed as she navigated the narrow path between the fields, a panting, comforting presence. *I am home. Reena. Holding her in my arms. The warmth of her. Real. Here.*

Vinod was at work. Shirin could hear the busy clatter of keyboards, a high-pitched female voice, laughter.

'Of course.' The smile in his voice caressing her down the crackling phone line. 'And you? Are you okay?' Concern.

'Yes.' And then, 'Come home, Vinod. I miss you. I love you.'

She carried his surprised bark of a laugh in her heart like a gift as she dialled Kate's number, wanting to hear her friend's voice.

'Oh, my God, Shirin, it's you. Hang on a minute; I'm going outside.' Clatter of keyboards receding. Bursts of conversation like voice-filled bubbles, a police siren whining, waning, gone. 'Shirin, you there?'

An image of Kate in her workaday uniform of pencil skirt and white dress shirt, phone glued to her ear, legs stretched out and crossed at the ankles, sitting in the smokers' corner on the only bench not covered in pigeon droppings. A sudden ache to be back in the ordered world of the office, fixing UAT issues, writing business specs, laughing with Kate over sandwiches and cups of tea.

'We miss you here. Justine's not up to managing your team. And, like a fool, I head over to your desk to tell you something and then it hits me. When are you coming back?' And then, softly, 'Just kidding. How is she, your mum? Did you meet Reena?'

'Reena is perfect. She knows, Kate. And yet, she came into my arms and it felt…' How to describe the feeling? As if she had been waiting all her life for that moment and it was everything she had expected and more… Her daughter in her arms had felt like… 'Like coming home.'

'And your mum?' Kate prompted.

Rage. 'I thought I could forgive her, Kate, but I find…'

'Thank goodness for that. I was beginning to worry you were like one of those martyred saints we were expected to emulate every Sunday at church; Saint Shirin— nice ring to it…'

A bubble of laughter pushed past the weight in Shirin's chest and escaped from her mouth in a surprised giggle. 'I miss you, Kate.'

When she disconnected the call, Shirin found herself at the church. She had walked out of the house blindly, punching Vinod's number on her mobile, wanting to hear his voice. And her feet, despite being shod in trainers and not chappals, despite being years out of practice, led her through the well-worn path between the fields, past the stream and up the hill, past Lenny Bai's compound and to the church without her noticing. Her feet had slipped effortlessly back in time to a past where they had made this journey a thousand times—it was her heart that was finding it harder, more painful, to make the transition.

A mass was in full swing when she slipped in quietly through a side door and knelt in one of the pews at the back. There were only a few people in attendance. They were singing the hymn preceding the second reading. It had been eleven years since she had last been in a church. But, she soon found, rituals drummed into one during childhood are not forgotten easily. She knelt down and made the sign of the cross. And, along with the rest of the congregation, began reciting prayers which came as easily to her lips as if she had been reciting them every day...

The priest was saying, 'Today's reading is from Colossians 3:13. Bear with each other and forgive whatever grievances you may have against one another. Forgive as the Lord forgave you. This is one of the hardest things God asks us to do, especially in the world today. Take the riots, for example, where poor Mr D'Sa was killed for no fault of his. This senseless violence makes us angry. It makes us want revenge. But the Lord asks us to turn the other cheek. The Lord asks us to count our blessings, to remember all those favours that He bestows upon us. All

He asks in return is that we forgive. As He forgave us, as He continues to forgive us every single day...'

It was all very well for the priest to stand there and sermonise, to blithely ask his congregation to count their blessings and to forgive. If only it were that easy...

Disillusioned, Shirin slipped out of the church and went to the cemetery to find her father's grave. The headstone said simply, 'Walter Diaz, much-loved husband and father.' Shirin sat beside it, beside the mound of earth that housed her father, and remembered the mound of his belly; how, when she put her ear to his belly button she heard churning and gurgling, busy sounds like the workings of a factory. 'It is a factory,' Walter had said, smiling down at her, 'It converts the food we eat to liquid so it can be digested easily. Isn't that amazing?'

She, Deepak and Anita had launched on him once, a mini mutiny, wanting to tickle him until he begged them to stop like he did to them. His laughter had started as a rumble deep in his chest and emanated in infectious waves until they were all laughing as they rolled on top of him, not sure who was tickling whom.

An aeroplane flew overhead, interrupting Shirin's thoughts with its low hum.

'I want to fly like you, Da,' she had said to him, hope shining in her eyes. He had lifted her then, swung her high above him and she had screamed, equal parts of fear and joy.

'There,' he'd said afterward, holding her close. 'You flew.'

'Not like that,' she'd put her arms round his neck, rubbing her cheek against his mostly white stubble. 'In an aeroplane.'

'It's not that different from going in a bus, you know.'

'It is! You get food in an aeroplane, in little trays. You told me that once.'

'It's not as tasty as Madhu's.'

Shirin had played her trump card then: 'You get to see clouds floating below you. You get to see heaven.'

He had put her down gently and smiled his dimpled, eye-crinkling smile. 'Ah. That you do.'

She held a fistful of mud in her hand, closed her eyes and tried to picture her father. And finally she saw him, hovering behind her eyelids: his almost bald head; his forever stubble; his round, benevolent face with the double chin that he had bequeathed her; the twinkling dimples; the kind eyes. He was smiling.

Are you in heaven, Da? Are you happy? My baby, my little girl, I saw her just now, Da. She's beautiful, all grown-up, without me. Is that how you felt when you visited every two years? Did you find it hard to reconcile the children in front of you with the images in your head?

And this was where Madhu found her, sitting on the mud beside her father's grave, talking to him.

Shirin was unsurprised. A part of her had known Madhu would come, had been waiting for her.

Madhu was panting. She must have run all the way. 'Ma'am is dying, Shirin. She had a heart attack after you left. Please come.'

'She turns her back on me. I leave the country. She summons me back eleven years later and I return to her like an obedient puppy. I have been her puppet far too long, Madhu.' Shirin stared at the mound of mud in her fist as if it held all the answers.

Madhu sat down beside Shirin and folded her into her arms like she had done countless times while Shirin was growing up.

'She's not faking the heart attack, Shirin,' she said gently.

Shirin burrowed into Madhu's arms and closed her eyes, slipping back with ease into childhood.

'Do you remember that one time when you asked me if I had children?'

Shirin looked up at Madhu. At her wispy grey hair. At the worn, lined face she so loved. 'You said you had a baby...'

'I was raped.'

'No.'

'I was fourteen. It was my uncle.'

'Oh, Madhu...'

'I had a daughter too. A perfect little girl. Ten tiny fingers and toes. Feathery black hair. I got to hold her to my chest for one long moment. Then they took her away. And I came to stay with your mother.'

'Is she...?'

'I don't know what happened to her, where she is, even if she is alive. All I wish is that wherever she is, she is happy...'

And then they were sobbing together beside Walter's grave.

'Oh, Madhu...' Shirin said again, after they had spent their tears.

'It happened a long time ago. In another life. But I still remember how it felt to hold her. How she scrunched up her little face and squealed like a kitten. How hard it was to let her go...' She paused, swallowed. 'Shirin, I of all people understand. I know how it feels to lose a child. I know how it feels to be abandoned and betrayed by the people you love...' She paused, and then, 'All those years ago, your mother had to make a choice, Shirin. And she chose wrong.'

The sun dimmed, preparing to set. The sky was orange going on black. 'It worked out so well for her. Her disgraced daughter banished from her life. Her beloved son getting the child he'd been denied, so she didn't have to bear the stigma of his childlessness. Her status in the community intact...' The words bitter in her mouth.

Madhu stroked her hair gently, as if by doing so she could stroke away the pain. 'Appearances always mattered to ma'am more than they rightly should. I was angry with her for a long time. I washed her clothes, cooked for her, gave her her pills, but hated her all the same for what she had done to you. And it ate away at me, the hate. But what she had done, it ate away at her too. She's suffered for it.'

Shirin looked at the headstones dotting the cemetery. Birds flew overhead in the twilight sky, making their way home. A dog howled mournfully.

'I know you, Shirin. You are not one to bear grudges. You will not be able to live with yourself if she dies before you have made peace...' Madhu said softly.

A cat jumped over the low cemetery wall and walked between the headstones. Its orange eyes glowed like headlights in the darkness. When it saw Shirin, it mewed and slunk away.

'She loves you, Shirin.'

Shirin watched shadows play on the headstones, performing a ghoulish dance.

'It's hard to forget, Madhu. To forgive.'

'I know. But you will.'

❈　❈　❈

Everyone was squeezed into Jacinta's little room, repeating the Catholic prayers recited at deathbeds after the priest. 'I went to the church first, asked the priest to come and administer communion to her before I found you,' Madhu whispered. Years of living in a Catholic household had made her wise to the rites and rituals.

The room was dark. The lone sixty-watt light bulb hanging from the ceiling flickered with the fluctuating voltage. Shirin's eyes picked out her daughter and her heart did a little flip of joy. Then she turned her attention to her mother.

Jacinta looked even smaller than she had just that afternoon. More frail. Her breaths came in loud, laboured gasps, their harsh sound somehow louder than the prayers being chanted by the rest of the family. The air was stuffy with grief and populated with ghosts whispering among the shadows. Outside the tiny window, lights from neighbourhood houses twinkled like beacons in the heavy darkness. The banana tree just outside the window swayed in the light night breeze. Ordinary sounds drifted in, only to be stifled by the heavy, oppressive silence weighted down with sorrow that had settled in the room, in the wake of the prayers, which, Shirin realised with a start, had ceased. In her white nightgown, silhouetted against the shadows, her mother looked like a pale ghost herself, already less of this world and more of the next.

The doctor had been called and sat beside Jacinta holding his bag, looking just as helpless as the rest of them.

'Too late for medical help.' He mouthed to Shirin as she squatted down beside her mother.

She nodded at him and turned to look at the slip of a woman who had once been regal, awe-inspiring, beautiful Jacinta. The mother she had been so proud of.

Jacinta moaned loudly, gasped for air and turned on her side. Shirin reached forward and gently laid her hand on top of her mother's cold, shrunken one. Jacinta's eyes opened, focused on Shirin. Recognition settled gradually into their murky depths. Slowly Shirin leaned forward and kissed her mother's gnarled cheek. And though it seemed to take every last ounce of her remaining strength, Jacinta looked straight at the daughter she had once denounced and smiled.

For Shirin, that was enough.

CHAPTER THIRTY-ONE
Kulfi Ice Cream

'Why did she give me away?' Reena asked. She was sitting on the rim of the well, her hands stroking the velvet moss growing up the sides. Shirin was in Bajpe meeting Vinod who was arriving from the UK. Preeti was inside helping Madhu and Aunt Anita sort through Jacinta's stuff. Deepak had come in search of her, bearing kulfi ice cream, holding out the green cone dotted with yellow pistachios like a peace offering. 'Want some?'

Reena had nodded, patting Gypsy's warm flank which sprawled across her lap, still unable to look directly at him. So many things had happened so quickly and she felt bruised all over, as if she had survived a crash. She liked Shirin and then she hated her. The rage she felt for her parents bubbled over like rice boiling in a too-small vessel, and during those times all she wanted to do was put as much distance between her and these traitors who had passed for her parents as was possible. She went for long walks in the fields, Gypsy keeping her company, trying to sort through her thoughts, her emotions. She felt she had grown a thousand years in the past weeks, suddenly shot up, and she was surprised that her clothes still fit. On the walks, images would come to her, suddenly, without warning. Preeti holding her during one of her nightmares; waking up delirious with fever to find her dad dozing by her side in a chair, startling awake to place a wet cloth on her hot forehead; Preeti comforting her when Gypsy's predecessor died; her dad lifting her up over a puddle, his arms strong around her, 'One, two, three, jump!'; rocking her on his lap and singing to her in his tuneless baritone when she was so tired she couldn't sleep; her parents coming to her school play where she had a bit part and clapping the loudest; her mother saying, 'Our special miracle.'

She felt shame at the thought of how she was conceived. She worried that she might be bad, like her father, remembering the monster that sometimes threatened to take her over, that had made her bite her mother that time. She was grateful that she had the parents she did, even though she was terribly angry with them, had lost trust in them. But the question that played most on her mind was this: Why had Shirin given her away? Shirin had tried to explain to her the day she found out, but that day was all jumbled in her head. And she wanted to hear her father's side of the story.

'You can ask her yourself of course…'

'I knew you would say that. I knew you wouldn't give me an honest answer…' The rage, always there, simmered. She jumped up, pushing Gypsy off, who howled in protest.

'I hadn't finished, Reena.' Her dad held her wrist, pulled her back.

'Don't touch me!' she yelled.

'Please, Reena.' Something in her dad's voice made her finally look up at him. Dark circles under his eyes, lines on his face, running into his stubble. Hurt in his eyes. This was her dad, the one who had taught her patiently how to play chess, who helped her with her maths, who even played hopscotch with her once, not caring how silly it looked. The dad who had marched up to her school and yelled at the head teacher for saying in assembly that Reena was not good with numbers. The dad who had tried to plait her hair and cook her noodles the way her mum did when Preeti had gone to visit a relative once. The dad who was always there for her, no matter how busy he was. The dad who made her laugh.

The dad who had lied to her all her life.

She sat down and Gypsy rolled back into her lap. '*When will this dog learn?*' she thought. '*I keep hurting her, but she keeps coming back. She trusts me implicitly. She loves me. What if I hit her repeatedly? Would she still come back? Everybody has their breaking point. I have reached mine.*'

'She called me, after you were born. I was living in Indiranagar, with Preeti. It must have taken great courage to call me, you see. We were all ignoring her; she was dead to us. Luckily for her, for us, Preeti took her call. She persuaded me to go and visit with Shirin. Shirin was broken, Rinu. She couldn't handle what she had done, what had been done to her. She begged me to take you. "Reena is the best thing that happened to me," she said. "She is perfect, unspoiled," she said. "She doesn't deserve me, I will not be able to mother her the way she deserves to be mothered," she said. "She doesn't deserve me," she kept repeating. "She needs someone who will love her, focus on her; not someone who is haunted, who doesn't have the energy to get out of bed."' Her dad paused. 'It is a hard thing to get your head around but there it is. She loved you. That is why she gave you away. She said something to me as she handed you over that I have never been able to forget.' He rubbed a weary hand across his eyes. 'She said, "If I had to go through all this again, I would, for the gift of her."'

He was quiet a long time. A crow cackled from among the fronds of the coconut trees. The air smelt of pineapple. A stone plopped into the well, a hollow sound.

'My biggest regret is that I let Shirin go, to live so far away, punishing herself, for so long. It just—it was the easiest thing to do. I fooled myself that it was for the best. Mai, Taipur society and all that. And of course we had you to consider. Innocent little thing caught up in all of this. Shirin was adamant that you were not to know. She did not want you to have to carry the burden of how you were conceived.' He paused, took a breath. 'Reena, look at me, please?'

His gaze, boring into hers, his voice firm, 'You are not to feel ashamed of who you are. Do you understand? A person is what they make of themselves; what they become, not what they came from.'

'Sometimes when I am very angry, a monster takes me over. It makes me do bad things.' She concentrated on scratching behind Gypsy's ears, head bent, not daring to look at her father. Gypsy moaned with pleasure.

'Rinu, sweetheart, we all feel like that sometimes. We are human, after all.' Her dad's voice was gentle. 'When I was six, I pushed Shirin into the stream. She hit her head and had to go to the big hospital in Manipal, have stitches. I went to mass twice a day for the two weeks she was in hospital, promising God that I would be good for the rest of my life if only she came home alive. We all get angry and we all do bad things sometimes. It's okay to get angry, Reenu. Look at me.' Her father's eyes, the colour of hot chocolate. 'I have known you since you were two weeks old and I can tell you one thing: you are *not* like Prem was. You don't have it in you. You are a better person already than Preeti and I, than any of us. Aunt Anita told me how you questioned her, how you championed Shirin's cause, how you made her feel ashamed of the way we all had behaved. You are wise, you are honest and you stand up for what you believe in. More than can be said of any of us.' And then, softly, 'Shirin loves you, Reena. Very much. As do we. You are loved, my darling. You are loved.'

The ache in her father's voice. The yearning. She had never heard her father speak so openly before, put so much of himself into his words. There was no point perpetrating regrets, she thought, continuing the chain of hurt and hate. She went up to him and gently, with one finger, brushed away the tears squeezing out of his eyes, pooling into his stubble. She rested her head on his shoulder and watched the ice cream melt to a jade puddle, watched Gypsy greedily lap it up and choke on the pistachios, her expression that of unabashed disgust.

CHAPTER THIRTY-TWO
Beginnings

Bajpe Airport. Twice in two weeks. Jostling for space among the crush of taxi drivers, rickshaw vendors and relatives, Shirin waited. Watching the new arrivals, their faces emerging from behind the trolleys, blink in the sudden blast of sunlight, their faces transforming as relatives jumped over the barrier and enveloped them in bear hugs, ignoring the harassed security guard futilely waving his baton. And she watched him walk out, wheeling one small suitcase behind him. He didn't see her, he wasn't expecting her. His face, that familiar face, was tired, new lines creasing it. He looked older somehow, and had he always walked with a slight stoop? His shirt was untucked. His eyes scanned the crowd, probably deciding which taxi driver to choose, and landed on her. The surprise in them, the joy. She watched as his face transformed. That smile that had won her over. He looked years younger. Her Vinod once more.

She went up to him, jumping over the barrier, ignoring the security guard's, 'Hey, miss!'; ignoring the calls of 'Sir! Taxi, sir, ma'am—where do you want to go?'

She looked up at him, his eyes soft as he smiled at her, his day-old stubble flecked now with more grey than black. She lifted her palms and cradled his face in them. His eyes widened, but his gaze never left her face. She gently lowered his beloved face down towards hers, ignoring the oohs and aahs and aiyyos from the crowd around them, ignoring the 'Oh, my God! Look. What is she doing?'; ignoring the security guard whose baton pressed into her back: 'Ma'am, ma'am, please, public place, ma'am,' he kept saying, thinking switching to broken English from Kannada might help, get the message across.

'I love you,' she whispered, just before her lips touched his, and then she was kissing him. She was kissing him and nothing else mattered—not what had gone before, not what was to come. All that mattered was this man, here, now, with her.

Afterwards, she inhaled the familiar smell of his sweat, rested her cheek in the crook of his neck. 'I missed you,' she whispered as the security guard shooed them down the steps, dispersed the onlookers with a flick of his baton, yelling, 'What are you gaping at?' and went back to guarding the barrier muttering, 'These people! Going to foreign countries and coming back with ideas in their heads. Kissing in public—and on the mouth, too! Ayyo devare…'

'I have waited so long for this, Shonu,' Vinod said as her hand found his and squeezed.

❋ ❋ ❋

Shirin smelt fish frying as she and Vinod neared the house she had called home for the first twenty-two years of her life. They had stopped off at the church, deposited flowers on Jacinta and Walter's graves and were now making their way home through the fields.

The air smelt of rain and earth and something else, something fresh. Perhaps this was the smell of seeds drunk on rainwater and soil, ready to sprout; the smell of new beginnings, of hope, Shirin mused. Her feet led her unerringly toward home, balancing with ease on the precarious path between the fields. Vinod followed, not balancing quite as well.

Dark clouds collected in clumps, staining the azure sky black, playing hide and seek with the sun. *Looks like rain.*

Her childhood home rose majestically above the fields on the hill. Smoke rose from the chimney in the bathroom, reminding her of dreaded scalding baths as a child. She could just make out Madhu in the kitchen, hunched over the gas as she used a spatula to flip the frying fish, stopping only to shoo the cat, Chinnu, away. The front door was wide open as usual. Shirin's eyes scanned for Reena and she found her sitting on the rim of the well, Gypsy sprawled across her lap, Deepak by her side. Reena's head was bent and she was stroking the dog's back. Shirin's heart did a crazy flip. Her daughter!

She quickened her steps, raced up the hill and Vinod followed, breathless. 'You need to get fit,' she said to him, winking. Vinod was too out of breath to think up a riposte. He bent double with his hands on his knees, panting with his mouth open, and she laughed, 'You look like Gypsy. Go on in. I'll be along in a minute.' She looked towards Reena. He nodded, understanding without her having to spell it out.

As she walked to the well, she watched Reena stand up, go to Deepak, put her arms around him, hold him close. Gypsy coughed out something she had eaten, bounded up to her with a low bark, danced around her legs. Reena turned, her face lighting up when she saw her.

'You came back.'

She came up to Shirin and put her arms around her, as naturally as if she had been doing it always. Shirin held her daughter, breathing in the scent of her. Over her hair, which smelt of coconut, she met Deepak's gaze. 'How could I stay away, Reena?'

'I want to talk to you about something.' Reena's voice sounded muffled.

'I'll go on inside, let you two catch up,' Deepak said.

As he walked past, Shirin held out her hand. Her brother took it, his eyes shining. She looked down at his hand—the hand that had snatched the note; the hand that had connected with Tariq's flesh; the hand that had cradled her child that rain-sodden night and sealed a promise; the hand that had raised the beautiful girl who was now ensconced in her arms. 'I'm so sorry, Shirin,' he said. She squeezed his hand hard once and watched him walk into the house, his back stooped.

'Yes?' she whispered into her daughter's hair.

Reena worried a loose thread on her sleeve. 'I do understand, sort of, why you gave me away. But... I am still very angry with you.'

Shirin gently tipped Reena's chin up with her finger. Her daughter's face, so like her own, was distressed. 'Reena, you have every right to be angry. Rage, fight; get it all out. Don't let it eat away at you.'

'Sometimes, I don't know who I am. I wake up frightened. If my parents are not really my parents, what else don't I know?'

'Reena, there will be no more secrets. All the adults in your life promise that.'

'And you expect me to believe it? You adults make a lot of promises you don't keep.' Her eyes sparkled with unshed tears. Shirin held her close, patted her back. Reena snuggled into her, drawing comfort. Her daughter. She breathed her in. She smelt of coconut shampoo, sandalwood, spices and dog.

'When I found that picture, I identified with you instantly… Since I found out, I often wonder… if you had kept me, not given me away, how things would have been…'

Oh, Reena. She wanted to hold this girl forever. She wanted this moment to never end.

'But…' Reena paused, swallowed. Whatever it was that she wanted to tell her, she was finding it very hard to say. Shirin was content to wait, while she held her close, like this. Overhead, thick smoky clouds spirited the sun away. Shadows played across her daughter's face. 'I don't want to hurt you,' Reena said finally.

Lightning signed in cursive writing on slate-grey canvas.

'Reena,' she said softly, 'I lived for eleven years missing you, aching for you. Nothing can hurt me as much as that, especially not anything you say. You are a gift, Reena. A precious, precious one. I have longed for you for what seems like forever and to have you now... It's a miracle...'

'They love me very much.' Reena's voice was soft.

There was a sudden playful growl of thunder. Gypsy barked, cowered under the banana tree.

'I know.'

Madhu rushed out of the kitchen to pull clothes off the line and from where they were sprawled on the aboli branches, a colourful awning. She stopped short when she saw Shirin and Reena. 'Shirin, when did you come? Come in—you must be hungry. I've made mackerel fry; I put lots of chilli and vinegar in the marinade, just the way you like it. And there is raw-jackfruit curry, and I made crab masala with ginger and tomato. It's going to rain. Why are you standing outside?' She frantically pulled off the clothes, gathered them in her arms.

'They are the only parents I have known.' Reena bit her lower lip.

This close, she could hear her daughter's heart beating steadily, drumming in time to her own.

The first drops of rain fell, bringing with them the sound of trees whispering blissfully, the smell of drenched earth.

'I know how painful it is to live without your child,' Shirin whispered. 'I will not do the same to your parents. I promise.'

'Come in. What are you doing there?' Madhu was standing on the veranda, gesticulating wildly, her arms full of clothes. 'You are both city people now, not used to the monsoon—you'll catch a cold.'

Her daughter in her arms, Shirin turned her head up to the heavens. The rain fell in a huge deluge, pasting her hair to her scalp in wet tendrils, running down her face, her neck, her arms, soaking her and the precious gift she held close. She opened her mouth, savoured this, her first taste of the monsoons after eleven years.

Her daughter stood on tiptoe, held her face in her palms and kissed her with rain-soaked lips. 'I love you,' she whispered.

That was reward enough.

THE END

Dear Reader,

First of all, I want to say a huge thank you for choosing *Monsoon Memories*, for accompanying Shirin and Reena on their journey and for sticking with them until the end. I hope you enjoyed reading *Monsoon Memories* just as much as I enjoyed writing it.

If you are not quite ready to let go of Shirin and Reena yet, there are more stories about them that I couldn't include in the book at my website: www.renitadsilva.com. Here, you can also read my blog – I chat about writing, reading, Indian fiction and about the wonderful, roller coaster ride that is being an author. Also, if you go to the 'My Supporters' tab on my webpage and sign up, you will get regular updates about my next book. You will be the first to see the cover and will also be party to exclusive material from the book.

Your feedback is valuable to me. I would like to know what you made of Shirin, Reena, Madhu, Vinod, Jacinta, Deepak, Prem and everybody else in *Monsoon Memories*. Do visit my website and pop me a note. I'll also keep an eye out for reviews on Amazon and Goodreads.

I look forward to hearing from you. And I hope you join Devi, Nisha and Shilpa – the protagonists of my next book – on their journey. I can't wait to share it with you.

Thank you.
Renita.

FIC DSILVA
D'Silva, Renita.
Monsoon memories

9-13

CPSIA information can be obtained at www.ICGtesting.com
Printed in the USA
LVOW07s1700180913

353041LV00019B/1148/P